# WALKING IN DARKNESS

# MORE FROM A.L. JACKSON

## Moonlit Ridge

*From Here to Eternity*
*Under an Endless Moon*
*At the Edge of Surrender*
*Beyond the Blue Horizon*
*On the Brink of Bliss*

## Time River

*Love Me Today*
*Don't Forget Me Tomorrow*
*Claim Me Forever*
*Hold Me Until Morning*

## Redemption Hills

*Give Me a Reason*
*Say It's Forever*
*Never Look Back*
*Promise Me Always*

## Falling Stars

*Kiss the Stars*

*Catch Me When I Fall*

*Falling into You*

*Beneath the Stars*

## Confessions of the Heart

*More of You*

*All of Me*

*Pieces of Us*

## Fight for Me

*Show Me the Way*

*Follow Me Back*

*Lead Me Home*

*Hold on to Hope*

## Bleeding Stars

*A Stone in the Sea*

*Drowning to Breathe*

*Where Lightning Strikes*

*Wait*
*Stay*
*Stand*

## Closer to You

*Come to Me Quietly*
*Come to Me Softly*
*Come to Me Recklessly*

# WALKING IN DARKNESS

A.L. JACKSON

Published by Montlake, Seattle
www.apub.com



EU product safety contact:
Amazon Media EU S. à r.l.
38, avenue John F. Kennedy, L-1855 Luxembourg
amazonpublishing-gpsr@amazon.com

ISBN-13: 9781662524950 (paperback)
ISBN-13: 9781662524967 (digital)

Cover design by Hang Le
Cover image: © Michelle Lancaster PTY LTD; © Guillaume Weiler, © K.-U. Haessler, © iMarzi, © KDdesign_photo_video / Shutterstock

Printed in the United States of America

# WALKING IN DARKNESS

# Prologue

## ARIA

Fear blanketed Aria's spirit as she tried to figure out where she was. Where she had been taken. Her surroundings felt completely foreign.

It was quiet there.

Small and enclosed.

Too still.

Even colder than Faydor, though a bright orb of light hung at the horizon.

A shape was in the distance.

A man standing, facing away with his hands clasped behind his back.

A blond man.

Her stomach plummeted when he slowly turned around.

His smile was both placating and malicious as he stared across at her as if she were nothing more than an artifact to be studied.

It was the man from the diner, who had at first appeared harmless, though something about him had set Aria off-kilter. Her anxiety surrounding him had only increased when she saw him again outside the fast-food restaurant. But she hadn't understood that he was truly something wicked until she followed the little girl out to the pond. Aria had jumped in to try to save her and had quickly realized it was a trap, her spirit and mind tricked as the little girl's face began to flicker between the man's and the child's in the frigid waters of the pond.

He sneered as he began to speak. "I've ended your kind for twenty generations. Did you really think I'd stop with you? No, Aria. You must die like the rest."

She was frozen where she stood, staring at the man, who grinned malevolently in her direction. Her heart drove in a frantic beat as she tried to process what was happening. Where she was and how she'd been pulled into an unseen plane she hadn't known existed.

How *he* was here.

He was . . . human. Aria had seen him in the flesh during the day.

Though she'd also seen him as part of the otherworld when the waters swallowed her in her sleep.

It was as if . . . he was both.

Human and ethereal.

Like her and the rest of her Laven family.

The ones who, when they fell asleep at night, woke in a different realm, chosen to fight the evils planted in human minds by the Kruen who roamed the bowels of Faydor.

She took a slow, faltering step backward, terrified that there might be no way to escape this place.

It felt both confined and eternal. The walls were made of rippling darkness that shivered and wept, though they kept her wholly bound.

She took another step backward, and her back hit the lapping barrier that held her prisoner in this unfound sphere.

She wanted to weep when the man took a menacing step toward her, though at least thirty feet still separated them.

Apparently, she'd been a fool to believe her danger had ended when she had extinguished the Ghorl, the most powerful of Kruen and almost impossible to defeat. It had taken hold of her father's mind, using her family as bait to lure her back so she would find her demise.

But she'd been wrong. So wrong.

She could almost hear Pax shouting for her from the other plane. Could feel his panic as he searched for her within Faydor, where they'd been hunting.

"What do you want from me?" Tremulous words fell from her tongue.

The man laughed, a vicious sound that slipped through her like ice. "You are all so clueless, aren't you? Cowards who hide away within the safety of their beloved Tearsith, then fall into Faydor as if you're actually going to make a difference. As if you stand a chance of stopping me."

He continued to approach, and Aria's attention darted in every direction, searching for any possible escape. But the blackened walls billowed and danced on all sides. A fortress of depravity.

There was nowhere to run. Nowhere to hide.

"Who are you? I saw you . . . in the day. While I was awake." She tried to demand it. To keep the quiver from her voice. He didn't deserve her fear.

But it was difficult to do when pure evil was glaring at you.

His head canted to the side as his grin grew. "This life is filled with many mysteries, is it not? A child lying in their bed, waking to a paradise unseen, believing they are a chosen one. But no . . . that paradise is only a shroud. A cover for the affliction we're to be given. A man walking in darkness, charged with a burden unlike any other would ever be asked. Asked to carry an albatross so great he's on his knees, both night and day."

Aria's mind spun through his confession. The hatred and bitterness that underscored the words he uttered.

"But why suffer when we can be so much greater than that?" He kept coming closer, and Aria's short breaths turned jagged with every step he took. Slow and purposeful, he erased the space between them. His presence slicked over her in the coldest wash of evil she'd ever felt.

She was trembling when he stopped a foot away, and he reached out and dragged a single fingertip down her cheek. It burned through her like a blade, a match to the way his voice sharpened in cruelty.

"Why succumb to the albatross of being a Laven when you can have everything?"

He suddenly had her by the throat. Her eyes went wide with the shock, and her hands flew to his wrist. She struggled to break free, both hands ripping against his hold. He only squeezed tighter.

She struggled for air, choking against the lack of oxygen, though she refused to stop fighting.

She couldn't go down like this.

Not after everything she'd already survived.

"Do you want to know who I am?" His voice curled with venom. "I am the one who will purge the existence of those who think they have a chance of standing in my way. I am the one who will put an end to your kind. I am Ambrose. And you, little Valient, have no power here. You may have prevailed against the Ghorl I sent, but you will not prevail against me." His fingers dug deep into her throat. "Because you are pathetic, just like the rest."

Aria read the truth in his icy-blue eyes as he added a second hand, squeezing so tightly she was sure he was going to crush her windpipe.

She may not have been able to die within the boundaries of Faydor, but she realized quickly that protection had not been extended to this place. To this stricken, abhorrent place. She could already feel her spirit being drawn from her body like vapor sucked into the nothingness. Could hear the moaning of her soul.

Agony clawed down her throat and clamped around her chest.

On instinct, she fought harder, and she tore at the backs of his hands and arms as she struggled to break free.

Writhing and thrashing.

Kicking and flailing.

He laughed at her efforts until she managed to strike him in the stomach with her boot. Even she was shocked when he flew back, soaring high in the air before he slammed to the ground ten feet away. He skidded along the hard, barren dirt, his body digging a foot-deep trench in the black-soot earth.

Shock blew his eyes wide as he scrambled up into a crouch, as if he could not grasp the action, before he was flying back for her in a storm of fury.

His speed was greater than that of any human.

Before she could prepare herself, his fist flew, colliding with her right cheek. Pain splintered across her face. She cried out, though she regained her footing and threw her own punch. He gripped her by the wrist before her fist could make contact, and he wrenched her arm backward.

Aria screamed.

"Little bitch. Cunt. Whore." He wheezed all the foulness that typically oozed from the Kruen. "You have no power. You have no power."

But she somehow knew that she did. She could feel it spark within herself. A glow that demanded that she retaliate.

Stand and oppose.

It was the *light*.

The same light that she'd used to battle against the Kruen in Faydor. It was how she extinguished them—binding them with the energy that raged inside her.

It was there right then, burning bright.

Pleading with her to use it.

She didn't take the time to question if it would work. She tossed her free hand out and projected the energy.

A shock wave of it rushed from her hand.

On a roar, he blew back, though this time, he landed on his feet.

Oh God, it wasn't enough. Not nearly enough to stop him. Panic rolled through her as she watched rage color him an ungodly red. It was as if he were consumed in fire and brimstone.

"You will die—die like the rest. You will not stand in my way. I will reign."

Aria had no option but to turn and run, but there was no place to run to.

He was right behind her, a frigid blaze that scalded her back. Sickness clawed through the air, which had become dense. Suffocating. She pushed with all her might, though she only ran in a circle.

No way to break beyond the bounds of this nefarious place.

That sensation rose in her again. The light building within her, demanding that she do something.

She held it tight, a glowing orb in the center of her chest.

She kept running as she tried to increase it.

Multiply it.

Searching for a power she'd never before possessed.

One she prayed might be enough to defeat this monster in this unfathomable place.

Hands slammed into her back, pushing her from behind. She stumbled forward, and with it, she could no longer contain the energy, and it blistered from her hands.

It pierced the black, rippling wall in front of her and sheared through the barrier. A gaping hole that writhed.

Aria couldn't stop the trajectory of her momentum.

And she fell through.

# Chapter One

## ARIA

Disoriented and gasping for breath, I jolted upright in bed, terror clutching my spirit. I blinked as I was blinded by the bright rays of sunlight that seared in through the gap in the long drapes.

It took me a moment to process. To understand that I was safe.

I was here . . . surrounded by morning light in the same hotel Pax and I had checked into last night.

One second later, Pax shot up from where he had been asleep beside me.

Those pale-gray eyes were wide with panic. With the torment of what he'd suffered while we'd been separated.

For one second, he stared at me, like he had to process that I was there, too, before he threw himself forward, gripping me in his arms, and holding me against the strength of his chest.

Heat burned through the cold that had held me hostage in that place.

"Aria," he rasped. "Fuck, I couldn't find you. I couldn't find you. And you're here. You're here."

His words came out in a torrent of dread.

In relief.

In confusion.

Frantic, he kept brushing a quivering hand down my head and back, as if it were the only way to assure himself that I was there.

"Where were you?" he finally demanded, his voice raw.

"It's not over." I choked on the words, pain still obliterating my throat as the harsh, horrible reality sank down into my spirit.

*It's not over.*

*It's not over.*

Those three little words pelted him, and I felt him stiffen against me before he peeled himself back and held me by my arms.

Fury contorted every line of his severe, glorious face. Every sharp edge hewn in brutality.

"What do you mean, it's not over?" he growled.

I gulped around the chaos that thrummed through my being. "It wasn't the Ghorl who was really after me, Pax. It was something . . . someone greater. The man. The one I saw at the diner and then outside the fast-food restaurant? The man whose face flickered between his and the little girl's? He was the one who sent the Ghorl. He is the one who was trying to stop me."

Rage clouded his expression. "You saw him again?"

My nod was shaky as my thoughts spiraled through what had transpired. "Yes. I felt something when we were hunting the Kruen last night. A force."

Confusion hitched my voice, and my brow pinched as I tried to make sense of it. "It was almost like the gateway from Tearsith into Faydor. How we know what direction we're supposed to go because we're called to it. But it was so much stronger than that. Irresistible. I couldn't do anything but reach out for it, and when I did, I was pulled through. He was there, in this . . ."

I swallowed around the throbbing thickness of my throat, the words a quiet rush of disbelief when I managed to expel them. "It was another plane. As if I were standing in the middle of a dark, frozen snow globe, stranded and completely contained. It was quiet. Still and cold. Tearsith's opposite."

But I also had a feeling it was Tearsith's dark mirror. A resting place for whoever this man named Ambrose really was. A plane that held his darkness.

Pax's palms trembled on my arms, and I could hear the grinding of his teeth. "You were dragged away from me? From Faydor and into this . . . ?"

He trailed off on a ragged breath. His eyes closed for a moment before he opened them to me. "But you're here. You woke up here."

He said it like the truth of it might ground him. Like it might be the only thing keeping him from flying off the bed and going on a rampage.

Though I wasn't sure that would remain true when his attention tracked the spot on my cheek and down to my throat, both of which I was sure burned a fiery red. A sound of wrath left him, yet his touch was gentle when he lifted his hand and caressed the spot where Ambrose had dragged a fingertip down my cheek. "Who is this monster?" Pax could barely grit out.

My mind spun through the things I'd learned, though most of it had only caused me more confusion. "He called himself Ambrose. He said he'd sent the Ghorl to end me. He . . . he called me a *Valient*, Pax." I nearly begged it. "He called me what Maria Lewis called me. What she'd believed her husband had been . . . the only one with the power to defeat a Ghorl."

Maria Lewis was the only person I'd ever heard use the title Valient. There had been no mention of it in our history, other than the vague intimation of a stronger type of Laven in the great book. Our teacher, Ellis, had only heard myths and tales of one.

"He said he'd ended my kind for generations. I think he meant Valients," I continued. "He said there was nothing I could do because he was going to end me, too. Right then. At least, that's what he thought he was going to do."

Turbulence rolled through Pax's being. "But you got away."

He said it as a statement, though I could hear the question behind it.

How?

How was I here?

How did I survive?

Above all that, I knew he wanted to berate himself for not having been able to stop it.

Blame himself.

But this was so much bigger than just the two of us.

"He tried to choke me. So casually. Like he thought he could just reach out and snuff the life out of me. He thought he was going to end me there. I know he did. He believed he would kill me last night. He told me I had no power in that realm, and he approached me as if he was the one who held it all. He was shocked when I was able to fight back."

Questions raced through Pax's features, though he brushed his thumb over my cheek, his words a scuff of praise as he murmured, "Of course you fought back. You wouldn't let that bastard win. You're too strong for that."

"I fought him off—physically, at first. I was basically just in a fight-or-flight mentality, and the only thing I could do because he was choking me was fight. But then I . . . kicked him, and he flew off me. *Flew*, Pax. I don't know where it came from, but it was like I had this strength I had no idea I possessed. Born in that place. For that moment."

As if that power had sprouted up through my vulnerabilities.

The corners of my eyes pinched as the memories flooded me. "It was the light. The energy that we have in Faydor. It was screaming inside me, urging me to use it against him. End him the way I would a Kruen."

My tongue stroked out to wet my dried lips. "It only knocked him backward a small amount, though, and he immediately attacked me again. But that urge was there . . . burning inside me. To fight. To harness the light."

I paused, then whispered, "And somehow, I amplified it—though I didn't know how to use it or if there was any way to use it to defeat him."

Air puffed from my mouth, and my head slowly shook. "It was all there, this ball of power that throbbed inside me. Then, all of a sudden, he shoved me from behind, and when he did, I was no longer able to hold on to the power. It flew out of me, pierced the barrier of his realm, and cut it wide open. When it did, I fell through, and I ended up here."

I'd been shocked awake.

Coming to, right in this place.

I peered over at Pax, whose expression dredged through a thousand questions. Through the fear and the turmoil. The confusion and the relief.

I struggled to grasp the significance of what had happened. To understand this brand-new piece in what felt like an unsolvable puzzle.

Pax gripped me by both sides of the face. "But you did it. You got out. You got away from that bastard."

I curled my hands around his wrists. "Yes."

He dropped his forehead to mine, the anguish he'd felt bleeding out. "Fuck, Aria, I was so scared. So goddamn scared when I couldn't find you."

He inhaled me, his eyes squeezing closed before he brought his mouth to mine.

His lips pressed firm and solid, both torment and an apology bound in the action.

I exhaled, whispering, "I'm right here," against his mouth.

He groaned, and his hand twined up in the fall of my hair. "I can't believe this is happening again. Aria, I won't let him get to you. I'm going to fucking tear that piece of—"

I pushed forward, stealing his words.

Begging him to focus on me. On the fact that I was there and whole.

He responded, kissing me deeply.

It was tortured.

Impassioned.

A promise and a petition.

Fire tore through my frozen body. Heat and comfort and need.

I trembled, and Pax's palms smoothed over me, chasing the chill away.

"Thought I was going to lose my mind," he rumbled against my lips, hauling me even closer. "Trying to find you. Searching through Faydor when you just disappeared."

"I could feel you," I whispered. "I could feel your panic from wherever I'd gone. Calling out for me."

"I hate this. Hate that I don't know how to put an end to this," he murmured through the kiss. "But we're going to."

Severity scored through him when he peeled himself away. White flames burned in the depths of those pale, pale eyes, his white hair a disaster from his toiling on the bed. His chest bare and heaving, his ashen flesh covered in the miseries he'd witnessed in his life.

The man fierce, potent volatility.

His hands were back to gripping my face. "I promise you, Aria. He will not get to you. I will do whatever it takes to make sure that doesn't happen, whoever this fucker is." Speculation pinched his brow. "Is he . . . Kreed?"

My soul shivered.

Kreed was a monster we only knew from the teachings that had been passed through our Laven family.

Kreed had once lived in harmony with Valeen, our highest one. He had betrayed her in an attempt to dethrone her from her great power. When he failed, their worlds were split in two, and he now ruled over the Kruen he had created. Forever seeking destruction. Bringing calamity on the world.

I could feel the frown pull across my brow. "I don't think so."

My mind spun through everything Ambrose had said. Through what he might have revealed in his ambiguous confessions. Through what I had felt.

A vague memory hinted at the edges of my mind. Somehow, it felt as if I should know him . . .

I fully turned my attention to Pax, speaking around the aching of my throat. "I think he's human, like us, but has gained some sort of power. He said . . ."

I closed my eyes as I pictured him.

What had roiled in his expression.

His hatred.

His greed.

"You remember I told you that he said he has been destroying Valients for twenty generations, and he promised he would put an end to our kind. It was like . . . he had to. Like whatever he has become hinges on it."

Apprehension rolled through Pax, though vehemence lined his features, the words like a mandate when he issued them.

As if he'd come to the same resolution at the exact moment as me. "And you are the only one who can stop him."

Uncertainty meshed with the verity that pulsed through my being. My nod was frantic when I realized the emotion I was trying to put my finger on. "I could almost taste his desperation when he realized I could fight him there. Could taste his fear. He was afraid of me, Pax. He was afraid of me. Which means he is not unstoppable."

I gasped the last sentence.

Hope rising up with the words.

Pax's fingers sifted through my hair, his palm on my cheek as his tone dipped to adoration. "No, Aria, he isn't unstoppable. Because of you. Valient."

I still didn't fully understand what that meant. Why or how I'd been chosen.

But I knew, right then, that I would accept it. Take it for all it was and stop this monster, because I somehow knew that was exactly what I was meant to do.

"I'm terrified, Pax," I said, though my chest glowed with determination. I rushed to add, "But I won't let that fear stand in my way this time. This time I won't run. This time I will fight."

# Chapter Two

## ARIA

It was strange to look at my family and suddenly view them in an entirely different light.

When everything changed in what felt like the passing of a single moment and nothing that any of us had known remained the same.

Sitting in the passenger seat of Pax's car and peering at them through the windshield where they were gathered at the small neighborhood park, I felt as if I were watching them through a distorted, clouded mirror.

The car idled in the cold, the heater was working overtime, and I couldn't seem to make myself move from the spot as I stared at the people I loved most.

People who had so misunderstood me.

Right then, it felt as if time and space were stretched between us. A million years passed. It seemed impossible that it'd barely been two weeks since the day I was placed in the mental care facility.

It felt as if, during that time, everything had been reconfigured.

As if I'd aged twenty years during that time. My eyes opened and my heart changed.

Theirs had, too.

I could feel it in my mother's gaze when she looked up from where she was sitting on a bench. It gave her a good view of my brothers, who played in a field at the neighborhood park near my grandmother's.

On the far side of the park, my younger sister, Brianna, sat on top of a picnic table under a ramada, her long brown hair whipping around her face, her downturned focus on her phone.

It was cold and dreary out, but when I'd texted my mother this morning after Pax and I had gone to the store to purchase a phone—since I refused to be cut off from my mother any longer—we decided this would be a safe place to meet. No walls surrounding us.

We were still on edge after Pax had broken me out of the institution, worried the local police might be looking for him, but after what had happened with my father last night, I needed to maintain contact with my mother.

She had stayed at my grandmother's last night, but I didn't want to deal with the pressure of others listening in on us. I wanted a place where we could talk.

Really talk.

Because for the first time in my life, I didn't have to hide my truth.

God, how many years had I ached for her to know me? To truly see me?

"You sure this is something you want to do?" Pax's voice was low and riddled with concern. He reached out a tattooed hand and threaded his fingers through mine.

Silent support.

I knew it would be a long, long time before he forgave them, if that was even possible.

Maybe longer before he trusted them.

I stared across at my mother, whose attention was fully trained on the car. I could feel her pain radiating out.

The regret.

The confusion.

More than any of it, her love.

"I can't imagine what my mother was feeling last night." My voice was wispy. "Can't imagine the trauma she went through before I got there. She had to have been *terrified*." My chest tightened with the thought of that type of trauma.

My father's mind had been taken over by a Ghorl, the strongest of the Kruen. It had been a manipulation to draw me back to my home so the Ghorl could end me. My father had held my mother hostage through the middle of it, and she'd had to witness him trying to kill me.

But we'd destroyed the Ghorl. Prevailed over its power.

"To witness my father that way? To have him treat her that way? Then to see what she saw? To see you?"

My mother had always believed Pax was a figment of my deranged mind. That he'd told me to hurt myself when they believed my scars from Faydor had been personally inflicted.

Then to find out my nightmare world was real? It had to have been so much for her.

Shifting, I let my gaze travel over his face, and I reached out and scratched my fingernails through the stubble that coated his jaw.

My fingers drifted, tracing over the deep scar that slashed down the right side of his face and down to the tattoos that climbed his throat.

Ink that spoke of the terrors we faced each day and night of our lives.

The man was my Nol, my soulmate, even though our Laven family believed it was forbidden for us to be together this way.

He gathered my hand and pressed my knuckles to his soft, plush lips. His words landed somewhere between an apology and a plea. "Thought I was going to steal you away from here forever. Thought you'd never have to return and face the judgment and disbelief you were subject to for your whole life growing up."

My head shook. "What we are is unfathomable, Pax. I don't blame them."

Old wounds swam through those boundless eyes, and pain clutched my chest. I could see what he kept hidden there, beneath the hard layers that covered him whole. His own childhood traumas and scars.

"The only thing I want is to keep you safe. From everything," he murmured.

I unwound my hand from his so I could cup his cheek. "You can't do that, Pax—but you can stand by my side, and that's the only thing I'm asking you to do."

When we were running, he'd promised so many times that he would have to leave me once I was safe. He'd told me it could only be temporary. But we'd come to accept that we were destined for so much more than that.

Purposed.

Placed here in this perfect time.

He gave a slight nod, and the faintest smile pulled at the edge of his mouth. "Guess that's good, because beside you is the only place I want to be."

He set his palm on my face and brushed the pad of his thumb over my cheek.

Softly.

Tenderly.

Just staring across at me.

"Through it all, Aria. We're going to get through it. Whatever is coming our way."

"I know," I promised.

He gave a slight nod, and I inhaled a steeling breath as I turned back to look out toward my mother, who waited. My hand flexed on the door handle, and I forced myself to open it and step out into the winter chill of Albany, New York.

My home for all my life.

Februarys here were always freezing. It was a different kind of cold from Faydor's, though. Warm rays of sunlight rained down and caressed my face.

A promise that even though it might feel that way to me, this world wasn't so desolate.

The soles of my shoes crunched on the long, dead grass as I made my way toward my mother.

She sat on the bench, her hair twisted in the same messy knot she so often wore, the grays interwoven in the browns now more profound.

I could feel the anxiety rolling off her.

Confounded waves that battered against me like an apology.

I stopped three feet away from her. My throat, still sore from the attack last night, grew so thick it was difficult to breathe.

I felt overwhelmed, looking at her like this.

The lines that had been carved so deep on her face, written in the horrors and the grief she'd found. Her entire world in shambles.

"Hi, Mom." I could barely force it out.

The tears she'd clearly been trying to hold back slipped free. Long tracks that streaked down her face and dripped from her chin.

"Aria. You came."

Nervously, I fiddled with my fingers. "I promised you that I would."

Her attention darted toward Pax's car, then slowly returned to me, her voice hoarse when she whispered, "No one could blame you for leaving this place and never coming back. No one could blame you for cutting us off and pretending like we never existed."

A lump of grief pulsed in my chest. "I never wanted that."

Sorrow billowed from her. "You only wanted to be believed."

The nod I returned was weary. "It was the only thing I ever wanted. To be believed. To be seen. For you to understand me."

She stared at me for the longest while, as if that was what she was doing—seeing *me* for the very first time.

Her gaze softened as her eyes traced over the exposed scars on my face.

Then she suddenly breathed out and lifted a blanket she had folded on her lap. "Here, I brought this for you. It's freezing out."

"Thank you," I told her as I accepted it. I unfurled the heavy wool and wrapped it around my shoulders before I sat down on the bench beside her.

Taking a beat of respite from the heaviness, I gestured at my little brothers playing in the distance. "Those two would never know it's even cold, though, would they?"

Mitch and Keaton were chasing each other, laughter rolling off them as they tagged each other back and forth.

"You're it!"

"No, you're it!"

Their sweet little voices carried on the breeze.

My heart fisted.

God, I'd missed them so much. Had worried so much, unsure if I'd ever get to see them again.

Mom let go of a mild chuckle. "They seem to be completely immune to anything but the other's antics. I asked your brothers and sister to give us a little time to talk. Asked them to keep themselves entertained, and of course, your brothers are out there bickering."

My laugh was quiet. "They might argue, but there's nothing truly malicious about it."

I could feel the weight of her cautious curiosity burn into my cheek. "And you know that? You can feel it?"

I dropped my head and fiddled with a piece of fringe on the blanket as I murmured, "I can."

Tension strained between us before she begged, "I don't understand, Aria. I don't understand how any of this is possible. I thought for years . . ." She trailed off, unable to say it.

That I was crazy.

Insane.

Hurting myself.

"You could only see what you could see. What you could understand. Every choice you made was because you cared about me. I know that."

Sadness bleared her eyes. "But it still hurt you."

Head downturned, I grabbed her hand, squeezing it so tightly that my knuckles blanched as I whispered, "You did. But I get it. All of this is . . . terrifying."

"I spent so many years being afraid for you, Aria. Terrified for the one I loved so much." Mom breathed out as she tightened her hold on my hand. "I spent years aching for you. Praying for a way to fix it. For a way to take away whatever tormented your mind, so you could be free. Live a healthy and happy life. And now . . ."

She gulped, her head shifting away, her chin quivering as she struggled with the truth.

"I don't want you to be afraid for me," I murmured.

She turned back toward me. Sheer adoration and devastation burned through her expression. "I could never not worry about you. You're my *daughter*. My beautiful, talented, amazing daughter."

She choked on the last word.

Mom paused for a minute before she seemed to gather up the courage to step into territory she was afraid to traverse. "It's real? The things you told me when you were a little girl? About that place where you would go to play, and your best friend you'd meet there? Pax?"

His name left her on a whisper of reverence, and her gaze drifted behind me to where he waited in the car.

My heart squeezed in a fist. "Yes. He's real. It's all real."

More tears streamed down her face. "The wounds . . . they came from that place. How?"

She nearly begged that.

"There's still so much about it that I don't understand myself. How I was chosen to go there. To fight there. But what I know is, there are things beyond us that most cannot see. Battles for our spirits. Battles for our souls. There are beings who seek to protect and those who seek to destroy. And somehow my soul was called to protect. I go there every night . . . since the day I turned sixteen."

She sniffled, and the rock of her head was filled with remorse as she came to an understanding. "The first time I thought you'd hurt yourself."

"Yes."

She shuddered. "And when you fight there . . . they . . . hurt you?"

I kept squeezing her hand, wanting to give her encouragement. Solace. For her to understand I was okay.

*At least for now.* I ignored the voice that echoed through me.

"Yes. They can burn me, but they can't kill me."

She hesitated, then whispered, "Are they, like . . . demons?"

My shoulder barely hitched. "I guess that's what they could be called. They're spirits, and their only purpose is to bring calamity to the world. And somehow . . . someway . . . those like me have been given the power to fight them in our sleep. To take some of the burden off the world. Without us . . ."

I trailed off, not even wanting to consider how horrible the world would be if there weren't Laven there to intervene.

She breathed around a soft cry. "I wish . . . I wish I could understand. I wish I could see."

"I would never want you to."

Silence stretched between us before she forced out, "Please help me understand what happened to your father. He just . . ."

Her eyes squeezed closed for a beat before she said quickly, "All of a sudden, he wasn't the same person. One moment he was worried about you, terrified and pacing the floor the same way I had been . . . And the next, he was this cruel, vicious person. Wicked. It was like the man I knew was no longer there."

A shiver rolled through her. Without a doubt, she was tormented by the memories.

"One of the evil ones took his mind hostage. Used him against me to lure me back here. They want me dead."

The words felt harsh.

Blows that hit the frosty air.

I wanted to shield her from them, but I also needed her to understand the severity of what we were facing. After what had happened last night in Faydor, the terrifying thought that the Kruen could use my family again still held fast.

Revulsion rolled through my mother, and a soft sob hitched in her throat. "I can't—" She inhaled a shaky breath, her grief palpable. "Is he still a danger to us?"

"I don't think so." Hope heaved out with the words as I thought of what I'd felt last night. When I no longer could hear or feel the wicked voices that had captured my father's heart and mind.

"I don't know how I can ever trust him again." She swiped the tears from her cheek with the back of her free hand.

"I don't know, either—and it's up to you if you ever do decide to trust him again. But at least I believe you're safe from him."

"So it's over. We're safe? *You're* safe?"

Apprehension gathered at the base of my throat. "I believe you're safe."

I felt the weight of her gaze on my cheek. "But you are not."

My head slowly shook. "We're trying to find a way to be. To stop the one who's after me."

Another wave of grief and pain rolled through her. "Oh God, Aria . . ."

"I know. But I promise we're doing everything we can. We'll find a way, but until then, I need you to know what is happening so you can look out for any signs. If you feel anything strange. If any thoughts infiltrate your mind or if anyone in the family starts acting strange. I need you all to be prepared."

She choked on her disbelief. "I don't know how to be prepared for any of this, Aria. Don't know how to stop it. I'm . . . not as strong as you."

I fully turned to her. "You are. Just be vigilant. Be careful. And if something happens, call me. You have my new number, and I need you to use it."

Her head bounced in understanding, though she whispered, "You're leaving."

"We can't stay here. Not right now."

She hesitated before she asked, "He came for you? When you were in trouble?"

She peeked over her shoulder at Pax's car.

"I know it's hard to understand, but Pax and I are tied. Bound in a way that others are not. We will always be together."

Tenderness filled her expression. "You love him."

"I always have."

Her hand tightened on mine. "If one good thing came from this, then I'm thankful for that. That he found you and you found him. That you were not alone." Her head tipped to the side as she studied me. "Is he good to you?"

Emotion pulled at my lips. "He's more than good—he's everything."

Her warm brown eyes brimmed with moisture, and she turned and wrapped me in her arms. Her mouth was at my temple as she murmured, "I love you so much. Please know that. Please take that with you everywhere you go. And I pray one day . . . one day that you see the fullness of it."

I held her close, nodding my head against hers. "I do. I already do."

Sniffling, she pulled away, and she squeezed both my hands before she wiped her tears, then waved over my brothers and sister.

Mitch and Keaton immediately stopped what they were doing and came sprinting in our direction, and Brianna slowly slipped off the table.

Wariness slowed her steps as she followed.

"Aria! Aria!" Mitch and Keaton shouted.

I stood, and they slammed into me. A flood of affection pummeled me as I curled my arms around them.

"I missed you!" Keaton said.

"I missed you even more," Mitch said, trying to one-up him the way he always did.

A soggy laugh left me as I hugged them to me. "I missed both of you. So much," I murmured.

With eyes the color of our mother's, Mitch peered up at me. A beaming smile lit his face. "Are you home forever now?"

Sorrow swam through me, and I brushed my fingers through his hair. "Not yet. I have to go away for a little while longer, but I promise I will come back to visit soon."

"You'd better hurry up, because it's going to be my birthday in six weeks!" Mitch said.

My spirit pinched, and I prayed it wasn't a lie when I told him, "I definitely can't miss that, can I?"

"You better not. It's gonna be extra fun because Mom said I get an ice cream cake."

"Wow, then I definitely have to be here."

I could feel Brianna approaching from behind.

Filled with caution.

My brothers released me as I straightened, and there was no missing the fear in Brianna's eyes. She was obviously old enough to recognize the trauma that had befallen our family in the last two weeks. No way to keep her from the pain and distress.

Her steps were slow, but the second I murmured her name, she broke. She ran to me in pure desperation, slamming against me in a tidal wave of relief. I hugged her tight as she sobbed. "I was so scared, Aria. I was so scared."

My heart groaned. "I know. I was scared, too. But it's all going to be okay."

It had to be.

She clung to me. "I want you to stay."

"I wish I could, but I have to go away for a while longer."

Last night, Pax and I had contemplated finding a place to settle. A place to make our home. But now . . . it felt dangerous to remain in one spot. Running was the only thing we knew.

Maybe one day I could return. Settle close. Become a constant in their lives. But not when so many questions remained around us.

Nodding, she peeled herself away. "I understand."

"I expect to see an amazing performance from your dance troupe as soon as I get back," I tried to tease, though it came out thick.

She fumbled over an uncertain laugh, her brown eyes shining as she looked at me. "I'll be practicing every day."

"I can't wait to see it."

"Would you mind taking your brothers back to your grandmother's house?" our mother asked her.

Brianna also seemed to have matured a decade since I'd been gone, and without argument, she took the boys' hands. "Come on. Let's go get warmed up. I think my toes are going to fall off."

She stalled and lifted her chin. "Come back to us."

My nod was jerky. "I will."

Without saying anything else, she turned to lead them away, though both my brothers were shouting, "Bye, Aria! We'll see you soon!"

Brianna glanced back once, her sweet face full of grief and belief, before she hurried across the street and down the sidewalk.

Once they'd disappeared, my mother stood, in disquiet, shifting from foot to foot. "How long will you be away?"

"I don't know. Until it's safe."

"Please be that, Aria—safe. We need you here. In our lives. We all love and miss you so much."

"I know," I promised, "and I'm so thankful."

She pulled me into the tightest hug as she whispered in my ear, "My beautiful, brave, awe-inspiring girl. Take care. I will be thinking about you every second."

We stayed that way for the longest time; then she was swiping at her tears as she forced herself to step away. She turned on her heel and took the same path my siblings had taken as she headed to my grandmother's house.

Though my mother . . . she never looked back.

I had a feeling it was too painful for her.

I stood there until she disappeared around the corner; then I turned, still hugging the blanket around me as I started for where Pax waited in the distance.

I was halfway across the field when I felt it—a shift in the atmosphere. The way ice crystals seemed to form in the gloomy air.

With it, evil crackled across the open space.

The hairs on the nape of my neck lifted in awareness.

I whirled toward the direction that I'd sensed it. A hundred feet away, a man had cut through the field, riding toward me on a bicycle.

It wouldn't have been all that strange a sight except for the expression on his face.

Pure, unmitigated hate.

That, and the piece of metal that glinted from his hand beneath the bright rays of winter sunlight, protruding from the handlebars like a sadistic appendage.

A knife.

Fear streaked through my being.

Then I turned, and I ran.

# Chapter Three

## ARIA

Terror battered my senses, and my heart thundered so hard in my chest that it was the only thing I could hear. The pound, pound, pounding that drummed through my senses on a wail.

A shout of instinct to protect myself.

Tossing the blanket from my shoulders, I took off in a sprint across the crispy, dead grass.

I knew the moment Pax realized what was happening. There was no missing the fierce pulse of protection that blistered through the air, cutting through the cold in a slice of lightning.

A bolt that struck in the middle of me.

My feet clapped on the hard ground and air ripped from my lungs as I raced toward the car.

I could feel the man gaining on me, erasing the distance in a flash. The tires of the bike crunched over the dead field as he pedaled, the harsh rasps of his breath growing closer with each second.

He was suddenly right there, riding his bike around me and cutting off my path.

Surprise tore out of me on a yelp, and I stumbled to the side. The only thing I could do was shift course, pivoting ninety degrees and driving myself away from the direction I'd been going in.

I got the sense the man was herding me.

Forcing me to run toward an acre of woods that rose up about fifty yards in front of us. He came up to my side, and he swiped an arm out, stabbing the knife toward me.

"Bitch. Whore. Did you think he would let you live?"

I ducked, and the blade whooshed by my face, missing me by half an inch.

Behind us, an engine revved and tires squealed, and I could hear the scraping of metal as the car jumped the curb.

Oh God. Pax was coming.

The car roared as he blazed across the field, coming directly for us.

The man was undeterred, his mind so gone to the evils that possessed him that he had no clue what was coming. "Little slut. You have no place. No power."

Pax was right there, swerving back and forth from behind. His power surged, though it was trapped, held back as he waited for the right moment to strike.

I could almost hear him shouting in my head, *Get clear. It will be my pleasure to do the rest.*

The man slashed the knife toward me again, but his bike wobbled with the angle. He missed me by a foot, and he cursed as he struggled to regain his balance.

It gave me the chance to sidestep, and I shifted course, making another sharp turn.

One the monster was unprepared for. One that Pax used as the perfect opportunity.

He gunned it, the engine screaming as he flew across the dead grass of the winter field. He clipped the rear tire of the bicycle before he slammed on the brakes.

The man was thrown from his bike, and he arced through the air.

Suspended.

Flying over the top of the car.

Airborne for the longest time.

Finally, he smashed to the ground, as if gravity had suddenly sucked him down. He tumbled at least three times before he came to a stop face down.

The passenger door whipped open, and Pax shouted, "Get in!"

My attention darted once more to the fiend who'd come from out of nowhere—a stranger who'd been sent to hunt me—before I ripped myself from the shock and ran for the car. I dove into the passenger seat and slammed the door shut.

Gasping, I looked out the passenger-side mirror in time to catch the man climbing to his feet.

During the fall the blade had impaled his side, and he ripped it out as if immune to the pain.

Barbarity filled his expression as he began to stumble our way.

Pax caught the action in the rearview mirror. "Motherfucker."

Jaw clenched, he shoved the car into reverse and rammed his foot on the gas. The tires spun before they caught traction, and we flew backward.

Pax shifted around so he could watch out the back window, keeping his purposed trajectory.

The man lumbered forward, no self-preservation left, and we slammed directly into him with a loud *thunk*.

A scream tore out of me when the car jostled and bounced as we ran over him, and my hands shot up to cover my face as if it could shield me from the sight.

From the horror of what our lives had become.

Because there was no chance the man was ever getting up again.

Then Pax shifted into drive, peeling out as he ran over him again, going in the other direction. Once he was clear, he tore through the field and out onto the street, the back end fishtailing as we blazed down the street.

I hung on to the dash and the door handle, trying to regulate my breathing. To climb back to sanity.

Pax was ten minutes across town before he finally looked over at me, viciousness carved in every line of his face. "Couldn't leave him, Aria. He would have gone for your family."

I swallowed around the turmoil, and I looked at the man who raged in his seat. "I know."

His expression was grim when he warned, "I will raze them all to the ground. Every fuckin' one of them. And I won't stop until there's not one person left to come after you."

# Chapter Four

## PAX

Aria was two steps ahead of me as she climbed the exterior steps of the motel.

Long black locks of hair blew in the breeze behind her, the scent of coconut and the goodness of who she was invading my senses.

My love for her gripped me.

She held herself so differently from when I'd first met her in the flesh. Since the moment I broke her out of the mental facility.

She'd been so fuckin' timid. Terrified of the burden this life had placed on her shoulders.

Sure she was going to succumb.

I'd sworn then that I would protect her. That I would go to any length to see to it that she came out safe and whole on the other side.

Maybe I'd been a fool to think the *other side* was going to begin last night. To think that she was finally free of the bonds that held her hostage. Free of the threats. I should have known it wouldn't be that easy.

Easy.

What a fuckin' joke.

It should have been apparent our existence was far more complex than I'd believed.

Twisted gnarls of mystery.

God, I didn't think I'd ever been so terrified as when I'd lost her last night in Faydor. No way to tell where she'd gone, though I'd been sure she hadn't been awakened.

It was different.

I had sensed her. Right there. Floating in the otherworld, but in a place unseen. In a place where I couldn't reach her.

It had nearly brought me to my knees, having no way to protect her after I'd promised it was the very thing I would do.

My purpose.

Now she walked like she'd found that purpose, and it was bigger than she ever could have imagined.

Because she was more remarkable than any of us had known.

"This is it," she said as she stopped in front of Room 237.

We'd gone east, following the same path we took the first time we escaped Albany, though we made it an additional four hours deeper into Pennsylvania this time.

Hated that I had to drag her on the run again, but I honestly didn't know what else to do except keep moving.

Stay one step ahead of the monsters that lurked.

Which was hysterical since those bastards would be waiting for us wherever we chose to go. But staying stagnant felt as if we were setting ourselves a trap, and I was doing the best I could do.

Aria tapped the key card against the reader, turned the handle, and pushed open the door to the motel room.

This one was a bit nicer than some of the dives we'd previously stayed in. Not so off the beaten path. Half of our issues had been solved once we no longer had to keep Aria hidden from her parents.

At least that part was a relief.

Problem was, I was pretty sure the only way we were going to get through this was by leaving a trail of bodies behind us, and I doubted that we would remain anonymous and unwanted for long.

But I'd lived close to half my life running as a criminal. Hiding my identity. My own sort of monster flying under the radar.

At least I was good at it.

We'd ditched my car outside of Albany. Thankfully, it had been registered to a fake name; we would have had a whole new set of issues if it hadn't been. There was no chance in hell they weren't going to link that altercation at the park to a car with my description.

I'd paid cash for a decent ride, telling the salesman at the used-car dealership that I was buying a gift for my girl. For once in my life, it hadn't been a lie.

Because all of it was for Aria.

Everything I did. Every moment. Every breath. Every single thing I had to give.

From here to whatever fucked-up eternity we found ourselves in.

Aria was stronger than ever, but old habits die hard and all that shit, so I still wound around her, murmuring, "Wait right there," as I swept the motel room.

"It's clear," I said when I was done.

The second I did, she stepped in and clicked the locks behind her.

She swiveled back to me, the woman so damned gorgeous that she knocked the breath out of my lungs every fucking time I looked at her.

Now that things had changed between us—now that I'd given in to what I should have known was coming all along—that feeling was overwhelming.

She slightly lifted her jaw, and the hazy light from the lamp illuminated the scars that marred her face from the battles we fought in the night. Scars that didn't do anything to sabotage her beauty, but instead marked her as extraordinary.

She watched me with those fathomless gray eyes, rimmed with the darkest lashes.

They roiled with intensity, emotion bubbling up from an endless chasm.

The energy that bound us pulling through time and space. Through realms and eternities.

"Sight of you, Aria. Ruins me every time. Leaves me standing here gaping at the beauty that you are. Leaves me wondering how I could get lucky enough to be standing in front of you. Lucky enough to be chosen for you."

A tremble rolled through her body. "It's the way it's supposed to be."

Frustration puffed from my nose, and I ran an agitated hand through my hair. "Yet I have you on the run again. I hate it, that you have no peace. I thought finally . . ." I trailed off.

Her brow pinched. "You're the one who's running because of me . . ."

"I just wanted to give you stability. A permanent place to stay."

The thought of it tore through me like a pained, blissful dream.

A home.

I had never really had one of those. Not the kind that spoke of rest and safety. Every memory I had of *home* was riddled with torment and pain. Had to squeeze my eyes closed against the assault of the voices that instantly poisoned my mind.

*You little fuckin' freak. Gonna beat it out of you one day. Won't have my son bein' some fuckin' pussy.*

"We'll have it one day. A home." Aria's voice jolted me from the memory, her words flowing as if she had a direct tap into my mind. "A place where it's just you and me. Where we don't have to be afraid that the other is going to disappear. I choose to believe, Pax. I won't count my days any longer."

"Is that what you want, Aria? A home? With me?" I asked as I took a step toward her, the woman a lure.

Shackles and chains.

I wasn't about to complain. I wanted to be bound. Tied to her in every intrinsic way.

Funny, it was only two weeks ago when I'd been terrified of seeking her out. Worried of breaking the creed given by Valeen that we never search for our Nol while awake. A warning given that it would only cause us more danger. That we might somehow turn on each other.

Our Nols were the ones chosen to fight beside us in Faydor. I wasn't sure if it was the case with every Nol, but I knew the connection I shared with Aria. Knew she was meant for me the way I was meant for her.

And I knew right down to the fabric of my being that there wasn't a chance I could harm her.

"Yes." She said it without hesitation.

"And what kind of place is that goin' to be? Tell me it'll be on the beach, Princess."

I let my words twist back to the fantasy she'd woven—one of us on some deserted island. One where, when we went to sleep, we didn't arrive on another plane to fight a war that was never going to end.

One that would go on through every generation.

A soft smile played across her tempting lips as she leaned against the door. "Hmm . . . our vacation home will be on the beach, but I think we'll have another house. Maybe one in Albany."

I took another step forward until I was standing directly in front of her. I slipped my palms onto her sides as I murmured close to her mouth, my voice rough with need, "Oh, we're going to have *two* houses, huh?"

Heat flamed at the contact.

Her tongue stroked out to wet those plush, tempting lips, and she peeked up at me with a sweet dose of playfulness swimming in her expression. "I am a princess, after all."

"My princess." My hands curled around her waist as I claimed it.

"Yours," she murmured. All the lightness vanished, and her voice quivered with the truth. "Just like you're mine."

Dipping down to capture her mouth, I kissed her slowly. Needing her to understand what she meant to me. I thought she did, though. I thought she was the only person who *could* get me.

A low whimper rolled up her throat as she pressed herself against me, all that soft sweetness against the hard planes of my body, every muscle coiled with need.

"Is it wrong that I want you? After what happened earlier today?" she whispered into the lapping shadows of the room.

Twilight just beginning to take hold.

Edging back so I could look at her, I ran my fingers through her hair. "Isn't it you who told me that we didn't know how long we had? That we had to relish every second? There is nothing wrong with that, Aria. You deserve every ounce of joy. Every bit of pleasure. And if that means eking it out in the few moments of quiet we have, then that's what we're going to do."

Except Aria and me? We were going to have forever.

I knew it.

Knew it in my soul.

Because I was sure then that mine didn't function without hers.

My heart.

My purpose.

My Nol.

"I think that sounds like a really good plan."

"Oh, I have plans for you."

She rocked her head back on the wood of the door, a shy, excited smile dancing over her lips. "Oh, really? Like what?"

She squealed when I swept her off her feet and into my arms; then I turned and tossed her onto the bed.

Then I peeled myself out of my shirt and tossed it to the floor. "Like this."

# Chapter Five

## ARIA—TEARSITH

She lay wrapped in Pax's arms, and her Nol held her close as they drifted to sleep, curled on the motel bed.

Their souls hovered and danced in the nothingness. In that bare space that always held them before they were taken to where they were destined.

Lights flickered and flashed in that glimmery second before they flew.

Carried away to the otherworld.

Aria emerged on Tearsith's boundary first.

Their sanctuary was surrounded by dense woods, the foliage lush and the air cool. Green grass and red vingas covered the ground, and her ears were filled with the gentle babbling of the brook that cut through the middle of the meadow.

Off to the side was the great tree she and Pax had played on as children, its massive arms coiled and twisted. A canopy of peace.

Previously, she hadn't given much consideration as to why there were no children there now, playing beneath its protection. Why she was the youngest of their Laven family. But now it struck her as wrong.

Ominous.

She didn't have much time to contemplate it, because one moment later, Pax manifested at her side. He didn't hesitate to thread his fingers through hers.

Energy erupted, stronger than it'd ever been.

It was as if a new force had been bred between them once they'd joined.

When their barriers had been stripped away and there was nothing left to separate them.

When they'd become one.

They shared a fleeting glance before they turned their attention to their Laven family, who had gathered near the stream at their great teacher's feet.

Ellis was giving them words to bolster their spirits. A reminder of their calling. The way he did every night before they descended.

But there was something in the air that left her unbalanced, something that felt off as they stepped out from the fringes and into the clearing.

Ellis immediately quieted when he noticed them.

"Aria and Pax. You have arrived." Aria had thought relief would shine bright in his expression. It'd been only the previous night that they'd defeated the Ghorl, and Ellis wouldn't know of the new world Aria had stumbled into afterward.

But no.

It was sorrow that twisted through his aged features. The weathered lines carved on his face deepening to ravines.

Aria's attention rushed to take in the faces of the rest of their family.

Grief.

She felt it fiercely. She felt it distinctly.

And she somehow knew it wasn't about her or her situation.

"What has happened?" she whispered hoarsely.

Ellis's expression dimmed further. "We've received news that Nathan has passed into eternity."

Shock speared through Aria. Nathan wasn't that much older than she was, only by four or five years. Aria and Pax had often played with him during their childhood growing up here in Tearsith.

He was a friend.

Family.

"No." It wheezed out of Aria on a bottled sob.

Margarethe, Nathan's Nol, stood from where she'd been surrounded by ten or so of their family members.

Dani, Aria's closest friend, the one who'd been her mentor when she'd prepared to descend into Faydor for the first time, kept an arm around her waist to support her.

Tears blurred Margarethe's eyes, and Dani curled her closer to keep her upright as she swayed to the side and struggled to form words.

"He didn't come for three nights. I became concerned, and I . . ." Margarethe hesitated as if she were afraid of admitting a mortal sin. "I knew his last name and where he lived, so I searched for him. I found a news article. He . . ."

She faltered before she choked around the confession. "He fell down the stairs at his house and broke his neck. His sister found him the next morning."

"Oh my God," Aria gasped around a clutch of sorrow.

But she knew that sorrow wasn't close to the magnitude of what Margarethe was experiencing right then. She could sense it.

A shattering of spirit.

A cleaving of hearts.

As if an actual piece of the woman had been carved from her being.

"I'm so sorry, Margarethe," Aria wheezed.

Dani met Aria's gaze. The two friends shared a moment's grief between them.

Margarethe squeezed her eyes closed, and a torrent of tears fell down her face before she shook her head in anger. "It . . . it doesn't make any sense. He was strong. A force. Completely stable. There was no reason . . ."

Death always seemed impossible. A vague threat in the distance before it reached you.

"You're going to be okay," Dani murmured, though the words broke. "You're going to be okay."

"Oh God, where is William?" Claire suddenly cried out from the edge of the crowd. As if she'd been trying to keep it bottled since she arrived. She turned in a circle, as if coaxing her Nol to step from the boundaries and into Tearsith. "He didn't come last night . . . and he still isn't here."

Ellis's Nol, Josephine, ambled over to Claire. Her spine was hunched with age, her limbs spindly and thin. She reached for the Laven, and she peered up at her as she took her hand. "Oh, Claire, do not be troubled. He must have had a change in his human life. He'll come. You must not worry."

Though Aria heard the quaver in Josephine's voice, could feel the unease ripple through the entirety of their family.

As if each of them felt that something was off.

Trepidation slithered through Aria, and Pax's palm twitched against hers, as if he had the same sense. The feeling that an axis had shifted.

Their entire Laven family gathered around Margarethe, their heads bowed as they surrounded her to offer their support.

No doubt, each of them wished for a way to bear some of it for her. To hold her up when she dropped to her knees and wailed. All while they clung to their own Nols a little tighter.

"No. Why? Oh, Valeen, why?" she wept toward the placid heavens.

Dani got down on her knees to console Margarethe the best that she could, and her Nol, Timothy, joined her.

Ellis moved forward, touching Margarethe's bowed head. Promising that Nathan was at eternal peace, that he could now rest and his duty had been served, though it did little to quiet the sobs that racked the woman.

When Ellis finally stood and turned in their direction, his features were piteous. They only dimmed in worry when he stepped toward them and Aria whispered, "I need to speak with you."

He ushered Aria and Pax away from the group, and the three of them gathered beneath the gnarled, twisted branches of the great tree.

Ellis glanced behind them to the group of their family mourning with Margarethe before he turned his full attention to them. "Tell me I should not fear. I'm not sure how much more this family can withstand."

It was a plea. They'd already been through so much.

Reticence filled her at sharing the news. "Unfortunately, it is not over."

Ellis blanched, and he reached for her and wrapped his bony fingers around her wrist. "How so?"

Wariness pulsed through Aria. "Last night, while fighting in Faydor, I was compelled into another realm."

Alarm rushed through his features. "What do you mean?"

Aria told him about what had happened. How she'd been drawn into the other realm. The things the man had said. How he'd told her he'd ended her kind for generations. The fight that had ensued. How she was sure he was responsible for the Ghorl being sent for her, and that it was only happening again as humans were clearly still hunting her.

"He called himself Ambrose. Have you ever heard his name before?" she begged.

Awareness nudged at her consciousness. She swore she should know. It was like the answer was right there, dangling in front of her but just out of reach.

Regret shook Ellis's head. "No. Nor have I ever heard of anyone of his kind. Of another plane. And he said Kreed gave him this *gift*?"

He might as well have spat it.

Aria's nod was withdrawn. "Yes."

"Maybe he welcomed Kreed into his heart in some way? Allowed Kreed to strip him of his humanity to use him on Earth? I don't know. This is . . ." He trailed off in horrified disbelief before he peered at her with sheer intensity, though his voice was soft with awe. "Sweet child, you are beyond anything we've ever known. I wish I had the answers, but I don't. I'm afraid I no longer hold the wisdom to be your teacher, but it will be you who is teaching us."

He gave a wary glance between her and Pax, worry seeded deep in his gaze.

Air puffed from Aria's nose, and she let her eyes travel their sanctuary. It used to make her feel safe. Untouchable. But now that peace felt thin. She was sure these realms were so much greater than she'd fathomed, and she couldn't help but wonder how much had been undiscovered.

"But the thing I do know is, you must figure out who this man is in the day," Ellis urged. "He must be human if he is walking on that sphere. Maybe that is where you have to stop him."

Uncertainty washed through Aria. It seemed unlikely that he would be vulnerable in the day. Susceptible to human weaknesses. His powers seemed far above that.

But if she was also vulnerable there . . .

She almost scoffed at herself.

Could she dare compare herself to him?

"Don't worry, I have every intention of hunting that bastard down," Pax growled from her side. "Every intention of ending him. Whatever it takes."

Ellis shifted in disconcertment, and Aria watched as his attention dipped to where Pax had her fingers woven firmly through his.

Refusing to let go for a second.

The old man slowly lifted his gaze to theirs.

"And you remain together."

He didn't phrase it as a question. It was a statement knitted in distress.

Pax didn't cower. He simply lifted his chin. "I'm not leaving her, Ellis. Know I made the promise to you that I would once we stopped the Ghorl, but I can't, and I won't. This thing isn't over. But even if it was, I don't believe that we don't belong together. And even if we didn't, it wouldn't change anything. I won't leave her side."

"It's a risk we're both willing to take," Aria told Ellis, her words twisting in a plea for him to understand.

Aria knew the mandate.

Nols were not to join in the flesh; Ellis had only given them a temporary blessing while they'd been trying to defeat that Ghorl.

But how could Valeen forbid this? This connection they'd been given?

She and Pax were so much more than temporary.

Another wail rose up from Margarethe, a mournful cry that echoed through their sanctuary.

Aria's spirit throbbed and thrashed, and she held tight to Pax's hand.

Praying that what they were was unbreakable.

# Chapter Six

## ARIA

When my lids fluttered open, I found Pax staring at me from where his head rested on his pillow.

We faced each other, tangled in the middle of the bed.

Bare light flooded the room, but it was enough to cast him in a spotlight. Rays spearing through the drab atmosphere and glinting over the sharp edges of his face.

Cheeks cut like razors, his brow proud, and his jaw a blade.

But I was the one who felt lit up in the spotlight right then. The way he gazed at me through the space, those icy eyes the softest I'd ever seen them.

It was as if I had become a beacon. The only thing he could see.

He reached out tattooed fingers and brushed back the matted locks of hair from my face. A sorrowful smile touched his lips.

"Morning." The word was rough as gravel.

"Good morning," I murmured, eyes flitting back and forth as I took him in. Absorbing everything I could.

The sorrow from last night chasing me here. Knowing what Margarethe was waking up to.

A hole that I knew ached so horribly inside her.

Pax must have felt it, because he set his palm on my cheek, so big that it nearly covered the entire side of my face. "Nothing better in the world than waking up next to you. Getting to have you in my arms. Knowing you're right here. This sweet body tucked right up against me."

"It can't be wrong," I whispered.

"It can't," he agreed.

Wistfulness pulled through me, and Pax's gaze tracked the motion as it pulsed through my expression. "You're hurting for her."

My hair swished around me as I nodded against my pillow. "I can't imagine."

"I know," he murmured. "Weird that I never gave much thought to giving thanks in my life—but lying here, right in this moment, that's what I am, Aria. I'm thankful. Thankful that I have you. Thankful that you're mine."

A warm buzz hummed in my chest, and redness rushed to my cheeks. I let my fingertips scratch through his stubble. "I told you that you were going to like claiming me."

It was a thread of playfulness woven with a ribbon of sincerity.

A rough chuckle scraped his throat. "Oh, you did, did you?"

"I just had this hunch," I teased with a lift of my bare shoulder, a lightness pushing through the gloom we'd been met with in Tearsith last night.

"Let it be known that there was never any question if I was gonna like it or not." His tone shifted, too, riding on the whisper of levity that curled through the air. A flirty taunt from his tongue that had me snuggling closer to him.

"Well, I don't know. I would have thought I'd have been irresistible the second you saw me."

A hot palm slid all the way down my side. Chills lifted in its wake. "Turns out, you are irresistible, Aria Rialta. God knows I tried."

"I guess I'm going to count it a positive that you were a total failure."

Mischief danced on my tongue. The joy we'd found together bubbling through my being as that energy rolled through the room.

Pax let go of a warm, rumbling laugh, and he edged close, his nose brushing mine as he murmured, "Total, complete failure."

I trailed the tip of my finger down his cheek. "You can take heart that at least you excel in one thing."

In a flash, he rolled me onto my back and hovered over me.

He was so viciously beautiful that my heart clutched, and my stomach twisted into a thousand needy knots.

He angled down and wisped his lips across mine. "Oh yeah? And what would that be?"

My teeth raked my bottom lip, and the teasing evaporated. "Loving me."

"That's right. Because loving you was what I was created to do."

He suddenly pushed back to kneeling, and the covers dropped from around his waist.

He rose high between my trembling legs, a fortress that towered over me.

A stream of light that cut through the slit in the drapes lit him in a dazzling blaze.

Every inch of him bristled with strength.

Skin scarred with our fate, covered with the violent designs he'd imprinted on his flesh.

Our truth.

But it was the first time I noticed what was hidden deep within the horrors inked on his abdomen. The first time I was this close to him in the light.

Veiled within a darkened expanse of red vingas.

The faint vestige of a face.

Gray eyes wide and long black hair whipping around the face.

With a trembling hand, I reached out and brushed my fingertips over the image he'd tattooed of me.

"Pax," I whispered.

His body quivered beneath my touch. "You see it now, Aria? I was always yours. I just hadn't quite gotten what that meant."

The air changed. A charge of static electricity.

All the lightness vanished, and those fathomless gray eyes somehow darkened as he stared down at me.

"Need to feel you, Aria. Whole and safe and real."

"I'm right here."

He hooked his fingers in the edges of my underwear, and I lifted my hips so he could peel them down. Then he wound himself out of his, and he came to me.

Pressed himself inside me.

Took me.

His big body curled around mine as he began to move. He watched over me the entire time, our eyes locked, our souls hinged.

I swore that I could feel myself glow. Swore that I could see it reflected in his eyes. Flames that leaped and lapped. And when the orgasm tore through me, shooting me to the greatest heights, beyond the realms that we knew, there was only Pax and me.

Lost to a place that existed only for us.

Our match, something beyond my comprehension.

It didn't matter, since what I understood was him.

Chest heaving for breath, he slumped down, though he immediately rolled us so he was on his back, and I was draped over him. A soft giggle got free. "So, I think you were totally wrong earlier. I think *that* is the best way to wake up."

Amusement vibrated through him, and he curled his arms around me as a smile spread across his mouth.

Joy.

Even in the middle of everything we were going through, I still felt it wrap us whole.

Then he bucked up, the playfulness resurfacing, jostling me against him. "Go get yourself a shower; then we'll eat."

"So bossy," I told him as I rolled away, slanting him a teasing smile.

He sat up, so intimidatingly beautiful in the middle of the bed. "Just taking care of my princess."

"Fine, just as long as you remember my favorite way of waking up."

His chuckle was dark as he raked his fingers through the crop of white hair on his head. "You think you're going to find me complaining?"

Heat flushing my skin and a tiny grin threatening my mouth, I slipped off the side of the bed, taking the top sheet with me, and dipped into the bathroom.

I showered quickly. It seemed ridiculous that I had a smile plastered to my face the entire time, but I wasn't going to feel guilty for it. As far as I was concerned, we'd earned whatever scraps of happiness we could scrape together.

Once I'd finished, I stepped out and wrapped myself in a towel before I headed back into the main room.

Though I froze when I felt the anxiety gripping the room the second I stepped through the door.

Pax was propped up on the bed, and his head was downturned, all his attention trained on his phone.

"What is it?" I croaked around the tension, not even sure I wanted to know.

Foreboding filled his features when he looked up at me and said, "William is dead."

# Chapter Seven

## PAX

"What? How do you know?" Aria begged from where she stood wrapped in a towel outside the bathroom.

In an instant, the bubble we'd been cloaked in earlier popped. Those threads of peace that'd been weaving around us stripped away.

Grief tugged at my insides, but it went so much deeper than that.

It was dread.

The heaviest kind of dread sank down to the pit of my stomach.

"Didn't know him well," I told her. "But I knew his last name and his hometown. Couldn't shake this feeling, so I looked him up."

I lifted my face so I could fully meet her gaze as I delivered the news. "He died of a drug overdose two nights ago."

"Oh my God." It gushed from Aria's mouth, and I knew her heart was immediately stretching out for Claire. Like she might be able to reach her on another plane and comfort her. Though I doubted there would be much comfort for this.

Aria blinked through the disorder, and I could feel it gather inside her. The same awareness I'd been terrified of recognizing last night. "You don't think it's random."

I exhaled heavily. "I can't say for certain, but this shit doesn't sit right. Two of our family in a week? Both of them young and healthy?

When we haven't lost anyone in years? And I don't buy that bullshit that William OD'd. He didn't strike me as a junkie."

And God knew I'd encountered many of them hunting the streets of Las Vegas.

I looked to the floor, processing, before I tentatively returned my attention to her. "What that bastard said to you . . . something about ending you all. You took it as him meaning Valients . . ."

It took her a moment of the same processing. "You think he meant all Laven and not just me."

She didn't phrase it as a question. I think we'd both arrived at the same conclusion a while ago. Or maybe we'd just known it was coming all along.

"I don't know for sure. But if it is? If these deaths weren't by chance?"

"Oh God, Pax." Tears blurred those pale-gray eyes.

"Maybe I'm being paranoid . . ." Sighing, I anxiously ran a hand through my hair. Nothing about saying that sat right. Fit right.

Slowly, Aria moved toward me.

A lure, because there was nothing I could do but shift around to sit up on the side of the bed. My hands went to her thighs, and I held on to her like she could be an anchor.

She breathed out. "We have to stop him. Find him here, on this plane, and stop him like Ellis said. And we have to do it soon."

Silence stretched between us.

"How the hell do we do that?"

She softly brushed her fingers through my hair, surety in her voice. "He'll come for me."

My arms curled around her waist, and I blew out a ragged breath where I buried my face in the towel at her belly.

Terrified that she was right.

# Chapter Eight

## PAX—TEARSITH

He and Aria remained at the motel that entire day, watching out the window for any sign of the depraved, wondering if and when someone would come for them.

When it'd been quiet for the entire day, they curled themselves together on the bed, where they fell through time and space to emerge in their sanctuary.

Only, when they stepped out into Tearsith, it was anything but a sanctuary.

It was a place of torment.

One of grief.

Claire sobbed from where she was huddled with Margarethe, while murmurings of distress rolled through their Laven family.

Five others had not come tonight, and the worry of what might have befallen them was distinct. Palpable as it rippled through the cool breeze.

Many paced, ripping at their hair. Others mumbled among themselves, their voices hushed and dripping with fear.

Pax held tighter to Aria's hand than he ever had in his existence.

Ellis moved to the spot near the stream where he stood as their teacher night after night.

He raised his frail arms out to his sides, fighting the horror that wanted to bring him to his knees; rather than succumbing to it, he lifted his chin.

"My children, I know this is one of the hardest days our family has ever endured. Coming here to this plane and realizing that William and Nathan have been stolen from us. The worry we face that others may have been ripped from us as well. I know what we're all thinking . . ."

He paused and let his attention drift to Aria, who stood at his side, before he began to speak again. "And no, I cannot deny that there is a chance that we are being hunted in the day. Picked off, one by one."

Gasps rolled through their family.

Ellis continued, "We know not for certain, but we do know that Aria has specifically been tracked by a man named Ambrose. Someone she has seen both in Faydor as well as walking in the flesh in the human realm."

Timothy met Pax's gaze, and the man curled his arm around his Nol, Dani, as if that single action could wrap her in a hedge of protection.

Ellis cleared the thickness from his throat. "This man had the power to pull Aria into another plane that none of us knew existed."

Another roll of overwhelming shock, and Pax's insides twisted at the thought of it. At the fear that at any moment, this monster could reach out and rip Aria from him.

"As you see, she was able to escape, but this man did threaten that he was there to end all her kind. She'd thought he was referring to her, to the special abilities she's been given. A Valient who can heal in the day."

They had filled Ellis in on what they had found out through Maria Lewis, the wife of another Valient. Told him about the theory that there was a special group of Laven who had additional powers. Even though Ellis didn't fully understand what it meant, he had shared it with the rest of their family previously.

Ellis inhaled a shaky breath. "But now . . . now we must question if he intended that threat to extend to all of us. To this family that we hold so dear. I fear Ambrose is controlling the Kruen, making them target us in the day."

A disturbance wobbled through the air.

"The only thing we can do is fight," he continued. "Search through the evils that the Kruen are whispering into human minds, watch for any ill deed they're trying to pour onto our brothers and sisters within their minds, and stop the carnage before it happens."

He didn't try to hide the truth of what they'd all accepted was happening.

Rage burned within Pax, and he tightened his hold on Aria's hand as he gritted his teeth. "We have to stop this monster, Aria."

"I know. And we will. We have to." She ran her thumb over the back of his hand.

"Be careful, my family. In the day, use caution wherever you go and with whomever you interact. And when you descend into Faydor, fight with everything you have. We cannot let them prevail."

Hundreds of Laven gathered together, each finding their Nols. Those whose Nols had not arrived or who mourned the ones who were forever lost remained huddled together on the grass.

Choosing to wait.

Praying for a miracle.

The pairs moved toward the gateway, which was hidden to the naked eye, invisible save for the energy that lapped and pulled. A force that drew them to the vile darkness that waited beyond.

To their calling.

Only now, their calling had changed. Their survival hinged on snuffing out those who sought their demise.

Or the *one*.

Aggression curled through Pax, and he and Aria followed the trail of their family who stepped through the portal, two by two. Their essences lit up in a brilliant, blinding light before they disappeared into the nothingness.

Dani and Timothy came up to their side, and Dani muttered, "Oh God," to Aria before she wrapped her friend in her hold.

"It's going to be okay," Aria promised, her voice firm, taking that truth on for its own.

Dani shook her head against her shoulder, the woman so tiny next to Aria that her head barely came to her chest. "I know. It has to be. We have to stop this. I can't lose you. You are . . ."

Emotion wound through Aria. The stark love she held for Dani. Her closest friend. The one who understood her in a way no one else could, Dani having gone through her own trials as she'd grown into adulthood. Trying to accept who she was when she went to sleep and be confident enough to live her life to the fullest while she was awake.

She'd been such an inspiration to Aria. Her confidante. Her teacher. Her supporter.

"That's not going to happen," Aria promised. Praying it was true. "We will defeat him."

"I know you will," Dani murmured as she pulled back. "You are so strong. Stronger than anyone I've ever met."

Affection pulled, and Aria squeezed her tightly for one more second before she stepped away and readied herself.

Pax and Timothy shared a look. Their own resolution.

"Be safe, brother," Pax told him.

"Always," Timothy returned; then he took Dani's hand, and the two of them stepped across the threshold in front of them.

Pax felt the shaky breath Aria inhaled as they stepped up to the rippling energy that lured them forward.

"Don't let go of me, Aria. No matter what you feel. You can't allow it to drag you away from me. We can't give him that control."

"I won't." The words were resolute, an oath she made herself, and they stepped forward, drawn into Faydor.

In an instant, they were consumed by the shearing cold as they fell through the darkness. Howls of the wicked intoned in their ears. The calls for the heinous that battered their souls.

They hit the barren ground with a thud, both crouching low as they adjusted to their surroundings.

Darkness spread over the wasteland, and a bare glow hung on the horizon. Wiry, leafless elms grew out of the frozen ground, and lightning cracked across the low-hung canopy.

Their Laven family darted off in every direction, and Pax and Aria did the same, their feet pounding over the depleted earth.

Kruen slipped as vapors around them, intoning the corrupt and debased. Feeding all forms of wickedness into the minds of the humans who were unaware of the manipulation they were under where they walked the Earth below. Oblivious to the sins that were being whispered into their minds.

Aria and Pax slayed the Kruen they passed, right after they'd tapped into their thoughts, searching through the visions they could see in their minds.

Searching for any sign that Kruen were targeting their family.

They pushed themselves hard, and their breaths were salient in the frigid, ice-slick air as they ran headlong into the chaos.

They fought for hours, hope in their hearts and despondency in their spirits as they failed to catch even a glimpse of any Kruen feeding thoughts that would cause injury to their Laven family members.

Until they rounded a massive boulder, and they stumbled in their tracks.

It was a Ghorl. The most powerful of Kruen. Something they'd believed mythical until one had been sent to end Aria.

They were nearly impossible to crush. It'd taken Ellis, Josephine, Dani, Timothy, and Pax to extinguish it, though he knew it had been Aria's strength—her ability to use her energy while awake—that had truly given them the power to end it. There was no chance they could have done it without her.

And now there was another.

It toiled in a mess of liquid and shadow. A writhing, pitch-black puddle.

Through it, Pax could see someone asleep in their bed.

Peter.

Peter, who was here in Faydor, on the hunt.

They could see him in the eyes of a man who watched him through a window, jealousy and bloodlust rushing through his veins as the Ghorl fed the wicked thoughts into his mind.

*"This is the bastard who stole your wife. He's the one she was sneaking off with. He's the one who seduced that slut. He told her you were beneath her. Fed her lies. He's the reason she packed her bags and left. He's responsible for all of your pain. Open the window and slip inside. Do you feel the weight of the gun? How good it will feel to lift it and pull the trigger? All sins have consequences. Death is his."*

"It's Peter." His name wheezed out of Aria.

"Do you think you can bind it?" Pax's question was barely a breath.

Laven had the power to bind Kruen in Faydor. To stretch out the energy inside themselves, striking the Kruen with it where they would be turned to ash.

Ruined.

Destroyed.

It was the purpose they'd been given. To hunt the Kruen in Faydor and end them as they fed all wickedness into human minds.

No, they couldn't stop them all, but it kept the world from falling into complete destruction.

Uncertainty and determination rolled through Aria on a wave, and she squeezed his hand. "I will try."

"I'll try to help," he mumbled, though he was sure his powers were a fraction of what Aria possessed.

They kept themselves hidden behind the boulder as they gathered their strength, something between a physical and a spiritual feat. Their focus was intent on the energy they could feel winding within themselves. It magnified the orb of light that gathered from the deepest places inside them, until it became almost impossible to contain it.

Pax was sure that within Aria, the power was even greater.

Aria gave him a glance, a dip of her chin, a silent *go*.

They rushed around the boulder at the same moment and let the energy go, hoping the impact of it would be enough to bind the Ghorl.

With a screech, it amassed as it sensed their attack. In one instant, the beast transformed from vapor to a solid, vicious being.

Its flesh was charred ash, though it was somehow transparent, so Pax could see the wickedness streaking through its writhing red veins. Its mouth was deformed. Twisted and gnarled with hate. The monster opened it to reveal jagged teeth as it snarled.

It reared back against their attack, though, unlike the Kruen—who would flee, shift to shadow, and escape as mist along the pitted, desolate ground—it lashed out, the beast flying in their direction as it sent a thousand fiery tendrils whipping through the air.

"Aria!" Pax shouted, jerking her to the left. They dove behind the boulder, hitting the ground with a thud.

The second they landed, Pax scrambled to cover Aria.

To protect her.

To shield her.

He had no idea what a burn from a Ghorl would do while they were in Faydor, but he refused to take the chance to find out. He couldn't allow her to be wounded when she was their only chance of survival.

Streaks of fire flashed over the top of them, sparking and crackling as the darts struck the ground, before they flickered out.

Aria pushed at his chest. "We have to stop it," she urged.

Reluctance pounded through Pax, but he finally pulled back, taking Aria's hand to help her up. They crouched low as they peered out around the boulder to the endless darkness laid out in front of them.

And the Ghorl.

It was gone.

# Chapter Nine

## ARIA

"Do you know how to find him?" I gasped the second my eyes shot open to the morning that had taken hold of the motel room. Pax was already awake, flying off the bed and dragging on his jeans.

Both of us had clearly woken up with the exact same intentions.

"Fucking hope so," he all but growled as he snagged his phone from the nightstand.

"Peter Conway," he mumbled, typing his name into the search bar. "Thirty-three. Indiana—at least, I hope that's where he still lives."

He started pacing as he scrolled through the results, anxiety ripping through him on tormented waves.

I sat forward, the sheet pulled tight against my chest as I waited. Praying that he would find something. That we could *do* something.

A heavy exhale whipped out of Pax when he landed on something. "Think I got him. Fort Wayne, Indiana."

Pax searched something else. "It's about six hours from here."

I threw off the sheets and jumped out of bed, limbs trembling as I hurried to get on my clothes.

"If we scared off the Ghorl, maybe its thoughts didn't have a chance to take hold and the guy second-guessed his plans," I reasoned. "Maybe we can get there to stop it before the Ghorl returns."

My stomach tightened. If Peter was still alive? If the man had taken off?

Then we had to do something.

The problem was, Peter wouldn't even know to be extra vigilant. Wouldn't know that he had been directly targeted, since he was hunting in Faydor through the night. Our Laven family had spread out and covered too much ground for there to have been a chance for us to find him during the night. At least Ellis had given the warning to be extra vigilant during the day.

My hands shook out of control as I zipped up my jeans, a frenzy lighting through me as I snatched the shirt I'd had on yesterday from the floor and pulled it over my head.

There was no time to delay.

Pax dragged on his tee, too, rumbling, "There's a number listed. Probably a long shot."

Still, he dialed it and tucked the phone between his shoulder and ear as he sat on the edge of the bed, grabbed a boot, and shoved his foot into it.

The sound was dull, but I could hear the faint ringing on the other end of the line.

"Hello?" a man answered.

"Peter? Peter Conway?" Pax said in a rush, the words an appeal.

"You've got the wrong number, man."

The line went dead.

"Shit," Pax spat, and in frustration, he threw the phone onto the bed as he pulled on the other boot, then pushed to his feet. He took a step in one direction, then one the other, continuously dragging the fingers of both hands through the locks of his white hair.

His eyes wild.

He looked manic.

Unhinged.

Likely the same as me.

"We have to get to him before it's too late," I said, stuffing my feet into my shoes.

"It's probably already too fuckin' late, Aria. The address I found could be as wrong as the number."

Gloom shrouded his spirit.

Rushing over to him, I fisted my hands in his tee and jerked him toward me. "Don't give up on me now, Pax. We have to try."

Remorse blustered through his expression, and his hand snatched my waist. "Not givin' up on you, Aria. I just don't know if I can protect you and the rest of our family, too. You're what's important."

I shook my head, just barely. "Every single one of them is important—and they have their Nols, who love them just as much as you love me. Don't forget that. This has never been only about us, and selfishness is not going to serve us now. We have to do whatever we can."

The tattoos on his throat bobbed as he swallowed. "Fuck, I know. I'm just—"

In a flurry of motion, he clutched me against him, his body a burning flame against mine. He buried his face in my hair. "This is all so fucked up."

"I know. But we can't lose hope in the middle of it."

Peeling myself out of his hold, I leaned down and grabbed our bags where we'd left them packed at the foot of the bed. "We need to go."

We made it into Fort Wayne a little before noon. Our nerves were frayed. We'd spent the entire trip on edge as we sped as quickly as we could without drawing too much attention to ourselves.

I could barely take in the quaint beauty of the city as I sat forward in the seat, though there was no missing that it was frozen.

Covered in snow.

I had the cell gripped in my hand as it gave directions to the address Pax had found, my attention rapt as he wound through the city.

My heart thundered and my spirit screamed.

We had to make it.

We had to stop this tragedy.

Pax made a right off the main road and into an older family neighborhood. Most of the houses appeared unique, each different from the others, the yards of different sizes and the paint different colors.

Some were surrounded by tall wooden fences, and others remained open to the ruddy river that ran on the opposite side of the road.

Trees soared, their branches stretched out like bare bones in the frigid winter, and the ground was completely covered in snow except for the sidewalks and roads.

The heater cranked through the vents, but it didn't do anything to allay the chill that suddenly slicked across my skin and sank all the way into my spirit.

Pax flinched, fingers twitching on the steering wheel.

"Do you feel it?" I asked, the tension suddenly so stark that I could barely speak.

A harbinger of wickedness.

"Yeah, Aria, I feel it," Pax grunted.

He sat forward in his seat, both of us peering out the windshield as we approached the address.

*Your destination is on the right,* the computer-generated voice proclaimed, though somehow it felt like it was issuing a sentence.

A penalty.

Pax slowed to a crawl, and ice slipped down my spine and a chill raced through my body.

Because up ahead was a two-story house painted a sage green with white accents, and coming down its walkway was a tall, lanky man who ambled along with his head down and his hands stuffed in his jacket pockets.

He was headed toward a gray truck parked in front of a closed garage.

Short, black hair and pale, pale skin.

"Peter," I rasped, blinking, unable to believe I was laying eyes on another member of our family.

But there was no relief in it. There was only a crash of desperation and a frenzy of recklessness when we saw another man step out from where he'd been hidden behind the truck.

Arm trembling as he lifted a gun and aimed it over the hood.

"Oh God," I wheezed.

In the middle of the road, Pax shoved the car into park and threw open his door. "Stay in the car," he gritted as he jumped out.

I couldn't help but do the same. Needing to do something. To stop this from happening.

Only it was too late.

Because the man uttered his name, and Peter looked up.

The second he did, the crack of a gunshot rang out.

It echoed and rolled.

Disorienting.

Everything set to slow as a scream locked in my throat.

Stunned, Peter gripped his chest.

"Fuck," Pax spat at the same second as he whipped his gun from his jacket pocket.

Shock covered Peter's face, though I thought I saw realization dawn beneath it. When he discerned that he had been the next fatality. That our family's twisted fate had brought him to his end.

Something close to sorrow billowed through his expression before he stumbled to the side, then dropped to his knees, slumping face down on the snow-covered lawn in his front yard.

Snow that turned bright red.

A rattled ball of grief lifted, but I pressed my hand over my mouth to keep it contained, knowing I had to get to the man before he knew I was there. Put my hands on him and pray I could extinguish the cruelty he had been given, all while wondering if it was too late for him.

If he'd fully succumbed and welcomed the wickedness. A willing vessel to inflict pain.

Only I had no time. There was nothing I could do but let that rattled ball of grief go when the man brought the gun to his head and pulled the trigger.

It rang out, and the man crumpled to the ground.

My legs wobbled from the horror, and I dropped to my knees on the pitted pavement.

Pax rushed around the front of the car, and he curled his arms around me from behind and tried to get me onto my feet.

"We have to go, Aria. We need to get out of here."

"Peter," I wept. "We were too late. We were too late."

"I know. I know. I know, baby." He mumbled it against the top of my head. "But we have to go."

I gasped through the tears that blurred my eyes, and I swore I could hear Ambrose's laughter roll through the trees. His satisfaction that he had taken another of us.

His words from that night infiltrated my mind. The vitriol.

*This life is filled with many mysteries, is it not? A child lying in their bed, waking to a paradise unseen, believing they are a chosen one. But no . . . that paradise is only a shroud. A cover for the affliction we're to be given. A man walking in darkness. Charged with a burden unlike any other would ever be asked. Asked to carry an albatross so great he's on his knees, both night and day. But why suffer when we can be so much greater than that?*

Awareness pulsed through my consciousness, and I rasped, "I remember. I remember where I saw his name."

# Chapter Ten

## PAX

I resisted the urge to speed out of the neighborhood like a maniac, instead gritting my teeth as I drove slowly, taking one quiet street and then another. The whole time, I kept one hand on Aria's thigh like it might be enough to stanch the shaking that wouldn't quit as she sat gasping in the passenger's seat.

Whatever epiphany she'd had locked on her tongue.

All while searching out the windows to make sure no one paid us any mind. Hoping no one had witnessed what had gone down between Peter and that bastard, and pinned us as being there.

It was one of the most painful things I'd ever had to experience. Trying to protect Aria the best way that I could, all while feeling like a piece of shit that I'd had to leave my brother's body in a pool of his blood on the snow-covered lawn.

I was too fuckin' late to save him, and unable to risk making an anonymous call. Could only hope someone would be out walking their dog or something soon and find them, or had maybe heard something and come out to investigate.

We finally made it to the other end of the neighborhood, and my heart hammered as I came to a stop at the intersection of two larger streets. I made a left and wound into the traffic, becoming one with the mass.

We hadn't traveled a quarter of a mile when sirens suddenly cut through the dense air. All the cars pulled off to the side as a cruiser came blazing down the street from the opposite direction. Four more followed, whipping by in a blur of flashing lights.

My hand tightened on Aria's thigh, and I glanced in the rearview mirror to see them all make a right into the neighborhood we'd just come out of.

Guessed it hadn't taken long at all for someone to find them.

Wasn't sure if I was relieved or worried.

"Do you think anyone saw us?" Aria whispered into the anxiety hovering over us.

"I don't think so. I would imagine it's going to look pretty cut-and-dried to the investigators." A murder-suicide they could easily wrap up. "They likely won't be looking for anyone else unless someone specifically saw us get out of the car."

Aria barely nodded as she sank lower into the seat.

I started to pull back onto the road, then had to immediately pull back off when an ambulance came barreling through.

"I hate this," she rasped through her grief.

"I know, baby. I know."

Once we got back onto the road, I started to take a bunch of turns, getting us lost in a maze of businesses and homes, before I finally broke back into the downtown area. I pulled off at a picnic stop that sat on the side of the murky river.

Everything was painted in a thick coating of snow. The tables and the trees and the roofs of the buildings.

It covered the park area, too, right up to the edge of the river that cut through.

I had planned on just leaving the car running so we could talk, but Aria tossed open the door and got out.

She lifted her face toward the bulbous gray clouds that hung heavy from the sky.

Long locks of black hair whipped behind her as she headed toward the edge of the river, leaving a trail of torment in her wake.

Chest as heavy as the fucking clouds, I climbed out, and I stuffed my hands in the pockets of my leather jacket as I slowly edged up behind her, feet crunching through the snow and withered grass.

I stopped a foot away, just breathing in her pain.

"He's going to hunt all of them, Pax. All of us. And he won't stop until everyone is dead."

Aria hugged her arms over her chest as she stared out over the muddy, stagnant river.

"Who is he?" My thoughts toiled with the possibilities.

She hugged herself tighter, and her head swept from side to side. "I don't know. But I remember . . . I remember where I saw his name. When we discovered Abigail Watkins at that library where we met Maria Lewis?"

When we'd been searching for any information on Laven and who we were, we'd found an artist who'd painted visions of Tearsith and Faydor. Abigail Watkins. She'd died more than 120 years ago in a house fire.

"Yeah?"

Aria slowly shifted to look at me from over her shoulder. Her face was pinched in doubt and speculation. "Abigail Watkins's husband was named Ambrose. That can't be a coincidence, can it?"

My mind spiraled back to that day, which felt like a lifetime ago when it'd been only a couple weeks. We hadn't had time to click on the husband's name since I was unsettled by a guy who was watching us, and we'd taken off.

With everything that'd happened, we hadn't done any more digging around Abigail Watkins. Figuring it was nothing but a dead end. Too far in the past for us to glean anything useful.

The dread that scorched through my chest told me it had to mean something.

"Not sure there's a world that small where that could be a coincidence."

She turned away and looked down, and I knew she was staring at the cell she had clutched in her hand.

I could feel her reticence. Like she wished she could squeeze her eyes closed and all this would go away.

That she'd finally—*finally*—wake from this nightmare.

But this nightmare was our lives, and I eased up to her side, bringing us shoulder to shoulder.

Vapor puffed from our mouths as we stood out in the glacial cold. Tension bound us, chains of uncertainty and trepidation, before she blew out the biggest sigh and tapped into the search bar on the phone.

She typed in the few details we knew about Abigail.

*Abigail Watkins, painter, Tearsith.*

The painting titled *Tearsith* populated first.

As if the chains had been loosened, Aria hurried to click on it, then clicked directly on Abigail Watkins's name; then from there, she scrolled down her history to her family's listing.

> Abigail Watkins was an American painter.
> Born: February 16, 1871, in Pendleton, South Carolina
> Died: March 4, 1902, in Charlotte, North Carolina
> Known for: Painting
> Spouse: Ambrose Watkins
> Parents: Robert Ray Smith, Beatrice Louise Remington

*Ambrose Watkins* was hyperlinked, and Aria stalled for only a beat before she clicked on it.

There was little information.

His name and date of birth.

September 2, 1863.

But there was a picture. A faded black-and-white picture that still held the power to punch the air from my lungs and sent Aria's free hand clapping over her mouth, though her whimper was clear.

"Oh my God, it's him."

# Chapter Eleven

## ARIA

I shivered as I sat with two of the car's vents pumping in my direction, trying to thaw what had gone cold inside me. It felt as if I'd been frozen from the inside out.

Seeing Peter murdered.

Remembering where I'd heard the name Ambrose before. That thread that had dangled in the periphery of my mind finally knitting into awareness.

But getting the confirmation that he had actually been married to Abigail was what had made me feel as if ice had formed around every organ inside me, a flood of bitter cold rushing from my spirit and spreading out to saturate every cell of my body.

A tremor rolled through me, and Pax turned his vent my way, too. Concern radiated from him as he put the car in reverse, then pulled back out onto the road.

"How is it possible?" I blinked as he made a right. "He was born in 1863. This is beyond—"

I clipped off, not able to process it, let alone voice it.

Pax looked through his side mirror as he hit the freeway before he glanced my way. Apprehension scored deep grooves into his forehead. "So, what, this fucker is immortal?"

His jaw clenched when he said it, and his tattooed hands covered with the vapor of Faydor flexed on the steering wheel.

Another shiver rolled through me at the thought. Uncertainty weaved a path through my senses. "He was *born*. You and I both saw him walking here, in the flesh. He has to be human."

"A human who's more than a hundred and fifty years old?" Speculation suffused the words. "A human who was able to drag you from Faydor and into a whole different plane? One none of us has ever known?"

Each instance he issued was like a stake being driven into the validity of Ambrose being human.

I tried to swallow around the unrest that quivered inside me. It had been hard enough trying to accept who I was. My fate. So many misunderstandings surrounding it.

And now it felt as if I was floundering through a brand-new world. A world in which all of us had been given a death sentence.

"And he told me he was the one who sent the Ghorl," I added on a breathy wheeze, trying to piece together the clues we had.

A harsh puff of air escaped Pax's nose, and he roughed a hand through his shock of white hair.

"He took on the face of that little girl we thought was a Laven," he started to reason. "Maybe he's taken on the face of Abigail's husband. Maybe he's bred of Kreed, some kind of Kruen that we've never encountered before, and his taking on the identity of a human is the only way he can be here. Hell, maybe he *is* Kreed."

I choked on the idea.

We'd all be dead then. But ultimately, wasn't he what we were up against?

Reaching across the center console, Pax curled a warm palm over the top of my thigh. "Fuck. Didn't mean to upset you. I'm just throwing out ideas. Trying to figure out what the hell is going on here. We don't have any proof of anything."

Doubt furled out of me on a small laugh. “You can’t upset me more than I already am, and you know you can’t tiptoe around me. Figuring this out together is the only way we’re going to survive.”

I shifted to look at him fully, determination in my voice. “And I think confronting him head-on is the only way we’re going to get proof of what he is. The only way we’re going to be able to get answers. The only way we’re going to be able to stop him.”

A roll of dread left him on a heavy exhalation. “And what exactly are you thinking?”

“I’m thinking we need to pick a spot and stay there for a little while. Let him come to us.”

“Aria . . .”

“I already told you I’m not running this time, Pax. I’m here to fight, no matter what that looks like.”

“It goes against every fiber of my being . . . thinking about putting you in the line of fire. You want to confront him, and the only thing I want to do is hide you from him.”

“I’m already in the crosshairs, and there’s no way to get out of them. I just need to figure out how I’m going to fight my way through it. I can’t sit around and allow something like what happened this morning to happen to any more of our Laven family. You and I both know Nathan didn’t fall down those steps on his own, Pax, and we know William wasn’t responsible for OD’ing. And then Peter . . . we had direct access to that Ghorl’s thoughts. *We know.*”

The question no longer lingered.

It was plucking us off, one by one.

“I have to do everything in my power to end this sooner, because if he continues, I’m not sure how many of us will have a later.”

It was late afternoon when we carried our bags up the stairs at a motel in a suburb of Indianapolis. The chill of Fort Wayne had followed us here, the winter in full force, the wind a blustery gale that cut all the way to the bone.

Darkness loomed on the horizon, ready to swallow the gray sky as the last vestiges of the sun melted away.

"Cold as fuck," Pax grumbled as we came to stand in front of Room 251. This motel had a key card that slid into the lock, and it gave when he ran it through. The orange door drifted open to a room that was decent compared to some of the other places we'd stayed.

A king bed sat against the left wall, and a flat-screen was mounted on the opposite. A larger round table was beneath the window, and the dressing area and sink were situated on the far wall outside the bathroom.

The decor was a bit dated, but the room was clean.

"Movin' up in the world." Another grunt from Pax as he dropped his duffel to the floor before he slipped inside and did his routine check.

"All clear, Princess," he said when he returned, and he swung the door open wide and grabbed his bag and took mine from me. He turned and dumped them both onto the foot of the bed.

I stepped inside and carefully turned the two locks on the door.

I may have wanted to draw Ambrose here, but I wanted to do it on my terms.

I just wasn't entirely sure how to make that happen. It was like he was right there, dancing along the fringes, taunting and provoking. Lording over those he had under his control.

It was that control I needed to shatter.

The heater under the window pumped, and a tremor rolled through me as the cold clashed with the heat.

"It's warm in here, at least," Pax mumbled as he unzipped his duffel and pulled out his toiletry bag. He kept his attention down as he dug around, and there was something in his demeanor that was off.

Unsettled.

Not that we weren't always on edge. But I could feel it. The strain that pulled right beneath the surface.

I'd felt it grow with every mile we'd traveled today.

"What's wrong?" I asked his back, my chest stretching tight in worry.

It wasn't as if there weren't a million things that were *wrong*.

But this was new.

Something that had emerged in the aftermath of what we'd seen and learned earlier today.

Pax hesitated, clearly not wanting to let me in.

"If there's something going on, you need to let me know. You can't keep me in the dark. There's enough of it already, isn't there?"

On a sigh, Pax stopped riffling through his bag and his head drooped between his shoulders.

"About out of money. I'm going to have to hunt. Track down some fuckin' monster who has plenty of it for all the wrong reasons and relieve him of it. That, and relieve the world of his burden."

He stayed that way for the longest time before he slowly turned to me.

Ferocity fueled the lilt of his chin, white fire in the flames of his eyes, though there was the slightest smudge of guilt that underscored it. That part of him that believed he wasn't good enough for me. That he was bad in some way. That he'd taint me.

"Then we go find him," I told him.

Simply.

Because I also understood his calling. Why he did the things he did.

A gush of rejection puffed out of him, and he let go of a caustic laugh. "Absolutely fuckin' not. There is no *we* to it."

The words were shards, scorn directed at himself.

I lifted my own chin in challenge. "I thought you said we were in this together?"

In a flash, Pax crossed the room, and he had my face framed in his hands before I could process the movement.

"You think I would ever want to subject you to that, Aria? What you have to witness is bad enough—the barbarity both here and in Faydor. But for you to see it coming from my own hands?" His face pinched in disgust. "When it isn't done to protect you? When it's done out of my own selfishness?"

"Out of your own selfishness?" Disbelief gusted from my lungs. "Do you think I don't know why you really do it? Do you think I don't know this is another way that you protect the innocent? That you're giving your entire life to stopping the evils that run rampant in this world? Both while awake and asleep? You think I would ever judge you?"

He dropped his forehead to mine. "I can't stand the thought of you seeing me like that, Aria. With bloodstained hands."

My forehead shook against his, and I clutched on to him as I whispered, "All of our hands are bloodstained. In some way. You're the one who told me that what is important right now is my survival . . . And if this is part of what it takes for that survival, then so be it."

He tightened his hold on my face. "No, Aria. Not this. Please don't ask it of me. Stay here and keep the doors locked. I hate leaving you, but it's so much more dangerous out there than it is in here. I'm going to leave my gun on the table. Do not hesitate to use it. I'll be back as soon as I can."

With that, he tore himself away, and he pulled his gun from where he had it tucked inside his jacket. Metal clanked against the wood as he set it down; then he pulled a large knife from his duffel and tucked that into its spot.

Anxiety rolled through me. The thought of him out there, on his own—every part of me rejected the idea of it. This misconception that he was supposed to take on more of the burden. That he had to protect me from the things he thought I shouldn't be exposed to.

We should have long since passed that.

"Pax," I said, trying to break through to him, but one second later, he stood in front of me again.

His hot hands burned on my cheeks as he begged, "Please, just stay here, Aria. Please."

Then he moved around me and worked through the locks. He scanned the area before he looked back at me with some sort of apology written in his expression, then fully stepped out and let the door drift shut behind him.

Hurt blistered through me, and a puff of incredulity escaped my mouth.

I began to pace, fingers twining in agitation.

Was that what he thought? What our partnership meant? What our relationship meant? That he could keep me out of the parts he didn't want me to see?

Only, I could see. Our connection was too great for his insecurities to shield it.

I didn't need to close my eyes to feel it.

Because an hour later, a sense was there, infiltrating my spirit. A sense that swelled inside me on a rising tide. A warning that he was in trouble. It invaded my mind with visions of darkness. The darkness he'd just stepped into.

# Chapter Twelve

## PAX

Fuck.

I felt like an utter prick leaving Aria that way. Just turning my back and walking out. It was the only thing I could do, since there wasn't a chance I could remain there and deny that she was speaking the truth. Her point was more than valid, but how could I drag her here?

To the seediest part of the city, where I knew I would find what I was looking for.

Some sick, deranged bastard getting rich off the weak.

Night had just fallen, and the dense clouds that hung over the city created a canopy. A darkened shell that felt as if it enclosed the wickedness, held it in captivity while letting it run unchecked.

The whole vibe made it feel later than it was, though the streets were crammed with cars that made their way through rush hour in an endless string of taillights.

A siren wailed from somewhere in the distance, and the cold, corrupt air was intermittently filled with the blare of a car horn and the revving of engines.

People bustled along the sidewalks, ducking into stores and restaurants and apartment buildings.

I wondered how many of them noticed the aura in the atmosphere. If they could scent it the way I did.

Nah.

Not possible.

They had to be wholly immune, or there was no chance they'd be dashing around as if all things were right. Not a care in the world when I felt the weight of that world's sin crushing down on my shoulders.

It was so heavy I could hardly breathe.

I followed it, winding through the city, taking back alleys and narrow streets, tracking my way into the places where the disparaged lived. The places only the depraved would seek.

It was then that I found what I was looking for.

Women.

So fuckin' young that bile burned in the back of my throat.

There were only two of them, loitering at the end of a street.

One had dark-brown curly hair, and the other was a bleached blonde.

They were dressed in next to nothing, their legs bare in the middle of the frigid winter. Each of them wore a cropped fake-animal-fur jacket, like that would be enough to keep them warm.

Both were clearly strung out.

Eyes devoid of emotion.

Detached.

No question, it was the only way they could stomach living this life, which they were likely forced into.

But they weren't really who I was looking for. They were just a sign. A beacon for the perverted.

The brown-haired girl didn't even look at me when she stepped forward in an attempt to get my attention. "You looking for someone to keep you company tonight?"

The younger one beside her looked up. The second she did, a bolt of disquiet moved through her when she caught sight of me.

Shaken from her stupor.

It was like my appearance was enough to drag her back down into a beat of reality. Green eyes widening with shock and a surprised sound spilling from her lips.

She stumbled back a step, trying to disappear into the shadows of the dingy building that stood high behind her.

Her fear was distinct.

Palpable as it radiated from her skin.

I ground my teeth, hating that she was afraid of me.

"Nah," I said. "But maybe you should go home. Get out of here."

The one with the curly brown hair laughed a hollow sound. "Oh, honey, this *is* home."

I angled around them, turning left at the corner they were standing at, and I stuffed my frozen hands into my jacket pockets and let loose a chill that tumbled down my spine.

Doubted it was the weather that had conjured the cold. It was just the sickness that roiled in the confines of the squalid street.

Knowing I was close to what I came for, I itched, nervous that I didn't have my gun. I was armed only with a knife, but there was no chance I was going to leave Aria at that motel without a way to protect herself.

Fucking hated that I'd had to do it in the first place.

"You sure?" the only one who'd spoken called behind me. "You look awful lonely."

"Yup," I said without looking back. Covertly, I let my attention swivel from left to right, searching the foulness that wormed through the night.

Vapor puffed from my mouth, and adrenaline thrummed through my veins.

This bastard couldn't be far.

I was halfway down the block when I spotted him. He was on the opposite side of the street outside a small restaurant. He leaned against the dingy brick wall like it was his post, flanked on either side by two other men.

He was probably in his late twenties and had dark, slicked-back hair. Wearing slacks and a striped button-down shirt.

I felt it swarm.

A cloud of lechery and self-indulgence all mixed in a vat of cruelty.

He was the one.

Didn't miss that his eyes moved to the girls at the end of the street—checking his *property*—before he slanted them back to me.

I could feel it burn into my side, and the raucous conversation the other two guys were having clanked off when they noticed where their boss had set his attention.

I kept facing forward, acting like I hadn't noticed them lurking across the street.

Minding my own business.

Oblivious.

Which wasn't the smartest game plan, either, considering the fuckers were likely to jump me, though I guessed there was something about me that kept them rooted.

Or maybe some lone bastard wasn't worthy of their time. They had more important crimes to keep them busy, like coercing vulnerable runaways into chains.

Violence pulled through my consciousness, and I had the urge to turn, rush across the street, and take all three of them out.

But I couldn't attack without a plan. I had to play this smart. Couldn't act so recklessly, the way I used to do. Running into situations with guns blazing, not really caring if I came out whole on the other side.

Nothing to lose.

Now I had Aria. Now I had this *completeness* that throbbed inside me.

Her face passed behind my eyes, and my stomach churned in disquiet.

The last thing I wanted was for her to feel like I'd disrespected her.

Belittled her.

That hadn't been my intention, even though I'd seen the offense and worry playing through those gorgeous eyes.

But it felt like my responsibility to keep her from this.

I couldn't imagine her walking down this street with me. Putting her in even more danger than she was already in.

It seemed risky and imprudent.

Unnecessary when keeping her safe was the only thing that mattered.

I had to do this on my own, and I had to get this piece of shit by himself.

Wait it out or come up with a way to lure him out.

Needed this fast and clean so I could get back to Aria.

So I kept moving, making a right at the intersecting road, walking all the way down the block before I made another right, winding around so I would come back toward the girls in the opposite direction from where I'd begun.

The whole time, I calculated.

Figured he'd either come to the girls at some point, or I could follow them back to whatever slum he was keeping them in. So I was going to need a place to hide out until the time was right.

Conceal myself in the shadows and watch.

I made it to the street I'd first come down, and I leaned against the wall and peered around the corner.

This end of the building was cast in a cloak of gloom, the single streetlamp on the other side of the road flickering the barest flashes of light.

The stench of corruption filled the air. As thick here as it had been when I passed by the monsters on the other street.

Blood drummed through my veins. Frustration and determination.

I slipped around the corner and started to slink up through the shadows, and I edged up to a large dumpster that kept me hidden but obstructed my view. I attempted to peer out through the back side of the dumpster near the wall, but it was too narrow, and I couldn't get tabs on the girls.

I had to get closer, or I was going to lose them at some point.

Only the second I started to edge around the dumpster, I felt a shift in the atmosphere.

Coming at me from both the front and the back.

A torrent of wickedness and a slosh of greed.

I glanced over my shoulder. My chest tightened when I saw the same two guys who'd flanked the man come rounding up the corner of the building.

But it was the fiend standing five feet in front of me who sent a stone sinking to the pit of my stomach.

They had stalked me.

Surrounded me.

The bastard in the front cocked his head.

Pure evil oozed from his pores as he flashed a knife and said, "No one plays with my girls unless they pay for it."

# Chapter Thirteen

## ARIA

I couldn't sit still as I rode in the back seat of the taxi. A taxi that had taken twelve minutes and fourteen seconds to arrive to pick me up. One that had nearly made me tremble apart while I paced in the motel lobby, anxiety ripping through my senses as I waited for it to show.

It wasn't like I had a credit card and could download a rideshare app. I had the small wad of cash Pax had asked me to stow in my duffel bag before we left Albany.

Now I clutched two twenties in a sweaty palm, peering out the rear-passenger window at the city slowly passing by. The taxi crawled through traffic as the driver carried me to some random address that I'd thrown out.

I had to get downtown. At least that part, I knew. At least that part, I could *feel.*

That awareness thrashed inside me, gripping me by the throat as we traveled deeper into the city.

Worry and anger at Pax leaving me the way he had flashed through my senses, and I clutched the handle of the gun that I had hidden in the left-hand pocket of my jacket.

I'd never held a gun before.

Had never wanted to.

Now, it trembled in my hand.

Proof that Pax had left himself vulnerable.

Susceptible.

Because why? Because he'd thought I was too precious to be exposed to what he had to do, when I bore witness to the gravest, most horrible atrocities each night?

A part of me got his reasoning, but the other couldn't abide him making this decision for me.

I would have been okay with waiting to hash it out with him when he returned.

But now? I couldn't sit idle.

He was in trouble. I knew it all the way to my soul. I could only imagine that sense was something similar to how he'd known I was in trouble when he'd come to rescue me from the mental facility. The way our connection howled through me like the battering of a storm. Pulling me toward a destination I shouldn't know but could feel like it'd been marked with a target.

We were stopped at a light, and once it turned green, the line of cars ahead of us began to move and the driver accelerated. We'd made it halfway to the next light when I felt it.

The awareness became so intense it was strangling, my throat closing off and my heart violently bashing at my ribs.

"Stop!" I shouted.

The driver tossed me a worried glance through the rearview mirror. "We still have two blocks to go," he said.

"It's okay. Just let me out. Please." The words hitched with the frenzy that burned through me like a flame.

He shrugged, likely happy to get the freak out of his car, and he barely pulled to the side when he stopped, the tail end of the car still angled into the road.

The car behind us laid on the horn, and I rushed, tossing the two twenties into the front seat before I threw open the door and jumped out.

Breaths haggard and panting as I stumbled out onto the sidewalk.

Disoriented but drawn.

I turned in a circle, trying to get my bearings, to tap into the tether that was hooked directly in my soul.

I instinctively turned toward the narrow road that cut between two tall buildings about twenty feet up ahead on my right. I rushed that way, dodging the people who bustled along the sidewalk.

I rounded onto that street, and I was nearly knocked off my feet by the swell of iniquity that slammed into me. A cold rush that whipped through my hair and gusted across my face.

There were far fewer people here, and it felt as if I'd been cut off from the hustle of the city and tossed into an entirely different realm.

It was like descending into Faydor from Tearsith.

Jarred from one existence to another.

Darkness reigned, and I lumbered deeper into its midst, through the vapor that pumped out the vents low on the buildings and misted the frostbitten air. Following the tether that pulled me in his direction.

My spirit screamed in awareness as I kept myself tucked as close to the walls of the buildings as possible.

I crossed one street, racing beneath the streetlamps of the crosswalk to the other side, before I was back to slinking through the pall.

It was freezing, the air spiked with ice, but I felt drenched in sweat. Consumed by an inferno that threatened to turn me to ash.

I clutched the gun inside my jacket pocket as I crept below the dull, hazy streetlights, the grip slick against my palm.

Too heavy.

All wrong.

I could feel my pulse accelerate, eyes sweeping as I took in everyone I passed.

Wary of anyone who might suddenly turn on me.

A young couple who kissed in a recessed alcove of an apartment building.

A woman who hurried across the street in front of me.

Two men who leered as they approached but were smart enough not to touch.

Breaths rasping from my lungs, I made it to the next street.

This one was nearly deserted, though there were two young girls on the opposite side on the corner. One had curly brown hair and was dressed in a miniskirt. The other appeared to be maybe three or four years younger than her, blond and wearing shimmery black shorts.

Both wore heels and were hugging their arms over their faux-fur jackets to provide some warmth as they waited to garner attention.

But it was what radiated from them that nearly stopped me in my tracks. What nearly made me switch direction and go straight to them.

The shouts of their thoughts.

Only they were dulled by the drugs I could almost smell running through their veins.

Sticky and sweet and vile.

But they made them no less profound.

The hiss of the Kruen that whispered the cruel evils into their hearts.

*"You were destined for this. This is right where you belong. With the foul. Did you think you'd make something of yourself? You were born this way. You're just like your mother. Disgusting and pathetic and weak. Ignorant and stupid."*

A wicked voice laughed low in the brown-haired girl's ear. *"Don't think you're smart enough to walk away. You owe your life to Thadeo. You wouldn't have a roof over your head if it wasn't for him. Your only value is your body, and he's paying you exactly what you deserve, which is next to nothing."*

She fought them. The thoughts that fired through the distortion that blurred through her consciousness. Fought to rise above them. To break through them.

And the blonde . . . the one who seemed much younger . . . She was close to succumbing, her thoughts torrid and bleak.

*"Of course it hurts. Because you deserve it. You earned it. Asked for it. Begged for it. Why do you think your mother's boyfriends came to you? You*

*were always a little slut. They could smell it on you. You'll die this way, and soon. You should just put yourself out of this misery. It's okay to welcome it. It's the only relief you will ever find. You can't take this any longer. It's time. It's time."*

I stumbled over her agony as her thoughts blistered through my mind. It was as if I could actually see her memories without touching her.

A terrified little girl. Man after man in her room. Telling her she was special. That she was pretty. That it was their secret. The pain. The prayers. The pleas.

Oh God, oh God.

Nausea coiled in my stomach, and my fingers tingled with an unbearable urge to touch. To end the battering mayhem in their minds.

It grew as their thoughts spiraled through me in a deluge of devastation.

It became impossible to turn from them, and I was moving, crossing the street without giving myself permission.

Drawn to them.

"You look like you took a wrong turn," the older one—the brunette—tossed out as I approached. "You should get out of here before it's too late."

It was like she couldn't tell if she wanted the warning to be spiteful or if she actually wanted me to run.

Except I was on the sidewalk, and my hand that wasn't gripping the gun stretched out with the need to touch, though there was still a foot of space between us.

"Stay here. Please don't leave. I'll be right back," I whispered to her through the disorder.

The screaming in my ears growing louder.

Both theirs and Pax's.

I could almost hear Pax chanting, *Hurry. Hurry. Hurry.*

A vague, fuzzy innuendo that he needed me.

Her laughter was a scoff. "What, you think you've got somethin' to offer me? Get the hell out of here, you clueless bitch, before your luck runs out and you end up right here next to us."

Terror flared in the other's green eyes when she looked up at me and saw the color of mine, and she whirled, looking around as if she were searching for someone else.

Pax had been here.

I knew it. Could feel it stronger than ever. The pull that tugged and compelled.

I felt torn, fractured by the instinct to stay and help, and the need to go.

*Hurry.*

"I'll be back," I promised again, pain leaching out with the words before I moved deeper into the darkness that reigned along the side of the dingy building.

The sensation grew with each step.

As danger echoed and chaos thrashed.

Pax.

He was near. I could feel his severity. The sharp cut of his aura.

Keeping my footsteps light, I hurried in its direction, trying to orient myself to the bedlam that flashed through the dense, hazy air.

Hostility and malevolence.

Then I stumbled when I saw the outline of someone up ahead in the distance.

A dark silhouette that rippled with a twisted sort of violence. Everything about him was sullied. No goodness to be found in the slick of immorality that dripped like sludge from his being.

"No one plays with my girls unless they pay for it," I heard him say, his voice a sadistic taunt as he took a step forward and disappeared on the other side of a large industrial dumpster that blocked the sidewalk. "You should have thought twice before you came sniffing around here."

There was the echo of more footsteps that grew closer, and I could feel the swell of aggression rise in the atmosphere.

My senses keened as I listened through the muddle to try to discern what was happening.

Men were surrounding him.

Circling him.

Hunting him.

Sucking in a breath, I crept forward as I pulled the gun from my pocket while I kept myself concealed against the wall. My heart pounded so loudly I was afraid they could hear the beat of it.

My own terror gripped me, thundering through my veins in a surge of adrenaline.

The gun shook between my quivering hands.

I hated that I couldn't see. That I felt blinded. Unprepared.

"Think right here is exactly where I'm supposed to be." Pax's voice was carved in animosity.

Menacing laughter rolled from one of the men. "Seems someone is looking for death."

"Nah, I'm just looking for some pathetic fucks who think controlling women actually makes them something special."

The second he said it, mayhem broke out. A rushing of feet and a pummeling of flesh.

It came from all sides.

Grunts and shouts and the scraping of bodies.

Anxiety beat through my thready pulse. Maybe Pax was right. I was so out of my comfort zone. Had no clue what I was doing, even though I knew I had to do *something*.

Tiptoeing forward, I pressed my back against the dumpster as I slowly skated around so I could see.

Pax was embroiled in a battle.

Kicking and punching and slashing a knife at the three men who surrounded him, all of whom were doing the same.

"You think you can come around here and disrespect us?" one of the men snarled, lunging forward and lashing out, the metal of his knife glinting beneath the hazy light.

The blade nicked Pax's wrist.

It didn't do anything but set him aflame, the man a fire that raged.

"You sick motherfuckers are going to bleed," Pax growled as he spat a wad of blood onto the ground at their feet from a wound that gaped on his lip.

The first man I'd seen chuckled a dark sound as he wielded his knife. "Ah, you see, it's fools like you who come around here thinking they can edge up on my territory. Saw the way you looked at my girls. You think you can have them? Can promise you one thing—you won't be walking out of here tonight."

He glanced at the other two guys and gave a jut of his chin in Pax's direction. "End this piece of shit."

He said it as if Pax were trash.

Expendable.

A problem to be disposed of, and he was going to take pleasure in watching it happen.

The two men obeyed while their leader looked on, slowly encroaching on Pax, who they began to back into the wall.

Pax seemed to comply, angling back, both his hands stretched out as if he were surrendering, though one still held on to the knife. "No need for that. I'll just go."

Except I could see the look in his eye. His intentions. Something neither of the men recognized through their arrogance.

They laughed. "Gonna make it easy on us, yeah? What's the fun in that? Think we'll take our time cutting you up."

Only as soon as one of them took him by the wrist to bend his arm behind his back, Pax attacked.

It was a flurry of movement as he spun around, twisting out of the man's grip and taking hold of his arm.

Pax held a knife in the other hand, and he jerked the man forward and drove the blade deep into his stomach.

Pax had already whirled around and was behind the second guy, taking him by the forehead and dragging the knife across his throat before anyone realized what had happened.

Both dropped to the ground in two quick thuds.

Motionless.

I fumbled through the dim light to turn off the safety and cock the gun.

I leaned against the dumpster, trying to catch my breath. To keep calm. To see through this madness.

With my back plastered to the rigid metal, I forced myself to move closer, my feet scuffing along the cracked sidewalk and up to the very end of the dumpster so I could peer around it.

Thadeo, the man who'd been in the girls' thoughts, stood between me and Pax with his back to me, and Pax was already hurtling around to take him down.

But he froze in his tracks when he found Thadeo pointing a gun in his direction.

"Motherfucker, you're gonna die."

There was no time to think it through. No time to contemplate or judge.

I shouted, "Pax, get down!"

I thought maybe he'd already sensed I was there. Anticipated the command. Because he dove to the ground at the same second that I pulled the trigger.

A shot rang out, the crack pinging and echoing against the buildings for what felt like an eternity, and I squeezed my eyes closed as blood splattered across my face.

When I opened them, I found Thadeo was frozen in place.

I stood behind him. My hand shaking and shaking.

He remained there for the longest time.

So still.

So silent.

Then he toppled to the ground, crashing with a thud with the rest of his friends.

Pax was on his feet and surging my way, arms frantic as they wrapped around me. "Fuck, Aria. Fuck."

I couldn't even respond. Couldn't process the jumble of words he issued at the side of my head. "I felt you. Knew you were comin'. I was so fuckin' terrified that you came here. But you're safe. You're safe."

I could only stare at the man who lay slumped on the ground, limbs bent at odd angles. Could only process the blood that oozed out from the wound on his back and saturated the blue-striped dress shirt he wore.

Shock confounded before it began to quiver through me in spastic quakes.

"It's okay, Aria. It's okay. Stay right there. Don't move."

Pax pulled away, and I could barely comprehend that he was kneeling beside the body, patting him down, pulling out a wad of cash from his pocket and tucking it into his. He did the same with the two other guys before he was back in front of me.

"Come on, baby, we have to go."

He finally jarred me out of the trance when he pried the gun from my tremoring hand and shoved it into his pocket. Then he grabbed that same hand and tugged. "We have to go. Now."

He started to run, dragging me around the dumpster and up the sidewalk. I fumbled along behind him, numbness soaking me through, though that awareness spiked in the middle of it. A ridge that formed in the depths like a mountain rising from the ocean.

An earthquake.

It drew me back to the purpose I'd been meant for.

The two girls had moved closer, though they were huddled against the wall. The older one shielded the blonde as if she'd taken on a motherly role. Their eyes were wide in the night, orbs of terror that swam in shock and relief.

Though the voices still reigned.

*"This means nothing,"* the voice intoned to the brown-haired girl. *"You think this is your chance? Don't be stupid and run. You know your place. Where you belong. You'll only end up worse off."*

The blonde shivered with the words that whisked through her psyche. *"You won't survive now. He was the only one keeping you alive. The only one who had the single thing that took away the pain. You have nothing now. Look how empty you are. How you're nothing. Just a body to fuck. End it. End it."*

Gasping, I staggered to a stop.

Confused, Pax pulled at my hand as he turned to peer at me with urgency slashed deep into his expression. "We have to go, Aria. Right now."

"I can't," I wheezed, and I yanked my hand free of his and moved toward the girls.

Drawn.

Hands burning with the need to do something. The energy a scourge that whipped and compelled.

"Stay back, you psycho bitch," the older one spat.

Her bravery boiled beneath the alarm, and she shifted on her feet, fighting the impulse to run.

I suddenly threw myself forward, and shock blazed through her when I grabbed her by both sides of her face.

At the connection, a chill streaked through my veins, a fiery cold that scorched me from the inside out. I nearly wept at her pain, which ricocheted through me, hot flames that charred my insides and made me feel as if I were being burned alive.

Still, a frigidness curled within it as the darkness of Faydor flickered and flashed in my periphery.

*A barren plane. Vapors and mist. Shadows rose and lifted and swirled through the wiry elms. The night thick, the sky low. Evil prowled across the lifeless ground.*

*Lightning flashed at the same moment that thunder cracked.*

The woman flailed and thrashed, trying to break out of my hold once she came to the realization that I was actually touching her.

"It's okay, it's okay, it's okay," I begged as I tightened, the plea tumbling from my mouth as I tried to peer deeper into her mind.

And it was there, the dark shadow that toiled in a misty pool on the dried, fractured floor of Faydor.

The Kruen formless as it swirled and writhed, as it fed vile lies into her mind.

Within it, a slew of her memories raced to infiltrate, to become one with mine.

A tiny girl sitting on the soiled carpet of her living room floor, brushing her doll's hair. Her mother coming out of her room in a skimpy dress. Her hand running down the little girl's head before she pressed a kiss to it and whispered, "Be a good girl. Momma needs to go to work."

The child at the counter in a dirty kitchen, dishes piled high in the sink, standing on a chair as she poured herself a bowl of cereal. The sour milk that she forced down anyway since it would be the only thing she would get to eat.

Sleeping on the couch while she listened for her mother's return.

How those nights grew longer and sometimes turned into days.

The loneliness.

The fear.

The isolation.

The hunger.

How she'd had to learn to survive on her own. But that survival had come at a great cost. Her dreams and confidence slowly chipped away, every opportunity tarnished and bashed.

*"These streets are your destiny. They're in your bones and in your blood."*

Venom dripped from the Kruen's voice, already twisting the circumstance in its favor. Driving her toward her ultimate demise.

*"Thadeo is gone. You can take that control and make his world your own. You always wanted to be better. To achieve something great. Now is the time to step up and take his place. There are plenty of girls you could guide. Become their master. Look at Sophie, shaking behind you. So pliable to mold. Make her yours. It's time."*

Confusion bound her, her thoughts a whirl, the hope she'd had to escape this life flickering to life by the greed that was offered.

Yet her conscience fought against it. She thrashed as I tried to keep hold of her, and I focused on gathering the light.

Magnified it within me. That power that came from the ethereal. From a place I was sure I'd never truly understand.

It grew and grew while the Kruen continued its assault.

I let it go, and it flashed down my arms and through my hands. Her dark eyes widened in shock as she felt it pass into her.

The Kruen sensed my presence right before the bolt of light connected, and through my mind's eye, I watched it rear up high in defense, its gnarled, gnashing mouth twisted in hate.

But it had noticed too late, and it was struck before it even had the chance to lash out.

It screamed, a piercing agony as it wailed.

And in a flicker of darkness, it disintegrated to dust.

"What the fuck did you just do?" the brunette rasped, gasping and choking as I released her and she stumbled back.

She wobbled on her heels, fumbling to the side before she sagged against the grungy brick wall.

As disoriented as I was.

Dizziness blurred my mind, the pain of the burn overwhelming.

My hands were singed and flaming red.

"Aria," Pax attempted, but I forced it back, sucked down the exhaustion that threatened to bring me to my knees and instead hauled myself forward, my arms trembling as I reached for the second girl, grasping her face.

The girl shivered and shook in abject fear.

It was the only thing she'd ever known.

Her traumas were so great that bile rolled up my throat as I touched her.

So great that I felt as if a speeding truck had slammed into me.

Her memories nearly blew me off my feet and into the air.

Abuses so severe that I could hardly fathom them. This girl, who was only fourteen.

Her mother, selling her out to the sickest of society since she was a tiny child.

A girl who'd run away only to wind up here.

"You didn't deserve this. You didn't ask for it. You didn't do anything wrong. Not one thing. You are good and wonderful, and you deserve to live. To find joy." I said it as if I could counteract the voice of the Kruen that spilled its toxic deceptions into her heart and mind.

I searched inside myself for any strength left, through the reserves of my faltering spirit. Agony shot up my arms and flashed through my body as I struggled to hold on, as I begged her to look at me with those green eyes and see.

On the fringes of awareness, I could hear the siren. Could feel the anxiety that tore through Pax. But he only set his hand on my shoulder and murmured, "Hurry."

It was as if his touch jolted a spark of it.

The light.

There was so little of it, but I squeezed my eyes closed and tried to magnify it the way I would in Faydor. To tap into the well.

I could only pray it would be enough.

"Please," I said, not even sure who I was begging.

Valeen. Maybe myself.

Or maybe I was begging the girl, because she pushed herself forward and angled her face outward so I had better access to her cheeks.

Giving herself over, as if she were asking for the sickness to be purged.

And the spark glowed, a rising flicker that I turned all my focus to.

Building it and building it.

Before I turned it on the Kruen that writhed in a shapeless pool on the barren ground in Faydor.

And I wondered if, in my exhaustion, it didn't feel the threat coming. Because it didn't have time to take form when I expelled the energy in a blinding flash of light.

Whipping through time and space and realms.

A shock of energy that struck like a lightning bolt in the middle of the toiling pool.

There was only a squeal of outrage and pain before it was consumed in the flame.

A pile of ash.

And there was nothing left.

I collapsed.

# Chapter Fourteen

## PAX

"Aria!" I barely caught her before she fully crumpled to the ground, and I swept her into my arms.

Holding her close while my heart beat at a manic pace.

What the fuck were we thinking? Standing here on this street doing this? But there'd been no chance I could try to stop her. Not when I knew it was her purpose. Not when I knew it was what she was meant to do.

My attention dashed left and right, searching for a place to hide us as I listened to the single siren grow louder as it approached.

We had to get the hell out of here, or everything we'd been fighting for was going to go up in flames.

Had to assume it was the single gunshot she'd fired that had caused someone to call and report hearing it. The single gunshot that had saved my life.

I pressed my nose into her hair, inhaling her coconut scent, trying to find a semblance of calm as panic flailed against the gratitude I felt.

The overwhelming awe I had for this brave, beautiful, unstoppable girl who was limp in my arms.

Completely drained because she was always willing to give all of herself to others.

To offer it all.

"This way. Hurry." I was surprised when the hushed voice hit me from the side, and I looked up to find the brown-haired girl hissing the words. She held the hand of the younger girl as she waved for me to follow them with the other.

I didn't hesitate. I followed them around the corner, jogging to keep up as they ran ahead of us.

Aria's head jostled from side to side with each thud of my boots on the sidewalk.

Harsh pants were ripped from my mouth by the exertion.

They hustled along the sidewalk before they stalled out at a tiny alley that cut between this building and the next.

The older one ushered me and the younger girl ahead of her before she ducked in behind us. The blonde teetered on her heels, trying to balance as she ran, her movements entirely different from before Aria had helped her.

That gaunt hopelessness was gone.

Now her gasps were sharp and raking as we raced between the two buildings all the way down to the intersecting road.

We stopped at the end of it, still hidden in its shadows.

The brown-haired girl pointed across the street. "Keep going between the buildings for three blocks. Once you get to the third street, there is a bar just off to the right. Catch a ride there, and tell them your girl is drunk and you want to get her home. We need to clean her up first." She pulled a tissue from her pocket and cleaned the droplets of blood that had splattered on Aria's face.

My throat thickened. I wasn't sure what the fuck I was supposed to say. I'd always gone it alone. But now, Aria had taught me that every fucking thing was different.

"Thank you." The words were gravel.

A sound of disbelief huffed from her mouth, and she dropped her gaze to Aria. A riot of emotion rippled across her face. "I don't know what the hell just happened, but I'm pretty sure it's us who should be doing the thanking."

She was back to clutching the other girl's hand, and she shook her head as if she didn't want to contemplate what she had just seen and felt.

"Go on. Get yourselves to safety," she said, urging me with her chin in the direction she'd pointed out.

I hesitated, then asked, "What are you going to do?"

She squeezed the blond girl's hand firmly in hers. "Soph and I are gonna start a new life. Right now. We're gonna disappear from this horrid place, just like I suggest you do."

I attempted to shift Aria around so I could get to the pocket where I'd stuffed the cash I'd poached from those fucks. She must have known my intention, because she gave a slight shake of her head. "No. We don't need it. We'll make it."

Aria groaned through the exhaustion, my name a garbled roll on her lips.

Both came forward and brushed their fingertips over the back of her hand before the older one sent me a knowing glance.

A clear understanding.

She was promising to hold our secrets.

Then they rounded the corner and walked away.

I watched them disappear into the thick mist before I darted across the street beneath the cover of night and into the next alleyway.

I kept Aria tight against me as I followed the brunette's instructions.

The pathway dumped us out exactly where she'd said.

Music and a drone of lifted voices seeped out of a dive bar that was on the right side, and a few people loitered in a roped-off section out front, smoking cigarettes and sipping beers beneath the orange glow of outdoor heaters.

I angled in close to that area like we were two more patrons, and I waited at least half an hour before a cab finally came by. Wasn't about to risk making a fake account for an Uber or some shit like that.

I hailed it, and the guy barely grunted at me as I gave him an address across the city. As far away from our motel as we could feasibly get.

Once he dropped us off, I did the same thing three more times, grabbing cabs and having them drop us off in random places.

Making sure the two of us disappeared without a trace.

I had the last driver leave us half a mile from the motel.

I paid him and stepped out, clinging to Aria, who had fallen into a foggy state of coherence.

She gazed up at me with those pale, pale eyes, cognizance as heavy as the clouds that covered us as I carried her the rest of the way to our motel.

I climbed the steps, let us into the room, and laid her out on the bed.

She blinked up at me through the bleary light. Sadness pooled there, all mixed with that glorious, unfathomable strength.

"I won't say I'm sorry." The words were hoarse when she whispered them.

I dropped to my knees at her side, gathered her hand in mine, and brought her knuckles to my lips. "No, baby, I'm the one who's sorry," I murmured against them.

She shifted so she could curl her hand around mine. "We're in this together, Pax. Wholly. In every way. It doesn't matter what the circumstances are. You can't protect me from this life."

My nod was tight. "I know. I keep thinking I can, but I end up making it worse."

I brushed the pad of my thumb over her sweat-drenched brow, while she trembled from the cold.

She was completely drained, though at least this time she hadn't been struck by either of the Kruen she'd encountered. It was strange that she hadn't been drained when she fought the Ghorl in her father's mind, but tonight she'd been completely zapped.

It was so hard to make sense of the difference.

"You think I wouldn't give everything to protect you, too?" she whispered.

"That's not the way it's supposed to be."

"Yes, it is. That's exactly the way it's supposed to be." She said it so quickly she nearly cut me off. Then she lowered her voice as she continued, "It's exactly the way it's supposed to be. You and me fighting for humanity. It's our fate, and we do it together."

"You shot a man tonight." It raked from my chest. A stake of guilt.

She gave a long blink. "I hate it . . . that people can be so depraved that it was the only option I had. Hate that I had to do it. But I can promise I'd do it all over again, a thousand times over. For you, Pax. Because I love you."

As I sat there on my knees next to her, the significance of the night sank through me.

"You saved me," I told her. I wasn't sure what the fuck would have happened if she hadn't come. If she'd listened to the bullshit I'd spewed.

My thinking had been faulty. I knew it now. Knew she was right.

"I needed you—*need* you in every way," I corrected. "In every aspect and every manner, and I promise you I won't try to keep you from the things I have to do ever again."

Her teeth raked over her bottom lip as she nodded against the pillow, all that black hair strewn around her gorgeous face.

"Because you and I are in this thing together, Pax. To the very end."

# Chapter Fifteen

## ARIA—TEARSITH

"Peter is dead." Aria heard Pax grit out the words from where he and Ellis were huddled beneath the great tree. His voice was grave. The words as dire and bleak as Aria felt, where she lay on the cool grass next to the babbling stream, seeking respite within the confines of Tearsith after she'd been sapped of her strength.

The rest of their Laven family sat just in the distance, their turmoil distinct as they awaited instruction.

Only Dani was at her side, sitting beside Aria and running tender fingers through her hair. Whispering, "You're going to be fine. What you did was so brave. I'm so proud of you. So proud of who you are."

Above Dani's encouragement, Aria could hear the hushed, brutal conversation between Pax and Ellis.

"None of this is chance. Nathan accidentally falling to his death and William overdosing? Doesn't fit either of them," Pax hissed. "It's too much to be a coincidence. And we saw the Kruen set on Peter's destruction with our own eyes. Saw it in both Faydor and while awake. Plus, the other five who did not show last night still have not arrived. We can't chalk that up to coincidence, and I fear the worst for them. We believe every single one of us is in danger."

Ellis sagged in sorrow, his frail, thin frame slumping beneath the weight. The soft breeze that usually provided comfort gusted like a veiled, baleful omen, whipping through the stringy locks of their teacher's stark-white hair. His pale eyes, which had witnessed so much torment and suffering in his lifetime, had dimmed to desolation.

"My children," he gasped, and Pax darted out both hands to support him as the old man swayed to the side, nearly overcome with grief.

Aria's own grief hit her on a swelling wave, crashing against her consciousness as she watched the scene. Dani whimpered and moved to wrap her arms around Aria.

"I'm sorry, Ellis. I did not want to deliver this news," Pax muttered.

Ellis gripped his arm with bony fingers. "I do not understand. Others have succumbed throughout the years . . . targeted as humans. Susceptible like the rest. But never like this. So many in just a handful of days."

Ellis wobbled again, and Pax's gaze cut to Aria from the side.

She wondered, in that split second, if he questioned the same thing she did. If he questioned if their joining had caused this. If what Valeen had warned had come to fruition. Except that danger had not only extended to Pax and herself but also their whole family.

Had they done this?

"We have to warn them. Do something to help them prepare," Pax urged.

"And how do we do that?" Ellis turned his gaze on his flock, who waited. Clearly, he was not asking for an answer, since none of them possessed it.

Grimly, the old man ambled over to stand in front of their Laven family. Pax followed him, standing at his side while Josephine took up the opposite.

Dani looked down at Aria in worry.

"Go to Timothy," Aria told her. "He needs you. I will be fine."

"Are you sure?" Concern creased at the edges of Dani's eyes.

"I'm sure. And I know your Nol needs you."

Reluctantly, Dani nodded before she dipped down and pressed a kiss to Aria's forehead, then murmured, "You amaze me, sweet friend. I am so thankful for you. For all these years. No matter what happens, I want you to know that."

Aria wanted to tell her they had many more years to share together, but she couldn't make the words form through her thickened throat.

She could only nod, gripping Dani's hand for a beat of deep understanding before Dani brushed the tears from her face and stood.

She moved to Timothy's side just as Ellis began to speak.

"My dear family, I stand before you tonight with more devastating news. It has been confirmed that Peter has been lost to us. He has gone on to eternity, and his own Nol has not come tonight. We also still have no word of Lisa, Ivan, Steven, Beverly, and Jakai, though it is our greatest fear that they have also been stolen from us."

A bellow of grief rode on the breeze, and Aria squeezed her eyes against the agonizing sorrow that gripped her family.

Ellis wavered, searching for what to say. "We don't know why this has begun, what has changed, but there is no other conclusion than we are being hunted in the day."

"It's because Aria and Pax came together. They knew the law. And they have broken it and cost us everything." The wail of words rushed out of Emilia, Steven's Nol, who wept in the middle of the family.

Her pain sharp and brutal.

Aria winced from where she lay on the grass, her heart faltering at the possibility. She couldn't imagine having brought this calamity on her family.

Her spirit thrashed, a wild clanging against her ribs, refuting the idea.

*"Together. Wholly,"* a high-pitched voice murmured through her mind.

Chime-like.

Delicate and wispy.

A voice she hardly recognized but remembered in the very recesses of her consciousness. She tried to clutch on to it, but another of their family, Katrina, called out, "I'm broken over your loss, Emilia, but I can't believe that. I . . . I have this feeling. Something is calling to me."

"Maybe we're supposed to go to our Nols like Pax and Aria did?" another said. "Maybe it is the only way we can be safe in the day?"

"And make it even worse?" another shouted, incredulity in their voice. "We know the rules, and look what's happening now that that they have been broken. I agree with Emilia."

Aria could feel the torment that rolled through Ellis, who stood before them and lifted his hands as if he could give them all peace. "I know we are afraid, but we must not fight amongst ourselves. We must be strong. United."

His gaze drifted over the hundreds who remained. The hundreds who sat in trepidation.

"Yes, I understand the creed that has been issued, but I have to believe Pax and Aria's circumstances are special. I believe she had drawn the attention of this Ambrose before Pax had gone to her, and she would also likely not be with us had he not."

Silence washed over the crowd, and Ellis wavered in uncertainty before he pressed on. "I would suggest that we share our information with each other so we have a way to track and keep in touch. To warn if we find something during our hunt in Faydor."

A ripple of agreement seemed to go up.

"Please be careful, my family. Stay in your homes if you can. Stay away from strangers and even watch for changes in your loved ones. We need you all to come back to us. Now, we must descend and fight."

A solemn understanding fell over them, and they all rose and began to pair off, though their voices were hushed as they each shared their contact information with those around them.

Aria wanted to get up and join them. Fight at their sides. But she didn't have the strength to even get to her feet.

Affliction assaulted her as she watched them go. She felt aggrieved at the thought that she could have done this. That her love for her Nol might have caused this.

Those stolen moments.

Their kisses.

Their touches.

Had she been that selfish?

A moan bottled in her chest, and that sense was on her again. The whisper of that tinkling, melodic voice.

*"Together. Wholly."*

It was a call that echoed through her middle.

Her family disappeared into the nothingness while Pax hugged Josephine, offering her his hope.

That voice whispered again, nudging in the deepest spot inside her. A call.

She had no choice but to heed it. To follow it.

Slowly, she rolled in the grass until she was on her stomach, then fought to bring herself to her hands and knees.

She gasped as she crawled in the direction she was led.

To the spring that rippled through the meadow.

The exhaustion was excruciating. Her joints felt as if they'd been pulled apart, her muscles sundered and riven.

She winced as she moved, grinding her molars against the agony of pressing her palms to the grass after they'd been completely scorched.

But she couldn't resist the lure.

The innate need to get to the stream.

To listen.

To see.

*"Aria,"* the haunting voice whispered when she made it to the brook.

Barely able to keep herself propped up on one hand, she stirred the fingers of the other hand through the cool, placid water.

*"Together. Wholly."* It was faint, nagging at the edge of her ear.

"Valeen?" she begged. Not for herself. For the others who had to be saved.

*"Rise up, dear Valient."* The words wisped through the air just as the hint of a face passed through the rippling water. *"You are the chosen. You must lead."*

"How? Show me how," she implored, hand diving deeper into the water as if she could hold on to the vapor that whisked by.

*"You hold the power inside you,"* the voice intoned, drifting farther away. Farther away into the nothingness.

On a frustrated cry, Aria slumped forward, practically sliding into the stream as her hand frantically swished beneath the water. "Please. How?"

"Aria, it's okay. It's okay." Pax rushed up behind her and dragged her into his arms as he sank back to sitting on the grass.

*"The answer is already written inside of you,"* the voice wisped before it fully drifted away.

Legs spread out in front of him, Pax tucked her onto his lap. Rocked her as he kissed her temple.

"Did you hear her?" she asked in desperation, wondering if she was hallucinating.

He curled his arms tighter around her, and he seemed to hesitate before he exhaled the admission near her ear.

"Only the last, when I was touching you."

# Chapter Sixteen

## ARIA

"I think this was the best idea you've ever had," I told Pax before I took a sip from my hot caffé mocha, then a bite from the gooey doughnut piled high with strawberry icing and sprinkles.

Pax let go of a rough chuckle from where he sat across from me in the small booth at the local doughnut shop. We were tucked in the corner, mostly out of sight of the rest of the lobby, though Pax had a direct view of the door so he could keep tabs on who came in and out.

It was midmorning, so it was fairly quiet, just a few patrons dotted about, and we'd felt somewhat at ease when we stepped inside.

People's voices were there, hovering at the fringes of my mind, but they were subdued. No true distress in the handful of people inside the shop.

"You're awful easy to please for a princess," he teased. "Besides, I think I picked up early on you preferring dessert for breakfast."

Pax tilted his head as he blatantly stared at me. Flames licked in the depths of his icy gray eyes as he made a slow pass over my face and down my neck.

Redness rushed in its wake. I wondered if I'd ever get used to it. Him looking at me that way. With unfettered desire. I'd longed for it forever and thought I'd never feel the full severity of it.

I'd thought what beat between us would be forever locked away by the laws that had kept us fractured.

My chest squeezed with the accusation that had been thrown out two nights ago by Emilia in Tearsith. One I'd understood she'd made in her distress. But after I'd seen that suggestion of Valeen's in the stream, I couldn't accept the assertion Emilia had made.

Valeen's words had weaved through me like a thread that healed.

*Together. Wholly.*

I didn't understand it, but at least I was sure that Pax was supposed to be right here with me.

This man a dream. The only good dream I'd ever had.

"Why are you looking at me like that?" I whispered with the hint of a smile tugging at the edge of my mouth.

It was my turn for my eyes to caress. Tracing the sharp angles of his face. The scars that marred him. The tattoos that rolled up his neck to touch the base of his fierce jaw. His hewn, lean body that pulsated with rugged, rough brutality.

So terrifying, and still my greatest comfort.

"Because you're the only thing in this world I really want to see, Aria. Because you're every picture in my mind. The imprint marked on my soul." His raspy, low voice filled the area between us. Then he sat back with a smirk. "Well, and on my skin, too."

No doubt, he was making reference to the tattoo I'd finally noticed hidden on his abdomen.

We'd lain low in Indianapolis for the last two days, allowing me to take yesterday to recuperate. Allowing me time to regain my strength and for the blisters that had risen on my palms to subside.

In it had been a small respite of bliss.

Pax and I locked behind closed doors.

It was both frustrating and a relief that no one had come for us during that time. Ambrose remained elusive, but it wasn't like we had been out and about trying to draw attention to ourselves.

"Get used to it, Princess, because I plan on spending my whole life staring at you."

Then he reached out and snagged a piece of doughnut I'd torn off and popped it into his mouth.

"Hey," I tried to admonish, but it was full of a giggle as he reached out to steal another piece and I swatted his hand away. I pulled the plate against my chest and curled my arms around it. "Don't you know to never come between a woman and her sweets?"

"Wouldn't dream of it," he said, aghast.

My brows drew together. "Says the guy who ate half my doughnut."

"What can I say, yours looked better than mine."

"That's just rude. You need to pick better next time." I tried to keep up the playful affront, but everything softened when Pax reached into the white bag on the table and produced a second strawberry doughnut.

He set it on my napkin. "Just because you're my princess, I got you two."

"You do love me," I murmured as I ripped it to shreds, then put the largest piece into my mouth.

I groaned at the sweetness that coated my tongue.

Pax suddenly leaned all the way across the table and grabbed both of my hands. He pulled them to the middle and leaned forward to get closer to me.

I did the same, moving in his direction, drawn to the intensity he exuded.

We both leaned so far over it that his mouth was a breath away from mine when he whispered, "If it was ever a question, Aria, I want to make it clear. The way I love you. The way it feels when I look at you."

His hands tightened around mine.

"It's like I'm shredding apart because I can't hold the magnitude of it inside. It's like there's not enough room inside me to hold the fullness of it. It is greater than anything I've ever known, and goes far beyond this reality and into the next. Far beyond this *life* and into the next," he emphasized.

Emotion pulled taut in his expression.

Gravity.

Passion.

Fervor.

"It's unending. Eternal. And whatever that eternity might look like, the only thing I know for sure is I will meet you there."

Moisture filled my eyes, and I squeezed back. "I will always meet you there. Wherever you are."

We stayed like that for the longest time, before Pax suddenly went rigid when the bell dinged above the door and it swept open. I peeked behind me to see a woman step inside.

A police officer.

Pax was far more exposed, and he slowly shifted so his face was better concealed, the backs of his shoulders angled in that direction. Peering around the side of the high booth, I held my breath, waiting to see what she would do.

We'd thought to leave two nights ago after what had happened in the city, but I'd been so drained that I couldn't move. We'd decided to stay here until I had rested.

Pax had checked the local news to find out if they were searching for us.

He'd found a news report of three men found dead outside a building. All had been arrested previously for drug possession and facilitating prostitution, and that article had speculated it had been some kind of deal gone bad.

I could only hope that belief remained.

It wasn't as if those three men were the only reason the police might be looking for us. Not after Pax had broken into the mental facility to rescue me. I still thought of Jill often, the nurse who'd believed there was more to my story than my chart claimed, and had helped me escape.

I knew her life had to be intrinsically changed; no hope for her ever working in nursing again. Plus, I had no idea if any sort of charges had been brought against her.

I could only pray that she was safe and okay. Pray she didn't regret what she'd done. I hoped some way, someday, I'd be able to repay her.

I carefully peeked around the back of the booth again, and I breathed out the strain when the officer moved to the counter to order.

I turned back to Pax, my voice quieted. "She's just a customer."

His nod was tight, and he busied himself by staring into his coffee. He didn't look up until the door swung open again and she exited.

On a heavy exhalation, he scrubbed a flustered palm over his face. "Fuck. This is getting messy."

My nod was slow. He grabbed his phone, and I knew he was searching the local news again. Antsy that something had changed. That someone had come forward and reported that they'd seen us. Had witnessed it all.

I expected there to be nothing, until Pax's pale face completely drained of color, blanching a pasty white. Anxiety jolted my heart into an erratic beat as I watched him from across the table, apprehension curling through my being as I waited.

His eyes frantically flicked back and forth as he read.

"Tell me what's going on," I pleaded, so quiet the sound barely broke the air.

He didn't answer. He simply turned the phone to me. It was an article, the headline reading Local man shot dead after closing pizza shop.

I wanted to scan the story. To take in the details that outlined what was known of the crime and understand what had caused Pax so much alarm.

But I didn't need any of that.

I only needed the picture to know.

Only needed the image of a man who was probably in his forties.

A man with the palest gray eyes.

A Laven.

And he wasn't part of our family.

# Chapter Seventeen

## PAX

"I can't believe this. I feel sick," Aria whispered from where she leaned against the headboard on the bed next to me, her legs drawn to her chest and her cell resting on her knees as she scrolled.

We'd been here for the last two hours, searching news stories from random cities.

We'd started close.

Chicago.

We'd been staggered when we found reports of three people, clearly Laven, who had been killed there that week.

All of questionable causes.

Violent.

Two gunshots.

One hit-and-run.

Their faces imprinted on the screen like blades driven into the centers of our chests. Unfamiliar faces we still could recognize.

So we'd extended the search, looking through news stories from both large cities and small towns. We'd seen the death reports of Laven after Laven stretched across the States.

The horror had only grown heavier when we found it extended around the world.

I could feel the sinking confirmation roll through Aria as she whispered, *"'I am the one who will put an end to your kind.'"*

Sadness pulsed through her features as she turned her gaze on me. "We knew he was hunting us, but I thought it meant *us*. Our family. I can't fathom the scope of this."

"He wants to wipe all goodness from existence. Anything that would stand in evil's way." My chest tightened with dread as I uttered it.

We knew next to nothing about other Laven families, except for a mention in the great book that they existed. Neither Aria nor I had seen any other of our kind throughout our lives. Not until we'd come together.

Now there was evidence of us everywhere. The force greater than I'd imagined.

But I was worried the force we were fighting was even greater. The hope I kept trying to latch on to getting quashed every time we turned around.

Except sitting right next to me was maybe the greatest force of all.

Aria turned her attention away, that same dwindling hope cut deep into her words. "How can we defeat him? This is impossible, Pax. Look at all these people. These Laven . . ." she trailed off.

Shifting toward her, I took her phone and set it aside so I could thread my fingers through hers. I lifted them between us. "I heard her, Aria. I heard Valeen when I touched you. I heard what she said. She said it is written in you." I squeezed her fingers tight. "You have the strength."

She blinked through the moisture that blurred her eyes. "And what if I fail? What if I fail our family? What if I fail the rest?"

She glanced at her phone, which sat face up on the bed. The screen was still open to a picture of what was clearly a Laven woman. Dead after a stabbing at a railway station in Italy.

"What if I'm not enough? And what happens if Laven no longer walk in Faydor? What happens when we're obliterated?"

I grabbed her by both sides of her face, palms holding her tight as I drew her toward me. I brushed the pads of both thumbs under the hollows of her eyes as I urged, "You can't lose faith."

Aria let go of a tremorous sound. "It's so much more than I ever imagined. For so long, our world was small. Our Laven family. And now . . ."

"And now we know how important Laven truly are," I stressed. "Now we know what is riding on stopping this monster."

Uncertainty passed through her expression. Desperation and despondency. "I want to. I want to believe that I hold that kind of power—but God, Pax . . ." She sucked in a shaky breath. "We know what it means if there are fewer Laven to stop the Kruen. More humans will die, too. It feels like too much."

She hesitated, then whispered, "And I'm just . . . me."

Tightening my hold on her face, I pulled her closer. Breathing her in. The goodness and the light. "That's right, Aria. You're just you. Amazing and wonderful you. You are so fuckin' powerful. I've seen it. Have felt it. And I think you know there is so much more inside you that remains untapped. We just have to figure out how to tap into it."

# Chapter Eighteen

## ARIA

It was unsettling, waiting for something to happen. For the tsunami I could feel building in the distance to finally hit land. A surging force that would eradicate everything in its path.

It was as if I could feel it lingering at the edges of this world. Trembling and vibrating as it gathered strength. And when it combusted, it would fracture everything this world knew.

That worry over my family had come back in full force, and I'd probably checked in with my mother too many times to make sure they were all safe.

They were.

Safe and still staying at my grandmother's.

I'd warned them to be extra vigilant.

I glanced around the grocery store, where Pax and I roamed up and down the aisles, grabbing a few things to stock our room with.

I couldn't help but peer at those surrounding us who went about their days without a clue. Some in torment, the voices so strong that it felt nearly impossible not to reach out and touch them as I passed by.

Others where their voices were only a slight drone.

None were without hopes and fears.

An elderly woman, her back hunched with a hump and her head permanently angled to one side.

A mother with three young children who was frazzled but still patient as she smiled.

A man who rushed in to grab a twelve-pack of beer.

The workers.

The patrons.

My spirit ached with what might happen if all Laven were erased. I couldn't imagine that society would stand. It would mean complete and utter destruction.

It would be impossible for life to go on the way it was meant to.

The precarious balance we tiptoed tossed from its axis.

"Ah, here we go. Doughnuts." Pax sent me a wry grin as he grabbed a plastic container from a display in the bakery.

A sad smile ridged my mouth. There was no stopping the melancholy. Finding proof of all the dead Laven earlier today had wrecked something inside me.

But I had to put one foot in front of the other and hope I could tap into whatever was trapped inside me, the way Pax had said. It just made it really difficult when I didn't understand any of it.

The hardest part was that this was no longer about my survival only.

It was about survival for all of us.

For Laven.

And I knew, without question, that extended into humanity.

Pax felt my unease, and he reached out and tugged me toward him. "Come here, Princess."

He tucked me between himself and the cart, and he started pushing it around the end of one aisle and up another, his mouth at the side of my neck as he murmured near my sensitive skin, "Remember when you told me we had to cherish every moment that we had? Make use of every minute of time that we're given? I'm gonna hold you to that right now. We've got too much to be living for . . . to be fighting for . . . for you to give up on me now."

I leaned against him, letting myself sink into the warmth he exuded. "I'd never give up on you, Pax."

"Good, because I'm never giving up on you." He let go of the handle with his left hand and splayed it across my belly, pulling me closer against the rippling strength of his body. "I have too much planned for you, Aria Rialta, for you to start looking like you're ready to surrender."

I turned in his hold, and he stopped moving. The two of us just stood in the middle of the cereal aisle, staring at each other. That energy wisped between us, the connection that bound.

"I'm not surrendering," I promised.

"Good girl." The words were a brush of air that he exhaled.

I fiddled with the collar of his tee as I gazed up at the ruthless beauty of his face. Heat danced just under the surface of my skin. "Are you trying to seduce me?"

"Is it working?"

"I think it might be," I said, playing along.

His smile turned to greed. "Think we should get back to the motel and put some of this time to good use."

He shifted me around so he had his left arm slung over my shoulders, hugging me to his side as he maneuvered the cart to the checkout.

More people were up front than in the rest of the store.

The voices crowding in and growing louder.

Pax could sense it as he grabbed the few things we'd picked up and ran them through the scanner, working quickly and precisely, the way he always did.

His eyes were keen, but today, they were keen on me.

Reading me.

Knowing me.

Getting me.

His voice was hushed as he covertly looked around, as if he were trying to figure out who I might be drawn to. "You have work to do?

Not gonna stop you, Aria, but you need to try to conserve your energy if you can."

My brows drew together in concentration. "I don't think so. I don't think anyone is in crisis."

Those were the ones I couldn't resist. The ones that compelled me to do something.

"Okay . . . You just say, though."

"I know," I told him as I helped place our purchases in a bag.

Two minutes later, we'd paid and were heading out into the day. A heavy chill sagged in the dense air. The clouds were so thick it almost felt as if evening were approaching, though it was the middle of the day.

A shiver rolled through the chill.

Something ominous that coasted down my spine.

I trembled, but tried to ignore the foreboding that swept through me.

Pax pushed the cart out to the car, and he clicked the locks. We piled the few bags into the trunk while I struggled against the sensation.

Against the awareness that pulsed.

"Mommy?" A scared little voice suddenly carried on the wind, and I straightened from where I was bent over the trunk to look out in the direction it had come from.

There was a young boy, wandering by himself at the far end of the parking lot. Up close to the sidewalk.

The street beyond it was busy.

Cars, trucks, and buses whizzed by, their drivers unaware.

Dread grabbed me by the throat, though my mind wavered, uncertainty pulling through me like threads driven by a needle that tugged at my spirit.

"Do you see him?" I wheezed, terrified I was hallucinating the way I'd done the night when I'd been coaxed from the hotel room. When the little girl hadn't been a little girl at all, but a manifestation of Ambrose.

"Where are you, Mommy?" The child inched closer to the street as his distress increased.

"Fuck . . . Yeah, I see him," Pax said. He didn't take the time to shut the trunk. He started sprinting in that direction, calling, "Hey, buddy, why don't you come away from the road, and we'll find your mommy?"

The child turned around. His eyes grew wide when he saw Pax running toward him. "No. You're a stranger."

"I won't come near you . . ." Pax stretched out placating hands. "Just . . . come this way so you're not so close to those cars. How's that sound?"

I jogged to catch up to them, but Pax was already at the end of the lot when I was only halfway.

Shock hacked through me when arms suddenly wrapped around me from behind. A scream tore up my throat, but a hand clamped over my mouth and stopped any sound from getting out.

Terror locked tight, and I flailed and struggled to get loose, kicking my feet into the air since I'd been ripped off the ground. Shouts bowled up my throat only to hit the barrier that kept them trapped.

A man who had to be twice my size snarled venom into my ear. "You little bitch. Where have you been hiding? He's been looking for you."

I gasped and choked against the scent of him. Something vile and offensive.

He dragged me between two cars, quickly and steadily moving across the lot. I could hear the immorality of his thoughts, the heinousness he'd fully given himself over to. "He promised I could have you once he was finished with you."

I kept trying to scream. To draw attention to what was happening. But no one paid any attention to us. Everyone's focus was on the commotion happening on the other side of the lot.

The screeching of tires and the blaring of horns and the shouts of horror.

Unquestionably, the child was being used as a decoy, and there was no one there to notice that I was being dragged around the side of the building.

A fence ran the length of it. Only three feet separated it and the cinder block wall of the grocery store, the area completely isolated and concealed from the front.

The man kept my back pinned against his chest, walking backward as he went. I kept kicking my feet, trying to set him off-balance. I clawed at his hands, so hard I was sure I had to be breaking skin.

He only laughed a menacing sound. "So feisty. That's good. I like it when they fight." He pressed his mouth harder against my ear. "But I like it so much more when they scream. Are you a screamer, little girl? But I guess you won't be screaming any longer once he gets finished with you. I'll have to make do."

Sickness roiled, and I could smell the stench of his memories. The horrid things he had done.

He hauled me all the way behind the building, where it was even more secluded.

I swore I could see the tumult in the sky. The roil of thunderous clouds.

Violent and cyclonic.

As if the heavens had begun to boil.

Awareness slithered through me. A horrifying recognition. It was Ambrose. I could feel him. The freezing cold he elicited.

"Release her," a low voice intoned.

A cold sweat slicked my skin, the fear so deep I felt it sink into my marrow.

The man who held me whirled around and threw me forward at the same time. I stumbled with the momentum, trying to find my footing, to keep from falling to my hands and feet.

I was barely able to steady myself when I lifted my attention and found Ambrose standing twenty feet away.

Blond hair darker beneath the darkness of the clouds that swirled above him.

A man who had appeared so benign and plain, but who I knew possessed the greatest wickedness.

Was possibly the epitome of it.

Or with the way his brown eyes seemed to glow, maybe Pax had been right. Maybe he was the embodiment of Kreed.

Maybe I was standing in front of the evil one.

I searched inside myself for the courage I'd found when I faced him on that unknown plane. For the conviction to fight.

It was harder here outside of the supernatural realm. When I was wholly human, and I had none of the strength and speed that I had in Faydor.

Except my spirit rattled and my fingers buzzed.

A reminder that that wasn't true. I was different. Some of the ethereal had followed me here.

A reminder that I'd promised myself I wouldn't succumb and, rather, would fight.

A reminder that I had to face him head-on or this was never going to end.

Laven would continue to die because of him—because of whatever or whoever this monster was.

"You bastard," I spat, unable to hold the spite back when I knew he was responsible for the deaths in our family. For every Laven who had been lost this week.

A thrill ran through his features, and he cocked his head to the side, his voice condescending. "Have you enjoyed my handiwork, little Valient? I wondered when you would notice. When you'd see that I meant it when I told you I was going to end you all."

He came forward then, the pavement below me rumbling with each step he took, thunder that rolled like a dark storm possessing the ground and sky.

"Every last one of you, and there is nothing you can do about it. This has been coming for a long, long time."

I lifted my chin, nerves clattering as I tried to stand my ground.

To hold on to hope when I was surrounded by sickness.

The disgusting presence of the man who'd grabbed me salivating with evil from behind me and the culmination of it in front of me.

"Since the day Abigail died?" I said it as a challenge. I wanted to set him off-kilter and make him stumble.

He only grinned. "Ah, you have been doing your research, I see. She was such a sweet little thing." He tsked like it was a shame. "Talented and beautiful. I loved her with everything I had. Your Nol will do that to you, though, won't they?"

It was me who stumbled. Me who was set off-kilter at his words.

Was that what he was saying?

That he was a . . . Laven?

But how . . . how had he ended up like this?

I gulped around the thickness that nearly closed off my throat. "You're a Laven."

But his eyes . . . they weren't gray.

His laughter was menacing as he began to circle me as if I were prey. I followed the path, trying to keep him in my line of sight.

All while my mind shouted for Pax. For him to feel me. Find me.

"I *was* a Laven," Ambrose hissed before his voice turned mollifying again as he continued.

"It's true what Valeen says . . . Your Nol is your greatest strength and your greatest weakness. I was supposed to take over my father's printing shop, but I didn't care. When I was seventeen, I traveled from Chicago to South Carolina to find her. She was the only thing I cared about in that horrible life I'd been sentenced to."

He kept moving, his voice drifting between malice and awe. "God, she was breathtaking. I was enthralled. I would have given anything just to be by her side. The smallest reprieve from a lifetime of torment. The voices? The burns? Those eyes? As if what we'd been given was supposed to be some gift?"

His scoff was discordant.

Jarring.

"I hated it and would have done anything to be rid of it. I would have given anything to be normal and go to sleep and dream at night. But Abigail . . . she embraced it. Her whole purpose was what happened once she went to sleep. And then one day she woke up changed . . . and she took on that purpose during the day. A *Valient*."

He snarled it as if she had committed a sin.

"No regard to anything else but giving herself to the pathetic, weak creatures of this earth, as if they deserved her time and care. As if they should have something better than what Kreed had planned for them."

His jealousy twisted around him, a tornado that spun as fast as the clouds overhead.

"She was pathetic, just like the rest. So it was easy when Kreed made me the offer."

A soft puff of air slipped from his nose. "Did you know if a Laven doesn't sleep for a week, he's brought before Kreed? Its soul so weakened by not returning to Tearsith that he now owns it. I wished I'd have known sooner so I could have been brought before Kreed earlier. It turned out, all I had to do was kill her in his name. Take one Valient's life, and mine would go on forever. I'd be removed from the burden that Laven were given. Given a true gift . . . one where I ruled the night. There was really no option."

He said it casually. Easily.

He circled me, coming closer with each rotation that he made around me.

"You should have heard the way she screamed inside that house when I set it afire."

*Pax,* I begged in my mind. I could feel his confusion and fear blistering through the air. He was searching for me.

Ambrose angled his head to the side. "Just the way every Valient I've hunted down over the years has done. One given to this world each decade as if they might have the power to stop me. And you, little Valient . . . you will be the last. Have you ever wondered why you were the last Laven in your family? Valeen has no power left to bring anyone into her fold. She gave everything she had remaining to you—creating the last Valient to stand. And it will be my pleasure finally bringing her vain attempt at stopping me to its end. You are the final one sustaining her, and once you're gone, Valeen will finally have lost the very last of her pathetic, wilting strength. I've been waiting for more than a hundred years, and now, once I remove you, I will reign here. No longer in the darkness."

His voice twisted and dipped, and my pulse careened as I tried to process everything he was saying.

"People will no longer fear what is in the shadows. They will fear what stands in front of them in the day. *Me.* They will bow at my feet. I have given my soul to Kreed, and he has offered me this reward. To rule both here and in Faydor. And there will be no Laven left to protect them from that. And you, little Valient, are that bridge. I will cross it when you come to your end."

The second he said it, he grabbed me by the throat and threw me to the side.

I flew off my feet and slammed against the block wall. My head cracked against the concrete.

Pain ricocheted through my body, and the air was knocked from my lungs. Gasping, I attempted to orient myself, to hold on to the memory that I'd beaten him in that realm. That I'd gotten away.

*He'd been afraid.*

Energy throbbed within me. Convulsing and rough.

I grabbed hold of it, but I had no time to focus on amplifying it before Ambrose was on me again. Gripping me by the throat and squeezing with both hands. "And that end is now."

Blackness clouded in at the edges of my sight, coming so fast I was unprepared.

Eyes bulging with pain, with the loss of oxygen, I tore at his wrists, but I was unable to budge him.

The other man danced around in the periphery, howling with deranged excitement.

And I thought that this was it. I really had met my end.

Except, in the middle of the desperation, the light within me suddenly glowed. Glowed so bright it was blinding. It built in a flash.

I struggled to harness it, to bring it to my hands and use it against the one man who would bring complete annihilation to the world.

I stopped clawing at his wrists and instead drove my fingertips into his sides.

He roared when the contact blew him back ten feet, as if my fingers were electric prods. The beast skidded on his feet, and it took him all of two seconds to right himself.

I didn't have time to process the exhaustion that wanted to bring me to my knees before he was flying back for me, though he'd produced a knife. "You little bitch. Whore. You think you're going to escape me the way you did in Baahg? It will not happen again."

He slashed the knife in my direction, and I lifted my hands to protect my face. A yelp rolled through my throat when it nicked the tip of my pinkie.

But that energy boomed. Bounding within me and becoming something brand new. I fought him with it, grappling as he lashed and whipped the knife. I kicked, sending him flying backward again, much the same as I'd done in that realm he'd called Baahg. In the place where he currently ruled.

Ruled the Kruen.

The Ghorls.

In the place where he commanded that all Laven be extinguished.

I had to stop him.

A shout ripped out of me as I dove for him. I knocked him back to the ground. He whipped the hand with the knife across the air, barely missing my chin as I ducked before I grabbed him by the wrist with both hands.

I tried to jostle the knife loose, and he roared, tossing me off.

I tumbled across the pitted pavement behind the grocery store, groaning when I landed on my back. My eyes pinched shut from the jolt of pain that rocked through my body.

The atmosphere simmered with evil, and my eyes peeled open to Ambrose standing over me. He turned the knife over, the blade pointed downward as he held it between both hands.

My heart was his target.

I could see it. The finality that gleamed in his eyes.

But the energy shifted, stirring through the air in a clamor of desperation. A thunder of footsteps raced up behind Ambrose, and Pax drove his shoulder into his ribs. The velocity knocked Ambrose to the side.

Pax's eyes were wild when he saw me on the ground. "Aria."

"Pax!" I shouted when the other man lumbered up behind him. "Behind you!"

Pax whirled, ducking just in time to miss the fist the man threw before he delivered a punch that knocked the monster onto his back.

I scrambled to my feet and ran toward Ambrose, who'd spun back around and was coming for me.

We met in the middle, and I grabbed the wrist of his hand that still held the knife while a tussle of shouts and kicks and punches thudded behind us.

I begged my spirit to comply. For the light to gather in a way that it never had before. To become something great. The power Valeen had promised that I possessed.

It glowed within me, and I gritted my teeth as I fought with everything I had to use it against Ambrose.

But on his face was a sneer. The amusement that I thought I could prevail.

Still, I tried to harness the power from Valeen and send it sailing into his being.

If it wasn't enough, then how could I end him here? Was it all futile? Worthless?

I gasped and choked as I tried to push against him. To break the knife from his hold. Turn it against him. Hopelessness rolled through me. Even if I managed it, it likely wouldn't do any good.

He was immortal.

A wave of strength erupted, and I managed to twist his wrist just a fraction away from me, turning it toward him.

His sneer turned to a snarl, and he pushed against the light.

Darkness enveloped, wrapping around me like the fiery tendrils of Kruen.

Pax was suddenly behind me, both hands planted on my back as if he was going to rip me away so he could stand in front of Ambrose.

Only the second he touched me, the light surged.

A shock wave that blistered through my hands in a burst of power.

The knife drove forward, and the blade plunged deep into Ambrose's stomach.

It blew him off his feet and into the air, and the monster slammed into the grocery store wall. The cinder blocks cracked and crumbled where he smashed against them.

He stumbled forward, dazed as he jerked the knife from his stomach.

Blood gushed from the wound—a thick, sticky red. Like the wounds Pax and I woke up with after being burned in Faydor. Shocked, he stared down at it before he lifted his malicious gaze to me.

I was frozen in it.

This thing that felt like a crossroads.

We stayed that way for a prolonged beat before he suddenly turned and ran down the far side of the building, far faster than either Pax or I could run.

Our own shock held us there, our breaths panted and harsh as we tried to make sense of what had happened.

Then Pax was in front of me, begging, "Are you hurt?"

I could hardly shake my head. "No. I barely cut my finger, but it's nothing. Are you?"

"No, I'm fine." His palms flew to my cheeks, cupping them as he stared at me. "Fuck, Aria, I was so fuckin' scared when I turned around after grabbing that kid from the street and you weren't there. Knew immediately what had happened."

"I'm okay. I'm okay. I . . ."

I looked back to where Ambrose had disappeared before I turned back to him.

And that was the second we knew. When we understood what our connection meant.

We were stronger together.

The bond between us that had pulled us through time and realm amplifying our power.

We were meant for this—for this love that, for so many years, we'd been told was forbidden.

But no . . .

No . . .

Joy spiraled with the intensity that ricocheted between me and Pax, and in a flash, Pax's mouth descended on mine, his kiss frantic as he twisted one hand up in my hair and clutched me against him with the other.

His mouth pressed and begged, his tongue stroking against mine in a bid of desperation.

Passion spiraled.

Speeding through our veins and whispering down into our souls.

Love and lust and every chain that had tried to hold us back.

He hoisted me up, and I wrapped my legs around his waist at the same time that I wound my arms around his neck.

I kissed him with the same fervency he kissed me with.

The need that boiled between us urgent and acute.

He didn't break the kiss as he stepped over the man who was knocked out, face down on the ground, and carried me around the side of the building.

His tongue sought and his spirit thrummed while I breathed this new belief into his being.

"Pax."

"Fuck, Aria, fuck," he mumbled frantically against my lips.

When we got to the front of the building, he reluctantly set me on my feet, though he took my hand, and we raced across the lot to his car. He whipped the door open and helped me inside before he ducked in to take another desperate kiss.

He broke it long enough to jog around the front of the car, and he jumped into the driver's seat; then he was reaching for me from over the console. Hot hands glided over every inch of my body he could get to, his mouth possessing mine again.

A groan rolled up his throat when he forced himself away. Ragged breaths jutted from his mouth, which remained an inch from mine. "Need to be inside you, right fuckin' now."

I leaned over the console, and I kissed up under his jaw and scratched my nails under his jacket and over his tee, searching for a way to sink all the way into him.

"And I need it. I need you to be. Right now," I whispered back.

His hand clamped down on the inside of my thigh before he threw the car into reverse and whipped out of the spot.

# Chapter Nineteen

## PAX

I could not make it back to the motel fast enough. That single mile felt like fifty as Aria continued to kiss along my throat and dig those nails into my skin as we traveled.

Her hair bunched up in my face, the scent of coconut and goodness filling my senses.

Her aura all around.

Whatever the fuck had happened back there was still pumping through our veins and driving this craze that encircled us.

I took a sharp left into the motel parking lot, careening across to a spot that was close to the stairs.

I barely had it in park and shut off before I was back to kissing her like our lives depended on it.

Wondered if they did.

If all this was dependent on the two of us being together, hinged on Nols' connections being so much greater than we'd ever believed.

The only thing I knew right then was this girl made me better. That touching her lit something in my spirit that otherwise would have remained dead.

Undiscovered.

Aria crawled across the console to wrap herself back around me. "Need you," she muttered at my mouth.

I tossed open the door and climbed out with her in my arms, kissing her mad, the way she was kissing me. Unable to stop, rasps of words making it out through the plucking and pulling of our lips. "You have me. You fuckin' have me, Aria. All of me."

I knocked the door shut with my hip, and without breaking the kiss, I let my attention slant around our surroundings for a single beat before I started up the steps with her in my arms.

She rocked against me, pressing her perfect frame to my overheated body as she fought to get closer. Hands yanking at my hair and nails raking down the back of my skull and to my neck.

Lust gripped me by the throat.

The desire severe.

Neither of us seemed to give a shit that we were out in the light of day, clawing to get to the other.

We made it to our door. Aria had a key card in her pocket, and she fumbled around to slide it into the reader as I held her with one arm looped tight around her waist and turned the knob with the other.

It swept open to the dimness of the room, and I carried her in, letting the door drop shut behind us. Our kisses remained frantic as I worked through the two locks.

Only made it a step deeper into the room before I pressed her back to the wall.

"Pax," she whimpered as she used those sweet, powerful hands to shove my leather jacket from my shoulders. I shucked out of it, letting it plop to the floor as I tore at hers, ripping it down her arms.

She arched forward so I could get it free, those tits covered by her long-sleeved tee brushing against my chest.

Fire lashed.

A lick of flames that singed beneath the surface of my skin.

I had her pinned by my hips, my cock straining between us as we tore at each other's clothes. I twisted her out of her shirt in one second flat, hands slipping around her to unclasp the hook of her bra and dragging the straps down her arms just as she yanked my tee over my head and kicked off her shoes.

The girl was hooked high on the wall, that lush fall of black hair raining around her shoulders. Her pale, pink-tipped nipples were puckered and peaked, her chest heaving for breath.

"You're so beautiful." The words rasped from her as she dragged her blunt nails from my jaw and down my chest in a desperate plea, and she reached down and frantically tugged at the button on my jeans.

My muscles ticked and bowed at the touch, abdomen rippling, the need to be inside her growing to unbearable. My palms skidded down her sides as I pressed my mouth to her neck and laved kisses along the delicate column. When I spoke, my voice was a gruff scrape. "It's you, Aria. You are the beauty. The fullness of it. Have never seen anything so right. The shape of you. Inside and out."

I shifted so I could loop my arm around her waist to support her, and the other moved to the button of her jeans. I popped it and dragged down her zipper. My palm snaked beneath the material, slipping around until I was gripping her ass.

"I need you," she begged through the fever that burned between us. She helped me rid her of her jeans, pushing them off her hips so I could get a hold of them to pull them all the way off her feet.

She shoved my jeans down around my thighs, freeing my cock.

"Please."

I didn't hesitate. I drove into her, taking her whole in one thrust.

She rocked up the wall as a delirious sound tore up her throat.

I grunted her name. The single word nothing but a prayer.

Praise.

I swore that I could see an aura glow beneath her skin.

The girl a beacon for a lost soul.

My guide.

The light that sustained.

Dizziness rushed through me at the feel of her grip.

Her walls clutching and that connection brimming.

Flames that lapped.

A firestorm that consumed.

"Fuck. So good, Aria. So good." The words were rasps, crazed and hazardous.

"Nothing could compare to this. The feel of you inside me," she whimpered.

"You feel it? The way you were made for me? The way we were made for each other?" I pulled out and pushed back in.

Deep and hard.

Air breezed from her lips, and she arched forward. "Yes. I've always known. Always. It's us. It's us."

Nails tore at my back as I began to move.

That frenzy sweeping back to hit us at full force.

I drove into her again and again.

Each thrust more desperate than the last.

I wrapped an arm around her waist and propped my other hand on the wall beside her head, angling her so I could take her how I wanted.

Unchecked and unrestrained.

Reckless.

Aria's mouth found mine, and those sweet, amazing hands fisted in my hair as she kissed me into oblivion, the girl rolling over me as we took each other whole.

The energy whipped and blew, our connection a storm that raged.

There were no senses left but this.

Her.

Us.

The way we meshed.

The way we met.

The sound of it filled the air.

Our moans and pleas and the greed of our bodies as my hips slammed against hers.

It rose with each thrust. Driving us higher. Into that existence that had only ever belonged to us. One I'd been a fool to think we hadn't been destined for.

"Pax," she gasped.

I could feel the pleasure gather around her. A rising tide that swelled in the distance. As distinct as mine, which prowled up and down my spine.

"Do you have any idea what you do to me, Aria? The way it feels to have this sweet body hugging my cock? Let go. Let me feel you come around me."

The moment I said it, I could feel her split. The splintering of bliss that spiraled through the middle of her, the clutch of her body as she rode me, taking me with her.

Pleasure cracked. Bursting through the fracture that opened up between us. Bright lights flashing as rapture streaked through our bodies.

Glimmering as it raced beneath our flesh.

And I wasn't so sure that we remained here, on this plane. Wasn't so sure that we weren't elevated beyond it. Above it. Tossed to a place far beyond the reaches of reality.

To a place where there was joy and hope and a love unending.

I kept her hovered there, the two of us soaring for the longest time, before she finally sank down in my arms and sagged against me.

Both of us panted and shook.

With a heavy exhale, I pulled her closer and let my fingers flutter through her mussed hair as I buried my face in the side of her neck.

Holding on to her as I tried to process the magnitude of what being with her meant.

"Aria." It was almost a question.

"I see it now," she murmured, so low, still clinging to me. "We are stronger together, Pax. A force. Just like we are in Faydor."

# Chapter Twenty

## ARIA

"It was a lie." I paced the small motel room from one end to the other. I'd dressed in a pair of sweats and a long tee, my feet covered in socks and my hair wet from the shower Pax and I had shared.

Beneath that hot spray of water, an understanding had swamped us.

But in it, there were so many questions.

"You think Valeen lied about wanting to keep us separated?" Pax asked as he ran a flustered hand through his damp white hair. He sat on the end of the bed, dressed only in jeans, his elbows propped on his thighs. There was no challenge to the question. He simply wanted to know if that was what I believed. "Misled us?"

"No. I think Ambrose bred that lie. I think it was passed through Abigail's Laven family. Her demise was blamed on her and Ambrose coming together during the day, and I think it's how the legend that Nols would turn against each other if they made contact outside of the otherworld came to be."

"Except it didn't have anything to do with them coming together. It was just that Ambrose was wicked through and through," Pax surmised.

"Yes." My brow pinched. "Do you think it's true of all Laven families? That Ambrose somehow spread this lie to keep them apart?

Or do you think we're a part of Abigail's family? That we're the only ones who've been misguided?"

Pax sighed. "I don't know, Aria. Wish that I did. But we don't know enough about Laven to begin to understand it."

I crossed my arms over my chest, rubbing my hands up and down them as I contemplated what we'd learned today, trying to process everything that monster had said.

"Ambrose was jealous, Pax. Jealous of Abigail's powers. Kreed obviously pinpointed that weakness and used it against him."

"Or maybe he was bad to begin with and welcomed it." Spite filled Pax's voice, rage still stark.

"Maybe. But I don't think that's what matters. I think what matters is that Kreed was able to turn a Laven in his favor. Use him. That he made him immortal."

I blinked, trying to wrap my head around it.

Because Ambrose didn't feel that way to me when I'd driven that blade into his stomach.

He'd been powerful. Extremely so.

But there was a vulnerability to him. Like that immortality hinged on something. Like it could be disrupted.

I wondered if Pax had a direct link into my thoughts, because he rumbled, "Asshole was shocked to find himself bleeding."

"Yes. I think he was. I think he was . . . afraid."

"Because of you," Pax said.

I turned to him. "No, Pax. Because of us."

"You're the Valient, Aria. You're the one who can reach through realms."

"Maybe," I said simply. Then the words turned profound. "But together, we're stronger. You felt it. I know you did, and I think I felt a speck of it when I was losing strength trying to help the second girl the other night. When you reached out and touched my shoulder, a surge of strength rushed through me. You let go quickly, but I think it was enough for me to bind the Kruen. Then today . . . that difference was unquestionable. With the connection, that power gushed out of me. And you heard Valeen when you touched me. There is something there, Pax."

He stood. Every sinewy muscle in his body rippled when he did, the tattoos written on his skin dancing over that menacing, vicious strength.

He cleared the distance between us and took my chin between his thumb and forefinger. He tipped my face up toward his.

"Are you saying you're better when I'm touching you?" There was an undertone to it. Something possessive that skittered through my being like the fluttering of wings.

A tremble rolled through me, and I couldn't stop my mind from rushing back to what had happened between us thirty minutes ago. The way it was every time he touched me. Took me.

The way it felt like we were dipping our fingers into the ethereal.

"I'm always better when you're touching me, Pax. Always."

I shifted course from the need that boiled between us. Something I was sure was never going to taper off.

"You and I are stronger together. So much stronger. What if it's true for all Laven? Maybe . . ." I trailed off, afraid to get ahead of myself.

"What are you thinking?"

My head barely shook. "That maybe if Laven join with their Nols, they might be able to stop the wicked ones Ambrose has been sending to defeat us."

Was it a long shot? Was I grasping at straws? Desperate for anything that might turn the tables?

"You're thinking Nols should come together until we figure out a way to defeat Ambrose?" Pax confirmed.

"Yes. I don't know if it will do anything. If it will help or stop any of this. But we have to try. Laven can't go on thinking they're in danger being together if they're not. There is a reason that lie was spread, and I can't help but think that lie was told to make us weaker."

Awareness swam through Pax's expression before it flashed in urgency. "We need to tell the others."

I glanced at the window. Sunlight burned around the edges of the drapes, the hour just approaching twilight.

"It's early," I whispered, twining my fingers in restlessness. "Our family won't arrive for several more hours."

Pax pulled me closer. Our bodies flush. Blood whooshed through our veins.

"I have an idea of how we can pass the time." Innuendo threaded the words, and the slightest flicker of a smirk kissed the edge of his mouth.

"Are you trying to seduce me?" I asked, repeating what I'd said earlier, though the forlornness I'd felt then had no position.

Hope had sparked to life in the middle of me.

Possibility quickening into existence.

Just as desire did when Pax suddenly picked me up and tossed me onto the bed, that smirk in full force when he crawled over me. "You said yourself that you're better when I'm touching you, Aria Rialta. Have a few different ways for us to try that out."

And when he peeled me out of my sweats and burrowed his head between my thighs, I was sure I didn't mind a bit.

# Chapter Twenty-One

## ARIA—TEARSITH

"Are you sure?" Ellis's question was wrought with worry. With the age-old wisdom that had been passed down from his elders, which he'd then passed on to them.

He looked at the flock of Laven on the grass near the stream. Tonight, they didn't sit and rest in peace. Tonight, they wandered in turmoil and roamed in their grief.

Two more of their Laven family had not come tonight, and their Nols paced the boundary of Tearsith, their souls pleading with them to show.

Except everyone there knew they would not.

Aria and Pax had told Ellis what they had found. That Laven from one end of the earth to the other had been slain, though it was doubtful that authorities would ever make the connection.

Not that it would matter.

Ellis had dropped to his knees at the news, and Aria had climbed down to hers in front of him and told him of the hope they'd found in the middle of it.

Her altercation with Ambrose and her belief that she and Pax being together had made them stronger, rather than weakened them the way they'd always believed.

Now he peered over her shoulder to the Laven who wandered the meadow.

Torn.

Racked and wavering with uncertainty.

She took his frail hands, and she pressed them together with hers as if she were issuing a prayer. "I can't tell you with absolute certainty, Ellis, but I do believe it with all of me. Plus, I know what I've seen. What Pax and I have experienced. I have to believe that we've been led astray. Kept apart to keep us from reaching our full potential."

Ellis's attention traveled to Josephine, who tried to console Jeremy as he wailed for his missing Nol.

Aria didn't miss the longing in his gaze. The wonder of what might have happened had he gone to her long ago. What their lives might have looked like if everything had been done differently.

Aria's spirit moaned around Jeremy's grief. The love that he'd forever tucked away. One she was sure he'd kept hidden.

"We have to try, Ellis." Her plea sliced through his yearning. "We have to do something before it's too late and every single one of us is gone."

Sadness pooled in his hazy gray eyes as he turned his gaze to her. "And what if it only makes things worse? What if I send them on a path to destruction?"

Aria leaned in closer, her voice hushed. "They are already on a path to destruction."

Aria could almost see the acceptance glide into his spirit, and he slowly stood, laboriously staggering to his feet. She was unsure if it was from the strain of what she'd told him or if it was his age that made his entire essence creak.

"Gather around, dear Laven," he called.

Aria took a spot at his side. She felt the energy wrap her from behind. The belief that burned out of Pax where he stood three feet behind her.

Their family moved slowly, as if every step they took caused them physical pain. When they'd come together, Ellis began to speak.

"We have already come to the disturbing conclusion that we are being hunted."

A slow wave of desolation moved through the crowd. A dull gravity that pulled them toward their fate.

"But it is not only our Laven family," Ellis continued. "It appears those of every other Laven family throughout the earth are being hunted as well."

Horror wheezed from their mouths.

"But there may be hope in the middle of it. I will not lie and say my heart does not fear what it does not know or understand, but I trust in our brother and sister, Pax and Aria. I know it was questioned last night—if their joining had possibly caused this fallout. But they say they have found strength together. Extraordinary strength that neither of them has ever known. And it leaves us to wonder if that strength might be extended to all of us."

Shock rustled through the bleakness, and the air shifted as they looked between each other, at their Nols, whom they'd been forbidden to seek.

Those who'd lost theirs wept, their shouts of agony piercing the air.

Bearing it was nearly impossible, the force that pummeled Aria's soul as she watched out over her family who had been battered and dwindled. She knew Pax felt it, too, and he was suddenly at her side, slipping his fingers through hers in staunch support.

"For so long I've warned you of the dangers," Ellis confessed. "But I can no longer stand here with confidence and continue in that vein. There is speculation that the edict we'd been issued to stay away from our Nols during the day may have been a fallacy. A legend that has been passed down from generation to generation. One that Ambrose fabricated to weaken us. One that I had taken as truth from my own teacher and passed on to you."

He let go of a shaky exhale as he lifted a weathered hand. "Each of you have your own lives beyond the safety of Tearsith. Some with families. Others have found this life easier to traverse alone. But always, always separating our two realities. And maybe we've kept them separated for too long."

He hesitated, then proclaimed, "Maybe it is time for those walls to come down. Maybe it is time for you to seek your Nol in the day, for we all know the grave danger that looms around us."

The mass stirred. Unsure, though Aria could sense the glimmer of excitement that clashed with the arduous dread.

"I will not pretend to give you this advice with complete clarity, so you must decide for yourselves. I will no longer try to stand in your way. The only thing we can do is try and pray to Valeen that it is enough."

Ellis squeezed Aria's hand, urging her forward, a silent tip of his head for her to speak.

Aria looked out over her family, her throat thick as she forced herself to open her mouth.

What could she say?

What promises could she make?

There was one she knew she could keep.

"I know this is terrifying." She struggled to keep the tremor from her voice. "I'm afraid, too. But I promise you, I will fight to my last breath to end the one who seeks to end us."

Her inhalation was jagged. "Until then, be careful. Watch everywhere you go and everything you do. Listen to your hearts and find the inner strength, because I believe we are all much more powerful than we know. And if you seek your Nol, tap into the connection that you have in Faydor. Use it to protect yourselves. I believe you don't only possess it here, but while awake as well."

Ellis lifted his bony hands. "Fight, my dear family. Fight with everything that you have. Both here and while awake. There is much work to be done . . . It is time to descend."

Aria tracked through the bowels of Faydor with Pax at her side. The bitter cold wrapped her whole, and the howls of the depraved echoed in her ears.

They slayed each Kruen they passed.

Pushing themselves harder than they ever had before.

Their goal was to end them quickly. Their efforts were crucial since so many Laven had been lost.

But there seemed to be even more Kruen to contend with. Evil sprouting up from the nothingness. Growing in its own strength.

The chill in the air was volatile.

As if Faydor trembled on a brand-new axis, too.

Waiting for that tsunami to hit land.

The whole time, they searched for any Laven who might be targeted in Kruens' minds.

Tracking over the desolate, barren ground, winding through the spindly elms as they raced through the wickedness.

*"Take the gun and go in the store. Just walk inside. It's easy. Point it at the cashier. She'll give you anything you want."*

Aria heard the intonation in her ear, just off to her left. "This way," she called to Pax. They shifted course and wound around a boulder.

She and Pax rushed up behind what appeared to be a young Kruen. They gathered the light, projecting it as they ran, never even slowing as they struck. The monster was obliterated in a flash and disintegrated into ash.

They continued to run. Deeper and deeper into the darkness that reigned.

She wasn't sure when she noticed it, when she felt the creeping of the darkness growing thicker around them. The air becoming tacky. Aria struggled to breathe around it, to shun the sticky awareness that seemed to enclose her like a shroud.

It was as if the filament was taking form, a rippling boundary that sought to box her in.

She pushed herself harder against it, her breaths salient as she panted. Pax fell a step behind her.

And then she felt it distinctly—the air beside her taking shape. A diaphanous barrier that stretched thin like a blackened balloon.

Horror seized her lungs when she felt the presence on the other side of it. One that ran alongside her, separated by that gloomy, translucent veil.

"Do you think you possess the power to defeat me? Do you think you can stop me? I will take such pleasure in ending you." The voice was hollow. A distant echo. But she recognized it completely.

She knew it, as sure as she knew the face that tracked along at her side.

Ambrose.

Lightning flashed across the horizon, a thunderbolt that streaked through the air just overhead. So close she felt it sizzle across her flesh.

"Aria?" Pax shouted. His boots thundered behind her as he raced to catch up. Anxious confusion twisted through his expression as he caught up and ran along on her opposite side. "What's happening?"

She couldn't speak. Couldn't answer. She could only run.

"You think you can stop me from ending them all?" Ambrose hissed as he swiped a hand in her direction. The boundary stretched thin as he reached for her, and Aria saw the flood of his thoughts as he did.

Only he wasn't feeding a command to a Kruen or a Ghorl.

It was him, standing outside a tiny white house with a small porch fronted by a green lawn.

He who held the knife when Dani stepped out of the front door and into the light of day.

Dani who bled out on the steps.

*No.*

Desperation gripped her, and Aria whirled as she ran, attempting to punch her fist through the gauzy barrier, compelling the light to bash through the ward. To leash the fiend. To stop him in his tracks here in the dungeon where he reigned.

But he only laughed as he drifted away. Out of reach. Untouchable.

Before he fully disappeared.

# Chapter Twenty-Two

## PAX

"What the fuck was that?" It flew from my mouth as I floundered upright in bed.

Aria was already sitting up, chest heaving as she searched for the oxygen she couldn't seem to find.

"What happened, Aria? What's going on?"

"It was Ambrose," she rasped as she tossed off the covers and slipped from the bed. Anxiety bound her in chains, her entire being vibrating with trepidation.

I scrubbed both palms over my face, trying to break up the confusion. To orient myself after being yanked from one reality to the other. One minute, Aria and I had been tracking through Faydor, and the next, she'd been distraught, racing into the nothingness.

A flash of a second later, we'd both tripped, like our spirits had snagged on a branch and we'd been sent toppling forward.

And we'd landed here.

Awake.

Still two hours before dawn.

"What do you mean, it was Ambrose?" The question cracked through the disordered air.

Aria rushed her palms up her arms as she hugged herself. "It was like he was right there, riding a thin line between Faydor and wherever he was. That place, I think . . ." She inhaled a shattered breath. "He called it Baahg."

"The place you'd gone to? That night?"

"Yes."

Rage and hate lit up my insides. "Was he trying to drag you back there? Compel you?"

"No," she wheezed, and her eyes slammed shut. Distress held her in a fist. "He was showing me what he was going to do." I shifted off the side of the bed, and I slowly rounded the end of it to come to stand in front of her. In front of this woman whose spirit was shaking so badly I could feel it battering into me. "What did he show you?"

"Dani." She choked on her name.

Dread spiraled through the center of me.

"He's going for her," I said, the words blunt.

Filled with the fury this bastard evoked.

I wanted to end him. I wanted to end him with my bare fuckin' hands. Destroy him for the destruction he'd employed. But I knew it was going to take so much more than me.

"He wants to hurt me. Make me suffer before he brings me to my end." Aria's voice tremored.

"Or it's a fucking trap. A manipulation to get you where he wants you."

"He can obviously find me anywhere, Pax. That was the whole plan, wasn't it? That I'd draw him to me."

"It worked before the bastard ran away."

"And I think he's changing tactics. He's filled with hatred. He wants to torture me. Weaken my resolve by stealing the ones who mean the most to me."

"Because he's afraid," I said. "Afraid of what you can do."

Aria blinked those pale, pale eyes in the dimness of the room. Sparks of white flamed in their depths. "I don't know what his twisted intentions are, but I can tell you I'm not going to let him get to her."

She went to her phone, which was charging on the nightstand, her face pinching as she input the number, faltering over a couple of them. She wheezed in frustration, "I don't know if I remember the exact number."

She made the call anyway. It rang and rang. Never doing anything.

"Dang it, Dani." Worried frustration rolled from her before she grabbed her duffel from the floor, where we'd left our things packed in case we had to leave quickly in the night. She tossed it onto the bed, unzipped it, and dug through to find a change of clothes.

"You know where she lives?" I asked.

Aria sniffled as she shucked off her sweats and dragged on a pair of jeans. "Yeah. I've always known she lives in Oregon, but I got her address the other night. She lives in a small suburb outside of Portland."

"Shit." That was almost a two-day drive straight through.

I paced the floor, roughing my hands through the mess of my hair as I toiled through my thoughts. I turned back to Aria, who was pulling a pink sweater over her head.

"Maybe he's manipulating you, Aria. Sending you on a wild-goose chase so you're distracted from your purpose."

"And you know I can't take the chance that he's not." She turned toward me, her hands fisted on her chest, agony whittled into every gorgeous line on her face. "This is Dani, Pax. My mentor. The one who was there for me through my entire childhood. The one who tried to prepare me for what it was going to be like when I first descended on Faydor. My friend. My *sister*."

It was horrible what was happening with our Laven family. To all Laven. But I knew there was a special bond between Aria and Dani, just like there'd always been one between me and Timothy.

There was no way Aria would turn her back on her. And I wouldn't be the asshole who tried to stop her.

"Do you have any idea when? What his intentions were?"

Dejection roiled in her spirit. "I just saw him outside her house . . . waiting for her. It was in the middle of the day. What day that was, I don't know, and I can't take the chance of waiting to warn her tonight."

My head bobbed as I calculated, and I knew there was only one thing we could do.

"Hurry and get your things together. We've got to go."

An hour and a half later, we were speeding along a remote narrow road that cut through snowed-over fields that lay dormant in the middle of winter. We were about fifty miles outside the city.

The sun was just beginning to peek over the horizon, spraying pinks into the dusky gray sky, and every so often, we passed by the sporadic farmhouse tucked within the croplands.

Everything was quiet and still.

It felt like we'd gotten lost in the middle of nowhere.

"It's beautiful out here," Aria murmured as we flew down the road. Lines weren't even painted on the asphalt.

"Yeah."

Seemed crazy that this threat loomed so distinct, yet here, in this moment, there was peace. Like the world hadn't gotten the message that things were about to go to shit. We had to keep it that way.

"In a quarter of a mile, you will reach your destination." That generic, generated voice came from the speaker of Aria's phone, and in the distance, we could see the metal buildings rising on the left. A few evergreens poked up around them, and in the emerging morning light, a small prop plane took flight, its low whine filling the air as it slowly ascended.

"Do you think this is going to work?" Aria asked, fidgeting with the hem of her sweater.

We couldn't take the chance of booking a flight on a commercial airline. No way we could leave evidence of us flying across the country. Not after I'd broken Aria out of that facility and the pictures on the news of her had been easily identifiable—not to mention the fact that we'd left a trail of bodies behind us.

"Don't know. Hopefully, if you're convincing enough." I quirked a teasing brow at her. A slight prodding question.

She huffed. "I doubt that I'm much of an actress—but I've had to tell plenty of lies in my life, so I suppose I'm pretty good at it."

I reached over the console and took her hand. "The lies you told were never malicious, Aria. They were told for your survival. Both for yourself and the ones you love."

"I know," she whispered.

I slowed as we approached the entrance to the regional airport, and I took the left onto the short path that led to a squatty building with a slightly pitched metal roof. It was fronted by glass and two double doors. There were only four cars parked in the lot. We took the fifth spot, and I killed the engine before I shifted to look at Aria. "Are you ready?"

She gave a clipped nod. "Let's do this."

She tossed open her door at the same time I did mine, and I rounded to the trunk, grabbed our two bags, then followed behind Aria, who was already jogging toward the entrance.

A slight edge of hysteria was wound into her demeanor. I doubted she had to dig too deep to find that facade, her anxiety from last night easy to exploit.

She burst through the door and went straight to the counter, since there wasn't a single person in the lobby except for an older woman behind a desk. She was dressed in jeans and a floral button-down top, her thin gray hair cropped at her chin.

Aria and I both kept our sunglasses on so that we wouldn't have to deal with the negative strike of setting someone on edge at the sight of our eyes, though they were likely to feel it anyway.

The woman lifted her head at Aria's approach. Concern immediately twisted her expression. "Can I help you?"

"I'm so sorry to bother you, but I'm hoping you can help me."

"Well, that's what I'm here for. My name is Madge." The woman had a tenderness about her as she stood from the desk she'd been sitting at and came up to the counter.

I could sense it. There wasn't a bad bone in her body. I let go of a fraction of the tension.

"What can I do for you?" she asked.

Aria's tongue stroked out to wet her lips. "My husband and I . . ." Aria glanced back at me in a flurry of exasperation before she turned back to the woman. "We're on our honeymoon. Touring both Chicago and Indianapolis. I got a call last night that my mom was rushed to the hospital with a heart attack . . ."

Aria croaked it, then stammered for a beat before she rushed on. "She lives in Portland, and we immediately purchased tickets to get back to her so we can be there for her surgery, but this morning, we found our car had been broken into. Our suitcases we'd packed, to be ready for our early flight, and my purse were stolen . . ."

Madge gasped in outrage. "That's horrible."

Aria pressed the heel of her hand to her temple as she wheezed, "God, I was so stupid to leave it sitting on the seat for them to see it. I was just asking for this to happen. But I was so flustered I wasn't thinking straight."

She swiped the single tear that had slipped down her cheek. "We couldn't board our flight because my license was in my purse. And we have all this cash that we got from our wedding. Luckily, my husband had it hidden in his duffel bag that we had in the hotel with us, and we just were hoping there was someone here who could help us."

Looking helpless and forlorn, Aria spread twenty hundred-dollar bills out on the counter. "It's probably not enough, but when we get there, I'll be able to go to the bank and transfer the rest. I promise. And my sister is working on getting me a replacement ID, but said it was going to be at least forty-eight hours to overnight it, and I really need to be there for her surgery today."

Aria let go of a strangled sob and pushed out, "I'm terrified I'm not ever going to see her again."

Sympathy seeped into the woman's expression, and she reached out and patted the back of Aria's hand. "Don't you worry, sweet thing. We'll get this sorted out."

Madge moved back to her desk and picked up the handset on one of those old-fashioned corporate phones that had a bunch of lines. She pressed a couple of buttons before she brought it to her ear.

Aria and I shared a look. Hope brimming full.

"Hey, Ken, how's it going out there?" Madge asked. She nodded as she responded to whatever he was asking.

"Oh, good . . . yup."

I itched while they shared pleasantries I couldn't hear from the other end of the line.

"Hey, listen, I've got this cute couple who are in our neck of the woods on their honeymoon, and they need a quick ride to Portland. Her momma is having emergency heart surgery today, and they got robbed last night. Poor thing doesn't have her license, and she's beside herself."

A pause, then she said, "Yup. I'll just have her fax me a copy once she gets it, and then I'll get the passenger documentation in order."

She nodded. "They have some cash those jerks didn't manage to nab . . ." She looked over her shoulder at us. "Two thousand?"

I gave her a quick nod of confirmation.

"That's right," she told him.

More words from the other end of the line; then she said, "All right, I'll bring them around."

Relief punched me in the chest, and I curled my hand around Aria's fingers, which were trembling. Trembling with her own relief. Both of us in disbelief that we'd actually pulled this off.

Had no fucking clue what the regulations were with tiny planes like this. Apparently, a whole lot of the security was left up to the pilot, but still, I'd worried this was a long shot.

Madge hung up the phone and turned back to us, a winning smile on her face. "Ken's got you covered. He's goin' to have to make a stop to refuel, but he'll get you there just as fast as he can. Not as fast as one of those big ones would do . . ." She chuckled. "But it'll be a whole lot faster than driving."

"That's fine. I'm just so thankful."

"We can't have you missing out on being there for your momma, now, can we? Let's get you going."

She came around the counter and gestured for us to follow her, and she led us down a short corridor to another set of double doors that led out to the back of the building.

Cold bit into our flesh as we stepped outside, and I looked over at the single runway as another tiny plane took off.

"Hop on." Madge gestured to a golf cart that sat outside the door.

We climbed in, and it lurched forward as she rammed on the pedal. She whisked us over to a row of three hangars like she was the one who was flying.

She headed all the way down to the third. Its giant doors gaped open, and the plane inside was facing outward. She cut a right and drove through the doors and came to a jarring stop beside the plane.

This one was still a prop, a single propeller on the nose, though it was a little larger than the first two I'd seen taking off.

Madge kicked on the brake. "Here we go."

We climbed out, and I grabbed our bags as a man emerged from where he'd been checking something on the opposite side of the plane. "Heard we have us a bit of a rescue mission," he said.

He had no fucking idea.

He was probably in his fifties, wearing a leather jacket and a ball cap. Green eyes keen, though I wasn't getting any malicious vibe. Went against every instinct I had, putting our faith in other people—when any one of them could turn on us on a dime.

But I had to trust in this, give this guy credit, because there was no way we were getting to Dani in time if we didn't.

"Oh my gosh, yes, thank you for helping us. I can't express what this means to me," Aria gushed.

"It's my pleasure. Besides, it's been a couple weeks since I've gotten to take a longer jaunt across the US. Think you're going to find this is the superior way to fly."

"Ken here thinks he's the best pilot in the country," Madge teased with a wink.

"I sure hope he is," I grunted.

The man laughed. "Been flying my whole life. Don't worry, I'm gonna get you and your pretty bride home safely. I need to get the flight plan sorted, so you two hop in and get comfortable."

"Thank you," Aria gushed again. She glanced between them. "Both of you."

I nearly blew our cover when the woman moved to Aria and hugged her.

Hit with the intense urge to rip her arms from Aria, not wanting anyone close to her.

But we had a part to play, and I couldn't go losing my cool.

Madge hugged Aria tight, and Aria actually relaxed into the embrace and hugged her back. "You came to the right place. Told you we'd take care of you."

"You helped in a bigger way than you could ever know." Aria exhaled heavily as she breathed the words.

Madge patted her on the back. "Well, it was nothing. You two take care of each other," she said as she stepped away.

"Always will," I promised low, though I directed that statement toward Aria.

Awareness spun between us, and Madge cleared her throat before she turned on her heel and headed back for the golf cart. "Have a safe flight, and I'll be sending healing thoughts to your mother."

She whipped the golf cart back around and blazed out of the hangar, and Aria gasped with relief as I moved to her. I pulled her flush against me, my arm around her waist as her sweet body pressed against mine.

Her warmth lit me through.

"We did it," she breathed.

"You did it," I murmured before I pulled back with a smirk. "Wife."

A blaze of redness climbed up her neck and pooled on her cheeks. She fell into a sway with me as her teeth tugged at the inside of her lip. Her fingers were soft as they played along the neckline of my tee. "I don't hate the sound of that."

Surprise froze me for a beat.

Not once in this grueling, torturous life had I ever given thought to being married. The idea of it was nothing but a fucking joke. Like I'd ever let anyone get that close to me. Like I'd ever care. Like I could imagine *this*.

And there I was, picturing this woman in a pretty white dress with flowers in her hair.

Love rushed through the darkness that had always tainted my insides, and I slowed, slipping my hand to her waist as I dropped my forehead to hers . . . just breathing her in.

Swarmed by her scent.

The coconut.

The goodness.

The light.

"One day, Aria . . . one day I'm going to give you everything you want. Everything you have ever imagined that might make you happy. A normal life where you're safe and you don't have to forever look over your shoulder."

We were going to make it through this. We had to.

Aria's fingertips fluttered across my lips. "I just want you."

# Chapter Twenty-Three

## PAX

We touched down at a small airport outside of Portland just after 1:00 p.m.

Here, everything was green and wet. A ton of trees covered the rolling hills, the area lush, though the surrounding mountains that peaked into the sky were capped in snow.

The second the tires hit the runway, the breath whooshed out of Aria, though her anxiety seemed to double down. The frisson of it snapped across the surface of her skin, that overwhelming desperation to do something so clear I was close to suffocating from it.

Her need my own.

"Told you I was gonna get you here safe and in time to be with your mother," Ken's voice crackled through the speaker as we taxied down the runway toward the hangars. This airpark was quite a bit larger than the last, and there were at least eight hangars stacked in rows that went all the way back to a perimeter fence in the distance.

"You don't know how much I appreciate it," Aria returned.

"Ah, made my day, honestly. The two of you seem truly connected to each other. Love to see it. I'm just sorry your honeymoon got mucked up with the news about your mom. Hope it all works out right, that she's good as new; then the two of you can get that time to celebrate together."

"Me, too," Aria whispered, and she glanced back at me, her eyes hidden behind her sunglasses.

Ken brought the plane to a stop in front of a larger building, and he said a few things into his mic before he pushed something on the dash and the propeller began to slowly wind down. Once it did, he popped his hatch and jumped down, and he came around to the other side.

He helped Aria out, then did the same to me.

"Just head in there through the doors. Here's my card so you can forward your information." He handed it to Aria.

Felt bad since the guy was cool and had saved our asses, but that was not going to happen.

"Thank you. I hope your flight home is safe," Aria told him.

I shook his hand, mumbling my thanks, before I set my hand on the small of Aria's back and guided her toward the door he'd pointed to. My attention swung back and forth, taking in the area as we went, making sure there wasn't already some twisted bastard here waiting for us.

Heat embraced us when I whipped the door open and we stepped inside.

A chill rushed down Aria's spine, though I wasn't so sure it was coming from the clashing temperatures.

"I already texted for a cab the second we touched down," I told her, hoping to give her some encouragement. Some belief that we'd made it in time.

I knew what was going through her head.

No question, she was replaying that horrible vision of the way we'd rolled up on Peter.

How we'd been one fucking minute too late.

We couldn't let this turn out the way it had for him.

Couldn't fathom what we'd do then. How it would affect Aria. The guilt and grief that would consume her sweet, beautiful soul.

So I refused to contemplate if it was even a possibility.

"That's great," she whispered.

Aria at least knew Dani's address since everyone had exchanged info the other night.

After I slung an arm over Aria's shoulders like we were a regular couple on a trip, we walked down a hallway covered in industrial carpet. The longer corridor was separated by a rope that ran down the middle—one side for arrivals and one for departures.

Aria breathed out in disbelief when we got to the end and saw there was a small security area where passengers had to show their IDs and run their bags through a scanner, plus walk through a detector to get clearance.

We would never have made it through had we been traveling in the opposite direction.

Not without our IDs, and sure as hell not with the gun I had in my bag.

"That was some kind of luck," I muttered, turning my mouth toward her ear as we pushed through a door at the end that let us out into the unsecured side of the small terminal.

"I just hope our luck hasn't run out," she returned, the words soggy with apprehension.

We moved to a large bank of windows that overlooked the front. Aria fidgeted as we watched, chewing at her thumbnail and shifting on her feet. She flinched every single time a car came around the curved drive to the drop-off and pickup area just outside the doors, her breaths shallow as she anxiously waited.

Relief clashed with the trepidation that boiled between us when I saw a sedan roll up with the name of the taxi company written on the side. "That's us."

"Thank God."

We rushed out into the damp, cold air. Vapor puffed from our mouths as we jogged to the car, which pulled to a stop at the curb.

We hopped into the back, and I tossed out the address of a café in the shopping center nearest to Dani's address. Didn't want any record of us being dropped off directly in front of her house.

I knew Aria probably didn't care; she would take any risk to get to Dani. But I had to protect her, too. Everything hinged on her survival.

"All right," the driver said, glancing at us in the rearview mirror. There was some kind of speculation in his tone, unease that glided through his being, no doubt picking up that we were different.

Something he didn't trust.

"Gonna cost you fifty."

I pushed three twenties through the plastic plate that separated the front from the back. "No problem."

He didn't say anything else when he pulled back around the loop and headed out onto the highway.

Aria twitched the entire way, apprehension rolling through her in waves. I had my hand on her knee, trying to keep her calm as we traveled.

About twenty minutes later, he took an exit off the highway. I could feel Aria's heart rate increase. Her anxiety ramped up higher with each second that passed.

The driver slowed and made a right into a parking lot that housed what looked like a few local businesses. He rolled up toward the small café that sat in a freestanding building up near the road. The brick walls were painted teal, and there was a flower mural on the side.

Aria had her door open before he'd even come to a full stop.

"Thanks," I said as I grabbed our bags and slipped out the same side as her.

I acted like I was going to drag the door open while the driver drove away. The second he disappeared down the street, Aria was moving, her breaths going haggard as she jogged toward the neighborhood road that was on the opposite side of the parking lot. Our path already plotted out, as we'd searched the navigation during the ride over.

Heavy clouds hung low. So low it felt like you could reach out and drag your fingers through them. Stir them up. Or maybe it was the frenetic energy that roiled in Aria as she took to the sidewalk.

"Hurry," she pleaded as she looked at me from across the sidewalk, and she began to run, her tennis shoes slapping against the sidewalk.

I was right behind her, searching the area as we moved.

It was quiet.

Still.

Tree limbs stretched out over the road to make an arch, some bare but others still green in the winter.

The houses were older, and each was on at least an acre of land, if not more. Set back from the road and fronted by lawns and more of those abundant trees.

"This is it," Aria rasped when we made it to the address about halfway up the street. It was a small white house with a porch out front. Potted plants overflowing with colorful flowers sat at the top of the steps on either side, and a huge barren oak grew proudly in the middle of the yard.

Aria didn't hesitate. She ran up the walkway and bounded up the stairs. One second later, she was pounding on the door. Her palm smacked against the wood while I shifted, letting my gaze rove over the area, searching for anything amiss.

Silence echoed back from every direction.

The area almost too calm for my comfort.

Aria banged again. The wood clattered against the force. "Dani! Dani! Are you in there? It's Aria. Open the door. Please."

A flutter of movement suddenly whispered behind the drapes that covered the window to the left side of the door. In it, a wave of intensity rushed through the atmosphere, and a second later, metal ground as the person on the other side worked through the locks.

The door flew open.

Big, pale eyes rounded with shock stared back.

Dani.

She staggered where she stood, completely bewildered at finding us there.

"You're alive," Aria seemed to beg before she threw herself at her friend.

# Chapter Twenty-Four

## ARIA

Relief blew through me on a gale force as I hugged Dani to me.

Fiercely.

So fiercely I thought I would break her in half. My tiny slip of a friend who was alive and breathing in my arms.

Whole and real and unharmed.

"Oh God, I was so worried." It poured out of me as I struggled to get her closer.

Relishing the slosh of the blood that beat through her veins.

Her cropped, short hair, which was normally a shock of white in Tearsith and Faydor, was dyed a bright pink, and the ends stuck up and poked me in the face. I had to suppress the urge to weep into them.

"Aria?" Dani wheezed into my embrace, squeezing me back just as tight. "You came? I can't believe this. I didn't think to hope . . ."

Clutching her, I breathed out the terror I'd been holding in since I woke this morning. "I thought I was going to be too late. We tried to call, but it just kept ringing. I was so afraid."

"What do you mean, 'too late'? What is going on?" Except I thought she must have anticipated it, with the chill I felt sweep through her.

Or maybe all of us could feel the threat that loomed. Dark clouds that churned and spun. But I swore I could feel the tiniest speck of light in the center of the storm.

Hidden and trying to burst free.

I gathered myself enough to pull back so I could look down at my friend's cherubic face. She had a giant scar slashed at an angle across the left side of her forehead, wore wire-rimmed glasses, and had her makeup done in a way that made her look like she might be a professional.

She was stunning and beautiful, and God . . .

Emotion gripped me, and I grabbed her by the cheeks, unable to stop myself from touching her.

Needing to feel the palpable, undeniable truth that we'd made it on time.

"I saw you . . ." My words were thick. "In Ambrose's mind last night while I was in Faydor. He came here . . . to this house . . . in the middle of the day."

Her pallid skin, which was covered in nearly as many tattoos as Pax's, blanched further, and she nodded in understanding. "I guess he's coming for all of us, isn't he? We all know something has changed, even though I'd hoped somehow, in the middle of it, we'd all be safe."

She breathed out a shaky sigh. "I've kept my doors triple-locked and the alarm on day and night. I wasn't about to come outside. I nearly lost it when I heard the banging on my door, thinking it was the end. That I was trapped. But then I heard your voice, and I peeked out . . ."

Her tongue stroked out to wet her lips. "For a second, I thought I must be being deceived into thinking it was you. But it is . . . You're here."

"I'm here."

"Ah . . . I see how it is. Already forgetting about me." Pax's voice was close to teasing, and I let her go and shifted around to look at him at the same time that Dani pushed out a tinkling laugh. Her gray eyes washed over him where he stood at the top of the steps, keeping guard.

They stared at each other for a beat.

Affection and disbelief clear.

For so long, each of us had been on our own. Never thinking we would meet another of our kind.

Forbidden to even think about it.

Isolated and alone.

And here we were, standing out in the light of day.

Together.

A moment later, a smirk hitched the edge of her mouth. "God, Pax, you're freaking terrifying. What are you trying to do, scare people out of listening to the voices in their heads?"

He was still foreboding in Tearsith and Faydor, but none of his tattoos or scars were visible there. I'd been struck by his intensity the first time I'd seen him, too.

I choked on a laugh, and Pax scuffed out a chuckle as he roughed a tattooed hand through that shock of white hair.

"Flattered." Sarcasm rolled off his tongue.

She widened appraising eyes. "You should be. Because you, my friend, are handsome as hell. No wonder our Aria here would shake in her boots every time you walked into Tearsith."

"I wasn't that obvious," I defended myself. There was no stopping the smile that played across my mouth. The joy I felt at being here, at seeing her face in the waking world for the first time.

Dani sent me a withering look, mischief lining her voice. "Oh, please. It was written all over you both. I'm surprised we didn't catch you trying to sneak off past the boundaries or behind a tree, your pants down for all to see. The number of times I've had to skip over and intervene before anyone else noticed Aria getting all hot and bothered was kind of ridiculous."

Softness flooded her as her gaze drifted between us. "But I'm glad to know we don't have to do that anymore." Lines furrowed her brow as the severity came rushing back. "Do you really believe it? That we're safer together?"

She scanned the area as if she were searching for the danger that swelled in the distance.

"We think so . . . or at least, as Nols, we're stronger together."

"I can't believe this."

Wonder and confusion filled her spirit.

The things we'd been taught.

Commanded.

No doubt, it was hard for her to wrap her head around the changes. Unquestionably, it applied to all of us. The revealing of much that had been hidden. Truths that had been secreted and concealed.

But I also knew that meant there were complexities that only brought us more confusion from the lack of answers.

It was as if a crack had been made in the well that contained all that we knew. Uncertainties and doubts leaking out with the new freedoms we were discovering.

Freedoms we'd barely found.

Freedoms we had to stop from being stripped away.

The low hum of an engine echoed up the street, and everyone froze as we turned to watch a pickup truck pass.

A sharp edge cut into the mood, each of us wary of everything and everyone.

A collective sigh rippled out of us when it didn't slow and drove by without incident.

"We should go inside," Pax suggested.

"Oh my gosh, yes, come in." Dani jumped into action, and she widened the door and gestured for us to enter. She shut it as soon as we passed, hurrying to engage three big locks and plugging a code into an alarm-system keypad on the wall.

I took in her space while she did.

The house was small and cute. Chaotic and cluttered.

Kind of like Dani.

The living room was crammed with an oversize, plush cream-colored couch that was pushed up against the left wall, decorated with a slew of throw pillows in every color. A black cat with a white spot between its eyes was curled up on the back cushion, and it only lifted its head to peek at us in annoyance before it went back to its nap.

There was a coffee table with a bunch of books scattered across the top, and white shelves boasting a gorgeous collection of hardbacks were situated on the wall opposite the couch. A flat-screen television was built into the middle of it, the glass surrounded by a white frame.

On the far side of the house was a round table that sat beneath the bright light that flooded in through the windows set into double French doors that overlooked the backyard.

It looked like the kitchen was to the left of it, and just before the wall that separated the kitchen was a hall to the left.

"Your phone not working?" Pax asked.

Dani huffed. "I've been so nervous that when my sweet girl Pixie"—she gestured to the cat snoozing on the back of the couch—"jumped up onto the counter behind me in the kitchen yesterday, I screamed and basically launched it into the air like I was about to be murdered, which apparently I was, since you two are standing here. It completely shattered the screen when it hit the floor. I emailed my mom and asked her to get me a new one because there was no chance I was going out there by myself."

"That's a good call," Pax said.

"Apparently so." She exhaled a heavy breath; then her eyes went wide again. "How about some tea?"

"Sure," I said.

She moved through the living room and disappeared into the kitchen.

Cabinet doors started banging, and I could hear the clatter of dishes.

"You'll have to forgive me. I don't get a whole lot of company," she called, almost sounding flustered. "Okay, let's be real—I get none except for my parents."

I glanced at Pax, who had set our bags by the door and now was peering back out at the front yard around the edge of the drape to make sure we were in the clear. Turning back around, I edged through the living area and followed Dani's path to the kitchen.

It was tiny, but bright and airy. Gossamer curtains bracketed a window over the sink that also overlooked the backyard. The cabinets were old and painted white, the floor checkered black-and-white tiles. There was a little jut out of the countertop that created a bar, separating the kitchen and dining area, and two stools were placed on this side of it.

She was already digging into the pantry when I stepped in. "What kind of tea do you like?" she asked.

"What do you have?"

She blew out a laugh. "Pretty much every kind. My mom gets me tea for every birthday since she doesn't know what else to do with me."

She pulled out a wooden box and lifted the lid to reveal a bunch of slotted spots stuffed with different tea packets. "Pick your poison."

"Earl Grey?"

"Living on the edge," she said with a grin. She moved to the sink, filled a kettle, and placed it on the stove.

"That's pretty much been my motto of late," I said.

She bit down on the inside of her cheek as if she was trying to halt the vision of it, speared by the reality of what had been happening while Pax and I had been on the run.

Then she turned toward me, the slight frenzy she'd been riding shifting to reverence. She blinked with her big, vibrant eyes. So big they seemed to take up half of her waifish face as she stared at me where I hovered at the end of the bar.

"I can't believe you're here," she whispered, the words hitching in warmth. "That you came here because you were worried about me. Aria, that seems . . . dangerous and imprudent. God, what were you thinking?"

My laughter was hoarse. "Did you think I wouldn't do anything to try to protect you? And don't you dare tell me you wouldn't do the same for me."

She sighed. "I know. It's just . . ." Her attention dipped before it was back on me. "You're important."

"And so are you, Dani. Every single one of us is. But you know you're especially important to me. I don't know what I would have done without you growing up. You taught me so much. You were there through so much of my confusion and questions. You've always been my best friend."

Affection ridged her expression. "And you've always been mine."

Dani paused, glancing around as if she were trying to find an anchor, before she turned her gaze back to me. "I still can't believe you're standing in my house. This feels . . . insane. Like maybe I've finally lost it."

She shook her head a little, her hair a strike of pink beneath the rays that slanted in through the kitchen window.

I fiddled with the hem of my sweater and shifted on my feet. "I thought I'd been losing it my whole life . . . And then there was Pax . . . and now there is you."

She blinked, and a tear slid down her face. "I've been so scared. Knowing all these Laven have been dying. Being here by myself and completely helpless. Not knowing what was happening. To my family. To you and Pax. To Timothy." She could barely get his name out around the knot that bobbed in her throat. "God, I hate this."

The kettle started to whistle, and she crossed back to the stove and filled three mugs that she'd pulled from a cupboard and set on the counter. She tossed tea bags into each one, grabbed a container of sugar, and set everything out on the bar. "There you go."

"Thank you," I told her as I pulled out a stool and sat.

I could feel Pax's presence. His stealthy movements as he came to lean his hip against the end of the wall that separated the kitchen and the hall on the other side.

Quiet and furiously protective.

Dani stood on the opposite side of the bar, and she stirred a teaspoon of sugar into her mug, lost in thought. The words were thin when she asked, "So, he's coming for me? I'm next?"

"No. You're not next." It shot out of me. "That's why we're here. We aren't going to let that happen."

"But you saw it . . . My death?"

I didn't want to give her the details, but I had no right to keep it from her, either.

"I think that's what he wanted me to see, at least. Whether it was the actual plan or a manipulation to send me on a different path than the one I was on, I don't know, but there was no chance I was going to take that risk. We came as fast as we could."

Steam wound up from my mug, and I blew it before I brought it to my lips and took a sip. Warmth spread through my chest and into my stomach.

Her brow pinched. "How did you see it?"

A disbelieving sound rolled out of me, and I told her about what had happened last night. How Ambrose seemed to be able to get to me in ways I'd never fathomed. Dragging me into the unknown.

"God. I feel like we're inside some kind of weird freaking movie," she said. "One of those horror-slasher kinds."

Air huffed from my nose. "We might as well be. The Kruen must be the origin of every terror that has ever been written."

Every fear and insecurity that people possessed.

Every evil that captured humans' minds.

Pausing, Dani stared into her tea, leaning on her elbows on the counter, before she looked back up, blinking at me from behind her glasses. "Do you feel it, Aria? This thing in the middle of you?"

She edged back to touch high on her abdomen. "It's ugly and foul. Ominous. Like I can feel something coming. Something changing." She wavered, then whispered, "But there's also a pulse in the middle of it. Something urgent. Like I'm supposed to do something, but I don't know what it is."

I knew exactly what she was talking about. I had felt it coming for weeks. That tsunami in the distance that gathered strength as it surged forward to consume the land.

"Yes," I said in a rush. "I feel it, too."

She shifted to look at Pax, who still hadn't taken his mug of tea, the man just standing there, observing us.

"Do you?" she asked point-blank.

Pax's nod was slow, his voice rough. "Yeah. I feel it. Like wickedness is rising up from the ends of the earth. Building in power as it is driven to one specific place where it all will come together. And when it does, there's going to be a catastrophic implosion."

"Where?" she asked in exasperation.

To all of us, herself included.

"Don't know. I'm afraid it's going to hit us from out of nowhere," he said.

"He wants to rule here," I murmured. "Out in the open. He said everyone would bow to him."

"How is that even possible?" Dani wheezed as her face pinched in aggrieved disgust.

"I don't—"

My words were clipped off when there was a soft thud and then a clatter on the outside of the house. Our attention whipped toward the wall the shelves rested against.

Our teeth clamped down and plunged us into silence, though I could hear the sudden ravaging of our hearts. The boom, boom, boom that thundered through the room.

We remained still, barely breathing as we listened.

We all heard it at the same time. The clicking of a latch.

*Someone's out there,* I mouthed.

"The gate that leads into the backyard," Dani muttered beneath her breath.

"Fuck," Pax spat, and he eased off the wall and pulled his handgun out from inside his jacket. I didn't know when he'd moved it from the duffel and into his pocket, but he lifted it then, turning off the safety and checking that it was loaded.

Horror ripped from Dani, though she clapped her hand over her mouth to cover it, and Pax mouthed, *Get down on the floor, both of you.*

Dani dipped behind the counter, and I slipped off the stool and climbed down onto my hands and knees so I could crawl over to her.

Dread pulsed and pulled, the uncertainty of what we would face stirring us into a frenzy. We wondered if Ambrose was here, in the flesh but so much stronger than any man. Or if it was another he'd sent. Someone he'd wielded his power over and bent to his will.

Dani gripped my hand the second I got to her. She was shaking so hard that she rattled in my hold.

"We're going to be okay," I promised, squeezing back.

We peeked around the corner, watching Pax carefully edge across the floor, keeping his boots silent as he moved toward the French doors. He leaned his back against the wall to the side of them, and he shifted to peer out into the sunlight that poured in through the panes through a break in the clouds.

"Don't see anyone," he rumbled, turning back to us. "Dani, need you to shut off the alarm so I can go check it out."

"I'm coming with you," I said, getting to my feet, though staying low.

Part of me had expected him to argue, but instead he muttered, "Ah, baby, like I'd go anywhere without you."

# Chapter Twenty-Five

## PAX

Dani hurried over to the keypad and turned off the alarm, and the second it beeped, I turned the top lock on the French doors. My attention darted all over the backyard, searching for whoever was out there.

There was no question in my mind that someone was lurking.

Hiding.

Lying in wait.

I just hoped they had no fuckin' clue what was coming for them. Had no idea that Dani was no longer here by herself.

There was no movement, just that awareness floating through the atmosphere. I slowly pulled down on the latch, and the hinges whined as I inched the doors open, then slipped through the crack and out onto the porch.

Gun drawn and swiveling from left to right, ready for any piece of shit to come charging toward me. Not sure what was going to happen if that beast turned out to be Ambrose. If he'd lured us here for this exact purpose.

Funny how we needed to get in front of him—fight him—if there was any chance of stopping him, but the thought of it was always wrought with terror.

Never knowing if he might prevail. If the only thing we were doing was setting Aria up for certain death.

Either way, it'd become clear that death could get at her no matter where she was, so the location didn't matter.

Unless the whole issue with the location was that he didn't want her someplace in particular.

It was a thought that had kept creeping into my head all day.

The distraction factor.

I kept thinking that maybe if he couldn't end her as easily as he'd assumed he'd be able to, he needed to keep her out of the way.

Still, my heart rate notched up by a thousand as I crept across the porch, which was maybe ten feet wide. The wooden planks creaked beneath my weight. I could feel Aria emerge behind me, that energy fierce and unrelenting, though she kept back, sticking close to Dani as I slowly glided down the three stairs to the damp grass below.

The backyard wasn't huge, but there was a fucking massive tree in the middle of it. The base of its trunk was at least five feet wide, branches stocky and substantial where they twisted out to create a canopy over the entire yard.

Plenty of cover to hide.

There was also a shed at the back of the yard near the fence on the left with a gap behind it.

But I was drawn to the right, where we'd heard the clanking. The hairs on the back of my neck stood at attention as I inclined my focus in that direction.

Gut told me there was a presence concealed on that side.

I wound around the porch and pressed up close to the back wall of the house. Slowly, I slunk in that direction with my back against the paneling, doing my best to control the breaths that pelted from my lungs.

I was two feet from the corner when I heard a twig snap.

Adrenaline jumped into my bloodstream.

No question, someone was there.

So I reacted.

I moved swiftly so I'd be the one benefiting from the element of surprise, and I threw myself around the corner.

A man was a foot away, his back to me as he started to reopen the gate, like he was having second thoughts about coming here. Or maybe second thoughts about his mode of entry.

Not Ambrose.

He was a tall, lanky Black guy, who whirled around when I emerged behind him.

Instantly, his hands flew up in surrender when he saw the gun pointed in his direction.

Pale-gray eyes wide with shock and fear.

My own surprise had me dropping the gun to my side. Relief punched me in the face, and the name was heavy as a stone as it toppled out of my mouth and onto the ground.

"Timothy?"

Air gushed out of him as he bent in two, resting his hands on his knees as he panted. "You scared the fuck out of me, brother."

Breathing heavy, I rambled, "Uh, yeah, I could say the same."

I uncocked the gun and turned on the safety; then I staggered forward and gripped the top of his shoulder as I bent down so I could fully take him in. "Can't believe it's you."

He surged forward, nearly picking me up off my feet as he hugged me and clapped me on the back. "You're alive. And here. Fuck, I can't believe it. Been dodging bullets all day . . . You're not the first person who tried to get a shot in at me. This shit is out of control."

"Didn't mean to freak you out. We thought you were . . ."

I trailed off when an overwhelming presence rolled over us, and Timothy fumbled back a step when he was struck by it, drawn to the side so he could see around me.

I looked over my shoulder to find Dani standing twenty feet away.

Nailed to the spot with an earthquake rumbling beneath her feet. A riot of energy fired in the middle of them.

The two of them just gaped at each other as their chests jerked and spasmed.

One second later, she was flying toward him and throwing herself into his arms. Without reservation, he hoisted her up, and she wrapped her legs around his waist and her arms around his neck. He had an arm looped around her lower back, the other rushing over her.

Her back.

Her shoulders.

Gliding up the back of her neck before his fingers were digging up into her scalp.

"Oh God. Oh God. Oh God," Dani whimpered as she looked down at him, her fingers trembling as she reverently touched his face. "It's you. It's you."

"It's me, baby. It's me."

Then he was kissing her. Wild and frantic. Like he'd just found the missing piece inside him.

My gaze moved, drawn to Aria, who waited near the side of the wall, her eyes soft as she watched them before they drifted to me.

My heart squeezed in a fucking fist.

Yeah. No doubt Timothy had just found his missing piece, and I was looking directly at mine.

# Chapter Twenty-Six

## ARIA

Pax stuffed his hands into his jeans pockets as he ambled my way. The breeze rustled through the white locks of his hair, and the slightest smirk played at the edge of his mouth, something knowing and tender written in the harsh angles of his face.

I didn't know if he'd ever looked so beautiful to me. So perfect and right.

It felt as if we'd just received confirmation of a theory we'd held on to for years. A loss that had throbbed. A vacancy that had gaped.

Wondering if others in our Laven family had felt the same way we did about each other. If we'd been marked on each other in greater ways than we'd been told, or if Pax and I were just an anomaly.

It seemed like an affirmation.

A promise that Pax and I had made the right choice in stepping out. Going against a rule that felt faulty. A blight carved in the middle of our souls.

"He didn't even try to resist her the way I did you," he muttered when he got to within a foot of me, low enough that it wouldn't disturb Dani or Timothy. The smile still fluttering across his plush red lips that seemed so at odds with the rest of him sent a crash of wings fluttering through my stomach.

"Dude couldn't keep his hands off her for one second." His voice was raw with adoration.

I couldn't stop my own smile as I swiveled so that we were hidden, to give Timothy and Dani a moment to themselves.

I let my hand slide beneath Pax's jacket, which was open in the front, my palm smoothing up the thin fabric of his tee and over the sinewy strength of his abdomen and chest. Warmth saturated me at the contact, the rush of his aura, which I swore weaved with mine.

I leaned back against the wall as I stared up at him, feeling light and airy within this sanctuary we'd found.

"Maybe he just wanted her more than you wanted me, and he couldn't help himself." I let a tease wind into the words. A taunt and a play. A moment's reprieve from the torment that haunted us.

For a few seconds, I wanted to get lost in the happiness I felt at seeing Dani and Timothy together. It spouted like a spring from within. A soothing balm, like something that had been set to wrong had been dialed to right.

An injustice rectified.

Mischief danced in the deep, fathomless depths of Pax's gaze, and he eased closer, boxing me in with all his heat. His nose brushed mine as he murmured, "You think that's even possible, Princess? Someone wanting another more than I want you?"

"Mmm?" I pretended as if I weren't quite sure as I toyed with the neckline of his tee. "He seemed awful happy to see her."

Pax's hand cinched down on my hip as he let his lips whisper down the angle of my jaw.

Shivers raced.

The perfect kind, that tingled through my senses on a streak of bliss.

"Think this thing I've got for you is far greater than any simple *want*. I thought I was going to die, not getting to touch you. Trying to endure the hunger that raged inside me. Feeling like I couldn't get a full breath of oxygen into my lungs whenever you were near. Fighting something that felt intrinsic. Like something I couldn't survive without."

The playfulness had shifted, and a stark severity wound into the breeze that wisped through the air.

Pax eased back, and he ran his thumb over the scar on my jaw. "Turns out, you were the blood in my veins. Because looking at you, Aria Rialta? I came alive for the very first time. It's when I understood the meaning of this life. Years spent denying it . . . forcing myself into accepting that you were only meant for me in Tearsith and Faydor. It was torment, Aria. Being without you was nothin' but torment, resisting you the most painful thing I've ever done."

Overcome by emotion, I raked my teeth over my trembling bottom lip as I reached out and brushed my fingertips down the long scar cut into the right side of his face.

His menacing, magnificent face that made my insides quake.

"And because of your bravery . . . because you were willing to sacrifice anything to get to me, you opened the gates for the rest of them. Because there is no question that remains in my mind that Dani and Timothy feel the same way as you and me, and I have to believe that's true for the rest of our family."

He took my fingers that were tracing over the lines slashed deep into his expression and pressed kisses to my knuckles. "No, Aria. All of that is because of you. Because of extraordinary, amazing you."

Then he grinned and edged in closer, the tease back in full force. "But for the record, there's no chance Timothy needs Dani quite as much as I need you. That's just not fucking possible."

"Sorry to break it to you, Pax, but I'm going to have to interrupt this little lovefest to respectfully disagree."

A surprised laugh choked out of me when I looked up and found Timothy grinning, him and Dani standing beside us.

Pax shifted enough to throw him a smirk, along with a wry quirk of his brow. "'This little lovefest'? That was quite the display going down right around the corner. Don't think you should be talking."

A blush rushed to Dani's cheeks, but she was still pressed tight to Timothy's side, their fingers locked, unwilling to let go.

"Hey, man, no shame here. Think it's clear there's a whole lot of love going around. As far as I'm concerned, it's about damned time," Timothy said.

"It's such a relief you're here," I said, slipping out from under Pax so I could edge up to Timothy's side, the one Dani didn't occupy. I wrapped my arms around his middle, and he curled his free arm around my shoulders and hugged me tight.

Affection billowed. Happiness uncontained.

"The second I woke up this morning, after you'd suggested that it might be safer to be with our Nol than without, I was on a plane," Timothy said. "Only thing I knew was, I had to get here. My heart was clawing its way out of my chest like it was going to make it here faster. Every piece inside was already sure that this is where I really belong. And I'm willing to bet that's been the case with a whole lot of our Laven family today. Reunions happening all over the place."

I pulled back, and Timothy cast a tender glance down at Dani. A thick sound rolled up her throat, her face blotchy from the tears that couldn't seem to stop falling.

Devastating joy and marked relief.

"I hope so," she whispered. "Because there is absolutely nothing better than this. No better feeling than you being here. Right beside me. That you're all here," she added in a rush of gratitude as she turned her attention to me and Pax.

We spent a moment relishing it—the hope for our family. But it was also tainted by the fact that there were those of us who would never have that chance. Their lives ripped from them before they could experience the fruition of the connection with their Nol.

It also wasn't lost on any of us that our rejoicing might be short lived. The celebration dampened by the threat we could feel lingering in the perimeter. Right on the outskirts of the peace we had found.

Dani cleared her throat as if she felt it, too. Right there. Hovering just out of reach.

She swiped the moisture from her cheeks with the back of her free hand as she urged, "Come on. We should go inside where it's warm."

She gave a little tug for Timothy to follow.

We all trudged back up the porch steps, stomping off our shoes on the mat at the door before we slipped back inside.

Timothy chuckled as he looked around. "How did I know exactly what this place was going to look like?"

Dani shrugged. "You've always known me best."

"Yeah, I have, haven't I?" He ran his knuckle under her chin; then she squealed when he suddenly swung her up into his arms. He cradled her as he strode into the living room and plopped down onto the couch with her on his lap.

Okay, so Timothy was not shy.

Pax and I shared a look, a tinge of embarrassment coloring my cheeks, unsure if we should excuse ourselves, or how to handle this. Remembering what it was like when I'd first seen Pax all over again, though our circumstances had been entirely different.

The pull that had dragged between us.

An undertow.

Waves of outright fear battering against it. Fear of the consequences of giving in to what we'd wanted so much.

"I'll grab our teas," I offered, and I slipped into the safety of the kitchen. Pax followed close behind. His lips twitched with amusement when we heard the murmurings echoing in from the other room, Timothy and Dani whispering things to each other that we couldn't hear.

Things that were only meant for them.

"Can I help with anything?" Pax asked quietly.

"We need another mug."

Pax searched through two cupboards before he found the one that held them, and he filled it with the still-steaming water as I went to the pantry Dani had been in and found the box of tea bags.

I opened one and tucked it into the mug; then Pax and I each grabbed two.

I peeked around the corner, worried I was going to interrupt something, before I eased around, clearing my throat to make sure they knew I was approaching.

Dani giggled and shook her head where she sat on Timothy's lap. Her arms were draped around his neck, my friend fully wrapped around her Nol. "I'm so sorry that you're in *my* kitchen getting us tea. I'm apparently a little distracted."

She glanced up at Timothy, who grinned down at her.

"Don't apologize. It's understandable," I said.

"Was it like this when you two first saw each other? I mean, I can only imagine, considering the way the two of you already were in Tearsith," she added.

Pax set the two mugs on the coffee table near them. "Safe to say, my foundation was rocked the second I saw her, but since I was breaking her out of a mental institute, we didn't quite have the time for a first encounter like yours."

"That, and he pretty much insisted on keeping at least twenty feet of space separating us." I gave him a mischievous roll of my eyes as I folded myself onto the floor, sitting with my legs crisscrossed. I wrapped my hands around my mug to warm them.

Pax grunted as he climbed down behind me, curling an arm around my waist and hooking his chin on my shoulder.

"Just was trying to be chivalrous." It was his own tease.

Dani peeked up at Timothy, her expression waffling between irreverence and awe. "Well, I, for one, am glad chivalry is dead."

"Don't worry, beautiful. I don't really intend to be polite," Timothy said, his intentions gleaming all over his face.

My lips pressed together. Nope. Definitely not shy.

Ease wafted around us, our smiles so wide they hurt, the same as our ribs, where our hearts pressed against their confines. Bursting free of the shackles we'd been given.

Given by Ambrose, who sought to steal. To ruin and destroy.

As if Timothy had heard the name uttered into his ear, he stiffened a fraction, his head angling to the side as his attention volleyed between each of us. "So now that we're all here, how are we going to take down this motherfucker?"

Pax exhaled a heavy breath. "We still aren't exactly sure, but when Aria came against him yesterday? She was the one who ended up with the upper hand, and he took off. Not sure if he was surprised, tucking tail because the fucker was scared, or if he was just choosing to divert and take a different route."

Timothy's eyes swiveled to me. "Do you think if you got one-on-one with him, you could end him?"

My rib cage expanded as I inhaled. "It's like I feel that I can. That it's possible. But also, I know there's something missing. Something I don't know or understand."

"And the problem is figuring out what it is," Timothy offered.

My nod was unsure. "It's like he keeps coming at me from different angles, and when he doesn't overcome me, he tries something else. Dragging me to different realities and realms. Sending others for me, and other times coming at me himself. It's like . . . the ground is always rocky. No way for me to fully figure out how to fight him because it's always brand new."

Timothy's expression turned appraising. Knowing. "And as long as you're scrambling, always disoriented, you won't be able to catch up."

*Distracted.*

It was there again.

"Maybe he's testing you . . . seeing what you're capable of?" Dani suggested, though it was clear she didn't want to.

"Like he's preparing?" Timothy phrased it like a question.

"He's definitely preparing for something," I said.

I felt Pax tighten his hold on me, his agitation at the thought rising high, before he murmured, "I promise you, that asshole won't be prepared for what is coming for him."

# Chapter Twenty-Seven

## ARIA

"Are you sure this will be okay?" Dani flitted around the small spare bedroom she predominantly used for her office, readjusting the bedspread that covered the full bed and fluffing the pillows. "I know it's cramped in here."

"If you saw some of the places we stayed in the last few weeks, you wouldn't be so concerned right now." I didn't hide the wryness as I stood at the doorway, watching her fret.

Her pink hair flipped to the side as she grabbed a decorative cloud-shaped pillow that matched the white-and-blue-polka-dot bedspread and tossed it onto the window seat that overlooked the front yard. "That bad?"

"I think we were trying to give *dive* a new definition."

I blinked through the fog of memories of the last few weeks. Days and nights that felt as if they'd been set to fast-forward, blips of cities and towns that we'd sped by imprinted in my mind in a black-and-white haze.

The endless slew of crappy motels that had all felt the same, though each was so distinctly different.

The beauties and horrors that had been found behind their doors.

It felt as if it all had transpired in a flash yet had stretched over years.

"But I didn't mind. And this? It's honestly perfect," I told her. "Your adorable house. Being here, *with* you and Timothy. It's better than anything I could have imagined. It feels like what home should feel like."

"A place where you're safe. Understood," she murmured, as if she felt it, too, her pale, pale eyes soft as she glanced in my direction.

My nod was slow. "Yeah. That's exactly it."

"Do you miss yours?" she asked as she straightened, and she leaned her hip against the white desk that sat against the wall opposite the foot of the bed. It was where she spent her days as a graphic designer for a local advertising company.

Three large monitors were arranged side by side, and a digital drawing pad and a keyboard sat on top. Colorful pens, markers, and notepads were organized in containers, and what had to be a thousand sticky notes with ideas scribbled on them were tacked off to the side of the screens.

An ache fluttered through my chest. "I do," I admitted.

There'd been a constant worry about them.

The worry that they might be targeted again, though everything had seemed to be fine the few times I'd texted to check on them. My mother and siblings were still staying at my grandmother's house since my mom wasn't sure how to handle my father.

How to trust again.

I cleared the roughness from my throat. "You know how much I love them. How I'd do anything for them. But this . . ."

She padded across the floor, and she reached up and hooked her fingers through mine. "This is your family."

Emotion gripped me. I nodded through the blear of moisture that rushed to fill my eyes.

"And I will forever be thankful that you brought us together. All of us," she said. Her long lashes fluttered behind the lenses of her glasses as she blinked through her thoughts. "Today was like being reunited with a part of myself that I only knew was missing but couldn't pinpoint exactly why it hurt so bad."

"It feels right, doesn't it?" I whispered.

"It feels like a dawning after being in the dark for my entire life."

She glanced behind me toward the low-pitched mutter of voices coming from the other room, where Pax and Timothy talked in hushed tones. "Seeing you and Pax in the light of day is so amazing. An experience I will forever cherish. But God, Aria. Timothy being here?"

The words cracked, hinged with the wash of confounded joy.

"That I get to experience this, even if it's just for a little while? Even if I only got to see him once? It means everything to me. It is the one wish I had ever made . . . the one true prayer I'd issued a million times that I never believed would be granted."

It was as if our spirits were peering into mirrors, her thoughts perfectly reflecting mine.

A tear slipped free of my eye, and she held my hand against her chest. "It's a gift, Aria. What we share. All of us. But especially with them. And this can't be temporary. It can't. We have to find a way."

Reaching out her free hand, she brushed away the moisture that lined my cheek, her voice soggy as she continued. "And I have faith that we will. Because even though I can feel what's festering in the air—the malignant—I can feel there's a solution. A remedy. Something bigger than what threatens to consume us. I can't believe we'd be here together if there wasn't."

Footsteps scuffed down the hall. We broke apart, and I poked my head out to find Pax and Timothy laughing under their breaths as they approached.

Though the air—it completely shifted when Dani stepped out into the hall.

Timothy slowed, just taking her in.

She couldn't be more than half his height, this tiny slip of a human who folded herself into him when he made it to where she waited. His mouth went to the crown of her head.

The energy begged between them.

Alive and real and eternal.

An understanding that surpassed all boundaries.

A bond that stretched beyond worlds.

"'Night, you two," Timothy rumbled.

"Good night," Pax and I returned.

Timothy slipped his arm around Dani and began to lead her down the hall toward her room at the end.

She paused only to slant me a knowing glance before she fully turned and stepped into her bedroom, Timothy right behind her.

The door clicked shut.

Pax and I watched, reverence in the air before our gazes moved toward each other.

That same connection billowed and weaved.

Though ours somehow felt familiar.

The soft smiles that fluttered across our lips.

Pax eased forward, his face cast in the bare light that shone from the sconce that hung on the hallway wall.

Striking, gorgeous angles.

He slipped an arm around my waist.

"It's good, Aria. It's fuckin' good." His voice was coarse. Grating with sincerity.

My fingers found the steady beat that pounded at the center of his chest.

"I know," I murmured through the fervency that thudded within mine.

A giggle echoed down the hall, and Pax smirked, though it was adoring, and he pressed a kiss to my temple as he wound an arm around my neck and muttered, "Come on, we should get some rest."

We stepped into the room, and Pax clicked the door shut behind us. He moved to the end of the bed where his duffel sat on top of the mattress. I'd already changed into sleep pants and a loose shirt, my feet bare.

Pax shucked off his boots and jeans and tee, all the way down to his underwear. He watched me the entire time where I hovered near the door, just as surely as I watched him.

He straightened, his body hewn in all that sinewy, defined muscle. The horrors were so clear where they were written on his scarred, disfigured flesh, though his aura skimmed over the top of them, whispering that things might not be so bleak.

He placed both our bags onto the floor, then moved to the side of the bed nearest me.

I flicked off the light switch, and it sent the room into darkness, though the faintest innuendo of light filtered in through the slats of the white wooden shutters from the porch lamp out front.

It was enough to make out his form, the way his back flexed and bowed as he dragged down the covers, then sat on the edge of the bed.

"Want to hold you." It sounded like a claiming, and rippled through the energy that tugged between us.

I didn't hesitate.

I crossed the space separating us and climbed directly onto his lap, wrapping myself around him.

He shifted to lie us down facing each other.

Chest-to-chest and breath-to-breath.

The sheets were cool and crisp, and a shiver rolled through me that Pax erased, his body a furnace that burned into mine.

Still, he pulled the blanket up, covering us as if it were a shield of protection.

"We made it," I whispered into the darkness, my face pressed up under his chin.

His palm smoothed up my spine and to the nape of my neck before his fingers threaded in my hair. "We made it."

"Thank you for doing it with me. For trusting me that this needed to happen."

"I will never doubt you, Aria."

He shifted onto his back, and I curled into his side and rested my head on his shoulder. "I wish we could stay just like this forever."

Soothing fingers stroked through the strands of my hair, his voice a low resonance that swept through my being. "You are my forever. Whatever that looks like."

I barely nodded, and a fog of exhaustion rolled through me in a disorienting haze.

"Sleep, sweet girl. I'll meet you there," he rumbled.

I snuggled deeper, sagging into the refuge I found in his arms. Into the steady thrum, thrum, thrum of his heart that soaked me like a balm.

I hovered there in the nothingness.

On that shimmery plane where I danced between asleep and awake.

In that weightless moment before my spirit would detach.

And I was there, in Tearsith, with Pax at my side. Descending into Faydor to fight the battle that I was terrified would never cease to rage.

Hours were spent hunting in the bowels of depravity. Slaying every wicked thing we passed while searching for any indication of Ambrose.

Until I was ripped from that realm.

Jolted awake by an explosion of shattering glass.

# Chapter Twenty-Eight

## ARIA

A scream tore out of me as shards of glass and fragments of splintered wood blew into the room and rained onto the bed, landing like tiny spikes against my exposed flesh.

The alarm screamed. So loud that I couldn't make sense of where all the sounds were coming from.

Pelting and piercing.

Chaos and confusion reigned, and I tried to orient myself to what was happening. To what had jerked us from Faydor and to an even more terrifying reality.

Pax scrambled to cover me in an effort to hide me within the darkness that shrouded the room.

"Aria!" he shouted over the disorder. "Are you—" His plea was clipped off when he was suddenly yanked away, taking the covers with him.

It left me whipping around on the bare bed, blinking into the mayhem and trying to process the obscured, darkened scene.

A cold chill snaked through the frigid air. It had nothing to do with the cold wind that gusted in through the broken window.

It was the evil that clouded the room.

Like dipping into Faydor.

Drenched in the sickness that curled and wept.

"Aria!" Pax shouted.

I gasped and flew up to sitting, peering through the hazy light.

Fear slicked through my consciousness when I found Pax.

I was barely able to make out his silhouette.

But he was there.

On his knees on the floor, next to the bed. Pale, pale eyes wide in the night, nearly glowing white with fury.

Only, his arms were pinned behind him by a man wearing a ball cap.

"Aria!" Pax roared against the restraint as he thrashed, trying to break free and get back to me.

Horror ripped through me when I saw the man restraining him lift a metal rod, and my heart seized when he brought it down hard against the side of Pax's head.

The crack ricocheted against the walls.

Another scream ripped out of me when Pax slumped face-first to the ground.

"No, no, no, no," I begged into the mayhem, rasps of terror cleaving from my lungs.

I scrambled to move.

To do something.

My mind whirring as I tried to figure out how I could get to him.

How I could help him.

How I could fight off the man, who towered over Pax where he'd fallen to the floor.

All while I prayed and prayed that Pax was okay. That he would get up.

Fight for himself.

"Pax." It clogged in a stagnant cry at the base of my throat when he didn't move.

A riot of pounding feet resounded on the opposite side of the door, crashing down the hall.

Timothy and Dani.

I tried to shout to warn them. To warn that there was a man right there who was turning toward the door to stop them.

But I was snatched by the ankle, caught unaware.

My attention flew to my left.

Panic pierced through me.

There was a second man in the room.

Alarm dumped into my system, hot adrenaline that flooded my veins and stirred me into venom. I tried to kick him off. Flailing and twisting, warring to free my ankle from his brutal hold.

He yanked me toward the end of the bed.

"You little bitch. Whore. Didn't you know we'd be coming for you? He'll be pleased, and his rewards are *generous*." He leaned over to hiss the last word into my ear, his sickness oozing out with the vile sound.

My spirit screamed, revolted by the stench of his malignity rather than compelled to heal it.

All hope was lost for his soul. His being was fully decayed and defiled.

The door blew open, and I found a shout, a scraping of desperation that I heaved from my throat. "Timothy, get back!"

But the man's rod was already coming down. It connected with the top of Timothy's shoulder and dropped him to his knees.

Roaring, he doubled over in pain.

And I could hear Dani sobbing, her cries as she rushed for him. She slid onto her knees at his side.

"Timothy. Oh my God. What's going on? Are you okay?"

Her confusion was thick as her attention swept into the havoc that seized the room.

Dismay widened her eyes when she saw the second man ripping me from the bed, though I tried to stop him, my fingers digging into the mattress, but I couldn't hold on.

He jostled me around and pinned my back to his chest, his massive arm as heavy as a steel band around my waist. The other he wrapped around my throat, that hand clinging to a knife.

Still, I clawed and kicked and struggled to break free.

To fight.

To get to my family.

"Aria," Dani wheezed as the man started to haul me back toward the window.

I flailed, kicking my feet in the air.

But it was no use.

Nothing I could do.

The man was fully overpowering me as he ducked us out through the opening. A jagged piece of shattered glass hanging from the broken frame cut into the back of my arm as he dragged me through.

A scream streaked up my throat.

Torment and a plea.

A meaty hand clamped down over my mouth to mute me just as the second man climbed through the opening behind us.

"You might as well not fight it, because you already know what's coming for you."

"No. No. You can't. You can't listen to him. You don't understand what's going to happen if he wins." But the words were nothing more than garbled pleas issued into his palm. Garbled pleas that continued to pour out of me as he hauled me across the yard toward a pickup truck idling out front.

Three more men were in the bed, each taken over by the salacious. High-pitched calls of their deranged excitement escaped their mouths.

The one who had me tore open the passenger door, the knife pressed up under my jaw when he dragged me onto his lap, then slammed the door shut.

The other man jumped into the driver's side, and the one holding me shouted, "Move!"

The driver gunned it, the tires squealing as he peeled out onto the road. Houses whipped by as he sped through the sleeping neighborhood, the night so thick and dark it didn't feel real.

It was as if the blackened sky had drooped down low, cloaking the earth in a deformed canopy of debasement. Dark, heavy clouds began to move, churning in a toil of wickedness.

A crack of lightning blistered through, and the man who held me captive muttered in my ear, "It's time."

While my spirit moaned, weeping as it called out, *Pax*.

# Chapter Twenty-Nine

## PAX

A tormented groan rolled out of me when I came to, face down on the floor. I struggled to push myself up onto my hands and knees. To get the fuck up. To get to Aria.

A bolt of pain stabbed through my head the second I moved, racking through my insides.

I fought to stay upright, and I gripped my head in both hands to try to stop the spinning.

To ward off the incoherency that pushed in at the edges of my consciousness, threatening to suck me back under.

Though the shout of Aria's soul was so much louder.

Breaking through the murky blur of my mind.

Screaming as it battered against my spirit.

*Pax. Pax. Pax.*

I could feel her calling for me.

Begging for me.

Blood gushed from a wound cracked high up on my skull, and nausea boiled in my guts, my sight nearly blinded. But I couldn't let it sway me. Couldn't let it stop me from my purpose.

*Aria. Aria.*

I could barely make out the fuzzy figure that was suddenly standing over me, something close to hysteria spilling from his mouth. "Oh, fuck, Pax. Fuck. They have her. They took her."

I could hear the shout of an engine tearing up the street, and I staggered onto my feet.

I floundered, and Timothy's hands landed on either side of my upper arms to keep me steady.

"You need to sit down, man," Timothy instructed, like there was a chance I would be able to comply. "You're bleeding like a faucet turned to high."

"You know that's not gonna fuckin' happen," I spat as I pulled away from him and stumbled to where I'd left my clothes in a pile on the floor. I bent down, jamming the heel of my hand into my eye when it felt like a hot blade pierced my brain, though I gathered myself enough to drag on my jeans.

Clarity began to infiltrate the daze with each second that passed. Each of those seconds warning that we didn't have one of them to waste.

It might already be too late.

Desolation yawned through the middle of me, though it was the panic surging through my bloodstream that rocketed me into action.

I snagged my shoes and shirt from the floor, and I glanced to where Dani was a stir of agitation at the door. "Tell me you have a car."

"I do," she rasped.

She didn't pause to wait before she darted down the hall. She was back two seconds later with her purse and keys, wearing a pair of sweats, a tank, slip-on Vans on her feet. "I'm ready."

"Need to grab supplies." I ripped open my duffel. I took the gun I'd left on top, plus the two large hunting knives I'd tucked in beside it, my insides rattling as I stuffed them into my pockets.

"Shit," Timothy grunted.

No doubt the guy's head was spinning since he hadn't lived the type of life that I had.

His life was devoted to children.

To the classroom where he'd instilled his own brand of hope into his students, though there was no question he knew enough from walking in darkness that he'd have a clue what we were up against.

"Hurry," Dani begged.

"Ready," I mumbled as I grabbed my boots, and Dani ducked out of the doorway and headed back down the hall. We ran out behind her, and dipped through the door closest to the living room that led into the garage.

Dani flipped on the light, illuminating the space that housed a newer four-door Civic.

The alarm still blared through the house, and I shouted, "Turn that off before the cops show."

I was unable to keep the harshness out of the command as I rushed to the car.

Though I knew she got it. Felt it. What was riding on this.

She nodded frantically, her pink hair sticking up all over the place, flustered as she punched the code into the pad next to the interior door right before she jammed the button to the garage to open it.

I'd already ripped open the door to the front passenger seat and was sinking down inside when she flew back around, jogged to the driver's side, and jumped in.

Timothy dove into the back behind her.

Our ragged breaths jutted into the cab as she pushed the button to start the vehicle and whipped into reverse. We flew backward out of the garage, tires screeching when she hit the street. She didn't even come to a full stop before she rammed it into drive and floored the accelerator.

Night was all around, the only illumination the few exterior lights that glowed from the porches of the houses that sporadically dotted Dani's street, mere outlines sitting way back below the trees.

Everything was too quiet and still.

Except for us.

We were chaos.

Calamity.

She blazed up through the neighborhood, already asking, "Which way?" before she got to where the street made a T at the main road. But I could feel the despondency behind it.

Her fear that we weren't going to find her.

That Aria was already gone.

Lost.

That urgency roiled inside me. The call that had led me to Aria the first time screaming so loud it was the only thing I could hear. Her fear and desperation in the middle of it, promising me that she was still alive.

I shoved my right foot into my boot as I shouted, "Left."

Dani barely slowed, and the car careened across the road as she made the sharp turn. The tail skidded, whipping far right, then left, before it corrected; then she was ramming on the gas again.

Timothy sat forward, holding on to Dani's headrest with both hands, his head poked between us. "Well, shit, it's a good thing my girl drives like her damn pants have caught flames. My mom's going to love you."

Dani croaked an incredulous sound. Disbelief that he was being light in the middle of this. Injecting hope in the midst of affliction.

"That is, if I don't kill us first," she mumbled as she flew down the road.

"Nah, baby, we're going to get through this. All of us."

I could feel his encouragement. The same encouragement he'd fed me when I was a kid, the man my guide for so long. Support and insight and the kind of love I'd never received from my real family.

Except this—this was my family. The center of it out in front of us, ensnared.

Held.

But I could feel her—could feel her rushing through my bloodstream on a plea.

"Yeah, we are," I promised quietly as I crammed my other foot into my boot, tying them tight before I shouted, "Right," when I was suddenly overcome by that sensation.

Swelling and rising.

We were getting close.

Dani gripped the steering wheel with both hands, jerking it hard as she took the turn far faster than was prudent. The tires screamed as we whipped around the corner. But she nailed it, the engine revving high as she blew down the road.

Not a soul was around. Businesses locked up tight, the neighborhoods quiet and dimmed.

Something about it felt different. Like we'd traveled beyond the limits of the city. Or maybe beyond the limits of this world.

The heavens too close.

The clouds, this tumultuous disturbance above. A bolt of lightning cracked through the sinister canopy that rolled in undulating waves above.

"What the fuck?" Timothy drew out on a whisper.

The energy shifted in the car as each of us became aware of the otherworldly.

"He's here," I said, gritting it out through the clench of my teeth.

A full-body tremble skated through Dani as she raced beneath it, the buildings becoming scarce, interspersed with open, rolling fields.

I thought she must have felt it, too—this connection with Aria—because she abruptly slammed on the brakes and jerked the wheel to the left when we came to a large open field.

The car pitched hard, and we hit the dirt at high speed. The front slammed against an embankment that sent us flying over the top. We caught the slightest bit of air before we bashed back onto the ground, the car jostling and lurching. The tires spun for a second; then we caught traction again and flew across the rough terrain.

The headlights were extra bright as the front of the car ate up the high grass we could barely see over, the sound of it grating beneath as it scraped on the underside.

When we crested a ridge, Dani smashed on the brakes as the scene came into view in the distance.

A pickup truck was parked out in the field, the headlights left on and illuminating a tree on a hill about a hundred yards away from it. A tree two men were dragging Aria toward, where three more men waited, each of them unable to sit still as they itched with bloodlust.

Ice sank down into the depths of me, freezing me in a vat of anguish.

"Oh God, what do we do?" Dani whimpered as she clutched the steering wheel and peered out the windshield.

"You two should stay in the car." It tortured me to suggest it, but this shit was clearly not stacking in our favor. Something about what was going down was so much bigger than anything I'd faced before.

The men who'd been sent to stop Aria previously had been fully human.

Sure, twisted, deranged, fucked-in-the-heart humans who had no other concern but her utter destruction—but still, human.

Mortal.

But there was something about this that felt off. Like maybe we were being lured straight into a trap, one I couldn't ask Dani and Timothy to step into.

Dani scoffed. "Don't even try to pull that bullshit with me, Pax. You act like I haven't fought in Faydor for longer than you. And yes, I know it's different. I know here I'm fully human and have all the vulnerabilities that come with that, but this is Aria we're talking about."

She flung her hand in Aria's direction.

"She's our family, Pax," Timothy rumbled from behind. "I know you want to protect us, but we're not sitting on the sidelines—just like you didn't when you believed Dani was in danger."

Lightning streaked above. A frisson of energy crackled through the atmosphere, a slow slide of iniquity that lifted every hair on my body.

"Don't know what we're up against," I warned.

"It doesn't matter. We're in this together," he said. "Now, you're going to give me one of those knives, and you're going to give the other to Dani; then we're going to go get our girl back. We'll creep in on either side of them, and you go up the middle."

"You're sure?"

They both gave me a resolute nod.

Dread thickened my throat, but I warily passed each of them one of the massive knives. Dani looked like she was going to puke when she clasped her hand around the hilt, her fear patent though her courage was vivid.

I clicked the latch to the door and slowly pushed it open before I cautiously stepped out into the howl of the whipping wind.

Wind that was crystallized. Frozen particles that stirred through the torrid atmosphere.

The clouds reeked with the stench of death.

But it was what was moving through them that nearly made me trip. The swirls of red and flashes of black.

Holy fuck.

It wasn't Ambrose.

These were Kruen.

# Chapter Thirty

## ARIA

Intonations whisked through the rumblings of thunder that cracked overhead.

*"End her. End her. Think of how she will scream. How her blood will feel drenching your fingers. She's the one in the way. He must have her heart, and you will have your reward. You will reign with us. Powerful beyond measure."*

Only the voices weren't in the heads of the deviants who'd kidnapped me. They were there. Above, in the clouds.

Flagrant and audible.

It was as if they were being played on a distorted record, the influence of the wicked so much more powerful as the Kruen dripped their poison into the ears and hearts of the men who danced around in deformed glee.

Oh God.

How was it possible?

The Kruen were here. In this realm. Unless I'd been intercepted again, taken to an unknown plane I'd never known existed.

But this felt so real.

Too real.

As if a fracture had opened up between Faydor and Earth.

It was all driven by Ambrose, who I could almost feel hovering in the distance.

The way it felt as if the blood in my veins had crystallized and frozen.

I could smell him.

The nasty smell that he emitted.

Fear clashed with the light that glowed hot inside me, an urge to do something. To release the power that burned deep inside.

So intense I could barely bottle it.

Could barely restrain it.

But I needed to be able to direct it. Control it in some way that assured I might be able to get away.

I still wasn't entirely sure how to use it. If I even *could* use it on humans like this.

A defense.

A weapon.

My mind spun through the scenarios. Worried if I loosed the energy too early—if they weren't close enough—I wouldn't be able to strike them all. Worried I wouldn't be able to incapacitate them all.

More than that, I was afraid I wouldn't be able to harness it again once I expelled it. That it'd be used up, and I'd be drained and completely weakened.

Then I'd be completely powerless.

I wasn't sure I could risk leaving myself that way. Not when I didn't understand the strength any of us possessed. How the impossibility writhing in a sky that sagged too low above me was going to affect the men. Not when I didn't know what would happen if I used the rage inside me that begged to be delivered.

I railed against the two monsters who held me by either arm as they hauled me up toward the other three, who frolicked like fiends below a colossal tree, waving their knives in the air as they chanted, "She's the one, she's the one."

I could smell the stench of alcohol that oozed from their pores, though it was bloated by something foul. Something sickeningly cloying that saturated the atmosphere in a thick mist that rained from the toxic heavens.

My spirit screamed as it called for my Nol.

*Pax, Pax, Pax.*

I could almost feel him racing along the fringes of my consciousness, his fingertips ghosting over my soul as I silently begged for him to be okay.

He had to be.

He had to be.

I couldn't believe I would feel him so strongly if that blow had killed him. And that connection had only grown stronger with each mile that should have taken me farther away from him.

Once we reached the clearing below the wide arch of the tree, the men restraining me threw me forward. It sent me stumbling through the mushy earth and grass toward the other three men.

The ground was cold beneath my bare feet. So cold it sent a chill curling up my legs. Frozen chains that clawed and sank in my flesh.

I whirled in every direction, and the long locks of my hair whipped around my face as I frantically searched for a place to run. Terrified of trying to fight them all off while something untapped inside me screamed.

Shouted that I must not succumb to the fear. To the horrors of a simple girl who wanted to drop to her knees and wail. To beg to finally wake up from this nightmare.

But there was no waking from *this*.

My purpose.

My calling.

My fate.

All five of them encroached, creating a large circle that caged me in, a writhing ring of barbarity. "She's the one. She's the one that he wants. He will be pleased when she bleeds."

*"She's the one,"* the voices sang overhead. One man stepped forward and slashed his knife. The tip just barely nicked my arm, which was

already bleeding from the broken glass, the loose tee I wore torn and tattered on that side.

On a jolted gasp, I spun away from him, the oxygen heaving from my lungs as vapor as I dove in the other direction. Only the man who'd struck Pax with the crowbar whipped it through the air. It whooshed in front of me, just missing my face.

I whirled again, around and around as I attempted to keep them at bay while the energy churned inside me. Stronger and stronger, it grew. Almost sickening in its strength.

The compulsion.

The need.

I put my hands out in front of me as if I were surrendering, while I focused on the light that brewed in the deepest recess of my being.

Focused on amplifying it.

A charge that I hoped would be enough to bring them all to their knees. Then I'd run for the truck that was still idling about a football field's length away.

I could do this.

I had to.

"You little bitch," the one who'd dragged me out of bed snarled, his lips twisted in a sneer. "I know what you're thinking. Go ahead and run; I'll enjoy the hunt. Will enjoy tracking you through these woods. I won't mind the taste of your fear on my tongue. You won't get far. You can't because your time has come. He told me you were mine."

"It's time, it's time," the other four chanted.

Terror clotted my insides, my blood turning to sludge, barely pumping through my veins. But I refused to yield. To submit.

And I swore I could hear it. A different voice that wisped through me on the trickling of fresh, clear waters.

*"Rise up, dear Valient. You are the chosen. You must lead."*

Valeen.

I wanted to shout for her. Beg her to finally show me what she'd promised I possessed. To reveal it.

Only there was something inside me that told me I was the one responsible for finding it.

Straightening my spine, I slowly turned in a circle, gauging each of the men, who came closer and closer with each pass. My hands were pushed up in front of me as if they might hold the power to create a barricade between us.

The glow inside me burned and burned. Gathering in potency and volatility. I allowed it to become larger than it ever had before. Coerced into what I prayed would suffice as a weapon.

And I was shaking. Shaking and shaking beneath the pressure of it.

When I couldn't contain it any longer, I let it streak down my arms and from my fingertips on a crack of energy. A shock wave that radiated outward. I wasn't touching any of them, but it threw each of them back at least ten feet. Shouts hurled from their mouths as they were tossed onto their backs, each vile beast hitting the ground with a loud thud.

But it wasn't enough. It wasn't enough to keep them down.

One by one, they climbed back to standing, disoriented and confused as they choked over the rush of debris and dirt that gusted across the land, though the bloodlust left them undeterred.

My body sagged with the wave of exhaustion that slammed into me. Heavy and crippling. I could barely lift my arms. Could barely stand.

I staggered to the side.

It was then that a call ripped through the middle of the confusion, a low growl of a voice cutting through and impaling me in a slash of deliverance. "Aria! Run!"

Pax.

He was there.

Relief thundered through me, pummeling and battering in the midst of the fatigue. I swallowed, searching inside myself for resolve.

For strength.

I started to stagger in his direction where he was coming up the hill through the high grass, but one of the men rebounded and stepped in front of me to block my path.

He slashed his knife from left to right, driving me backward toward the rest, who were right behind me.

A clash suddenly broke out.

A rush of footsteps and a clattering of spirits.

Chaos as Timothy and Dani emerged from the shadows just as Pax raced toward the man who had edged me backward. He slammed the butt of his gun across the back of his head. The man roared, but he didn't fall—he only spun and flung his knife toward Pax.

Pax used his gun as a shield, battling him back.

Grunts and shoves and punches thudded and echoed, and I slowly turned, my muscles mush and my mind hindered.

Timothy fought with two of the men, each warring for dominance.

But it was Dani, standing off to the side of the clearing, who sent an alarm hurling through me.

She was trying to draw one of the men toward her.

The blade of the knife she held glinted beneath the strikes of lightning, and I could see it trembling in her hand. Could see what she was willing to sacrifice. Could see the depravity in the glimmer of the man's aura as he turned toward her, his voice twisted and not his own as he wheezed, "You're one of them. It's time to meet your end."

From above, the voices chanted their agreement.

*"End her. End her. End them all."*

Frantic, I gathered what strength I had left and forced myself to run. To do something. To stop this.

I hurtled across the space, my bare feet sinking into the damp dirt. Spindly roots that jutted up from the ground and the weight of my limbs fought to hold me back, but I pushed through as I searched for the light inside. For the energy to amass once again.

But I couldn't conjure it. Couldn't invoke it.

The only thing I could do was slam into the man from the side, throwing my full weight at him as I rammed my shoulder into his ribs.

Distracted by his debased thirst, he was unprepared for the impact, and it knocked him to the side. He skidded on his boots, and one heavy sole caught on an exposed root and toppled him to the ground.

"You're dead, bitches. Both of you," he grunted as he started to climb back to standing, then immediately dropped back down. But how long he would remain there, I didn't know.

I grabbed Dani's hand, begging, "You have to get out of here."

"I'm not going anywhere without you. Without all of you. We're in this together," she argued. A lash of worry cut into her brow when she took me in, her entire face pinching in concern. "Are you hurt? Did they hurt you?"

I blinked through the sluggishness.

"Drained," I wheezed, panting into the disordered air.

"Oh God," she mumbled. She curled her arm around my waist to support me. "Okay, okay, we've got this," she promised.

I leaned against her, inhaling deep, massive breaths into my deflated lungs.

A spark of energy lit—the barest flame, but it was there.

"Aria, get to the car! Both of you get to the fucking car!" Pax shouted as he fought with one man. Another was on the ground, groaning beside him.

Timothy still warred with the other two, though I could feel him faltering.

Failing.

His own exhaustion from the type of battle he was not accustomed to slowing him down.

I thought Dani could feel it before I could. The peril that Timothy was in. Because she suddenly drew in a haggard breath, whispering, "No," before she released me and bolted forward, screaming as she ran.

She didn't slow or hesitate when she drove her blade deep into the thigh of one of the men who was overtaking her Nol.

Wailing, the man dropped his knife and gripped the wound with both hands. His voice dipped between his own and the rasped frenzy that the Kruen incited above. "You fuckin' cunt. Whore. Bitch. I'm going to make you bleed. Slice you up. He'll be pleased."

Forgetting his injury, he snatched his knife from the ground, jaw clenched as he went for Dani. I found enough strength to catapult myself in their direction, and my hand clamped down on her shoulder to push her out of the way as I drove my palm forward and into his chest the second before he got to her.

I released the bare sparks of light at the same time.

He flew back at the impact, catching five feet of air before he slammed to the ground, his body cutting into the earth as he skidded another three feet.

Dani gasped in surprise and relief, eyes wide with disbelief. "Holy shit, Aria. Did you seriously fry that bastard with your bare hand?"

I swayed, and when Dani realized I was about to fall, she rushed forward and curled around my waist. "I've got you."

Timothy kicked at the single man he was fighting. His foot connected with his stomach, and it sent him sailing back into the tree.

His skull knocked against its trunk. Hard enough that he slid down to the ground, giving Timothy a reprieve.

The second he realized both men were down, he came running for us, shouting, "We have to get out of here. This is something different than I can explain. These assholes have more than human strength."

As if to prove a point, the man I'd just sent flailing through the air climbed back onto his feet, and the other one Timothy had been fighting pushed to his, the two coming together as they turned back toward us.

Their faces were twisted in the ruthlessness that oozed in their veins.

"We have to go." Pax was suddenly there, gripping me by the hand. A shock of his energy rolled through me.

Bolstering.

Sustaining and fortifying.

"Can you run?" he wheezed.

"I think so."

He whirled us around with the clear intention of racing us back toward where they'd come from.

But we froze when we saw that the men he'd toppled had risen, as well as the third one, who'd been so close to getting to Dani.

Their features distorted, and their skin seemed to crawl and writhe over their bones.

The air around them trembled. Whirring and whirring.

More Kruen.

They spun around their bodies in a violent, cataclysmic storm.

The men closed in on us from behind, moving around to create a circle.

Trapping us.

Fear raced.

Disbelief and dismay.

A palpable wave that rolled through us all.

Pax still clung to me, and Dani held on to my other hand. Timothy was behind us, his back pressed to mine while we all watched the men come closer.

The four of us remained connected.

Our spirits clinging to each other.

It was a flicker at first. So slight that I wasn't sure for one second before it was there—the light.

It resurfaced within me and quickly began to glow. It seemed to gather strength as fast as the Kruen spun around the men.

The circle of men edged closer as the darkened clouds opened above us.

Lightning crackled, and I swore I caught a glimpse of Faydor.

More Kruen were taking shape, their monstrous forms dripping down from the blackened heavens as if they could reach out and control what happened below.

I was punched by incredulity.

By shock.

It was almost the exact same picture as the one I'd seen that day in the library when Pax and I had first discovered the paintings by

Abigail Watkins. One that she had painted of Kruen reaching down and devouring the innocent below.

One that I'd thought had been part of her imagination. A metaphor for the evils they cast into the world.

Had she seen it? Had she known what was to come? Did she sense the wickedness that had been borne in her husband?

Did she possess this energy that seemed to howl beneath it?

Expanding and deepening, becoming something beyond anything I'd ever felt before?

It trembled through me, shivers racking through my body as I tried to hold it in.

My hands burned with the need to do something.

This need intrinsic.

It seemed to feed off the contact.

Off Dani and Timothy.

But even more so, off Pax.

Spurred by the calamity that raged overhead.

And still, something told me to hold it.

Harness it.

Pax flinched as he gauged the men who inched closer. Every muscle in his body flexed with hinged restraint. Violence skated along the surface of his skin, sparks of volatility, and the gun he held in his left hand trembled.

"There's no good left in them," he muttered as if he were giving us a warning.

As if it needed to be said aloud.

A judgment.

A verdict.

A penalty.

"I have to do this."

He started to lift his hand to fire when the force inside me became unbearable. When I could no longer keep it contained.

Before Pax could shoot, I ripped my hand from Pax's and Dani's.

And I let it go.

It was an earthquake.

A burst of lightning.

Blinding as it surged out in every direction.

It struck the men in a flash of light.

They flew.

Blasted backward a hundred feet.

They seemed to be airborne forever.

Immune to gravity.

Before they finally came careening back to the ground like darts shooting from the sky.

Dust gusted and whipped, and it was seconds later before it cleared and we could see where they'd landed.

Their bodies were bent at odd angles. Contorted and mangled.

A sob wrenched out of me when I realized what had happened.

Their deaths marked.

I choked on the sickness that curdled in my stomach, and the overwhelming weakness that rushed through me sent me staggering two steps forward.

Disoriented and grieved at the truth of what had to be done.

"Oh my God, oh my God." I could hear Dani whimpering, and Timothy whispered something to her that I couldn't make out.

Because the world spun and spun.

The darkened clouds continued to writhe, and a torrent of ice-spiked rain suddenly pelted us from the gaping hole ripped in the heavens.

The Kruen above howled their rage.

One rose high, its gruesome face warped in hate as it peered down at me from the toiling clouds.

And there was no time to devise and plan.

No time to deflect or anticipate.

None of us were prepared for the fiery tendril that streaked from the sky.

One that struck me in the side, as deep as a blade.

# Chapter Thirty-One

## PAX

The tendril whipped out of nowhere, striking down from above, aimed directly at Aria, who was a few feet out in front of me.

"Aria!" I shouted, my chest in a clutch of anxiety.

But the warning came too late. There was no way for her to get out of the way before the belt of fire struck the lower left side of her abdomen.

Horror squeezed my heart as I watched her grip the spot where she'd been hit.

Her hands pressed to it as blood gushed from between her fingers, her eyes wide with shock and pain as she stared at me like she couldn't make sense of what was happening.

We were both held in it.

In this devastating awareness that passed between us as evil hovered overhead.

One second later, she floundered one step to her left. A blip away from losing consciousness.

It snapped me out of the trance.

I ran for her, but I didn't make it before she toppled over, landing hard on her side, then flopping onto her front.

Unmoving.

Panic assailed my spirit as I dropped to my knees beside her.

"Aria! Aria!" Frantic, I rolled her over.

Nothing.

No movement.

I patted her cheek to try to get her to open her eyes.

"Aria. Please. Baby, please," I begged as my fingers went to her neck. Couldn't get them to stop trembling as I searched for a pulse.

It was present, but thready and bare.

Terror slicked down my spine, and I ripped up her shirt to reveal where she'd been struck, and a gush of distraught air blew from my lungs.

"No." It raked out of me on a low cry. "No, baby, no."

The wound was gaping, but different from when we were burned in Faydor. It was deep. Flayed open. Blood pouring out.

I pressed my hands against it to try to stop the flow.

"Oh my God," Dani rasped from where she'd run up behind us.

I blinked through the agony. Through the torment. "We have to get her to the hospital."

It was a terrible fucking option. She'd be ripped away from me. Incarcerated or committed after what had happened at the mental facility. She'd be vulnerable, and Ambrose or whoever he sent would get to her.

Every fucking ignorant hope I'd let bloom inside me lost, but I couldn't give in to all the turmoil that wanted to hold me back from taking her there.

Because the alternative wasn't acceptable. She had to live. It was the only thing that mattered in this moment.

Saving her.

I'd deal with figuring out the rest later.

I tore off my shirt and balled it against her stomach, pressing hard as I scooped her up in my other arm and stood.

She felt too heavy and too light.

Those sweet, delicate arms didn't wrap around my neck the way they normally did.

They were limp. The same as her head, which bounced listlessly as I ran.

Ran through the fields toward Dani's car.

Dani and Timothy were right there, racing beside me, their gazes slanting to me with every pounding footstep.

Dread poured from their beings.

Heavy and harsh.

We ran through it, Timothy pushing himself faster so he could get the door on the rear passenger side open to have it ready when I got there. I ducked through it with Aria on my lap.

Timothy slammed the door shut and hopped in the front passenger side. Dani was already inside and had the car started and in gear. The tires spun in the dirt as she gunned it, and she made a U-turn in the middle of the field, the car jostling back across the uneven terrain as she headed for the road.

While I held Aria in my arms. Begging and begging her. "Stay with me. Please, you got to hold on. You can't leave. This world needs you. I need you."

I hugged her to me, rocking her, my mouth at the top of her head as I kept breathing the unintelligible words into her.

Begging her to stay.

Pleading with her to be okay.

Her wound was pressed tight against my abdomen. I could feel the sticky warmth of her blood saturating my stomach and crawling down into the waistband of my jeans. Could feel it spreading with every second that passed.

Dani flew, even faster than she had the first time. Though there was silence in the car as we blew down the two-lane road. A baited disquiet that clawed through the dense, suffocating air.

"What the hell is that?" Timothy asked as he sat forward, peering through the windshield.

A woman was in the distance, pulled off to the side of the road. She came up fast since we were traveling at such a high speed.

She stood at the back of a big white work van.

Flares in both hands as she waved them overhead.

At the sight of her, something unsettled rolled over me.

"The fuck is she doing? That would be a solid no, even if we did have time for that," Timothy muttered.

That unsettled something convulsed.

Pushing and prodding.

Dani moved into the middle of the two lanes and blazed right past her.

It took me two more seconds to realize where I'd seen her.

Short, curly brown hair and desperation on her face.

It was the nurse who'd helped us escape the facility.

Jill.

Maybe I was being a fool, but I suddenly shouted, "Stop!"

"What?" Doubt tore through the single word as Dani glanced at me in the rearview mirror like she was wondering if I'd lost it.

"Pull over. That woman. She helped me get Aria out of the institution back in New York."

Had no fucking clue how she was here. But it had to mean something.

Worry passed over Dani's features, but she hit the brakes, skidding to a stop in the middle of the road. She threw it in reverse and flew backward to come to a stop in front of the van where it sat on the shoulder.

Timothy hopped out and jerked open the rear passenger-side door. I angled out, shifting Aria around so I could keep her secure in my arms. My heart beat a thousand miles a minute, anxiety and alarm pooling thick in my consciousness.

Jill came around the back of the van as I was running for her, blinking in disbelief when she saw me carrying Aria, who was quickly bleeding out.

I didn't want to recognize it, but I could feel it—her spirit fading.

"How are you here?" Grief twisted my mouth to the side as I demanded it, unable to fathom what the hell was happening.

Her head shook, clearly not able to fathom it, either. "I . . . I don't know. I haven't slept since you broke her out, and the few times I did, I kept dreaming . . . dreaming that I was supposed to be here. In this place. That I was supposed to be doing *something*."

She moved toward the back of the van. I was right behind her as she flung open the double doors. Surprise rocked out of me when I saw it was set up as some kind of makeshift ambulance. A stretcher in the middle and a bunch of medical supplies sitting along the side.

"Get her inside. Hurry," she urged, looking behind us toward the road that remained barren, the howling from the skies having ceased.

Didn't find a whole lot of comfort in it. Figured the Kruen were satisfied that they'd gotten what they'd set out to do.

I lifted my leg high so I could get my foot on the end of the bed. I grunted as I hoisted us up into the back, cradling Aria as I bent over so I could stand beneath the van's low roof, terrified one wrong move would make things worse.

Jill climbed in behind us, her demeanor purposed and sure even though I could feel the chaos radiating around her. I laid Aria on the stretcher, which was lifted from the floor a fraction.

Dani scrambled in behind her, and Timothy remained outside at the gaping doors.

I gripped Aria's hand, looking at her face, which was a different kind of pale than normal.

Gray and ashen.

Her lips turning blue.

"Keep pressure on her wound. Push as hard as you can," Jill instructed, already in action, placing the earpieces of a stethoscope into her ears and pressing the chest piece over Aria's heart.

I let go of Aria's hand and pressed both of mine over my tee, which was completely soaked in blood.

She listened for less than fifteen seconds. She tried to cover it, but there was no hiding the bleakness that filled her expression.

I moved so I was angled up close to Aria's head, words tumbling from my mouth as I begged near her ear, "Hold on, baby. Stay with me. Stay right here. Listen to my voice. Help is here. Jill. You remember her? She helped us before when you were at the facility? Remember how grateful you were? How you felt seen by her? She's right here. She came for you. You're going to be okay."

"What can I do?" Dani begged.

"Go to the end over there." Jill gestured with her head toward the interior part of the van. "There's a cooler. Get me a bag of blood stored in there." She kept her voice even as she reached into a box and pulled out what looked to be supplies for an IV.

Dani squeezed around behind me, the space cramped and tight, our breaths heaving and raking in the confined area. Her hand slid over my shoulders as she passed. No question, she was trying to offer me comfort. To give me some hope in the middle of the torment.

"You." Jill glanced at Timothy, who hovered at the door. "Get inside the driver's seat in case we need to move her. Shut the doors so no one can see if they go by."

"On it." Timothy slammed the doors shut and, a second later, was sliding into the front seat while Jill pulled a plastic cover from off a long, thick needle. She leaned down, biting the inside of her cheek as she felt for a vein in Aria's wrist. When she found one she could use, she pushed the needle through, then taped it into place.

"Here," Dani said in a rush, passing her the bag of blood.

Jill pulled the cap off, attached the wire, then hooked it on a peg that jutted out up high on the van's wall.

Red glided down the tube and into Aria's arm, and Jill quickly added another bag, one that was filled with a clear solution; then she fumbled around to find something in another box. She produced another needle, which she injected into some nub down near the IV by Aria's wrist as she mumbled, "Painkiller," under her breath, keeping me apprised of what she was doing.

Then she ordered, "Switch places with me."

I kept pressure on Aria's abdomen, leaning down low as I swung over the stretcher at her legs to get to the other side.

Jill scooted around her front, coming to rest on her knees on Aria's injured side.

She nudged my hands away and peeled back the sopping fabric.

"Oh God," she wheezed beneath her breath, blinking one long blink before she swallowed hard and leaned forward so she could inspect it.

It was still gaping. Flayed open wide. But it looked like maybe it'd begun to clot. Like maybe the singe of the tendril had cauterized it in some way. I almost laughed at the thought that any of this bullshit could be counted as a benefit.

"It's deep," Jill muttered as she pulled it apart and prodded inside with a gloved finger. It was like she could hear the shouts of questions that whirred through my mind, like she thought I deserved to know the answer.

The outcome.

"It hit the small bowel."

"Can you repair it?" I begged, back to hanging on to Aria's limp hand. My other arm was curled up around her head so that I could hold her the best that I could.

"I don't know," she admitted. Dread pooled in her being, her breaths shallow and dragging with her concession. "I'm not a surgeon. She needs to be in an emergency OR."

"But there's a reason you're here," I grated through the clench of my jaw. "A reason you were led here. You wouldn't have set all this up if you didn't understand it. You know what's going to happen to her if she shows up there like this. You can do this. You *have* to do this."

Grooves cut deep into her forehead, and she nodded like she was trying to reassure herself; then she started tossing out instructions to Dani and me, asking for different supplies, half of them things neither of us had heard of.

"You, find her pulse in her neck. Watch the clock on the wall across from you, and every thirty seconds, I want you to tell me how many beats, okay?"

Dani bobbed her head, and she came forward, her fingers searching for Aria's pulse. Her pale gaze met mine when she found it, though there was a foreboding in it.

A dread seeded so deep we were drowning in it.

Sweat drenching her brow, Jill moved quickly.

Fear rolled and banged against the metal walls of the van.

A pressing and pulsing slammed into me with every errant beat.

So thick in the enclosed space that it was difficult for any of us to move in it.

Timothy remained completely quiet in the front, though I could feel the weight of his gaze as he kept peering through the rearview mirror at the commotion happening in the back.

Nausea convulsed in my gut as I watched Jill using a curved needle she held in some kind of metal tongs to sew up Aria's insides, the fingers of both hands deep in the wound.

Not because I was squeamish at the sight of blood, but because my entire fucking existence couldn't stomach the thought of Aria not being in it.

*Stay with me. Stay with me. We need you. This world needs you. You can't give up. Your purpose is too great for that. Do you feel it, Aria? It calling for you?* I silently pleaded as I kept hold of her.

The numbers Dani muttered every thirty seconds became a mark that promised Aria was still alive.

Though I knew she was. I could feel her, even though she was distant and drifting with each passing second.

Jill kept working, carefully yet efficiently placing stitch after stitch. Tying up all the meaty tissue that was exposed, then pulling the skin together to make a jagged, mangled seam.

She gasped when she placed the last suture, air rushing from her lungs as she sank back for one blink of relief before she was grabbing the stethoscope and placing it over Aria's heart at the same second that she started throwing out instructions again, looking at Dani first. "I need bandages from the box near the rear of the bed over there, and a blanket."

Then she turned to me. "Get another bag of blood from the cooler. Pull the tab out of the old one and attach the new. Do you think you can do that?"

"Yeah." I scooted on my knees on the metal floor to where the cooler was in the corner. I reached in and grabbed one and did as she instructed, fumbling with the tube as I tried to change it as fast as I could. The whole time, she continued to listen to Aria's heart, inhaling sharp breaths that she tried to keep controlled.

Fear rebounded when I turned around and saw the gloom that colored her face.

Crushing.

Excruciating.

The way whatever was in her eyes sucked the hope out of me.

I moved right back for Aria, taking her hand again and placing my other palm close to the spot where Jill still had the chest piece.

She stilled, frozen, before she whispered, "Don't move your hand."

Confused, I asked, "What?"

"Don't move your hand. I think she feels you. When you touched her, her pulse grew a fraction stronger. It's not possible, but . . ."

My fingers splayed wider, like I might be able to grip Aria's spirit and keep it on this plane.

In this reality.

"None of it is possible, though, is it? This? Us? You coming here and knowing what we were going to need? Being here in the exact spot and at the exact moment that we needed it?"

"No," she murmured as she sat back. Her warm brown eyes searched my face from where she remained kneeling. "No. None of this is possible. But it was too powerful to ignore. It was like I was being called to something. Something that was irresistible, even though I knew it was completely insane and reckless."

"That's exactly what it is . . . It's irresistible," I agreed.

Dani remained quiet, her gaze jumping between the two of us as she passed a box of large bandages to Jill. "Here."

"Thank you," she said.

It must have been the first time Jill really looked at Dani. At her eyes, which were the same color as mine and Aria's.

So pale they were nearly white.

Otherworldly.

Jill held her gaze for one beat as another layer of acceptance rolled through her before she dug into the box and placed a large bandage that covered half of Aria's abdomen; then she had Dani help her cover her with the blanket.

"What do we do now?" I asked, my words shards as I uttered them into the sudden silence that took over the van.

Everything was too fucking still after the frenzy.

Disquieting and unnerving.

Jill slumped back against the opposite wall. "We wait."

I knew exactly what she was implying.

Wait to see if she would heal.

Wait to see if she would survive.

"We should probably get her someplace where it's warm," she added.

"Do you think it's safe to go back to my house?" Worry saturated Dani's question.

"No place is safe, Dani." It had been proven time and again, and that threat was only growing. Getting worse with each twisted fuck Ambrose sent our way.

I didn't know how we were going to survive more of them. If we were even surviving at all. Because without Aria . . .

My throat nearly closed off.

"We should take her back there then," Dani said.

*And hope that no one else comes for her tonight.*

I could almost hear her saying it even though she left it off.

"Do you want to leave your car here or drive it back?" I asked.

"I'll drive it back. I'll follow you guys."

"Okay."

She pulled the latch to the double doors. A cold blast of air gushed in, cut off just as quickly when she jumped out, then secured the doors.

I met Timothy's eyes through the rearview mirror. His expression was both sharp and soft. Overwhelmed and staunch. A silent promise that we were all in this together.

A second later, he put the van into gear and slowly pulled back onto the road. I remained at Aria's side, touching her in every place I could, hand still splayed wide over the quiet but steady thud of her heart. Still on my knees, I leaned forward and rested my cheek on her shoulder while Jill's stare burned into the side of my face.

"What's happening?" she finally asked, her voice held on a tremulous whisper.

My chest knotted with trepidation over what had transpired tonight.

I was utterly unable to wrap my head around the fact that Kruen had been here. Part of me wanted to ascribe it to some sort of hallucination. That all of it had been a fabrication of our minds.

Some kind of fucking sorcery Ambrose had cast, which I was sure was the case, but I was also pretty sure it had become a thread in this reality. That he'd brought them here. How, I didn't fucking know.

I breathed out a sigh riddled with a boatload of uncertainty. "Think this already fucked-up world is about to completely go to shit. It seems our two worlds are merging."

"Two worlds." It wasn't a question. It was a deliberation. A pondering of transience and death and things everlasting.

Her brow pinched as she turned her soft gaze to Aria. "What are you?"

"Did you read her chart?" I asked.

She gave me a clipped nod. "I did."

She said it like she hadn't given herself permission to believe what was written in it.

"Then you know."

She blinked through the disbelief she was grappling with before she whispered, in a tone that sounded like acceptance, "Laven. I saw that word written in her chart, along with . . ."

She slightly shook her head through the riot of doubt and wonder. "That when you sleep, Aria believed that you fought a war to keep us safe. A war that none of us know is happening."

It was why Aria had been institutionalized. Because she hadn't been able to keep that truth from flooding out.

"It's true. Everything she said, it's true." I swallowed hard. "And I'm afraid that war has come here."

# Chapter Thirty-Two

## PAX

Aria was wrapped in the blanket from the van as I carried her into Dani's house. She was still limp. Still unconscious. But her chest lifted and fell with each breath. Breaths I inhaled like they sustained my own life as I held her close.

Even though it was dampened, I could sense Aria's aura all around me.

Coconut and the most extreme sort of goodness.

Pure and right.

This woman who was so powerful. So strong. Clinging to life. A life I tried to cling to with the surety of my arms.

Timothy had already scoped out the inside of Dani's house, ensuring it was clear. That, for the moment, it was safe and we could rest.

"Take her into my bedroom," Dani instructed. "Timothy and I are going to sleep on the couch."

I didn't argue. I just carried Aria down the short hall to the door at the end. The faint light from the bathroom illuminated the space as I laid her down in the middle of the bed. I touched her forehead, her cheek, her chest, while Dani clung to her hand.

"She's going to be okay," she murmured, the promise made to me. To us.

Silence washed over us for a beat before Dani looked up at me from across the bed. "This is insane, Pax. I can't—"

She clipped off like she couldn't give it voice, her brow twisting with the magnitude of what had happened tonight. Everything we thought we'd known had been smashed to shit. The feeble ground we'd stood on fractured, a cavern opening up in the middle of the fragile truth we had been hanging on to.

"She's strong enough," I rumbled like my own plea. She had to be. There had to be a way to end this. To stop the atrocity of what was happening and keep her safe.

Dani opened her mouth but clamped off whatever she was going to say when Jill appeared in the doorway. She hovered at the threshold, unsure of what to do, a medical bag hanging from one hand.

"Come in," I grunted as I gathered Aria's hand and pressed it against the pulse of my heart, begging hers to follow it.

"I'll let you two have some privacy," Dani said, excusing herself and quietly creeping across the room and back down the hall while Jill came to stand in the same spot where Dani had been.

She set the bag onto the floor beside her before she straightened. The two of us drifted in a long silence before Jill murmured, "She's amazing."

She reached out and stroked her fingers down the side of Aria's face.

"I knew in that facility that there was something about her. Something that didn't fit into the mold they were trying to force her into. Something that was radiant, though it was dulled by the lies she had to tell to protect herself."

"She was so grateful to you. She knew what you were sacrificing to set her free."

Tears blurred Jill's brown eyes as she looked down at Aria, who was motionless in the middle of the bed. "I think I knew it the first time I saw her. I had this sense that wouldn't let me go. A sense that things weren't what they seemed. That we were missing something important.

I could feel it . . . a depth to her that didn't exist in anyone else. Then I saw you . . ."

She lifted her gaze to mine. "I saw you, and I knew."

Air huffed from her mouth on a soggy chuckle, and she sniffled. "Of course, I didn't want to believe it. I mean, God, it's terrifying. Terrifying to think of those scars littered all over her body and how she sustained them. Terrifying to think of what you've seen and what you all endure. Terrifying to think that any of this is real."

"I wish it wasn't," I admitted.

She shifted a fraction as she processed what she'd witnessed both while Aria had been in the facility and tonight. The magnet that had refused to let her go in the time between.

"When it was clear that janitor had been after her, I knew what I had to do." Her head bounced slightly.

A reaffirmation.

A bolstering that the choice she had made had been the right one.

"And after that?" She rolled her bottom lip between her teeth. "It was like that single act had tied me to her in some way. As if a tether between us had formed."

"You saved her." The words were gravel. "Twice."

Silence stretched between us for a moment before she spoke, her voice broken when she asked, "What does it mean for me?"

I blew out some of the strain on a long exhalation. "Only thing I know is, you were meant to be a part of her life. A piece of this. How or why?" I shrugged, though it wasn't casual. It was heavy. Weighted with all the questions of this life. "I don't understand it any more than I've ever understood why we were chosen. How it is possible. But I know it's important. That it matters."

"Can you stop . . ." Her entire face pinched before she forced out, "Can you stop whatever is happening? This merging of two worlds?"

Stop the *end*.

She didn't need to say it aloud for me to hear it. For me to feel it.

Because it was out there, the awareness of what we were coming up to.

The end of this life as we knew it.

Maybe the end of humankind altogether.

"I don't know." Despondency filled the words. "Not without her."

"She's going to be okay. I can feel it. Like you said, there was a reason I was drawn here. I have to believe it made an impact. Changed a path the way it changed mine. A wrong that was righted."

"Thank you for listening to it. I don't know what would have happened if . . ." It died on my tongue, the trauma of it too much to bear.

It'd been close.

Too close.

Since the day I'd come to her in the flesh, Aria had said over and over again that she didn't know how much time we had. Had urged that we couldn't waste a moment of it. While I'd refused to give her end any consideration.

But it'd been right there, dragging her into the nether. One second from stealing her away from me.

"What will you do now?" I asked.

Jill shifted on her feet. Sadness flooded the movement when her shoulder came up to touch her ear. "I'm not sure. My nursing days are over."

"But it doesn't seem your saving days are."

Tenderness weaved through her demeanor, and the words were soggy when she answered, "Maybe they aren't."

Then she cleared her throat, picked up the bag from the floor, and placed it on the bed. She pulled out the stethoscope and the blood pressure cuff. She checked them both while I waited, antsy for even a bit of good news.

I breathed out some of the angst I was holding when she delivered it.

"She's stable, and her heartbeat sounds even stronger than the last time I checked. I'm going to give her a shot with an antibiotic to keep her from getting an infection."

She pulled a syringe from the bag, uncapped it, then filled it from a small vial. She pulled the blanket down far enough so she could tug the hem of Aria's sleep pants down to her hip and gave her the shot. Then she set an orange prescription bottle on the dresser.

"If she wakes up in pain, give her two of these. She can have two every four hours. I'll come check on her tomorrow, but you . . ." Her eyes were intense. "Stay close to her. She needs to rest, but I think she needs you more."

My nod was tight. "I'm not going anywhere."

"Good."

Then she packed her things and headed for the door, pausing for a moment to look back at us.

Emotion brimmed in the space. The tether that tied her to Aria stretching taut.

Then she turned and disappeared down the hall.

A minute later, Dani came in with Aria's duffel. "We should clean her up."

I gave a tight nod, and Dani helped me undress Aria, ridding her of the soiled, tattered fabric.

Dani balled all of it up and stuffed it into a plastic bag, which she tied off to be discarded.

Then she moved into the en suite bathroom and returned with two warm washcloths. Together, we carefully cleaned up the blood that had dried all the way across Aria's stomach and sides and down her legs, avoiding the large bandage where Jill had already cleaned her.

Then we re-dressed her in only a T-shirt, keeping her as still as we could, no words said as we worked together in a quiet, fluid understanding.

Aria moaned from the depths of her sleep. It might have been incoherent, dull and distant, but I thought it might have been the most beautiful thing I'd ever heard.

Dani stayed with Aria while I showered. I had to wash off the blood I was covered in.

Red-tinged water pooled at my feet, swirling as if it were trying to suck me down with it before it disappeared down the drain.

While I fought the dread that bound and festered.

The fear of what was coming.

A sense that buzzed at my spirit's periphery.

The truth that it was coming, and it was coming fast.

I stepped out of the shower, dried off with the towel Dani had left for me, pulled on a fresh pair of underwear and a pair of jeans, then walked back out into the bedroom.

Dani was on the bed on her side, curled around Aria.

When she noticed me there, she pressed her lips to Aria's temple and whispered her belief to her friend. Her sister. Their bond so great that I could feel it filling the room.

"You can do this, Aria. You are so strong. I've witnessed it my whole life. Have felt how special you are. But this? What happened tonight? You are extraordinary. You hold the answer, and you cannot let them win."

Without saying anything else, she climbed down from the bed, walked out of the room, and quietly snapped the door shut behind her.

Then I crawled into the bed and curled myself around Aria the way Dani had done.

Breathed my faith into her.

My hope.

My need.

Praying the connection would keep her anchored.

That she'd know where she belonged.

With me.

# Chapter Thirty-Three

## PAX—TEARSITH

Pax emerged in Tearsith with Aria in his arms. His bond so strong that he was sure when he'd fallen asleep, he had somehow carried her spirit there.

She was still limp, though her steady breaths filled him with the hope that he'd thought he'd lost.

He stumbled out into the meadow. None of their Laven family was there. All of them would have long descended to fight the battle in Faydor.

Pax sank down to the soft grass with Aria in the nest of his arms.

He rocked her there with her on his lap, his face tilted toward the placid sky that always welcomed them like an embrace.

His spirit moaned, begging for an answer.

*How do we stop this? How can we win this when we don't understand what we're fighting against?*

He didn't expect an answer.

Valeen had always been a mystery to him. Maybe even a fable. Fabricated to give them answers for who they were. For the existence he had never understood.

But sitting there, rocking her in his arms, he thought he knew. He thought he might understand, even if it was obscured.

And within it, the softest voice tinkled in his ear. Somewhere at the edge of awareness.

A voice that whispered, *"You must rise with her. Stand at her side and never let go."*

# Chapter Thirty-Four

## ARIA

I woke up curled in the safety of Pax's arms. Warmth radiated around me. A fire that burned at our connection, where he was pinned to my side.

A cover.

A shroud.

An embrace.

Groggy, I blinked my eyes open to find his right there. That pale, fiery gaze tacked on me in all its ferocity as he stared at me from where his head rested on a pillow.

I got the sense that he'd remained in that exact position for the entire night.

The man was a guard.

A sentry.

Wishing for a way to be my savior.

My chest constricted at the pain that also roiled in that gaze as he looked across at me.

Deep, dark, and haunted.

Though there was such relief mixed in it that I felt myself floating in the sanctuary of the murky depths.

Held there.

Uplifted.

A buoy and belief.

His palm was already on my cheek, and the pad of his thumb brushed along the curve of it before it wandered over my chapped lips.

"Hi," he murmured. The single word was raw. Brittle and cracked.

I swallowed around the sticky thickness that nearly closed off my throat. The faintest hitch of a smile wobbled at the edge of my mouth, the amount of love I felt for him in that moment overwhelming. "Hi."

He kept looking at me that way, unrelenting, drinking me in as if he'd been afraid he'd never get to see me again.

It'd been close.

Even though I felt disoriented—almost numb—I knew it. I remembered feeling myself drifting away into the nothingness.

He blinked. Studying. Adoring. Half grieving. "The way it feels to see those beautiful eyes staring back at me."

Reaching out a shaky hand, I curled it around his wrist, the words tacky as I forced them from my tongue. "The way it feels to wake up and the first thing I see is your face."

So fierce and awe-striking.

Its harsh angles carved in my memories and forever written in my mind.

His lips plush and his nose sharp.

And his heart . . . I could feel it thundering through me.

"I was so afraid, Aria," he gritted out. "So fuckin' afraid."

The movement was slight as I nodded against his palm. "I was afraid, too."

Understanding passed between us before he shifted around and grabbed a cup from the nightstand. He maneuvered so he could bring the straw to my lips. "Here."

I sucked down the cool water. Probably a little too fast. But my mouth and throat were parched.

When I'd nearly drunk the entire thing, he set it back on the nightstand, then turned right back to me.

"How do you feel?" His voice scraped out the question.

I searched inside myself for the answer, my mind right back to when I'd been struck out of the blue. A dagger from the sky. The obliterating pain, so severe it'd blinded me before I was just . . . out.

Right then, I could feel the large bandage that covered my abdomen. I knew it covered the spot where I'd been burned . . . or . . . stabbed, really. This wound was different from anything I'd sustained before. At least that much I knew for certain.

But somehow, I felt . . .

With a frown, I shook my head slightly. "I'm not in any pain."

Three severe lines slashed into Pax's brow. "You don't need to play it off as nothing, Aria. What happened last night . . ."

He trailed off, unable to say it.

"I'm not. Truly. I feel a little groggy and out of it." I blinked to process it. "And I'm aware of the area. Like . . . it's kind of tingling. But other than that, I think I'm okay."

Reticence filled Pax's expression. Wanting to distract him from it, I quickly asked, "How long was I out?"

"It's just after four in the afternoon. You were out for about fourteen hours."

"You held me the whole time?" Softness filled my tone.

His nod was slow, his touch tender as he kept running the pad of his thumb over the angles of my face. "As much as I could. I left you to take a shower and then use the restroom this morning. Dani sat with you in the moments that I couldn't."

"Was I there? In Tearsith?"

For the first time in my life, I'd roused in this realm with no memory of where I'd gone during my sleep. The entire time I was out had been completely dark.

"Yeah. I emerged in Tearsith with you in my arms, and I held you there, too. For hours. Then when I woke up, I was right here, with you still in my arms."

"I don't even remember."

"You were never coherent during any of it."

Emotion curled through my senses.

"But I think I could feel you. I think I felt you the whole time. An anchor in my soul. A beacon that kept me guided," I whispered.

"I refused to let you go." It ground out of him like a claim. A proclamation.

"How could I go anywhere without you? Not when you're the other half of this heart. The other half of my soul." I could barely speak.

Pax shifted so he had each side of my face framed in his hands. Intensity blazed from his being. "I would have followed you wherever you'd gone and fought for you there."

His love was a wave that washed through me, wisping through all the broken places.

Healing as it passed.

Because I could feel myself coming alive beneath it.

Hope searing through my insides where he'd refused to leave me in the depths.

He kept us there for the longest time, the two of us locked, before I forced myself to turn my focus to the questions that marred the peace in my mind. "There were Kruen here, Pax. Here. And they . . . they were in those men. Not just in their minds. They were . . . possessed. I could physically see them writhing beneath their skin."

His eyes squeezed closed for a beat. "I know," he ground out.

"They're coming for us." My response was haggard.

Pax warred in the middle of it before he rushed out, "Yes. But Valeen is here, too. At least, some part of her is." He hesitated before he tightened his hold on my face. "Because Jill is here, Aria."

In confusion, I rocked back an inch. "What do you mean?"

"The nurse who helped you escape. She was here. In Portland. She kept having dreams that she had to come here. That her purpose with you wasn't over. And she saved you. She's the one who patched you up. Gave you blood after you'd lost so much."

"Oh my God."

It was a whisper.

Awe.

A blooming of hope in the middle of my faith that kept getting trampled.

Pax threaded our fingers together and lifted them between us. "There's a reason, Aria. Something we're supposed to do. We just have to keep you safe until we can see it through."

"It was different last night," I told him.

Words started to fly out as the memories came flooding back.

"With you all there. When I expelled the energy the first time, I was drained . . . exhausted beyond my boundaries . . . but when Dani wrapped her arm around my waist to support me, a flicker of the energy returned. We already knew that happened when you touched me. Believed it would be the same for all Nols. But, Pax . . ."

I gulped as the realization came battering into me. "When all four of us were standing together. It was powerful. Extremely. There's no chance that bolt of energy would have come out of me if all of you hadn't been right there. With me. Touching me."

*It was the contact.*

*It was the contact.*

Awareness careened, a frenzy that blistered through my insides and sank into my spirit.

Bolting upright, I tossed off the blanket and sheet that covered us, and I started to tear the bandage free from my abdomen.

"Aria, what the hell are you doing?" Pax flew up to sitting, scrambling to stop me.

"No, Pax. Don't. Just listen. Look."

I could tell he didn't want to give in. That he worried I was delusional.

Fevered.

I was, but not in the way he was thinking.

He relented, and I grimaced as I peeled the bandage away to expose the wound.

A wound that was still there. The skin puckered and red and inflamed. But it was healed in a way it shouldn't be. The skin that had been sutured was closed. Not just by the stitches, but by the mending of the flesh.

Beyond the fathomable.

"How is this possible?" Pax muttered, aghast as he looked at the laceration.

"Because it was a lie to keep us weak."

A lie we'd been fed.

One I was sure Ambrose had created. Because he knew . . . He knew the power Abigail had possessed when they'd been together.

I could only imagine the ways he'd used it against her.

"Valeen showed you, Pax." My words rushed in urgency as the truth weaved together. "She showed you that we belong together by allowing you to feel that I was in trouble. In danger. She gave you that sense that you had no other choice but to find me. And we already know together this power is far greater than we thought—and now, after what happened last night? I have to believe it is even stronger with the four of us together."

No question our Nol was our greatest strength.

But there was power in these numbers.

In *us*.

In this family.

Excitement burned a path through me, and I gasped as Pax stared at my healing wound for the longest time before his eyes flicked up to mine.

Awareness flared at the connection. Our breaths shortened and heaved.

"We're stronger together. All of us," he murmured.

"Yes." Then I threw myself at him, lifted up high on my knees as I wound one arm around his neck and braided the other through the longer pieces of his stark-white hair. "Together," I murmured.

He was sitting, a leg drawn up in front of him and an arm looped around my waist. His gorgeous face was turned up toward me as I gazed down at him.

Each of us held.

Kept.

Then all reservations broke.

He pushed up to capture my mouth.

In an instant, we were fire.

A frenzy.

Desperate hands and beseeching kisses.

He wore no shirt, his chest and back and abdomen bare, and I dug my nails into the designs that covered the rippling, sinewy muscles of his back as I struggled to get him closer.

Need rose up inside me. A tidal wave I had no intention of escaping.

"Aria," he murmured at my lips.

My name praise.

Bliss.

Truth.

Calloused hands slid up under the enormous T-shirt I wore. He was careful not to touch my wound as he rushed his hands up my sides. Gliding over every rib until he was palming my breasts.

I arched into his touch.

Flames seared.

"I need you," I begged. "I need your touch. Your love. Your belief."

"And I need your everything," he rumbled back, his lips devouring mine, his tongue delving deep.

That fire leaped.

Pax climbed onto his knees, too, and he angled back for a second to peel the shirt over my head.

The air was warm but still, and a shiver rolled through me. Chills that lifted in the wake of his ravenous gaze.

"Are you sure you're not hurting?" The question was stone. Purified by his care.

"I'm not. I'm not," I promised, and he had me around the waist and was laying me out in the middle of the bed. He remained on his knees, that gaze severe as he looked over me, attention tracking over every scar and blemish.

As if every marred inch was his perfection.

I knew it. Felt it in the weight of his gaze. In the weight of his love that sagged in the room.

"Everything, Aria," he said again, and he reached out and hooked his fingers in the sides of my underwear.

I lifted my hips from the bed as he peeled them down.

"Look at you," he groaned.

"It's you," I returned, reaching out, not quite close enough to drag my trembling fingers down the rugged terrain of his chest.

Because he hovered there, at my knees. Every inch of his beautifully brutal body raged with need.

Desire flooded us. A deluge that filled the room.

He slowly wound out of his underwear, pulling them down and freeing himself.

A gasp got free. A whimpered "Yes," as he climbed down and wedged himself between my thighs.

And we were bare.

Whole.

One.

My entire being arched into him when he pushed inside me.

He wound a hand in my hair as he grunted in the opposite ear. "Did you know you fuckin' glow when I fill you, Aria? Did you know you become pure fucking radiant light?"

"I feel it. Just like I feel you speeding through me. Through my veins and my spirit and reaching all the way down into my soul."

That connection alive. Growing brighter and brighter.

Pax eased back, gazing down at me as he withdrew, then nudged himself even deeper. My fingers sank into his shoulders, holding on as he began to move.

Fervency rippled around us, a furor that sparked and danced, though he filled me in slow, measured strokes. One arm was banded around my back and the other had our fingers knitted together, our hands pressed between us.

Never once did he take those eyes from mine.

He held me as he loved me.

As he silently promised me so many things.

*Everything.*

*Everything.*

Bliss gathered. A rising, building storm.

He worked me into a writhing, panting puddle, my mouth parted and tiny gasps raking from my lungs.

He inhaled each one before he would turn around and breathe himself right back into me.

And it climbed. Climbed and climbed.

This pleasure that rode in on that storm.

Before it suddenly splintered. A thunderclap.

Rending through the middle of me with the force of a bomb.

It was a breaking.

A bonding.

A joining that could never be undone.

I stifled a cry as it rolled through to consume.

To race and touch and devastate.

Joy and ecstasy.

It was a rapture unlike anything I'd ever known.

He only pulled me closer when he came, his harsh brow twisted and his mouth parted on silent, jagged rasps. The tip of his nose just touched mine as his body went rigid.

Lean muscles flexing and bowing as he jerked and shook.

Sparks of pleasure billowed and broke. Shock waves rolled over us again and again.

And in it, we were endless.

Boundless.

Infinite.

And he kept me gathered that way as we struggled to catch our breaths. To come back down from the paradise where we'd been lifted.

Those eyes burned.

White flames that tethered me to him.

He tightened our fingers that were woven together, and he brought our joined hands to his chest.

The words that fell from his mouth were a rasp. As essential as the oxygen that'd grown dense, a desperate swelling in the room.

"I don't want to spend one minute without you, Aria. Not here or in Tearsith or whatever other plane we may be taken to. You are mine for eternity. In every reality. In every life."

I blinked, emotion riding thick on my chest.

Intensity radiated from him.

Potent and all consuming.

Though his face twisted in sincerity. In a plea.

In that thing that had come to life between us the first time I'd seen him standing in the doorway of the room of that facility. When the man had stood in front of me in the flesh, and I knew, in that second, that nothing would remain the same.

"Marry me," he murmured, the words gruff.

I couldn't get the gasp of surprise out before he continued. "Marry me here and marry me there, because I want to belong to you in every single way."

Tears blurred my eyes, love overflowing—there was no way to contain it where it erupted inside me.

This man who'd been nothing more than a fantasy. My everything. The only one I'd ever wanted and the one I'd thought I could never have.

"Pax." It was a whisper.

Adoration and awe.

"Marry me," he begged.

"I'm yours, Pax. You have all of me. Every promise. Every minute. Every oath that I could make."

"So, you want to make this one with me? This oath." He brought my knuckles to his lips and kissed them.

My teeth raked over my bottom lip, and I whispered, "I do."

His nod was soft.

Ardent.

Filled with a joy that neither of us had ever imagined we would find. Even if it was fleeting. Short-lived. If we only had this moment, it didn't matter because it belonged to us.

"Don't move," he told me with a half grin tugging at his mouth, and he slowly peeled himself away before he moved to the edge of the bed.

His attention hunted through the room before it settled on whatever he'd been searching for. He stood, and I shook all over again when that glorious, fierce body was fully on display.

The man hewn and carved.

His skin a canvas of our lives.

His scars a covenant given to this mission.

He crossed the room to a floating shelf where there were a few things on display, including a candle encased in glass that had a black ribbon tied around it.

He tugged the ribbon free, and he turned around. A mix between an adoring smile and a smirk was tacked on his face as he sauntered back to me.

He climbed onto the bed on his knees and took my hand. His eyes flicked between me and my left ring finger as he started to carefully tie the ribbon around it.

No words were said between us when he did, but my heart was shouting.

Singing.

*My heart. My love. My Nol. You are mine eternally.*

Once he had it secure, he ran his thumb over the ribbon, staring at it for a moment before he lifted his gaze back to mine. "This ribbon is temporary, Aria, until we get through this mess, but the promise it represents is not."

"We're going to make it through this." I sat up, and Pax leaned forward and fisted his hand in my hair, tipping my face up to his as he looked down at me.

"We will, Aria. We will get through this, and you're forever going to be mine on the other side."

# Chapter Thirty-Five

## ARIA

Jill came to check on me. She was shocked by the amount of healing I'd done, though she said she shouldn't have been. She examined me before showering me with her love and belief, then reluctantly said she needed to return to her family.

I hugged her for the longest time, thanking her over and over again, before I got into the shower after she'd said her final goodbye.

I washed and stepped out, drying quickly before I changed into leggings and a fluffy black sweater.

The ribbon still adorned my finger. I lifted it as I looked at my reflection in the mirror.

There was a chance that I might not ever take it off.

It was the sweetest gift I'd ever received.

Though it wasn't hard for me to piece together how this man who was so forbidding—a minister of violence—could still remain so gentle underneath.

His deeds had been defined by the purpose he'd been given. By this life that had forged us into the people we were.

And I realized then I would never want to change that. I wanted all facets of him. All his rough, steely intimidation and the soft caresses he worshipped me with at night. His gruff words and his undying devotion.

I wanted his everything. Every single thing he'd just offered to me.

Clearing my throat, I forced myself to finally move, and I tied my damp hair up into a messy twist, then slipped from the bathroom.

Pax was dressed, leaning over with his elbows resting on his thighs where he sat on the edge of the bed.

When he felt me there, he lifted his head. Worry had edged back into his features, as if the few moments without me had set him off-balance. "How do you feel?"

"I feel like I'm standing in front of my future." It billowed from my mouth. My own promise that it was us.

That I wanted it.

Forever.

He pushed to standing, his feet bare, the man so beautiful he stole the breath from my lungs. I wondered if there'd ever be a day when that would change. When he would stop having this effect on me.

I doubted it, with the burn that slipped through my body when he reached out and took my chin between his fingers. Wonderment was etched into every stark line of his expression. "You astound me, Aria. The resilience inside you."

"And you're the one who's still standing at my side when danger tracks me everywhere I go. *That's* resilience."

Dedication and loyalty.

His thumb brushed over the scar on the left side of my mouth. "Ah, Princess, don't you know the only place I want to be is at your side?"

My teeth raked my bottom lip, my own playfulness sliding into the tease. "I thought I was your fiancée?"

Softness hooked at the side of his mouth. "That's right. And I can't wait until we make that *wife*."

He grabbed my hand and threaded our fingers together. "Come on. We need to get you something to eat. Make sure we keep your strength up."

"I'd rather stay here in this room with you all day."

"One day, Aria. One day we won't be dealing with all this bullshit; then it'll just be you and me."

I gave him a small nod, and he started to walk backward, taking me with him, still wearing that grin on his face as he led me toward the bedroom door.

"What are you doing?" I whispered.

"I don't want to take my eyes off you."

Affection crawled into my cheeks on a bout of redness. "You're ridiculous."

"Nah, baby—I'm enamored."

That flush only deepened, a sheet of warmth that slipped around me like an embrace.

Then Pax clicked open the door, and he shifted around to face ahead as he led me down the hall, though he kept glancing back at me from over his shoulder as if he meant exactly what he'd said.

We slowed as we made it to the end of the hall, and we peeked out to find Dani and Timothy on the couch. Timothy sat on one end, while Dani lay across it, her head resting on his thigh and her cat curled into her belly.

She ran her finger through its fur as she and Timothy quietly chatted, the man's arm draped over the top of her waist to keep her close.

There was a peace that radiated around them.

A glow that kept them contained.

Another affirmation that what I'd come to believe was true.

When Dani noticed me standing there, her head popped up from Timothy's lap. "Oh my God, you're awake." She untangled herself from him and the cat, then hopped off the couch and came fumbling toward me.

Then she slowed, her actions pulling up short. "Wait. What are you doing out of bed? How are you even standing?"

A frown twisted her brow, and her tone slipped into disbelief. "And did you shower?"

Appalled, she looked at Pax, clearly asking for an explanation. Or maybe silently demanding that he sweep me into his arms to carry me back to her room.

"I'm fine," I answered before Pax could say anything.

"You're fine?" She basically screeched it as she flung a hand at me, her pink hair sticking up all over the place. "You were nearly ki—"

She stopped, as if she couldn't bear to say it, before her voice turned to a whisper. A fluttering of the residual of her fear. "We nearly lost you last night."

Stepping forward, I took both of her hands. "And I'm almost completely healed."

Doubt raced through her expression, so I hurried to speak. "It's us, together, Dani. All of us. Pax and I had thought being together as Nols made us safer. But it's more than that. You all gave me the strength to end those men last night, and I think you gave me the strength to heal as well. I think being together gives us all that power."

Her pale eyes widened behind her wire-rimmed glasses, and three long seconds passed as she seemed to work toward understanding. Then a stunned puff of air left her as she pressed her fingertips to her lips, awe bleeding out. "Last night, Jill said your heart beat stronger when Pax touched you."

My nod was shaky. "It's the key. The key to us. To who we are. And I think that Ambrose twisted it. Used it against us to keep us weak. To defeat us."

Timothy stood. "So that means we can beat this motherfucker."

My nod was frantic. "I think we can. We have to."

But after what happened last night . . .

Horror weaved in with hope.

A violent clashing of doubt and relief.

There were only five men last night, and it had already been close. How many more of them could he send against us? An army? A legion?

And where was he? Why wasn't he here, trying to take me down himself? He'd been tracking me for weeks. Showing up in random places.

"We have to find him," I said.

Uncertainty pulled deep into Dani's brow. "I thought he would come to you?"

Thoughts spun through my mind. "I thought so, too, but . . ."

"But you defeated him when he thought you couldn't." Pax's voice was low, his words speeding darts.

He angled forward to come up to my side, and the four of us were drawn together to create a circle. Hovering close.

The energy shifted. Grew in the intensity that we possessed.

Pax looked between Dani and Timothy before he set his full attention on me.

"He thought he would end you when he dragged you to that other plane when you had been in Faydor. Then he thought he would again behind that grocery store. He was afraid, Aria. You saw that he was afraid—shocked—that your demise wouldn't be simple. I saw it, too, that afternoon."

"Is he running?" Dani asked.

"That, or he's keeping us distracted with all the rest of this bullshit while he's working toward something that will make him unstoppable." Spite filled Pax's voice.

"He is somehow allowing the Kruen to break through the barriers of the otherworld and into this reality . . ." A heave of air pressed out from my lungs as the weight of the consequences fell over me.

"Which means he's about to take control of this world," Timothy surmised. "Fully."

"He told me he would rule it." I hadn't understood the fallout of what that'd really meant when he'd declared it. Had never deigned to imagine it might come to this.

I couldn't even fathom what that would mean for humanity. If the skies were busted apart and Kruen crawled out to run rampant on Earth.

The two worlds colliding.

The one thing I knew for sure was this one wouldn't last long.

It would be trampled.

Crushed.

Devastation strewn from one end to the other. Complete ruin left in its wake.

"We can't allow that to happen." Agitation curled through Pax's voice as he roughed a hand through his hair, the man itching with the need to hunt. To slay the evil the way he'd always done.

"We won't," I asserted, and I reached out and took Dani's hand, sharing a look with the woman who had been my mentor for so long. My sanity when I'd been so confused as a young adult. Support through all the trauma and fear.

My best friend.

My sister.

She took Timothy's hand, and I reached out and grabbed Pax's.

It linked us all like a chain.

And I could swear that, deep inside me, the light flared, and with the way everyone inhaled sharply at the contact, I was sure it did in them, too.

"Together," I said.

"Together," they reiterated.

Then surprise rocked out of Dani on a huff, and she cocked her head at me with those pale eyes wide. "Um, not to interrupt this whole pact to save the world that we're making here, but what the hell is that?"

She cast a pointed look between Pax, me, and the ribbon tied around my left ring finger.

Pax shifted his attention to me, a cross of resolve and affection on his face before he shifted it back to Dani. "Aria and I are getting married."

Then he squeezed my hand and murmured, "Tonight."

# Chapter Thirty-Six

## PAX—TEARSITH

Pax held tight to Aria as they eased out from the dense foliage that hedged in their sanctuary. The air was pleasantly cool. Perfect as it murmured across their flesh on the temperate breeze that rustled through the boundaries of Tearsith.

The massive, magnificent tree stood proud in the distance. Limbs forever full of dense leaves stretched out to create a canopy of green. A tree where he and Aria had played as children. Where they'd laughed and giggled and chased each other.

That was in the years before they'd understood the perversion and obscenity. The wickedness that reigned, that one day they would war against. Before the scars and the traumas and the fear.

This girl who'd been his very best friend. His only friend. The one who'd become his anchor when he felt as if he were perpetually lost in the ravages of a deep, toiling sea.

He glanced at his Nol then. At the sharp, defined angles of her face. Cheeks and jaw whittled like blades. Eyes sharp and keen, yet so unbelievably kind. Real and steeped in her desire to help those in need.

He had no question that she would be willing to sacrifice it all, even if it only served one person.

One soul.

But her mission had become so much greater than that. The scores she'd been given to protect. Every life. Every being.

The charge that had been her burden had become essential.

Basic for all survival.

The whole fucking weight of the world riding on her shoulders.

But for one night—just one night—he wanted to give her a reprieve.

A moment that only belonged to her.

A moment that only belonged to them.

Beyond where he and Aria stood on the soft grass at the edge of Tearsith, on the bank on the crystalline brook that weaved through their haven, their Laven family had begun to gather at their great teacher's feet.

Pax's chest tightened when he saw that Ellis had grown weary. His shriveled frame sagged even more than it had just a week ago.

Brittle beneath the great losses that had befallen their tribe. Their family, who were being picked off one by one, their numbers dwindling with each day that passed.

A quiet sorrow quivered and moaned through the flock, though in it, Pax could feel a new strength that had emerged. Nols sat closer, tied in a way they'd never been before, clinging to the other in relief that both had arrived in Tearsith that night.

That they'd made it another day.

"How many of them do you think have joined?" Aria asked beneath her breath as she stared out over the crowd. "How many do you think have found their Nol in the day?"

"I imagine that most of them ran to find the other, if there was any possibility of doing it," Pax rumbled.

"I can only wonder if them finding each other is what has allowed them to come here tonight. If it's what's kept them safe." Aria's voice was laden with caution, and he could feel her grief. Her pain over the ones who'd already been lost.

She suddenly trembled. "Do you think it's because of me? Is it because of me that Ambrose has been seeking the demise of us all? He said I was the last one standing in his way. Would he stop this slaughter if I was no longer in his way?"

Ferocity filled his spirit, and he turned to her, his words emphasized. "No, Aria . . . I think you're here because this was going to happen. Because Ambrose was going to try to merge the worlds. End our kind and likely every person on the planet. I think you've been sent—purposed for this time—because you're the only one who can stop it."

She inhaled a shaky breath, and Pax ran his thumb over the object tied to her left ring finger.

Another impossibility.

Because they never crossed realms with any human properties. Not clothing, or jewelry, or even their scars and tattoos. They emerged in Laven's uniforms, clad in brown pants and jackets and boots.

And there his promise remained on her finger.

The ribbon.

She exhaled before she tipped him a timorous smile, and the two of them slowly moved across the meadow to where the rest had settled. Dani and Timothy were already there, Dani tucked beneath Timothy's arm and pressed to his chest.

". . . of the utmost care . . ." Ellis's instructions trailed off when his regard landed on the two of them. His eyes were now nearly completely gray, as if the irises had spread out to stain the sclera, yet his gaze remained impossibly warm. An embrace from afar, though there was torment written in it.

Josephine hovered near him. Strands of stringy gray hair hung limp around her aged, weathered face.

"Aria . . ." Ellis said with an exhalation of relief. "Dani and Timothy told us what happened last night. It's all so much to handle and believe. I'm so sorry this burden has befallen you."

His expression went grim. "And the Kruen . . ."

"It was terrifying," she whispered. "But we made it out, and I am well and whole."

By the time they'd curled up together in bed, she'd nearly been healed, the wound resembling a scar more than anything else.

"Thank Valeen," Ellis murmured on the breeze.

Aria's nod was slow, though Pax could feel the gravity behind it. "Yes, thank Valeen. She was near."

"Then she has not abandoned us." Ellis's whisper held the weight of a prayer of deliverance.

"No, she has not. And I've come to believe that she is urging us toward one another. To stand together. More than here and in Faydor, but in the day. I believe we are not just stronger with our Nols, but together as a whole."

A ripple of surprise wound through the throng of Laven, their chattering held in uncertainty. But a current rode through it. One that struck a chord in their spirits.

As if they'd all become attuned to one another. As if their spirits recognized what Aria was saying.

A middle-aged woman named Stephanie climbed to standing in the middle of the crowd, her hair as black as Aria's, her skin just as pale.

She blinked with the severity of her confession.

"I had a dream. The same one two nights in a row. A dream telling me I'm supposed to leave. It's as if I'm being called somewhere else but I'm lost in the middle of it, not sure of where I'm supposed to go." Her voice waffled with uncertainty. "And I never have dreamed before. Not once in my life. Not until now. When I close my eyes, I always come here."

Two more asserted the same.

The confused certainty that they felt they were supposed to be somewhere else, though they had no indication of where they were supposed to be. Riddled with a feeling of being misplaced.

It left them all unsettled and unsure.

"Maybe it's calling us toward our Nols?" another speculated.

Stephanie's response shot down that theory. "But I was already with mine."

Hundreds of eyes turned to Aria, seeking guidance.

Pax could feel the anxiety roll through her. Her wish to be able to give something real. To be able to protect each of them. To provide a solution. A miracle.

"We all feel it . . ." Aria said. "Something inside us urging us to do *something* or a change is about to happen. And I wish I knew exactly what that was. That I could tell you exactly what to do. I can't, but I do get the sense we're supposed to wait for clarity. That we will know when the time comes."

Aria fisted her hand over her heart. "The one thing I can say with certainty is, I've been called to end Ambrose. How? I don't know. But I have faith that it will be revealed to me. That Valeen wouldn't bring me to this time and place only to leave us helpless."

Her chest shuddered as she inhaled. "And I promise you that I will go where she calls me. Do whatever she asks. Whatever it takes. I won't surrender or submit. In the meantime, I think you need to find whatever Laven live closest to you and go to them. Stick together. Not just with your Nols, but with anyone else that you can."

Apprehension rolled through them all, and Ellis lifted a bony, spindly hand. "I know it's hard to process, to accept when we've been instructed to live so differently, but I believe we must trust in what Aria says."

Agreement seemed to move through the crowd, and a chatter rose through the ranks as Laven moved toward those they knew lived closest to them, their conversations hushed as they made plans to meet in the day.

Ellis let them talk for a time before he cleared his throat. "My children, even though we must pivot during the day, we cannot become distracted from our original purpose. Finish your plans, and then we must prepare to descend. The time is coming near."

Pax edged forward, and he pushed a hand out to stop their family from rising, silently asking them to stay back as he brought Aria to stand directly in front of Ellis.

"Not yet, Ellis. I need you to do one thing for me."

Confusion knitted the old man's brow, though in it, Pax saw that he was willing to do anything.

"What do you ask?"

"I want you to marry me and Aria. Tonight. Right now. In front of our family."

# Chapter Thirty-Seven

## ARIA—TEARSITH

They gathered beneath the great tree. Verdant branches stretched out overhead as if hands were reaching out to cover them with a blessing.

Facing each other, Aria and Pax held each other's hands. Their bodies remained a foot away from each other, though they couldn't be closer.

Their gazes locked, their shallow, choppy breaths meshing with the energy that glowed in the bare space that separated them.

She felt it as a weaving.

As a knitting together of their beings.

Body, mind, and soul.

Ellis stood to her left, and the rest of their Laven family sat on the grass on the other side.

Love surrounded them.

A bright, unending glow.

How strange that just weeks ago she'd harbored so much guilt and shame over her love for her Nol, guarding it like a dirty secret.

Yet here they now stood in front of them all, boasting of who they were.

Ellis had not discouraged them, but Aria had still sensed his reticence. It was hard to dismiss nearly a century's worth of conviction. Hard to accept his own loss as his wary gaze traveled to Josephine in a whisper of longing.

Then, without a word, he had led them to this spot beneath their sacred tree.

"Dear Laven family, I stand before you today, entrusted with this commission. A commission I'd once believed would lead to devastation. To certain death. But our vision had been shortsighted. Skewed. Hindered by the lies we'd been fed—lies that I'd unknowingly then transferred to you."

He lifted a quivering chin as he continued, "It leaves me both aggrieved and gratified. Anguished and heartened. But for now, for this one moment, I'd like to turn from the sadness and instead focus on the overwhelming joy of bringing Pax and Aria together. As Nols. As partners. As lovers. As defenders. As everything they were meant to be."

A rush of that joy sped through Aria as Pax squeezed her hands even tighter, the man drawing her forward another inch.

Those gray, fathomless eyes swam with their own gladness. With desperation and devotion.

With a love unending.

With everything she'd dreamed of him one day watching her with.

Ellis looked between Aria and Pax with a self-conscious grin. "I've attended many weddings in my lifetime, but it is safe to say that I have never officiated. Please forgive me, as I may not have all the right words, but my meek soul tells me that Valeen has given me the authority. And that authority may be given here—in Tearsith—but this binding transcends all realms."

His gaze was intense as it settled on Aria. "So, Aria Rialta, as you stand in front of Pax Morrison, do you accept him as your husband? Both here and on Earth?"

Her attention drifted back to Pax. To his striking, unforgettable face. This man the very thing that possessed her thoughts and mind.

Her throat was thick as she whispered, "I love you, Pax Morrison. Forever. So I accept you as my husband, both here and on Earth, and far into the afterlife."

Emotion rushed from Pax. A gush of it that breached and pervaded. It wound through her with threads of reverence and need.

Their connection thrashed between them.

Ellis turned to Pax. "And do you, Pax Morrison, accept Aria Rialta as your wife, both here and on Earth?"

Pax stared at her.

Intent.

Vivid.

Stark and hard and so utterly soft.

His voice was gravel when he spoke. "I was told since I was a child that my Nol was only meant for me in one way: as a partner in a war I'd been picked to fight. But I should have known all along that she was meant for so much more than that. That she was everything that ever meant anything to me."

He swallowed hard, and his thick throat bobbed. "She was the light that burned inside me. A beacon. My only destination. And when I found you, Aria . . . when I saw you for the first time standing in front of me, you rearranged everything I'd thought I'd known. Every part of me. You brought me to life in an instant, when I'd long accepted that the only thing my meager days would encompass were gore and violence and death."

Tears blurred Aria's eyes, and her chest expanded as her Nol laid himself bare in front of their entire Laven family.

"And then you showed me that I had it all wrong. You showed me there was so much more to live for, and the one thing I was made to do was live this life with you. For you. So yes, I accept you as my wife both here and on Earth. Through every storm and sunrise. In the chaos and the peace. In all of eternity."

A deep fervency swathed them all as their family watched, rapt.

The energy she and Pax shared wound and glowed.

Ellis cleared the coarseness from his voice before he again lifted his chin and said, "Then it is my great honor to declare you husband and wife. In every way."

Pax didn't wait to find out if Ellis would tell him to kiss her. His arms were already around her and a hand was already twisting up in her hair, holding tight as he possessed her mouth in a mind-bending kiss.

One that trembled the ground beneath her feet and rocked her to her soul.

Commanding.

Proclaiming.

A vow that he sealed.

One that could not be undone.

She felt branded by it. Uplifted and taken.

Whole in every way she could imagine. The hollowness and vacancies and loneliness that had wept inside her for so many years had been completely obliterated.

Lights flickered and flashed behind her eyes, a blinding warmth that surged through the clearing.

And she wondered if the others felt it, too, as a chorus of soft gasps echoed around them, before there were shouts and claps cheering them on as everyone began to stand.

A gathering of hearts.

The hearts they were fighting for, only she knew that number was far greater than the small group that had come to shower them with love and well-wishes.

Aria and Pax finally parted, though their spirits remained tied, their gazes entrenched in the truth that vibrated between them.

*Forever.*

*Forever.*

"Now we must descend. Our work is far from over," Ellis said, breaking into the rapture. Pax and Aria gave him their assent.

He was right . . . they had much work to do.

They had all of existence to save.

# Chapter Thirty-Eight

## PAX—FAYDOR

They hit the floor of Faydor with a thud, both crouching low as they slammed against the frozen ground. They used their positions to catapult themselves forward and into a sprint, though their hands remained forever twined.

Except the second they'd stepped through the gauzy portal that lured them toward the sordid, Pax had known something was off.

He'd still been impaled by the cold slice of the frigid atmosphere, but there was something missing.

Something that left him feeling unsettled and agitated.

It took him a second to catch up to what it was.

To what sent a slick of apprehension clawing beneath the surface of his skin.

The howling.

The howling that whispered calamities into the ears of the weak.

The howling that imparted deviant thoughts into the subservient below.

It had been quieted. It was there, but it was different.

At the realization, he and Aria both skidded to a stop, their expressions troubled as they shared a confounded glance before their attention turned to race across the barren terrain to take it in. The Kruen were in a frenzy, racing as vapor across the pitted, rocky ground.

It was like they were lost.

Searching.

Their thoughts had mutated as they flailed.

*"It's time. It's time. It's time."*

The beasts chanted the chorus, no longer pausing to drip their venom in the minds of the willing.

Pax might have found comfort in it if it weren't for the sickening sense that crawled over him, penetrating flesh and bone.

His gaze scanned their surroundings, and he noticed that many of their Laven family had also taken off in different directions where they would walk in the darkness. Where they would fight. Only they'd also halted, rooted to the spot in varying states of confusion.

Turning in circles as the Kruen swept by them.

*"It's time. It's time. It's time."*

"What is happening?" Aria wheezed. He could sense her horror. The questions that spiraled through her mind.

"Don't know." It was a low rumble of caution.

Aria inhaled a steeling breath before she whispered, "We have to find out."

She yanked at his hand before she darted out into the nothingness, taking him with her.

Running.

Tracking.

Searching.

Despairing when they ran for what felt like for hours through the Kruen who seemed to seek the same thing. All being driven toward one place.

Until they came upon it.

In the distance.

They once again careened to a standstill, their boots skidding over the coarse, jagged rocks as they stumbled in shock.

Gasps of disbelief jutted from their aching lungs as they gaped at the affliction set out before them.

It was a giant fissure.

A crack that buckled through the cragged, rutted floor.

A fracture that opened directly to Earth below, and Kruen were slipping through it.

# Chapter Thirty-Nine

## ARIA

*"Rise up and go."*

*It was the faintest voice. A high-pitched tinkling in her ear. Dragging her through the nothingness where she typically hovered between sleeping and reality.*

*That moment when she was neither human nor ethereal.*

*"Do you feel it? The call?" the voice whispered. "You were made for this. Rise up and stand for the ones who cannot stand for themselves. End the one who seeks to destroy. Only you can. It's time. It's time to lead."*

*The call howled around her, dragging her spirit in a direction she didn't understand. The only thing she knew was she had to heed it.*

*And the sky opened up in the distance.*

*A magnet.*

*A lure.*

*The gravity a hook deep in her soul.*

*And in it, she saw his face.*

*Ambrose.*

*And Valeen's voice whispered again, "Go."*

A cry ripped out of me as I flew upright in bed, disoriented as I held the blanket covering us against my chest.

My mind was a hurricane. Still stuck somewhere between Faydor and the fog where I'd drifted right before awakening.

Where I'd been removed from Faydor, and rather than being catapulted back to this reality, I'd been held in a dream.

Pax jolted up by my side, as if we'd been attached, both of us waking at the same moment. He grabbed for me the second we were both upright, palms rushing out to frame my face.

"Did you see it? Did you feel it?" he demanded. "Were you dreaming, too?"

My throat was too thick to speak, so I only nodded, croaking out a bare "Yes."

There was a sudden pounding down the hall before a fist battered at the door. One second later, Dani threw it open. She stumbled in, pink hair a mess, desperation written in her expression. "I had a dream," she gasped, "and so did Timothy."

"We did, too," I managed to force out.

"It feels like we're being called somewhere else. Someplace specific. But where?" she begged, her desperation bleeding out onto the floor, the echo of her words climbing the walls with her urgency.

"That's exactly the way I feel," I told her.

But I thought we all already knew it. That the dream had been the same for each of us.

We were being compelled.

I blinked, trying to process what the visions meant. Where it was leading us. "I'm not sure . . . but . . . I think the area is close. I think I can feel it. Maybe a few hundred miles away."

It was only then that I heard the wailing of sirens. So many of them in the distance. That and the *thwomp, thwomp, thwomp* of helicopters as they flew overhead.

Dread soured in my stomach. It had started. The chaos we'd known was coming.

Timothy suddenly appeared in the doorway, a tower behind Dani. "We gotta go."

His features were a contortion of grimness and determination.

"I know."

"We need to think about this." Pax's words slashed into the air, and he shook his head as if he could throw off the disorder. "We don't know what we're going to come up against. There was a crack in Faydor, and Kruen were jumping through it."

Dani wheezed, "Oh God."

"Yeah. We found it deep in the recesses of Faydor. It's why the Kruen were acting strange. They were drawn toward it. No clue how many of them we're going to encounter. What kind of strength they're going to have on this plane. We can't take them all on ourselves."

Pax's teeth ground as he said it, anger spilling free. The memory of what we'd come upon last night in the farthest reaches of Faydor.

The crack.

The rending.

The ruin we knew would already be waiting for us.

"We don't have any other choice." I tossed off the covers and hopped out of bed. "We have to go. Now. It doesn't matter what we come up against. You know we're fated for this. You know it's the reason we're all standing here together. There's no cowering now."

Pax radiated his reservations. The need he felt to protect me butting up against the truth of what we were destined for.

My guardian.

My shield.

*My husband.*

The one who saw everything inside me. My purpose and my dreams.

The one I knew already had his answer, even though he wanted to fight against it.

He scrubbed both hands over his face before he gritted out, "If we're going to do this, then we'd better fuckin' show up prepared."

"Ah, now I like the sound of that." A big grin spread across Timothy's face.

"What the hell does that mean?" Dani glanced between the two of them.

Pax shoved off his covers and stood from the bed, too. "It means we do whatever it takes."

The four of us looked at each other as reality sank heavily on our hearts.

We either stopped Ambrose today, or we'd meet our end.

Thirty minutes later, we were peeling out of Dani's garage in her Civic. Pax and I were in the back, Timothy in the front passenger seat, and Dani at the wheel.

It was early, dawn just breaking at the horizon and cracking through the sky.

A sky that was intact above us, though I still shivered at the sight.

Dani rammed on the accelerator and flew down the road, again wiping tears that dripped down her cheeks when she glanced at the house that sat up the road from her own.

It was where she'd left Pixie. Dani had taken her to her elderly neighbor's and told the woman she had an emergency and needed to leave town for a while.

She'd promised she'd return as soon as she could.

Only I'd felt the wavering of the lie.

The way she'd been unsure if she would see her cat again.

If she would make it back.

If she would even have *anything* to come back to.

It was where our own humanity collided with our purpose. Where we struggled with our mortality.

Struck by the magnitude of the uncertainties that stretched around us.

A foreboding so thick in the cab of the car that it was difficult to breathe. Our lungs heavy and tight. Tremors of alarm and trepidation ripping through our bodies and shattering our spirits.

Pax clutched my hand as Dani flew down the street.

"Where exactly am I going?" she asked.

"East" was all I could say.

It was the only thing I was certain of.

The tugging at my spirit that guided our path.

A different place than the men had taken me last night.

"Yeah, east," Timothy agreed, no doubt getting the same indication.

"I know," Dani whispered, the words barely audible. "I just . . ."

Timothy reached out and set his hand on her thigh, trying to offer some of the peace that had seemed to slip away with each second that passed.

But any hope of peace had been torn away when Pax had turned on Dani's television as we ran around packing the few things we could bring. When we'd seen the carnage that had begun to spread across the world.

The complete panic and turmoil the world had been cast into.

No answers for the tragedies that befell the world. The murders and the fires. Wars started between allies and friends. Every manner of crime right out in the open. As if the reasons for hiding sins had been stripped away.

So far, we hadn't seen any reports of strange beings, but there was no question the Kruen we'd seen breaking through the two realms were responsible.

Pax searched for a route on his phone, and I could feel him scouting around within himself, looking for his own lure. For the power inside him to discern where to go. "Take I-84," he finally said. "We need to make a pit stop first. There's a camping and hunting store three blocks up. We need supplies."

Disquiet whirled around us.

From the opposite direction, three cop cars approached at high speed. Red and blue lights flashed, and their sirens blared.

Dani pulled off to the side of the road, and we were all silent as they whizzed by.

An ambulance and fire truck came from the west, crossing at the intersecting road and continuing in that direction.

We held our breaths as the world spun out of control around us.

Once they had all passed, Dani mumbled, "That is, if there is even a store left," before she pulled back onto the road.

# Chapter Forty

## PAX

I'd spent most of my life stealing from the scum that wandered the earth. Pillaging what they had stolen. Money they'd attained through whatever vile, heinous crimes they preferred to commit. Feeding their wickedness into the population.

Drugs and prostitution.

Thieving and deceiving.

Exploiting the vulnerabilities of others to sustain their greed.

Had sworn to myself that I would only ever take from the ones who had taken, but I'd never imagined that it would come to this—and some things just had to be done for the greater good.

Besides, I doubted any of these businesses would remain standing for much longer if something wasn't done.

If we didn't find a way to intervene.

To stop the madness that had so clearly infiltrated the world.

There was just this vibe pervading reality.

A lawlessness that had merged with the oxygen. So distinct I could scent the evils that coursed through the atmosphere, wisping and winding as they sought to lay siege.

Dani flew into the nearly empty parking lot at warp speed, her little car tilting to the left as she curb-checked the back wheel. The tires skidded as she cut across the lot, not taking the time to follow the aisles.

I sat forward, and from over her right shoulder, I pointed at the narrow lane between two stores that would lead around to the back of the building. "Go in down the side right there."

Dani jerked the steering wheel, and the car whipped to the right as she took it fast. She barreled between the two buildings, the thick gray bricks of the walls blurring by on each side.

The second she rounded the corner at the rear of the building, she skidded to a stop.

I threw open my door and jumped out. Timothy was quick to follow, slamming his door shut and rounding to the trunk.

I thumped my hand against the top of it.

Dani popped it, and I dug around on the right side, where I'd stuffed a crowbar I'd seen on a workbench in her garage.

I tossed it up, testing its weight.

"That going to be enough?" Speculation lifted Timothy's brow.

"It's gonna have to be." I strode over to the door as I felt Aria climbing out from her side. Both she and Dani ran up on their toes like they needed to remain covert, when we were assuredly getting ready to let the whole fucking neighborhood know we were there.

Right at where the lock was located on the door, I stuffed the crowbar into the tiny gap between the doorjamb.

I pulled with everything I had.

Metal bit against metal, a high-pitched groaning that pierced through my head as I put all my weight into it, teeth gritting as I tried to break the fucking industrial lock.

Even in the cold of the winter morning, sweat instantly beaded on my forehead and slid down my back.

I kept trying to work it, moving it up and down the slot, throwing myself against it.

It didn't budge.

Timothy jumped in and gripped the end of the rod. Grunts rocked out of each of us as we tried to force it open.

"Come on, man," he said through clenched teeth. "We need to get this bastard open."

Could feel Aria itching. Her attention wandering the area, watching for anyone who would notice what was going down.

"Hurry," Dani said.

We pushed harder; then I felt the shift. The force of Aria's presence as she came up between us. She placed her left hand on my shoulder, and with the other she reached out and grabbed hold of the rod, too.

A bolt of energy suddenly streaked down the metal, and the lock popped with a small boom.

Timothy chuckled under his breath. "Now, why the hell didn't we think of that in the first place?"

We didn't have time to contemplate it, because the second the door burst open, the siren started shouting.

Deafening.

Disorienting.

Lights flashed from the ceiling, doing their best to chase us out, like we hadn't been expecting their welcome.

"Hurry. We won't have much time before someone shows," I growled.

Unless the authorities were too busy dealing with all the alarms that no doubt were going off all over the city.

"We've got this," Timothy said, and he snatched Dani's hand and made a beeline up the aisle, heading in the direction we'd already planned.

Any weapons we could find were going to be at the back of the store.

Dani and Timothy were assigned to knives and bows.

I grabbed Aria's hand. The heat of her slashed up my arm the second we connected, a jolt to my heart. A zing reminding me that we had to do whatever was required to see this through.

"This is insane," she wheezed as we sprinted down the aisle.

"I know, baby. That's what happens when the world goes crazy."

I hooked a left at the end of the aisle. Releasing Aria, I snatched two big duffel bags displayed on an endcap and tossed her one.

"You can do this," I shouted above the blaring, feeling the bleak desperation that poured out of her. The siren was so loud that it thundered our pulses into chaos. Doing its best to drive us out.

"I know. We have to," she said as we broke apart.

I ran straight for the glass cases that displayed a bunch of handguns. But what I was interested in was the wall of rifles on the other side.

The area was blocked off, only intended for whatever employee worked this section.

I planted my hands on the top of the case and used it to propel myself over, while Aria rushed to a tall display case where a ton of ammo was displayed off to the side. I could feel her frustration when she found it was locked, and she spun around, searching for something she could use to bust it open.

Relief gushed out of her when she saw what she was looking for, and she ran two aisles down to where mallets used to drive in tent posts were set up on an endcap.

She grabbed one and came hurtling back up to the case. She swung it back, then smashed it through the pane.

Glass shattered, crashing onto the floor at her feet.

I could feel her frenzy as she searched for the specific bullets I'd instructed her to get, a full disorder pummeling the air as she frantically stuffed them into the bag.

While my gaze scanned, then pinpointed a bunch of rifles that fit the ammo.

I snagged the wire cutters from my back pocket, and I was quick to cut through the small wire ropes that attached the guns to the wall. I tossed the duffel onto the counter behind me, and I loaded in as many as would fit in the bag.

Then I turned to the case behind me, bashing it in with the butt of a rifle and grabbing as many of the handguns inside that I could.

Timothy and Dani came running up, weighed down with the huge duffels they'd filled. "We got everything," Timothy rushed, his chest heaving with his breaths.

"Good." I zipped up my bag just as Aria was zipping hers. "Let's get the hell out of here."

The four of us raced back out of the store.

Relief slammed us the second we stepped outside, the earsplitting blare of the alarm cut to a dull roar.

Only we were hit with the peals of sirens coming from not that far in the distance.

I inclined my ear toward the sound.

Fuck.

It was coming from the other side of the building, and getting closer with each second.

"Hurry!" I shouted, and I tossed my bag into the trunk. Dani tossed me hers and I caught it, throwing it in as she ran to the driver's seat and turned over the ignition. Timothy flung his on top and rushed to his seat.

Gasps raked out of Aria as she shoved her bag on top of the pile.

"Is it going to fit?" she begged as I tried to slam it shut.

A curse ripped off my tongue when it didn't latch.

"Just get in the car, Aria," I grated as I tried to compress the bags, and she wavered for one beat before she hurried around and dove in.

Jumping up, I tossed myself onto the trunk and used my weight to slam it down.

Relief gushed out of me when it finally caught.

Though that relief didn't last long, because I could hear the roar of the cruiser, and it was coming down the same cut-through we'd taken to get back here.

Adrenaline pumped through my bloodstream, and I ran, diving headfirst into the back seat of the car.

"Go, go, go, go!" I shouted.

Dani rammed on the accelerator before I was even fully inside. The tail of the car swung hard as she hooked a sharp right into the high grass that grew up along the back lot of the shopping center.

We bounded down into a drainage ditch with at least half a foot of water running through it. The water split in two and splashed up on the sides as the little car tore through it.

I finally managed to sit upright and drag my door shut as she flew up the other side, wheeling a left as she took an alley that ran along the backside of a fence that closed in the yards of the houses in a neighborhood on the opposite side.

None of us dared to even breathe as she took three more sharp turns, then looped back onto the road.

I finally chanced a look behind us through the back window, and I heaved out a sigh and rushed shaky fingers through my hair when I saw it was clear.

"Is anyone following us?" Dani's words were abraded as she glanced at me through the rearview mirror.

"No. You lost them."

Deliverance poured out of her on a wheeze, and Timothy reached over and clamped a hand down on her thigh. "Damn, my girl is a badass. Not that I didn't already know it."

Pink hair whipped everywhere as she shook her head. "What are you even talking about? Total computer nerd over here."

"Who must have been playing a slew of those driving games." He gave her a waggish grin.

She choked on her amusement, the sound hitching with the stress that still clamored through our bodies. "Never."

"Does that mean you always drive like this?" Aria asked. A hint of a smile kissed the edge of her mouth as she struggled to steady her own breaths.

Dani giggled. "But of course."

Timothy let go of an unrestrained laugh. "You should have seen her the other night when we were coming after you, Aria. She was not about to waste a second. I might have lost consciousness once or twice from the G's she was pulling."

A chuckle rolled out of me. I couldn't believe he was joking in the middle of this, but I appreciated it more than he knew.

I sank back into the seat, struggling to tame the way the blood slogged through my veins.

"Shit," I finally forced out, the word heaving from my lungs like a thousand-pound weight I was shucking, and I scrubbed both palms over my face as I tipped my attention to the roof of the car. "Wasn't sure we were going to make it out of there without cuffs slapped around our wrists."

Timothy fully shifted around so he could look back at me, an arrogant smile pulled onto his face. "O ye of little faith. How could you have ever doubted us? Our beautiful Dani here is not the only badass around—our whole crew obviously has mad skills."

Then he sobered as he glanced between the three of us. "A good fucking team is what we are."

I caught Aria's eye as she reached over and threaded her fingers through mine, and she locked sight with Dani through the rearview mirror before she turned her attention to Timothy and gave him a nod of agreement.

"Yeah," I added. "We're a good fucking team."

We had to be.

Because it was one we were staking all our lives upon.

# Chapter Forty-One

## ARIA

We'd been driving for more than five hours.

We'd crossed into Idaho and the scenery had become the most desolate stretch of road that we had traveled since Pax and I had first come together, and we'd spent more hours than I could count driving roads where it felt as if we might be the only ones on them. The houses and small towns that had been sporadically placed along our routes.

The rare cars and trucks we encountered during that time had made it feel as if we'd been secluded from the rest of the world.

Maybe lifted and elevated above it.

For a few moments, given a reprieve from the dangerous force that had tracked us for weeks.

This was an entirely different sensation, though, driving toward the danger we could feel compelling us forward. A danger that grew thicker and more menacing with each mile that passed.

The few moments of levity we'd found when we sped out of Portland had quickly evaporated.

In their place was something ominous.

A foreboding that crowded overhead as the terrain blurred by through the windows we each warily watched from. A river had followed us nearly the entire way, weaving along the side of the highway as we cut through the low range of mountains that appeared more like hills than anything else.

The knolls and rises nearly void of trees.

A landscape of snow-covered fields that had rolled on forever, the same as the heavens seemed to roll overhead. Laden with heavy clouds that hung low from the sky.

For a hundred miles or so outside Portland, the clouds had at least been pale gray, rimmed in fiery whites from the sun, which struggled to shine from behind them.

Though now, that light had lapsed.

The clouds growing denser the farther we got from the city. Every ounce of the sun obstructed as a storm had gathered from every direction, sitting heavy on the horizon.

Amassing as the clouds thickened.

Their bellies bloated and bulging, sending darkness curling over the earth.

Dimming the air in an omen we could taste.

It felt as if my spirit was being crushed by it. Flattened and mangled by the ugly, unbearable weight. Though something within me flailed to break out from under it, urging me toward the destination where we were being called.

I glanced down at my phone, warring before I tapped out another message to my mom. I'd texted her that morning to make sure they were fine and encouraged her to stay inside for the day without giving any real details.

She'd promised they would.

But I still couldn't settle.

Me: Is everyone inside and safe?

It took a second for a return message to blip through.

Mom: Yeah, we're all here. Locked inside. Except for your father. I did text him and asked him to lay low as well.

I could feel her love for him amid the wounds my father had carved deep inside her.

Me: That's good. I'm glad you did. Is it . . .

I hesitated before I finished the thought.

Me: Do things feel normal there?

Mom: I wouldn't call it normal. We turned on the news. A ton of tragic things are happening. I mean, there always seem to be a ton of horrible things happening. But this is entirely different.

A moment passed before another text came through. I didn't need to hear her voice to feel her terror.

Mom: What is going on, Aria?

Pax peered my way, his concern patent as I wavered with what to give my mother. I didn't want to freak her out or scare her unnecessarily. But this was too urgent to tiptoe around. I glanced at him, my chest compressing in the love that I had for them all.

With this hope I couldn't let go of, no matter how much it felt as if we were traveling toward destruction.

I turned back to my phone, fingers trembling as I gave the only answer I could.

Me: This battle we've been fighting has become something greater than any of us have ever known. We are trying to stop it, but I have no idea what is going to happen today. So please be careful. Stay inside for as long as possible. And know how much I love you and I'm fighting for you. For all of you.

A car suddenly whizzed by at high speed on my side, even faster than we were traveling, snapping up my attention.

A blip of black that flew past in a blink.

A few minutes later there was another.

Then another, and another.

It felt as if they were coming out of the nothingness that surrounded us.

I exhaled a shaky breath, and Pax shifted uncomfortably in his seat. Agitation eating him alive as he was forced into waiting.

"Do you think we're going the right way?" Dani asked into the tension as she gaped out the windshield, hands tight on the steering wheel, which I was sure was slicked with sweat.

The question was choppy and didn't need an answer, but Timothy rumbled, "Don't think we could even force ourselves to go anywhere else."

The sky toiled above, roiling over a lake that appeared to the left of the freeway. The water, which should have glistened, was covered in a dingy bleakness. A few spots of colored lights flashed in the distance, no question ambulances and police cars responding to pleas for help.

Because I could feel it—the cold slick that slipped over the surface of my skin.

The evil of Faydor.

"It's close," Pax grunted from beside me.

The air shifted, and harsh gusts of wind began to blow across the hills.

Harsh gales that seemed as if they might toss the car from the road.

Dani fought against it, trying to stay in her lane.

A semitruck bowled up from behind us, coming from out of nowhere, careening by in the other lane.

Fear clutched my chest when it suddenly cut back to the right and its trailer swept into our lane.

"Dani!" I shouted in warning, and she slammed on the brakes and jerked the steering wheel to the right.

Rumble strips roared in our ears as we hit the shoulder, and the tail end of her car skidded back and forth. Hands fisting around the wheel, she managed to steady it and pull back into the lane behind the truck.

"Shit. What the hell is that asshole doing?" Timothy wheezed before he cut his attention to Dani. "Are you okay?"

Her nod was wobbly, her attention fully trained out the windshield. "Yeah. I just . . . I don't know how to navigate in this. It's all . . . so new."

*Terrifying* was what she meant.

"I know, baby," he said. "It's going to be all right. We've got this team surrounding us, remember?"

The truck never slowed as it barreled deeper toward the darkness that loomed ahead. Toward the cloud bank that convulsed and smoldered, appearing as if it would consume everything in its path.

Flashes of lightning struck within its blackened depths.

Blinding flares that burst in front of our eyes.

"This shit is wild," Timothy muttered as it built and compounded over the top of us.

Pax only shifted closer to me, as if he could be a shroud of protection for whatever was coming.

Rain began to pelt us from the sky. Large droplets that suddenly turned to sharp spikes of ice that pinged against the windshield.

The sound grew louder and louder as hail began to pound, the sky spitting out what amounted to small rocks. They slammed against the car, so hard they bashed dents into the metal.

I cringed with each impact that battered the car. My lungs tight, my stomach twisting in the dread that churned through me as we approached our destination.

The chaos I'd felt coming for so long was right there.

Winding and whipping right in front of us.

A magnet.

Gravity.

I thought we could all feel it.

The consuming presence that overwhelmed. The darkness that reigned. The evil that silently intoned.

Beckoning anyone who would listen.

More cars flew past, some erratically, weaving back and forth across the lanes, and others seemed to wield caution.

"Get off the freeway at the next exit." Pax's voice was gravelly, carved in apprehension as he studied the map. "There's one in two miles. Merge onto that intersecting freeway on the left, then take the next exit on the right. There's a town about half a mile off the interstate where a couple roads juncture."

I could hear Dani gulp around the thickness in her throat. "I'll get us there."

But it was what we'd face once we arrived that chained us in trepidation. What slicked our skin in cold sweat and thundered our hearts into disorder. I swore that I could hear each of them—the hearts of this family.

The violent thrumming that thrashed within us.

It only increased when the exit came into view and Dani flicked on her blinker. Five cars exited in front of us. It was then that the train of headlights and taillights on the same route came into view.

A slew of cars barely creeping along as we merged onto the other freeway.

Dani didn't let it sway her. She pulled out around the traffic onto the left shoulder, and she sped up the freeway to where there was a gap in the cars. She cut into it and sped across two lanes to the second exit.

The traffic was fully stopped there, and Dani slammed on her brakes behind a pickup truck.

Her attention darted back and forth, searching for a clear path. "What do we do?"

"Since you're no stranger to off-roading, I'd suggest right there." Timothy pointed at what looked to be a pasture off to our right, down a steep incline and surrounded by a barbed-wire fence.

Dani hesitated for a beat before she threw her car into reverse, pulled back enough so she could make it out from behind the truck, then shouted, "Hang on!" as she rammed it into drive and floored it.

Pax curled himself around me as we flew, barreling down the sharp embankment. A shout ripped out of Dani as we raced toward the fence.

Metal pinged as we busted through the barrier.

Our gasps were harsh as we jolted forward, the tires peeling out and flinging dirt as we wheeled over the field.

We'd made it halfway across when Dani slammed on her brakes. We all stared, panting, the engine running and the headlights spearing the darkness that had crawled over the earth.

A forged eclipse.

None of us were able to move.

Frozen beneath the sight that writhed right over the very center of the town in the distance. Maybe a mile away.

The clouds boiled and seethed. Churning and twisting with depravity.

Whirring and whirring in a vicious cyclone that gusted across the land.

And in the middle of it was a crack.

The same fissure Pax and I had stumbled on last night.

And every sort of Kruen crawled out from it, clinging to the clouds before they dropped to the ground below.

# Chapter Forty-Two

## ARIA

All four of us clicked our doors open at the same time and climbed out of the car.

Frigid air gusted across the field. It was a chill that sank straight to the bone as spikes of razor-sharp rain pelted our flesh.

Each of us hung on to the top of our door as we peered up at the calamity that had been waiting for us.

This reality was something I'd prayed would never come to fruition. But I think I'd known the entire way here that we were going to be met with the impossible.

With the horrible.

I could feel the disbelief radiating from my family as we gaped up at where the sky was split open over the center of the small town in Idaho that I doubted many had even heard of, though now it would earn the most significant title.

The birthplace of the end of the world.

Because hopelessness shuddered through my being as I looked up at the onslaught of Kruen that continued to pour into this plane.

"Fuck," Timothy breathed.

The sight confirmed everything we'd feared when we saw the Kruen broach the barrier of the realms, their tendrils lashing out as they'd fed their degeneracies into the men who'd come for me.

This would be a massacre.

An absolute, complete massacre that would spread out to infect every inch of the world.

Tortured screams cleaved through the air, carried on the wind to taunt our ears.

"I can't believe this," I finally whispered. Tears blurred my eyes as I succumbed to what the surety of this meant.

There was no way the four of us could defeat them. No way we could stop them. And I was sure, in that instant, that the cars that had raced to this town had been called here for a single purpose.

Their drivers were going to be used as vessels for the Kruen. I should have known it then, that night when I'd thought I'd seen the monsters rippling beneath the men's flesh as they surrounded us.

"We can't lose hope," Dani murmured, trying to keep the trembling from her voice. She looked back at me, her big eyes wide and despairing. "We can't."

"I'm not giving up." Just because our fate was likely sealed didn't mean I wasn't going to fight until my final breath.

Pax met my gaze from over the roof of the car. White flames glinted in the depths of his eyes. My chest expanded. And I remembered his words from when we'd first met in person. How he'd already believed in his purpose—that he'd been sent to give his life for mine.

And I wanted to save it.

His.

Ours.

Everyone's.

From here to the next existence.

But how could we overcome this?

I shifted when I somehow felt the movement off to my left, and I scanned through the dim haze that coated the air, looking out into the dead, high grass that covered the field.

Alarm pitched through my body and adrenaline thudded through my veins in a convulsion of trepidation when I saw a man coming up through the pasture, pushing through the grass as he made his way toward the town in the distance beyond where we'd stopped.

Drawn that way.

There were more behind him. It appeared a ton of people had abandoned their vehicles in the gridlock that remained on the main road and were going on foot.

Emerging behind the cars and coming in our direction.

"Aria, get back in the car," Pax growled. "You need to stay away from these bastards until we can figure out what's going on."

But I was frozen.

Stuck as the man got closer and I was finally able to make out his face. But it wasn't his face that had me riveted to the spot.

No.

I'd never seen him before.

It was his eyes that burned through the chaos.

The palest gray eyes, which were wild and confused as he trudged across the damp ground.

"Oh my God." It whimpered out of me when I came to recognition.

"Do you see him, Aria?" Uncertainty filled Dani's murmured question, and she sent me a look of disbelief. One of shock.

"Laven," Timothy said from his position.

But he wasn't from our family.

The man seemed to cower, slowing his approach when he realized we were staring at him. Emitting turbulence and fear. His brow knitted in something between solace and grief when a stake of his own recognition seemed to strike him.

Though he remained there, wavering, unsure.

Worried it was a trap.

A loud explosion suddenly erupted from the middle of town. A shock wave blistered through the air and trembled the ground.

A yelp ripped from Dani, and we all dropped to our knees to take cover as a bulbous plume of fire rolled high into the heavens. Lighting everything up for one disturbing beat, our vision going red and our skin glowing with the heat.

Terror rebounded as a slew of screams carried on the gusts of wind.

Moisture burned at the back of my eyes, and my nails sank into the damp dirt below as I tried to catch my breath. To press out the panic that threatened to keep me pinned as ash rained down, turning pasty as it mixed with the icy rain.

Pax was suddenly right there, curling an arm around me where I was hunched at the side of the car.

"Are you hurt?" His hands rushed over me, palms smoothing as they shook, searching to see if I'd sustained any injuries.

"No." I gulped. "I'm fine."

Timothy remained low as he scurried around the car to get to Dani, whose breaths heaved as she whimpered through the bedlam.

"Is everyone okay?" Pax hollered.

"Yeah. Just startled. Don't think any of us are prepared on how to handle this shit," Timothy replied.

The man we'd seen lumbering through the field was suddenly right there, staying low as he came toward us, crying, "What's happening? Are you . . . ? Oh my God, are you Laven? How are you here?"

Twisting out of Pax's hold, I forced off the trepidation as I faced the man. Revealing to him the distinction of my eyes.

A gasp choked out of him, and he ripped at his hair, mumbling, "I have to be losing my goddamned mind. What is happening? I don't . . ."

"We are Laven. All of us." I stretched a hand toward him. "It's okay."

He warred for another second before he scrambled the rest of the way to us, remaining crouched down as he warily looked between us.

"You're a Laven. And you came?" It flooded from me on raspy astonishment.

We weren't the only ones being called to this place. There were others.

A spark of faith flickered within me, coming to life when the hopelessness had nearly trampled it out.

My gaze rushed over our surroundings, finding more and more people wandering through the fields.

Laven.

They were here, as disoriented and confused as they were drawn.

The man in front of me frantically shook his head. "I couldn't not. I had this twisted dream three nights in a row, something telling me that I had to do something. Demanding that I get up and move. It was like there was some kind of rope attached to me and I had no choice but to follow where it was pulling me."

"We had the same," I told him.

Disbelief puffed from his mouth, and he roughed a hand through his hair, which was as white as Pax's. The man was probably in his early forties, wearing jeans and a tee and a thin rain jacket. A large scar marred his right cheek, and another sliced through his left brow.

"And what the hell did we come to? I don't understand what's happening."

My throat was thick as I hurried to explain, "The Kruen have broken through the realms. They're here, which we believe makes them much stronger than when they're only feeding wickedness from above. There's a man . . . Ambrose . . . He used to be a Laven, but he betrayed his Nol and earned immortality through Kreed. He's been ruling in Faydor but has also been walking on Earth, and now, he wants to rule here."

"And why are *we* here?" The words trembled from his lips.

Pax stood, rising up to his full height, hands curled into fists. "To stop it."

"Stop it?" Skepticism creased the man's brow.

"Yeah, we're going to stop him. End this piece of shit now. End them all," Pax gritted.

Pax moved to the trunk. "We need to move. Get closer and make a plan." He thumped the metal. "Can you open the trunk, Dani?"

"Yeah." She shifted around, still on her knees as she reached in and pushed the button to release it. The trunk popped open, and Pax started taking out the bags we had piled inside and dropping them onto the ground.

I rose, too, a frenzy pulsing through me as I realized what was happening, the sensation urging me to move.

Valeen had sent an army. We weren't alone.

Her voice drifted through my mind.

*"Rise up, dear Valient. You are the chosen. You must lead."*

*You must lead.*

I wasn't alone.

I was only meant to lead. To stand and to guide. Another vessel in the midst of this war.

A charge I was going to fully give myself over to.

My hands shook as I moved to Pax, who'd bent over and unzipped one of the duffels, though he straightened when he felt me come to stand beside him.

He slipped his hand onto my cheek. His palm burned with our connection as he stared across at me. Every brutal edge of his face seemed to sharpen, his words coarse as he forced them from his tongue. "You have the power to do this, Aria. We wouldn't be here if you didn't. None of these people would be."

"*We* have the power," I said, emphasis lining my voice. "All of us. Together."

Those eyes flashed—pure, burning flames—and he threw himself forward and captured my mouth, his lips desperate as they pressed against mine.

And I swore, for one fleeting second, the darkness was swept away as he poured everything into this one singular moment.

Every oath.

Every promise.

All his love.

Then he cleared his throat and peeled himself back, though he clung to my arms as he gritted out, "Let's go get this motherfucker."

Dani, Timothy, Pax, and I all looked at each other for a moment. Taking one heartbeat for this family. A glance of eternal love and loyalty we would forever carry for one another.

Timothy finally dipped his chin and rumbled, "Let's go."

We each grabbed a bag and slung the straps of the heavy duffels over our shoulders, and we began to trudge through the high grass in the direction of the crack that hovered over the town.

The Laven man stuck close to us as we weaved across the field.

A throng of others had amassed.

An instinctual gathering as a stream of Laven made their way toward the town, heading in the same direction we were.

I could feel them coming.

Hundreds . . . maybe thousands who'd flocked from every direction and made their way toward the call that had been issued.

Strangers who'd been drawn.

Some spoke in English.

Others in different languages.

Brought here from every end of the earth.

It felt as if each of us had been inscribed on one another in some secret way. Our souls recognizing each other as wary, uncertain glances were cast. As understanding dawned and hope blossomed in the crux of the turmoil that awaited us.

The heavens continued to writhe, thrashing with insolence and the intonation of the immoral.

It only grew thicker the closer we got. Like sludge had filled the atmosphere.

The coldest chill slicked through the middle of it, gusting across our faces and whipping through our hair.

We slowed once we made it all the way across the field, our breaths heaving as we came to the fence line. On the other side was a road locked with cars. Most had been abandoned, many with their headlights still gleaming into the darkness that obliterated the day.

Beyond it was a gas station that looked as if it typically catered to semitrucks. The parking lot was large, and it now overflowed with pickups and cars that had been left at odd angles.

Huge diesel-fuel tanks were lined along the backside near the tall canopies that protected the pump stations.

And it was here that we saw the others. Those who'd been called for a different purpose from ours.

A slew of people charged through the abandoned cars and trucks.

Enraged.

Violent.

Barbaric.

Running amok on the streets as they flocked toward the crack where the Kruen crawled out from above.

My stomach toppled.

It was what I'd feared most.

Laven weren't the only ones who had been coaxed to this place.

The corrupt who had fully given themselves over to the nefarious and vile had come in scores.

We all crouched down at the fence line, taking in the scene. The complete chaos that had befallen the land, so much worse than it'd been back in Portland, though I was sure it wouldn't take long for this virus to spread.

For it to advance and expand and decimate.

"They've all gone mad," Dani whispered where she knelt at my side.

"It's what happens when there is no good left," Pax grunted as he peered out. "We've seen it time and again since we've been on the run. These monsters who give themselves over to the wickedness that possesses their minds. They'll do anything to see it through without any thought of consequence."

"Can they resist it?" she whispered, her heart bleeding out. Not wanting to harm someone who had no choice.

"I think they could if they wanted to," I whispered. "I can feel it . . . when I'm struck with the compulsion to reach out and heal, and when it's useless to try. The way it was with those men who abducted me the other night."

When the gift I'd been given became a weapon.

I could feel it smoldering inside me then. Rising up from deep within. A whisper that echoed through my spirit to fight.

Dani wavered for a moment before she seemed to come to a resolution; then she inhaled a shaky breath as she unzipped her bag and pulled out a bow. Her words were hollow as she muttered, "Well, I guess it's a good thing my parents made me do some kind of sport in high school and I picked archery. Never thought I would use it for this."

"You don't have to do anything you don't want to do," I told her.

She stood, a new ferocity taking over her expression. "Yes, Aria, I do. I owe it to the people we have always fought to protect. Now that fight just looks a little different."

She tossed the strap over her shoulder, then pulled out a quiver filled with metal-tipped hunting arrows. Her movements were quick and concise and proficient as she prepared her weapon.

Timothy did the same, pulling out a crossbow and a large knife that was sleeved, one that had a sling that hung around his waist.

Then he dug back into the bag and pulled out more, passing one to each of us.

I quickly strapped mine on.

Pax was quick to work through the guns, his actions focused and succinct as he loaded them. Then he stood, tossing two rifles onto his back and handing another to Timothy. He'd already given him instructions on how to use it on the long drive here.

"You sure you have it?" Pax asked.

"Yeah, man, I've got it—at least, the best that I can." Timothy slung the rifle onto his opposite shoulder; then Pax turned to the Laven we'd first seen who'd stuck close to us as we crossed the field.

"What's your name?" Pax asked him.

"Keith."

"You know how to shoot, Keith?"

"I've gone hunting once or twice."

"Good." Pax shoved a handgun into his chest, then packed up the rest of our things, voice clipped as he issued instructions. "Everyone, stick close. Right up to Aria's side. Our job is to protect her at all costs. She's the one who holds the power to end Ambrose. She has to get to him."

Grunts of understanding went up, and Pax gestured with his chin out toward the mayhem. "Let's do this."

He set his boot on a low rung of barbed wire, pushing it all the way to the ground and lifting the one above it to create a larger opening. Timothy ducked through, then stretched out his hand to help Dani; then Keith slipped under.

Pax's gaze met mine. One moment shared.

*Together.*

I ducked under, feeling the stir of energy curl around me as I eased over to the other side. Pax was right there, following close behind.

Then we stepped out into the madness.

# Chapter Forty-Three

## PAX

We hustled out into the bedlam that had taken control of the small town, keeping low as we weaved through the cars and trucks that had been left in the middle of the road, headlights still on and engines still running.

Doors had been left open where the slew of degenerate humans had crawled out to bend to the will of the wicked.

We slunk for the cover of the convenience store on the other side, the sky fucking alive and boiling with death above us.

A fissure ran straight through the middle of it.

From within, Kruen peered down, colossal, rising from vapor and amassing in their monstrous forms.

Their faces were void, innuendos of shape and holes for their eyes that led down into the eternal nothingness within them. A pit of darkness and despair. Fiery limbs stretching out to touch on the babel below.

They poured their inhumanities into the willing ears of the people who ransacked the streets.

Running wild. Lighting fires and bashing windows. Wielding weapons and throwing fists, unaware of who they were even attacking.

*Destroy. Destroy. Destroy.*

The vitriol being spewed wasn't even specific. It was just a command for complete destruction.

Some people's skin seemed to bubble and palpitate, red streaks lighting up beneath their flesh. No question, they were fully possessed.

"They're completely blinded. Taken," Timothy said as we crept forward, hugging the gas station wall as we did our best to keep concealed.

"Yeah. And if we don't do something to stop them, they're going to pour all of this out into the rest of the world."

Not that it already hadn't started.

Not that we hadn't seen it in the news reports and felt it the second we'd stepped out Dani's door this morning.

But it would get worse. The entire world would be given to this.

*"End her. She's the one."*

Chills lifted the hairs at the nape of my neck when I heard the command uttered from above, raining down onto the heart of a man who'd been running parallel to us.

Suddenly, he straightened, rigid for one second before he shifted course.

Rising tall as he craned his neck and peered through the dingy haze that wafted through the street.

His attention immediately landed on Aria. Aria, who started to stand like she was going to handle him. I set my hand on her shoulder. "You need to conserve your energy."

This one was on me.

I didn't even hesitate.

I stood, lifted my rifle, and shot.

Took three bullets to take the bastard down, each piercing him in the chest, his lanky, tall form rocking as he struggled to keep coming for Aria before he finally toppled to the ground.

"Holy shit," Keith said from beside me, and I sent him a glance.

One that warned him there was going to be a whole lot more of this. The threat was going to come at us from every direction.

"We need to move," I said, and we all rose a fraction, still hunched over and gliding along the wall, our breaths shallow.

*"End her. End her. She's the one."*

This one came howling on the wind, and three degenerates who'd been running toward the epicenter stalled and turned in their tracks.

Two men and a woman.

They came our way like fucking zombies or some shit.

Aria stood and released her power before I had the chance to aim and take fire again. A flash of light streaked out and slammed into them. They flew back into the wall of a building on the other side. The bricks crumbled where they struck the wall before they fell in a mangled heap on the ground.

She gasped, and I could feel the exhaustion threatening to bring her to her knees. My hand shot out, gripping her shoulder, while Dani curled her arm around her waist from the other side.

In an instant, she straightened.

Buoyed.

Fortified.

"What the fuck was that?" Keith wheezed as he stared at Aria.

"She's the one," I said, because the Kruen were fuckin' right. She was the one. The one who meant everything. To me. To all of us. The one who possessed the strength to see this through. "She's the one who was sent to save us."

"This way," Aria mumbled, and we ducked out from behind the store and ran across the street to a strip mall on the other side.

It was the same here.

Chaos reigning.

People who'd been possessed wandering around and inciting whatever misdeed they could conjure.

But Laven were in the middle of them.

Fighting them.

Physically, because they didn't possess any other power here.

One Laven woman screamed when a man suddenly pulled a knife out of the back of his jeans and thrust it into her stomach. Blood gushed when he ripped it out.

For one moment, she swayed before she fell face-first to the ground.

From behind, I clamped a hand over Aria's mouth before she could release her own scream.

A shout of grief.

Besieged by the horror.

By the atrocity being meted out right in front of our eyes.

I pulled her against me, my mouth at her ear, words grinding as I said, "I know, I know, I know. But you can't save them all."

Her spirit flailed against that, no way for her to accept it. This burden that she'd been given.

"Ambrose. Ambrose is your goal, Aria. Your target. You end him, and you end all of this."

She nodded frantically against my palm, and I released her and moved in front of the group. My attention darted in every direction to see if I could find a clear path to move deeper toward the middle of the town.

While shouts and screams lifted and rose. Explosions and gunshots. Complete mayhem.

"This way," I said when I saw a break in the swell, and the five of us cut across the road and around the side of the strip mall.

Then we all froze when we saw it.

An old man wandering across the street. His body frail as he hobbled toward a woman who stood out in the middle of the turmoil on the other side.

My fucking heart seized.

Ellis.

And he was moving toward Josephine.

"Oh my God." It was a whimper from Dani, just as Aria's spirit thrashed.

A brand-new kind of fear tore through us as we watched him stagger in her direction.

A mutant turned, the human's skin bubbling with the fire of the Kruen that writhed inside him, the monster going straight for Ellis.

"No!" Aria shouted just as a swell of protectiveness rose up inside me, so severe that it closed off my airflow.

I stepped out into the middle of the street, cold spikes of ice raining from the darkness that continued to pelt us from the sky.

"Ellis, get down!" I shouted as I lifted my gun and aimed.

He turned toward me, surprised by the call of his name, and I was running his way, throwing myself on top of him one second before the bastard got to him.

Curling my arms around him in the hope that I would protect him rather than hurt him as I took him down.

We hit the ground hard, and the second we did, two shots rang out.

One piercing the monster in the chest before the next struck him in the middle of his forehead.

He dropped to his knees, and I glanced back at where Timothy had stepped forward and taken the shots.

Relief surged between us, and the whole group came running as I carefully unwound myself from him.

Ellis.

The man who'd been my teacher for my entire life. The only real father I'd ever had.

I gripped him by both sides of his neck as he sat up. "Are you hurt?" I begged through my fear, though the words were harsh.

He nodded. "I am uninjured."

Air heaved from my lungs.

"Thank fuck."

Then Aria was there, throwing herself around him, weeping as she hugged him. "Ellis. Oh, Ellis. I can't believe it's you."

Joy rolled out to clash with the alarm as she helped him to stand.

Then the energy shifted.

A whirring of warmth that blasted through the cold as he shifted toward Josephine, who'd come three steps closer.

For a few suspended moments, the two of them just stared at each other from five feet away while the savagery raged on around them.

Josephine's stringy gray hair whipped around her weathered face. A face that was littered with a thousand scars.

The most gentle, beautiful woman. Battle worn.

The same as Ellis.

His thin, feeble frame downtrodden, flesh covered in the wounds from his years fighting the battles of Faydor.

But there was a strength beneath it.

A stoic ferocity that burned between the two of them.

Then they both stumbled forward and met in an embrace.

A fierce, unrelenting embrace as they hugged each other with the force of a thousand lives. An embrace that went on forever, no words said as they shared a moment that could only belong to them.

We surrounded them as they did, creating a barrier of protection, each of us facing out to ensure no one could get close to them.

When they finally parted, Aria and Dani moved, hugging them both and whispering their love and belief in each other.

"I can't believe you're here," Aria wheezed, the love she felt for them clogging her throat.

"We dreamed, too," Josephine told her. She didn't even need confirmation from Ellis to know that it was true.

"Many have arrived." Awe filed Ellis's voice as he stepped back, his expression carved in the wisdom he'd forever carried.

"More than we can count," Dani said. "And they're still arriving."

"Not only our family, but I would imagine from every family that can reach us," Aria added.

Emotion washed through Ellis, his nearly white gaze both pallid and uplifted.

The amount of time he'd spent believing we should be apart.

Living these meager lives in solitude. Without the ones we'd been purposed for.

He turned to Josephine.

His Nol.

And he took her hand. "Valeen has summoned us. Come, we must fight."

"It's not safe for you and Josephine to be here," I spat. "You need to take cover until this over."

It was bad enough when they fought within the bowels of Faydor. But this? This was on the plane of humanity. Where their mortal bodies could be defeated. Just as easily as that woman two minutes ago.

Ellis turned to look at me. Devotion burned in his depths. "Pax. My sweet boy. My son. We were called for a purpose. First for Faydor and now for this. And together we will fight. I will not sit it out."

"They're slaughtering." My teeth ground together as I said it.

"My life has been dedicated to humanity. To safeguarding the lives of the vulnerable. And that mission has never been more important than now."

"Ellis . . ." I pleaded, his name cracking as I said it.

"I know, Pax. I know." His nod was slow; then he turned and took Josephine's hand, and she shifted to slant a glance at me from over her shoulder.

Knowing.

Adoring.

Determined.

"We need to keep moving," Timothy said, turning in a circle, his gun lifted but aimed toward the ground a few feet in front of him as he kept threats at bay.

Hesitation brimmed in me, but Aria reached out and threaded her fingers through mine, her touch both gentle and firm as she looked at me with those eyes. Eyes that shone with her own wisdom.

This was a call for all of us, and I had no right to try to sway Ellis and Josephine from heeding it.

I gulped around the impulse to argue and instead squeezed her hand.

My own surrender.

*Together.*

Timothy passed large hunting knives to both Ellis and Josephine. "You're going to need a weapon."

The dip of their heads was succinct.

Accepting.

"This way," I said, and I gestured toward a large industrial building across the road. We kept low, hiding ourselves in the shadows as people continued to pour down the street from the fracture that roiled in the distance, held in a constant barrage of lightning strikes and thunder.

The ground trembled with each, sending tremors underfoot.

A gush of wind rolled over the top of us, so strong that we slowed, hunching our bodies against a frigid squall we could hardly move through.

Wicked voices intoned within it.

*"She's the one."*

*"Stop her."*

*"End her."*

At least twenty-five of the wicked who were streaming toward the crater stopped in their tracks. Shifting course. Craning their necks as they felt for her.

As if they could sense her presence.

No question, they could, the way they suddenly turned and came running our way.

A whole herd of the deranged.

Crazed as they screeched with bloodlust. Their faces contorted with perversion.

"No more hiding. It's time to fight this shit out," Timothy said, and he stepped out first, taking aim and firing. He hit one at the front of the pack, sending the asshole flailing backward.

It tripped up two others, who struggled to get back to their feet.

I did the same, lifting and firing as we all moved in their direction.

Taking them head-on.

I fired quickly, taking three down.

A woman broke from the pack and came sailing for Aria, her voice shrill as she hissed, "End her. She's the one. He will be pleased."

Aggression burned through me. The need to protect.

But I didn't have time to shoot before Dani had lifted her bow and set an arrow free.

It arced through the air and skewered the fiend in the center of the chest.

A shrill scream ripped out of her as she dropped to the ground.

We kept firing, taking them down one by one.

Ellis and Josephine faced the other way, swishing blades outward toward anyone who made it far enough to get around us.

Only they seemed to multiply, more gathering around us with each one we defeated.

*"End her. End her."*

I popped off a shot at an old man who was coming for her.

I swiveled, pointing at a bastard who launched himself in Aria's direction, my finger tugging at the trigger.

Fuck. I was out of ammo.

Fear gripped me by the throat when I realized I wasn't going to get to him in time—until an arrow flew through the air.

Dani, striking him through the shoulder.

But we were surrounded.

The crowd surging. So thick it was nearly impossible to hold them back. The mayhem so fucking loud it was confounding. People everywhere, fucking flying and dropping. Ravaging and protecting.

"Aria, we need you," I gritted out as I struggled to reload as quickly as I could.

"I know," she wheezed, and I could feel her focus.

Could feel her gathering the strength required to garner another surge of that energy.

Another piece of shit slashed a knife as he came toward her.

"Aria," I shouted, finally getting the mag loaded into the gun, but not before he was right there, two feet in front of her, when another shot rang out.

A bullet pierced him in the temple and sent him reeling sideways.

I looked in the direction of where the shot had come from, and Keith gave me a dip of his chin in acknowledgment before he took aim at others.

Ellis and Josephine pressed their backs up against Aria as they kept her shielded on the opposite side, and Aria ducked her head and pulled from their power as they poured what they had into her.

"Get down!" Aria suddenly shouted, and we all ducked when she released it. A blinding shock wave of light blistered out, cutting through the horde that amassed around us.

It sent every piece of shit surrounding us sailing backward.

Bodies flew high through the air, their shouts of rage climbing into the atmosphere and echoing through the false night before they were extinguished when they slammed into whatever surface they met. Walls crumbled and collapsed with the impact.

The road and sidewalks fractured into splinters.

A shuddering of vengeance against the depraved.

Aria slumped forward the second the energy left her, and we all moved to her.

Surrounding her.

Touching her.

Protecting her.

Doing everything we could to support her in this fight.

She inhaled a shattered breath and forced herself to straighten. Those pale eyes met mine, glints of devotion in the storm. My heart clutched with it, the connection roaring between us.

We had to do this. We had to push through.

She peeled her gaze from mine and shouted, "We have to find Ambrose. Now!"

We all started running up the middle of the road, keeping a barrier around Aria as we moved. Close enough that we were touching her while still fighting off any monster that came our way.

People surged. Streams that gathered in the street and flooded toward the epicenter of the destruction.

Both Laven and the possessed.

Battles raged through the chaos that seemed hooked on one destination.

We circled Aria as we fought, making a living hedge of protection around her as we moved deeper into the turmoil. Dani fired arrow after arrow, and once her supply had been spent, she pulled out the hunting knife.

Timothy and Keith fired away, and when some asshole got too close, they would kick with their boots and physically fight them off.

Ellis and Josephine were in the throes of it, stabbing and cutting and fighting the way they did in Faydor.

Without reservation.

A woman grabbed hold of Josephine's long hair. Vileness oozed from the woman's mouth. "You're one of them. You must die. We must end you all."

Josephine whirled around, knocking the woman back before she drove her knife between two of her ribs.

The woman's eyes widened, glowing red flames, before she was taken in the stampede of people, her lifeless body trampled underfoot.

Disbelief battered me, my entire body burning with the exertion. My spirit screaming with the compulsion to see this through.

We couldn't falter.

We were in such a crush that it became difficult to shoot, so I pulled the machete Timothy had given me from the sheath at my side.

I lifted it and began to strike. Slashing across the riot of bodies that fought to get to us.

Blade slicing through each vile fiend we passed.

Grunts of pain and shrieks of barbarity pierced through the frigid air that seemed to have come alive around us.

Spikes of ice still pelting us from above.

While the circle defending Aria seemed to grow, Laven coming together to create a larger circle that pressed farther down the road.

It was as if they instinctively felt it. Knew what they were supposed to do.

And the sky continued to swirl and rotate above us, growing denser with each second that passed. The crack made through the two worlds seemed to enlarge, splintering with the number of Kruen that continued to escape the confines of Faydor.

The Kruen weren't just possessing the humans who'd come in their wicked acquiescence.

They were taking form and shape on the ground. Manifesting as the Kruen we fought on the other plane.

Beasts that were at least seven feet tall. Their flesh blackened to char, though the evil was visible, thudding through their veins.

Red, fiery streaks pumped beneath the gore.

Their faces were contorted and gnarled, mouths mangled and disfigured, stretched wide to bare sharp, jagged teeth.

While the incantations whipped and whirred, coming from each of them as they raced into the disorder, chanting, "She's here, she's here. End her. End them all."

"Kruen." I felt the breath of the word that Aria exhaled rather than heard it. But I also felt the light burning inside her, rising higher and higher as we continued to battle our way toward the fracture above.

"It's happening," Dani cried above the din as she dashed the hunting knife at the toil of barraging people.

Panic infiltrating.

The horrible reality of this bleeding from her in her cries.

"They're here. They're real."

"Don't lose ground, Dani," Timothy shouted, his grunts hard and palpable as he slashed his own machete across the neck of a man who'd lunged for him. "Remember why we're here. You know what we're meant for, baby. We've got this."

People fell all around us.

Both Laven and the abhorrent.

And our circle became larger and larger, growing in strength and magnitude as the torrent of people undulated closer and closer to the magnet that pulled us all toward our destination.

The fissure.

Up ahead, Kruen began to run rampant through the mass.

Tossing people out of their way, rising high as they slashed with fiery tendrils, unconcerned who was in their path, though it was clear *exactly* who they were trying to get to.

"Oh God," Aria said as we pushed our way through the havoc. "We have to find Ambrose. There's too many of them to fight off. We have to get around them, cause a distraction somehow."

She closed her eyes for a beat before they whipped open with a new severity. "Keep pressing forward. He's here . . . I can feel him."

A loud engine suddenly roared over the commotion, and shouts of terror echoed over the crush before it was riddled with cries of pain.

"What the fuck is that?" Timothy bellowed, turning a worried glance my way.

I struggled to see over the heads of the people.

My heart sank like a rock to the pit of my stomach. "A tractor."

A big fucking tractor that someone was using to bulldoze the throng as it came in our direction.

Ellis slashed the belly of a woman who tried to claw at his face. Then he turned to me, belief in his eyes. "Do something."

I gulped, not wanting to leave Aria's side for a second.

"We have her," Josephine promised.

I met Aria's gaze for a beat.

An eternity.

My love pouring out before I gave a succinct dip of my chin, then ducked out of the huddle and ran for the edge of the sidewalk, where there were fewer people.

Here, the buildings were closer together, what likely amounted to their main street. The road was narrow, but angled parking spots were situated in front of the shops and restaurants.

I ran alongside them, jumping over garbage cans and flowerpots and dodging any fucker who tried to get in my way, shifting my body so I could glide around them, ignoring the assholes who were busting out windows and wreaking whatever havoc they could find.

One objective in mind.

Metal screeched as the tractor tore through the cars that had been left in the middle of the street, busting through them as well as any people in his way, both Laven and the deranged.

A man sat at its helm, his skin bubbling and blistering, appearing as if he were getting ready to explode. Nothing but evil twisted his malicious face, no thoughts other than the one that had taken over his mind.

*"End her."*

*"End her."*

I could almost hear it radiating from his spirit. Crawling out of the vile depths of his being.

I was not going to let that happen.

I finally made it far enough up the sidewalk that the tractor was nearly parallel to me.

It was old, the color a faded yellow with a big metal scoop attached to the front, no tires but instead those giant metal tracks that marred the ground.

Thank fuck there was no cage on it to protect the driver.

Turning on my heel, I began to run toward it. Winding between two degenerates who were so far gone they were fighting each other, I jumped onto the hood of a car in front of me and used it to propel myself over the heads of the fiends who writhed around the tractor.

I landed with an *oomph* on the back fender that covered one of the enormous metal tracks.

I didn't hesitate to throw myself on the bastard's back, knife drawn and ready to drag it across his throat.

But he flailed. Motherfucker was stronger than I was prepared for. He pushed to standing, and he swung me left to right as he dug his nails into my forearms.

Adrenaline surged, aggression curling through me as I tried to hang on. To end this monster, another who would do anything to hurt the one person who meant everything to me.

The one who meant everything to humankind.

Everything depended on her survival.

And that love poured out with the hate. With the violence that thrashed inside me. "You piece of shit. I'm going to end you," I growled in his ear.

"No, she's mine. She's mine."

He roared, a sound that wasn't human, a booming of the Kruen that reigned inside him. He clawed at me, and I fought, trying to tighten my hold, but he managed to rip my arms free.

With a bellow of rage, he tossed me off.

I flew backward.

I fought to regain my balance on the small metal platform when I landed, but the momentum was too great, and I tumbled over the backside. I barely caught myself before I fully hit the ground, elbows hooked on the metal frame of the tractor and my feet dragging on the pavement behind me.

I fought it.

Fought with all the strength I possessed, reminding myself of my purpose.

Of the one thing I'd been sure of when I'd first sought Aria out.

I'd accepted it from the beginning.

My fate already sealed.

I would gladly give my life if it meant she got to live.

If there was a chance for peace and harmony.

Something better than this horror that had become our lives.

Something better than the horror that had become this world.

Muscles straining with the effort, I clawed my way back up. No doubt, the driver had believed me long gone and was back to focusing his ill intent on plowing through the cars and people in his way.

And I could see them just up ahead.

The ring that surrounded Aria.

At least a hundred Laven, who had gathered around her to create a barrier of protection.

Gratitude squeezed my chest in a fist. A sudden overwhelming thanksgiving that almost made me want to weep.

I could feel their goodness radiating against the evil that encircled them.

As they moved below the cover of foulness that churned and swelled over them.

The ones who walked in darkness.

Willing to sacrifice everything.

And I knew I stood in those ranks.

I would give it all.

Without giving the fucker the time to anticipate my return, I fisted a handful of his hair and jerked his head back, and I dragged the knife across his throat before he even knew I was there. Blood gushed, and I tossed him off the seat.

He toppled off the side of the tractor, just another monster getting consumed by the swarm.

I jumped into his seat, and I fumbled around to find the brake, hitting it hard once I did.

The tractor ground to a halt.

A couple of the demented tried to climb onto the tractor in their hunger to get to the wicked destination they were heading toward, and I stood, kicking them off as they scrambled to get on from all sides.

Then they were right there, twenty feet in the distance.

Aria and the rest.

Nothing but a living, thriving ring.

Aria caught my eye from the middle of it.

Energy crackled. Riding between us on a keening bow. Invisible but so bright it was blinding. A mark forever written on my soul.

Hope blazed from her.

Belief.

Faith.

Conviction.

I swore she scored it into me, and I turned and sat back on the seat. I gripped the old gearshift, and metal groaned and protested as I tried to put it into reverse. Took me three times before I got it; then I backed up, smashing into a car behind me as I turned it around in the middle of the street.

By the time I finally got it righted and was facing the other direction, Aria and the rest had made it to me, and I began to drive the tractor up the center of the road, clearing a path as we moved up the street.

I didn't slow.

I ran right over the depraved who came sprinting my way without thought while I shouted warnings at Laven to get out of the way.

Laven who gathered and gathered, quick to come to the realization that they were meant to stand with us.

Each of us tied.

Strength in our unity.

Something that scum Ambrose had tried to keep hidden.

But that tether was too powerful between Aria and me for him to keep it bottled up. For him to keep it from us.

Because she and I? We were meant for this.

I carved a passageway for the slew of Laven who now marched together; then we all stopped when we'd made it to what appeared to be the town square.

It was a large, rambling park with an assortment of benches and a playground on the opposite side of a big, grassy circle.

The road looped around the entire area, and four roads jutted out from its juncture.

Right smack in the middle of it was a gazebo.

And the sky?

It was open directly above it.

# Chapter Forty-Four

## ARIA

I'd never seen anything so gruesome. Anything so grisly or appalling.

The atrocity greater than anything I'd ever witnessed, including what I'd seen in the minds of the Kruen as I'd fought in Faydor.

Not until this.

Pax was right.

They were slaughtering.

Slaughtering and slaying and butchering without thought.

Blood and limbs and bodies were strewn everywhere. Some had been set afire. Others moaned and begged to be relieved of their fatal wounds.

The stench of the carnage filled my nostrils and sent nausea swirling through my stomach.

But I staved it off.

We didn't have time to weep or mourn. We had to meet the brutality blow for blow.

My heart raced in the middle of it. A thunder that drummed through my spirit and rushed through my veins.

An awareness so viscous and heavy that I felt it as weights around my feet.

The wickedness that crawled this plane.

Noxious.

Toxic and foul.

A cold slick that slipped across my flesh as we moved toward the place where I knew Ambrose would be.

Josephine and Ellis held my hands as we moved within the sanctuary that had been created by the other Laven.

Their loyalty and ferocity feeding me strength.

Timothy was in front of me, and Dani was behind.

While Pax carved a path for us with the tractor up ahead.

Then everyone suddenly stopped.

Froze.

It felt as if the temperature had dropped by a thousand degrees.

Even the deranged had ceased to fight, and instead turned toward the origin of the suffocating power that held the oxygen in its cruel, vicious fist.

Pax shut the tractor off, and the loud roar of the engine was suddenly silenced.

And in it was a quiet howl.

A howling of the wind.

A howling of the wicked.

A profane whispering that curled through the air.

*"He will reign. He will reign."*

Pax hopped off the back end of the tractor and pushed his way toward me. His breaths were haggard as he stepped into my space.

Energy rushed.

Frenetic and intense.

A tether tied so deeply within us that, in this moment, we felt the same.

One.

Our fabric completely woven together.

"She is safe and whole," Josephine murmured in adoration as she released me so Pax could take her place.

"I knew that you would protect her." Pax's voice scraped with the adrenaline I could feel rushing through him in waves.

"With our lives," Ellis said.

Pax slipped up to my side where we were still hidden behind the tractor, and brand-new power streaked up my arm when he threaded his fingers through mine.

"Aria," he murmured.

A balm.

Belief.

Love.

I squeezed his hand.

"Together," I told him.

Ellis edged behind me so he could get to Josephine's opposite side. Then the four of us were linked as we held on with everything we had.

And all those who'd been summoned by the sinister suddenly broke apart and surged forward to surround the park.

In tandem, the Laven filed around the tractor, marching forward so we could see, still drawn and unable to do anything but come to stand where we had full view of the town park.

And the oxygen gushed from my lungs when I saw the depraved had dropped to their knees.

Bowing in reverence when Ambrose suddenly appeared from the shadows.

Anxiety rippled through the Laven, so severe that I thought they might scatter. Yield to the fear that crested and swelled.

But no.

They remained staunch, guarding me without anyone having told them why they should.

And my spirit wept and pleaded, begged with Valeen to give me strength. Begged that she would not have led us here if we didn't have the chance to defeat the monsters that loomed in front of us.

*Rise up; you must lead.*

Violence skated through Pax on a palpable wave, fury and rage lighting him through as he saw Ambrose standing like some kind of twisted savior on the steps of the gazebo.

Ambrose, who himself was not the same human I'd faced over the last few weeks, even though his power had been greater than any other human I'd met before him during that time.

Now his own skin had become translucent. Veins of fire twisted and twined beneath his flesh. His eyes were the same blackened holes that led down into the eternal void as the Kruen.

Eyes that led into nothing but devastation and desolation.

The sky spun above him, the clouds revolving and agitating the air into a cyclone.

Ambrose lifted his arms, and the words he emitted pulsed through the frigid atmosphere. "I have spent many years waiting for this moment. For the moment when I would stand in front of you to give you each the freedom you have been searching for. For the moment when I would get to end the mindless cycle of those who seek to stop what has been coming all along."

He stretched his arms out even wider.

"I've been waiting for this moment, when I would finally stand in front of you to lead you into a brand-new day. A brand-new life. One where we will rule together."

Then I felt the force of his gaze land on me.

Evil crawled across my skin.

"But I know that you know . . . know that you can feel it . . . that we have Valeen's chosen one in our way. She has come. Stand, my children, and bring her to me."

There was a stir of the possessed, and every single one of them returned to their feet as the charge was issued.

*Rise up; you must lead.*

Valeen's voice trickled through my mind again.

A prodding.

An urging.

*You, you are Valient.*

Valient. Power surged as I realized what it meant. The strength she'd given me to lead. I lifted my chin and shouted above the howl of the wicked, "We may fear, but we will not falter. We may be outnumbered, but we will not surrender. Look inside yourselves for strength because it is there. You possess so much more of it than you know. We are Laven, called for the good, to protect humankind, and together we will purge the wickedness that wants to consume. We will not relent or bow. Together, we will fight."

There was suddenly a new roar that deafened all ears. A shout of survival.

And one second later, all Laven burst forward and ran headlong into the wall of wickedness that had risen up to devour them.

# Chapter Forty-Five

## ARIA

Pax and I started running the same way we did in Faydor, hand in hand, directly into the war that had erupted.

In one instant, the thousands of people who'd gathered collided as they surged into battle.

Our boots pounded against the frozen ground as we launched ourselves into the mass of the depraved that rushed out to meet us.

A mix of humans who had completely lost their souls, their hearts calloused and cold, and the Kruen that had manifested in their full forms.

Metal bashed and clanged as each used whatever weapon they possessed. A riot of gunshots rang out, piercing the air as a toil of bodies swarmed and clashed.

It was chaos.

Pure, violent chaos.

Battle cries rang out, mixed with shouts and screams and pleas.

Desperation echoing through the riot that had descended.

Horror filled my heart with the sounds, that this was happening in the flesh, but I pushed myself into the tumult because it was the only thing I could do.

Pax shifted away from me for a beat so he could fire off two shots at a man and a woman who came running toward us. He hit each of them with a bullet to the chest. Their bodies convulsed as they dropped to the ground.

A Kruen was ahead of me, rising high and whipping around in my direction when he sensed I was there. Its gruesome face twisted in a snarl as its thoughts filled my ears.

*"She's the one. She's the one standing in the way. End her."*

It sped toward me rather than splitting apart and scattering into vapor to flee, the way they normally did in Faydor.

Its goal was no longer its survival, but to end me.

I gathered the same light I used when I tracked through Faydor and propelled it. A flash of energy rushed from my hands and struck the Kruen. It thrashed and wailed before it disintegrated.

Ash.

A slog of exhaustion threatened to drag me down, but I couldn't sit idle or even contemplate it before Pax shouted, "Aria, behind you!"

On a jagged exhale, I spun around to find a man rushing up from behind.

No weapon in his hands, but hate on his face.

Refusing to slow, I hurtled toward him, drawing the light and letting it go when I was within two feet of him.

It flashed through the space, and when the light struck him, his body blew backward, flying through the air before it crashed down onto two other deviants who were moving toward a Laven twenty feet away.

Each toppled, limp when they smashed to the ground.

I gasped for air, for strength, and I focused on the light that I could feel lapping inside me.

Dulled but still real.

I willed it to build. I needed to be able to wield it. Over and over. For it not to fail.

To my right, Pax warred with a slew of the corrupt, fighting them off one after another.

My attention roved over the mass that battled and raged, searching for Ambrose in the middle of it.

I had to get to him. It was the only way.

Darkness sat heavy on the earth, and the whirling clouds continued to spit spikes of ice from above. I blinked through it, trying to find the monster who no longer stood on the gazebo steps.

Frantic, I searched.

There was no sign of him.

Though what I did see sent a buoy to my spirit.

Laven.

They'd begun to pair with their Nols. Their hands bound for a few moments before they would split apart.

And they were splitting apart to bind the Kruen that battered through the horde with their tendrils whipping as they lashed out at any Laven they passed.

But the Laven were prevailing.

Throughout the crowd, I saw it. The wails and writhing of the Kruen before they were left to dust.

Annihilated.

Pax raced up to my side and grabbed my hand. A flash of warmth streaked up my arm. It rushed through me.

A stark rekindling of my strength.

"Do you see it?" I muttered in disbelief as we ran, diving toward a seething knot of people to our left. "The Laven. They're binding the Kruen in the day. While awake. Together. They just needed their Nols to be able to do it."

Because that was what we were when we joined.

Powerful.

Unstoppable.

Pax's hand tightened on mine as he exhaled a rasping breath. "You were right, Aria. You were right."

"But it's so much more than I had ever thought or imagined."

"It's why Ambrose was afraid. Why he tried to end you all those times. Why he sought to distract us and keep us from coming here," he said, voice grating from his ragged breaths. "He knew what would happen if we came together."

"But we were all drawn here anyway." It was awe. A blustering of hope swelled from the deepest parts within me.

The despair that had riddled me when I'd first seen the number of mutants drawn here was eradicated in a burst of belief.

An echo of Valeen's voice whispered in my ear, a reminder of what we'd been sent here to do.

A Kruen suddenly surged out from the mob and thundered our way.

This time, Pax just held my hand as we gathered the strength.

The light.

We released it at the same time, and the Kruen roared when it was struck before it combusted to dust.

A disbelieving laugh ripped out of me, and Pax almost smiled as we shared a look.

An understanding.

Pure awe that rippled through us before we threw ourselves back into the riot.

To my left, a man burst through the crush, a screech flying off his tongue as he drove a knife into a Laven who battled with another beast. On a shock of pain, the Laven woman fell, trampled underfoot.

I felt torn, rent in two, the one second of levity we'd found now extinguished in the dismay of what this battle would cost.

Those who had already fallen.

My spirit ached as I watched the woman meet her death. I wanted to lean down. Pick her up and hold her as she breathed her last breath.

But there was no time. Nothing I could do.

I could only drive deeper, searching through the disorder for the one I had to bring to his end.

Internally, I begged for my family to be safe.

Josephine and Ellis.

Timothy and Dani.

The four of them swept into the tumult.

Plus, in the chaos, I'd recognized a few faces of other Laven from our family. More who had come when they'd been called.

I wasn't shocked. I understood now. What had been pressed on all our souls.

Pax fired at a woman who was clawing her way to me.

Though his hand on mine ensured that the reserves inside me built and built. A burn within that raged, pressing in on my psyche and gathering in my limbs.

One of the debased suddenly wheeled over me from above, propelling himself off a tree. His boiling skin had begun to peel. Sickness twisted through me. He appeared as if he were being burned alive, his screech vile as he launched himself toward me overhead.

Aiming high, Pax fired off another shot. The man howled as he was hit, and his body convulsed as he fell.

He landed on top of me, limp and heavy when he slammed against the back of my head and shoulders.

Gasping, I whirled to shove him off.

"Are you hurt?" Pax shouted.

"No, I'm fine." It was haggard. Grating. Cutting as the energy that gathered inside me neared overwhelming.

I was consumed with the need to emit it.

To end the horrors that surrounded us.

"Keep moving!" Pax's voice vibrated over the clamor. "We have to find Ambrose."

"He's still here," I muttered. I could sense the distinct stench of vileness, which poured its toxin out on those who were slain because of his call.

"Fucker is hiding. Knows he's met his match," Pax grunted as he kicked a boot out to deflect the fall of a possessed woman who lumbered backward, already struck by a knife in the side by another Laven.

The battle raged on, the deviants and Kruen destroyed, one by one.

I could feel the belief being renewed.

Restored.

Conviction pulsed from the Laven, feeding into one another. Sustaining our strength.

*"End her. End her. End her now. She must not prevail."*

It became a screech. A rash cruciality that stank of fear.

He was afraid. He was afraid.

And he was near.

For a flash of a second, I closed my eyes so I could listen to the call that had led me here.

And I felt it.

Spearing into me. A dark, bitter blade.

My eyes flew open, seeking its source, and my attention whipped back to the gazebo.

Though now he no longer stood on the steps, but rather atop the roof.

His arms were outstretched with his bellowing command: "End her! Bring her to me! The one who stands in our way."

He didn't need one of his servants to bring me to him.

I was already on my way.

Rage pulsed through me, and I shouted to Pax, "This way!" as I bolted toward the gazebo.

Pax was instantly at my side, one hand in mine and the other fighting off any beasts that got in our path. Our boots thundered across the snow-covered ground.

Ambrose's focus turned to me. The deadened depths of his eyes filled with hate.

Pure, absolute hate.

His flesh was translucent, fiery veins curling up his neck and face. His short blond hair gusted with the storm that raged right above him.

The hole to Faydor was gaping and wide, throbbing and appearing as if it might swallow up the earth.

"Do you think you can defeat me, Valient?" His voice took on a different intonation. Curling and twisting with the otherworldly, then seeping back into his normal human voice.

There was something in it . . . something that nearly made me trip.

My head spun as I processed. As my spirit listened to the inflection.

It didn't take much to realize that Ambrose had merged.

He had become an extension of Kreed.

Oh God.

Fear sent my knees quaking, but I refused to back down. Refused to succumb when I knew why I was here.

"Don't you see that is exactly what we've been sent to do?" I did my best to keep the tremor from my voice.

The words grew brittle, though they were still filled with the determination that we could see this through.

Hollow laughter rolled. "So brave, little one. I see why she chose you. But Valeen is weak. Just like the rest of you."

"That is where you are wrong. Do you not see what's happening around you? How we are defeating the army you've gathered?"

In my periphery, I noticed Pax's movement. He was slinking around to the back of the gazebo, slithering within the shadows.

Keeping himself hidden as he went.

It took everything inside me to force myself to keep my attention ahead.

Not to shout at him to stop or be careful.

Not to draw attention to my Nol, who had stealthily begun to climb onto the gazebo railing. Once he found his footing, he jumped high, his arms outstretched as he grabbed on to a beam on the edge and used it to drag himself up.

He threw himself on top of the roof, his feet light as he landed in a crouch.

*"Pax."* It was a whisper from my soul, and my pulse stampeded when I realized his intentions.

He was suddenly charging.

Charging at full speed before he rammed a shoulder into Ambrose's back.

Ambrose was so consumed by the spite he had fastened on me, on the challenge I'd thrown up at him, that he was caught unaware. He stumbled forward, unable to stop himself before he hit the edge.

His arms pinwheeled as he tried to stop his fall, but he couldn't stop the momentum.

Was still vulnerable because he was still partially man.

But not completely.

My heart sank when I realized maybe not at all. Not anymore.

Because he landed with a roar and on his feet.

It placed him mere yards away from me.

The distance separating us churned with frigid, ferocious air.

And the light . . .

The light bottled inside me swelled and burned, and my hands tingled with the need to fight. With this purpose that I'd been given.

One I'd struggled with my entire life to understand, but now, in this moment, fully grasped.

It built and grew, manifesting into something so powerful I could barely contain it.

When holding it in became too much, I let it go.

A bolt of energy arced between us and blasted into Ambrose in a flash of blinding light.

I nearly sagged in relief until the dust cleared, and I found Ambrose just standing there with his mouth twisted into a sneer.

Malicious laughter rolled from him as he slowly moved in my direction.

His words a taunt that danced with the frozen spikes of rain.

"You're going to have to do a lot better than that." He tsked. "It's pathetic, really, that you came here thinking you could conquer me. It's time to surrender."

"I will never surrender." It was an oath. A promise to humanity.

I waited for the right opportunity. For the moment when Pax silently eased up behind Ambrose and gave me a telling nod.

As one, we rushed him from both sides, and we slammed our hands on him at the same time.

We let go of the light. The energy that burned and raged within us.

Streaks of power that pelted through him like darts.

Ambrose howled, though he retaliated, and a surge of his own energy blasted us back. I flew, my feet ripped out from under me, airborne for five seconds before my body was thrown to the ground. A surprised cry jutted out of my lungs; nothing I could do to stop myself from skidding fifteen feet back, cutting into the cold, frozen ground as I went.

Pain lancinated, every muscle in my body aching, but I refused it. My breaths were choppy as I staggered back to my feet.

Pax was already on his, and we shared a look.

*Together.*

The mass still battled behind us. Cries and shouts and the clashing of weapons.

While Ambrose smirked. Smirked like the wicked bastard he was.

And that rage billowed. Coming at me from all sides. All the depravities I'd seen through my years. The torture and the torment.

He couldn't win. He couldn't.

Teeth gritted, I ran back for him, desperate to focus on the light. Praying it would regenerate. That I would have the strength to see this through.

It faintly flickered, and with each thud of my feet, it wicked back to life. Growing quick. Combusting to a boiling point.

In a flash, I could no longer contain it.

My arms were stretched out in front of me when Pax and I hit him again, though this time, we held on, trying to inject as much energy as we could into his body.

Into his spirit.

Unsure of which needed to succumb first in order to end him.

Praying that ending him was even possible at all.

That his immortality didn't actually mean that he would go on forever.

Because this had to end.

It had to.

We couldn't allow this infestation to spread across the globe. Couldn't imagine the pain and suffering.

My family's faces flickered through my mind as I struggled to hold on. To pour everything I had into burning out his soul.

My mother.

My brothers and sister.

My father, too.

Those who'd been manipulated and used. Targeted and violated.

For all of them.

For *everyone.*

"Don't let go, Aria," Pax wheezed, trying to hold on as well. Our limbs shuddered and shook from the effort, from the energy that surged and passed between the three of us.

Ambrose thrashed, trying to buck us off.

Pax's brow furrowed, a warning that he was going to shift, and for a second, he let go with one hand and withdrew a blade from the sheath attached to his waist.

He lifted it and drove the blade into Ambrose's side.

Ambrose howled with rage. With a fury unlike anything I'd ever heard.

His fist suddenly flew from out of nowhere. I had no time to prepare before it cracked against my jaw.

I was knocked from my feet before I could even process the agony that splintered through my head.

A moan of misery jolted out of me when I landed in a heap twenty feet away, my chest feeling as if it was going to cave in.

Blackness threatened to take me whole. Consciousness fading in and out. I blinked through it, clawing my way out of the delirium that wanted to pull me under.

I choked as I fought to catch the breath he had knocked from my lungs.

A haze billowed over the area, disorienting and dark.

A veil that tried to cloak my perception. To push me toward the surrender Ambrose had demanded.

But I wouldn't give in.

I forced myself to sit up, but a sob ripped from me when a shearing pain suddenly tore through my thigh. A wild throbbing that nearly dropped me back to the ground.

I reeled when I realized a broken piece of wood was sticking out of my upper leg.

Nausea rolled through my gut, and my hand was shaking out of control as I wrapped it around the blunt end of the plank.

Then I yanked.

Hard.

A scream tore out of me as I pulled it free. The wood was bloody and sharp at the tip. Hand fumbling, I dropped it to my side, gasping for air, for resilience, for the strength to get back to my feet when everything hurt so badly.

I made it to my hands and knees when my gaze traveled, and it landed on Pax, who was coughing as he climbed to standing at least a hundred feet away.

Thrown across the park as well.

Then my attention jerked away from my heart and slanted back to Ambrose.

Ambrose, who stood at the base of the gazebo, staring at me.

Death in his eyes.

Lightning flashed above him in the toil of clouds, and a clap of thunder shook the heavens and rumbled across the ground.

Footsteps suddenly pounded up beside me, and a hand darted out to my shoulder. "Oh my God, Aria, are you okay?"

It was Dani.

Dani.

I struggled to speak. "I think so."

Dread carved Dani's brow when she noticed the blood saturating my pant leg. I shook my head to cut off her worry. "It's fine."

We didn't have time for it not to be.

"Okay, but you've got to get off the ground. Right now." Dani fumbled around in front of me and stretched out her hand.

A moan rolled from my throat at the rush of pain that clawed across my thigh, but I managed to stand.

Pax rushed up and held me in those strong, unrelenting arms.

"Aria. Baby," he wheezed at my temple.

Torment seeded in the words.

I wanted to sag into his care. Into his embrace. Into the promises I knew he wanted to make.

But this wasn't about my well-being.

So I gripped him for one second, relishing the warmth, his scent and ferocity and everything that he was, before I peeled myself from his hold and straightened.

With my chin lifted, I slowly swiveled toward Ambrose, who still hovered by the gazebo.

Dani and Pax were on either side of me.

It was the first time I noticed that the sounds of the battle no longer resounded, and I became aware that Laven had begun to gather.

A force that had assembled from every direction of the earth.

Surrounding me as they began to amass.

Timothy stepped up to Dani's opposite side, and Ellis and Josephine were on the other side of them.

Then all Laven who remained standing, one after another, pressed in to create a vibrating throng that faced Ambrose.

The Kruen and their hosts had been destroyed.

Relief gushed out of me with the realization that Ambrose was the last one.

The beast who stood in front of us, his face twisted in wickedness.

The sky swarmed above him, vicious swirls that churned and howled. The fissure that cut through the realms throbbed, pulsing with brutality.

And on a thunderclap, it began to crack wider, a splinter that stretched wide across the heavens.

Horror ripped through me when at least a hundred Ghorl jumped through the crack, falling through the chaos that whirled from above and landing on the ground to gather around Ambrose.

Soldiers that assembled.

Enormous and obscene. My insides shuddered as I took them in on this realm. They were as big as buildings, towering high over Ambrose where they'd come to protect him.

Massive beasts.

Bodies of char and flame.

Radiating dominance and debauchery.

They were the strongest, oldest of the Kruen. So powerful that we'd barely been able to stop the one who'd hunted me, the one who'd sought my end through my father.

The *one.*

Now there was a host of them, standing whole on this plane, their mouths gaping open as they raged.

Smugness filled Ambrose's expression, every vile thought he'd ever possessed so clear on his face.

The greed.

The thirst for power.

For recognition and adulation.

To be greater than those around him.

His jealousy of Abigail was so distinct that I nearly choked on it. The hatred it'd bred, the way he'd opened himself up to the greatest of evils.

Because of it, Kreed had so easily been able to use him for his endgame.

And the goals of Kreed's endgame were right there, the monster taking human form so he could stand and rule this world.

No longer from the bowels of darkness, though there was no question that the darkness would spread to stain everything.

"It's time to meet your end, little Valient." Ambrose's voice was low, thunder that rolled across the field. "Just like the rest, though you will be the last—because with you, Valeen will die, as well as every Laven in existence. There will be nothing left of your kind."

His statement punched through me with a devastating blow. A sword driven through my soul. Puncturing and boring.

*Valeen.*

Ambrose laughed—a morbid sound, though his voice was more human than Kreed's. "Didn't you know? Her well has run dry. Her strength depleted. No power left because it's been gifted to me by Kreed. Kreed, who has drained her, feeding off the foolish love that she never stopped giving him for all this time. And once her strength is gone? So is yours."

Then his voice boomed, a reverberation as Ambrose rose higher, wickedness glowing from the depthless chasm of his eyes. "And now, her power is mine."

*"Rise. Rise. Rise."*

The whispering voice fell on my ears and infiltrated my soul.

*Valeen.*

I wondered if the rest of them could hear it, too. If they experienced the urging that pushed at their spirits.

Because a tremble rolled through the multitude of Laven. A rippling of power.

And it hit me so hard and fast. A tsunami that nearly knocked me off my feet. A swelling of light that swept them in an undertow.

Hands were suddenly touching me everywhere. Every single Laven who could get close enough to set them on me. Those who could not, placed their hands on the Laven in front of them.

Until they were all linked.

*Together.*

*Together.*

Everyone understood it then. It was the only way Ambrose—Kreed—would meet his end.

*Together.*

*Together.*

And that power built and built. Energy crashing and surging, growing stronger and stronger as it gathered between all of us.

Amplified.

Magnified.

The compulsion to expend it became nearly unbearable, and with Pax's hand in mine, Dani's in the other, I stepped forward, leading the group closer to Ambrose, whose expression twisted in cynicism.

In hate and disgust.

Though it flickered with the fear I'd recognized. The desperation he'd felt when he realized I couldn't be so easily defeated.

And I wondered if he knew that, with us together, he could not prevail.

Because I felt it.

The sheer force that begged to be released.

As if the world moaned to be freed of his chains. As if the hearts of the oppressed begged for this retribution.

We all moved as one as it gathered to a breaking point.

To one tiny pinpoint of volatility.

My insides screamed from the pressure of it.

The feeling as if I might explode. Rend apart to become one with the light.

True fear streaked across Ambrose's features, and he suddenly shouted, "End them!"

The Ghorl thrashed, their fiery tendrils lashing out at the same second that I dropped Dani's and Pax's hands and released the energy.

A shock wave flashed across the area.

A sonic boom.

Seismic.

It was a collision of light and darkness.

A wall of energy that clashed and clawed to overpower the other.

I braced against it, the power pulsing and pulsing from my hands as I pushed every drop from the well inside me.

All my strength.

All my will.

The will of every single Laven who stood as a fortress around me.

It was deafening.

Blinding.

A battle of flame and light.

Our bodies bowed as we poured out every last drop from our souls.

And the light suddenly burst.

Rupturing in a violent explosion. A streaking, tangible resonance that cut down everything in its path.

The wails and snarls of the Ghorl pierced the air. An agony that tore through the realms.

But my focus was on Ambrose.

I could see the flames behind his translucent skin. As if he were burning from the inside out while rage blistered through his features.

"No." It was a snarl of the otherworldly. "You have no power. You have no power. Little Valient. You must die."

It was a shriek that was devoured when the flames licked higher, spreading out from within to consume his body.

A blaze that grew high as he was fully set afire. He writhed and thrashed within it, his wails barely penetrating the air: "No. Slut. Whore. Bitch. You will not win. I will find a way to—"

He suddenly combusted. Splitting apart on a thunderous boom that cracked through the heavens.

Ash the only thing that remained.

Ash that was caught in a cyclone that touched down from the storm that raged above and consumed the mass of Ghorl in front of us.

Devouring the wicked.

One second later, they were all swallowed by the crater above, the chaos sucked into the nothingness before the fracture closed, the clouds that had obscured everything taken with it.

And in an instant, it was silent.

Still.

Only the ragged panting of Laven gasping for breath filled the air.

Relief and torment raked from our lungs.

I must have been in shock, because the only thing I could do was turn around to look out at the aftermath of the battle that had besieged the town.

At the carnage and ruin.

Buildings had been completely obliterated.

Everything rubble.

But it was the bodies strewn from end to end that clutched me in grief. They were littered across the park and out on the crumbling streets.

Laven wept where they stood over their Nols or begged on their knees at their bodies.

And it became a grief I could not bear when I kept moving, in slow motion, as I turned all the way around to where Pax should have stood.

But instead, he was on the ground, those pale, pale eyes wide and unseeing, a deep gouge in his chest where he'd been struck by a Ghorl.

# Chapter Forty-Six

## ARIA

"Pax!" His name cleaved from my mouth on a plea, and I dropped to my knees at his side.

"Pax. No, no, no," I begged. My hands shook uncontrollably as they fluttered out to touch him. To feel him. To find him.

He couldn't leave me.

*Please, don't leave me. Don't.*

"Pax. Please." It was garbled. Incoherent.

I managed to get my trembling fingers to his neck, and I fumbled as I searched for a pulse. A frenzy grew inside me when I couldn't find one, and I pressed harder.

Searching.

Desperate.

A thousand pounds weighed down on my chest. The pain so brutal I couldn't breathe. I wheezed, the air jerking in and out of my failing lungs as I searched the other side, begging and begging, "Pax, please, look at me. You have to look at me. Please."

Dani was suddenly there, on her knees on the other side of him. "Oh God, Aria," she choked.

I pleaded, desperation scraping up my ravaged throat, "Pax, please, look at me!"

Her pink hair got in my line of sight as she leaned over him, and she tipped it so her ear was to his chest, watching and listening for anything.

For any movement.

For a breath.

For a heartbeat.

She remained there for too long.

Doing nothing.

"Dani, hurry, we have to help him."

She sat back on her heels. Anguish pulsed through her features, and she slowly shook her head. "I'm so sorry, Aria."

I shook mine back.

Frantically.

Refusing what she was trying to say.

"No. No, Dani. No!" I screamed, and I pressed my hands to his chest.

Feeling.

Feeling.

Feeling.

No heartbeat.

No movement.

But I could feel *him*.

I could feel his spirit, which had always lived inside me.

That intuition—that awareness—that had thrummed between us. No matter the miles or distance or spheres that had separated us.

Our connection, which would bond us forever.

Tears blurred my eyes as I leaned over him, touching him everywhere as the frenzy of words poured from my mouth. "Pax, come back to me. You can't leave me. Not now. We did it. We did it. Together. Together. The way we were supposed to. Listen to my voice, to my heart."

I took his hand and placed his palm flat to that thunder that battered at my aching chest.

"You promised you would always find me. You promised. You have to. You have to find me. Wherever you are, you have to find me. You're my partner. My husband. My *Nol.* I need you."

The cries raked out of me.

Misery.

Anguish.

"Oh, fuck. No, man." From behind Dani, Timothy gripped his head with bloodied hands, the gore of the battle we'd just fought written all over him, before he dropped to his knees.

He nudged Dani aside. "Let me see."

He cut me an agonized glance as he unzipped Pax's jacket. He peeled it back, revealing Pax's shirt, which was ripped from the burn he'd sustained.

The fabric was completely saturated with blood. The wound was right on the center of Pax's chest, so deep that I feared I would be able to see his stilled, lifeless heart. A hole that was at least five inches wide.

Carefully, Timothy set both hands on Pax's sternum, just below the wound.

He began to pump. To pump blood through Pax's veins for him when he couldn't do it himself.

A frenzy lit inside me. Hope that bloomed in the middle of the torment.

Pax and Dani had saved me. They'd saved me when that healing had been impossible. When I should no longer be breathing. Because they were there. Because they'd poured their power into me.

I had to believe.

I had to.

Tremors rocked through my hands when I pressed my palms right over the wound.

Dani seemed to realize it at the exact moment, too, and she scrambled around so she could place her hands on each side of his head.

And we breathed our belief into him.

Our life.

Our love.

Over and over, I begged him to stay.

"Pax, I'm right here. Find me. Find me the way you always have."

Timothy pumped and pumped. Exertion strained his arms, but he refused to give up as Dani and I called him back.

As we begged and prayed that the energy we poured into him was weaving something inside.

A healing we couldn't see.

We refused to falter or give.

Our breaths were harsh and ragged as we gave him everything we had.

And I knew it when I saw the stirring of his eyes.

The slight fluttering of his lashes.

"Pax, Pax! You hear me. I know you hear me." Tears gushed down my face as the words rushed from my mouth.

"Come back to me. I'm waiting. I'm right here."

His chest suddenly arched off the ground as he sucked in a jagged breath.

Timothy heaved out a delirious, surprised laugh. "Yes, that's it. That's it!"

He pumped two more times before Pax jolted, flying upright as he coughed and choked, his hands gripping his wound as he inhaled oxygen into his lungs. One second later, those pale, pale eyes were on me where I was on my knees in front of him.

Those fierce, terrifying, beautiful eyes.

They were whole and knowing.

Pure and right.

*Together.*

And together it was done.

I threw myself at him, curling around him as he wrapped his arms around my waist. He released the heaviest breath into my neck as he locked me against his chest. "Aria. I heard you. I heard you."

"You've always heard me." It was a sob of praise. Of respect for this affinity. For the gift we'd been given.

For this love.

Ellis had always told us who we were would be a blessing and a curse.

But this? Having Pax? It was a treasure.

I held him against me as tight as I could, clinging to him as he breathed me in. Sharp, deep gulps that he pulled into the well of his lungs.

Then he peeled back, his palm soft as he set it on my cheek, his expression racked with devotion, words rough as he uttered them into the air: "You did it, Aria. You fucking did it. I knew you could. Knew you had the greatest strength in you."

He curled me back in his arms, murmuring in reverence, "You did it."

Energy swelled, the connection binding. Warmth that blistered through my body and sank down into every recess inside me.

A knowledge that seeped into the marrow.

"We all did it. All of us," I whispered over the swelling of perfect relief.

A shock of a laugh flew out of Dani, a lightness in the middle of the burden that still weighed down our spirits. "Oh, come on, Aria, did you miss the freaking bolt of lightning that came out of you?"

My laugh was soggy, and my limbs were numb, every muscle in my body mush.

But in it, there was strength.

Belief.

Hope.

*We did it.*

*We did it.*

And we were free.

"We really need to try to bandage that wound," Timothy urged.

I basically had to pry myself away from Pax, not wanting to let go, though I kept our fingers twined as Timothy shrugged out of his heavy jacket, peeled off his tee, then tore it into strips. He wound them around Pax's chest, tying them tight, before he pulled his jacket back on.

"Thanks, man." Pax's voice was coarse. "For everything."

Pax's gaze swiveled between Timothy and Dani, then back to me. "To all of you."

"Always." Timothy squeezed his shoulder, then swallowed hard as his attention moved over my shoulder to take in the desolation. "We need to get the hell out of here. This place is a straight wasteland."

As soon as he said it, a feeling swept over me. A cold wind of awareness that shivered all the way down into my bones. I slowly pushed to my feet as the sensation overtook me. The realization of what was missing.

Frantic, my gaze scanned, searching through the Laven scattered about the park. So many of them were wailing and weeping, while others embraced loved ones who had been spared.

Then I froze when I found who I was searching for.

Josephine.

She was there, in the distance, sitting on the ground. Holding Ellis's hand where he lay beside her. Strands of stringy gray hair blew around her face. A face that was wrought with the starkest grief.

"Ellis," I whispered around the agony that clutched my ribs, and I started to run, ignoring the pain in my leg as I clambered over the devastation of bodies and debris that littered the ground, pushing myself as hard as I could to get to them. A cry tore out of me when I made it there.

The front of his jacket was completely ripped, revealing a gaping wound that covered almost all of his abdomen.

And the blood.

There was so much blood.

"Josephine," I said, her name cracking on my tongue as I dropped to my knees. Frantic, I searched for something to use as a pack for the injury. "Put your hands on him. Hurry. We can save him."

Josephine shook her head gently as she tipped her attention up to me. A single tear streaked down her cheek. "No, my sweet child, we can't. He's already gone."

"No, we have to—"

Reaching out with her opposite hand, she set it on my forearm, stalling my frenzied movements as I tried to shrug out of my jacket. "He's gone. I can feel it. I know. There is nothing we can do. He has been called on to eternity."

"No," I cried, and I tried to push up on my knees, to reach out.

To do something.

But I felt it, too.

A cavern that had been carved out in the middle of me.

One that gaped from the woman who sat stoic at his side.

Agony.

Misery.

The sheer breaking of her heart.

The rest of our family rushed up behind us, grieved exhalations heaving from them when they stumbled on the loss.

I could feel the weight of his pain when Pax set his hands on my shoulders.

Could feel it spilling. A torrent that gushed through us all.

Tears streaked down my face as I reached for Josephine's free hand, squeezing it tight as we all knelt around the man who'd loved us so fiercely.

The one who'd watched over each of us as a father.

The one who'd carried the weight of us all on his shoulders.

His devotion forever and complete.

# Chapter Forty-Seven

## PAX

I think we were all numb as we pulled into the hotel in the next city we came to, about thirty minutes outside of where it'd all gone down.

I'd driven since Dani had barely been able to walk after we'd found Ellis, and the whole ride here, she and Timothy were completely silent, curled up in the back seat.

Aria sat in the passenger seat next to me.

In a spot she'd so often been over all these weeks.

Weeks that felt like a century.

An eon.

Our worlds merging and our axis cracking apart.

A lifetime.

A beginning.

An end.

A reemergence.

I could almost taste the questions that swirled through the car. The uncertainties.

The loss.

The relief.

The pure absolution I felt when I put the car into park outside the lobby of one of those chain hotels found along every highway, and turned my gaze on Aria.

Aria, who would never fail to steal my breath.

My partner.

My Nol.

My wife.

The one who'd saved me. The one I knew with every part of *myself*.

My soul's destination.

She was war-torn. Clothes shredded. Hair matted and clumped, blood smeared all over her striking, beautiful face.

But it would always be those eyes that got me. The palest gray eyes that speared all the way through flesh and bone to what was written in the deepest parts of me. This woman who'd always seen.

Sorrow lanced across her sharp brow, though there was so much more in her expression.

Freedom.

Deliverance.

Exoneration.

The chains that had bound us for so long were gone. The fear that had hunted us extinguished.

And the hope—the hope that she'd held had been found.

Fulfilled in the truth that we saw—people wandering around, confused yet whole; rays of sunlight beaming across the sky, warming the bitter cold that had frozen everything over.

Moisture filled her eyes as she stared over at me. So much emotion clogged her spirit that I could tell she didn't know if she wanted to shout with joy or drop to her knees and weep.

Because with the triumph had come tragedy.

With the victory had come misery.

Reaching out, I set my hand on her cheek and brushed the pad of my thumb beneath the hollow of her eye. My head barely bobbed. The slightest moment that promised that I got it. That I understood.

Understood that there was still a burden in the fulfillment of her purpose.

Dani choked on a sniffle, her voice a raspy moan that infiltrated the car. "How could we just leave them there?"

Josephine had refused to leave Ellis's side. Had refused to come with us. Had demanded we go.

We respected her enough to give in to that request, even though it had torn every single one of us apart.

"Because she needed to be there with him. Alone. To seek whatever peace she could find." Timothy's words were soft, issued with encouragement and his own sorrow.

We were reeling with the truth that this was the only time the two of them ever had. That they hadn't gotten the chance to know each other outside the battles we'd forever fought in Faydor. Their only meeting in the flesh had been this—their souls drawn together for the shortest amount of time.

But I think we also knew Ellis's heart. Knew he would have gladly sacrificed himself. Hell, he'd been sacrificing himself all along.

"I'm going to get us a couple rooms. I'll be right back," I finally said, knowing we needed to rest.

Heal.

Actually fully breathe for the first time in weeks.

Aria brushed her fingers down my arm in a silent agreement, and I clicked open the door and stepped out into the chill, though the howl of the wind had ceased. I glanced at my reflection in the window of the car.

I was covered in blood. My clothes saturated and my hair matted in thick clumps. Face streaked and stained red even though I'd wiped it with a towel Dani had had in the trunk.

The scars written under it.

Painted in the gore that had been my life.

I looked terrifying. Like the dangerous freak my biological father had believed me to be. And yeah, I'd faced many terrors in my years.

Had inflicted them in my own way. Had thought myself only worthy of imparting death and judgment to those who'd wielded their sins.

But now I saw something different reflected back. Saw something beneath the scars and disfigurement.

I saw the man I was destined to be.

The man who'd been brought here to stand beside the one who would save us all.

Aria caught my eye through the window. All that affection and goodness radiating out.

*Together.*

Giving her a soft tip of my chin, I blew out a sigh and scuffed a hand through the disarray of my hair as I strode toward the automatic lobby door.

It opened with my approach, and I walked inside to find three employees huddling around the registration counter.

The four flat-screen TVs that hung on the lobby walls were all tuned to a news station that was covering a local disaster.

A tornado that'd ripped through a small town and destroyed everything in its path. Emergency crews were just descending on the scene, but reports said the death toll was expected to be significant.

Footage from a helicopter played over the screen. The sheer devastation that had been wreaked—every building demolished. Rubble was piled high, and they tried to blur out what was clearly a slew of bodies strewn all over the streets.

In the scrolling text beneath it were reports of other calamities throughout the world. The rash of crimes that had befallen every city in every country. The terror that had run rampant.

Terror I had a hunch had gone silent.

The employees watched, rapt, their voices hushed as they whispered about the destruction.

A woman looked up when she heard me approach. Shock widened her eyes when she saw my state, her fear apparent as she inched back a step.

I cleared the roughness from my voice, forming the lie that had to be told. "I didn't mean to startle you with my appearance. We just got in the middle of a really bad storm. Wind was so bad we got thrown off the road. Bashed myself pretty good."

I gestured to a fresh cut on my forehead.

Another employee pointed at a television behind me. "Was a full-out tornado that destroyed an entire town. Looks like you got lucky."

I swiveled around to look, heart gripped by the sight, by the number of Laven who'd been slaughtered. By the people of that town who'd been wiped out before we arrived.

My words were thick as I released them into the sticky air: "Yeah. Looks like we definitely were."

Had the urge to place my hand over the wound I'd sustained. A wound that was almost healed because of my Nol. Because she'd always been my destination, where my soul belonged.

The one who'd led me back. Her spirit a call that I would forever heed.

Forcing it down, I spoke again. "I need a couple rooms, if you have them. We'd like to get cleaned up and rest before we take a chance of getting back on the road again."

"Smart move. Who knows if some freak storm is going to come out of nowhere again. The whole sky was black. Freaked me out, if I'm going to be honest." The desk clerk tapped into a computer as he rambled under his breath. "That was some apocalyptic shit."

He glanced up at me. "Do you have a room-type preference?"

"Kings, if you have them."

"You're lucky again, my friend. I have two available."

"Thank you."

"Rate is $115.99 a night, plus tax, bringing you to a total of $263.19."

I dug my hand into my pocket, and I pulled out the one credit card I had to my name. The one that would mark me as having been in this spot.

And I had no trepidation about doing it.

Because we were no longer running.

We were no longer hiding.

He ran it, then told me about the free happy hour and breakfast in the morning before handing me two little folders with our keys. "Hope you enjoy your stay." He gave me a genuine smile. "Glad you made it out okay."

"Yeah, me too. Glad it didn't hit here," I returned, voice gravel as I thought of what could have happened. How what had happened in that town could have spread out.

Far and wide.

How life as we knew it could have been eradicated. The sheer number of those who would have perished. The evil that would have roamed the earth.

Ruled it.

I stepped back outside, and immediately my gaze landed on Dani's little red car, attention focused on Aria, who watched me through the windshield.

God, the number of times I'd walked out of a motel lobby to find her just like that. Watching me with those eyes. With that love she always held for me. Embracing it without shame. Sharing it without reservation.

Chasing it when I'd been so fucking afraid.

When I'd been terrified of what returning her love would mean.

Terrified of what it would cost.

Turns out, that love had given us everything.

A chance at a life that neither of us thought we could have.

I moved to the driver's-side door and climbed in, and I passed a key card back to Timothy. "Room 212," I told him.

"Thanks, man."

I'd left the car idling, so I drove around to a spot near a side door.

Timothy slipped out, then ducked back in to help Dani out. He swung her directly into his arms. I didn't know if she was spent or wounded or too full of grief to walk, but he knew what she needed.

For so long, I'd wondered if Aria and I were the only ones who shared the scale of this connection. I knew better now. Recognized what we'd been taught was a sin was actually a gift.

Timothy didn't say anything—he just carried Dani up the sidewalk before they disappeared through the door.

I moved to the trunk, grabbed our duffels, then wound around to Aria's side.

She stepped out the second I got there.

Everything about her was overpowering. So perfect and right that a knot tightened at the base of my throat.

We didn't say anything, either, as we made our way up to our room, as I touched the key card on the reader and let us in to the warmth that billowed from within.

We slowly—carefully—undressed each other, ridding the other of tattered clothes marked with the carnage of what we had faced.

She gently brushed her fingertips over the wound on my chest. A gash that had clotted over, the jagged seam sealing with the belief she, Timothy, and Dani had poured into me.

I took her hand and led her into the bathroom, and I turned on the shower. It took only a second for it to heat, and the second it was warm enough, I stepped in and helped her inside.

We stood beneath the spray as hot water pelted us from above, our arms wrapped fiercely around each other, holding the other up.

And Aria sobbed.

Sobbed and sobbed.

While I ran my fingers through the knots in her hair, whispering against the crown of her head, "I know, baby, I know. It's okay. It's over now. It's over."

When the tears finally subsided, I washed her hair, fingers massaging through the locks before I lathered a washcloth and ran it over every inch of her gorgeous body.

Over the scars and the curves and the history that had been written on her.

Did my best to remove any visible traces of the traumas we had endured, though I knew the true scars could never fully be erased.

Then, with trembling hands, she did the same for me.

Once we were both clean, I turned off the faucet, grabbed a towel, and wrapped her in it; then I stepped out so I could pull her to me. Lifting her off her feet.

Lush locks of black curled around her shoulders and chest, sticking to her damp skin, while the slender arms that were the strongest I'd ever encountered were locked around my neck.

I'd once thought her too thin and frail, as if the life we'd led had whittled her down to skin and bone.

But no.

She was fierce.

Formidable.

The strength the world had been waiting for.

I dragged down the covers on the bed, then laid her down in the middle of it before I climbed in beside her. I propped myself up on an elbow and took her hand with the other and splayed it over the thunder that ravaged in my chest.

A ravaging that beat because of her belief.

"You saved me, Aria."

She blinked up at me. That gaze an endless well of sincerity.

"And you saved me," she murmured.

I moved her hand, shifting so I could link our fingers together and lift them between us, scattering kisses over her knuckles as I whispered, "I guess we saved each other."

"I think that's exactly what we were meant to do. What we were all meant to do."

"Yeah. I think you're right."

She fought the moisture that resurfaced in her eyes. "We lost so many."

"I know." The words were gravel. "But you have to think of the multitudes that were saved."

Aria wavered, her throat bobbing, emotion thickening her voice. "Is it really over?"

I ran a thumb down her cheek. "I have to believe that it's over. Have to believe we're free, Aria. You're free."

Her lips trembled, giving way to a sorrowful, soggy smile that was still wrought with joy. She released my hand so she could trace her fingertips over the edges of my face.

"I was so scared." Her confession was choppy. "When I thought I lost you."

I ran the pad of my thumb over the scar on the left side of her mouth. "I don't think I could have gone anywhere without you."

"But it seems so unfair. For Josephine and Ellis. I wanted . . ." She trailed off, unsure of how to phrase it.

"We all did, but we can't know all things. We can't know the full purpose of Ellis's path. Of his journey. But the one thing I do know is he would have been proud to have given his life like this."

Silence covered us for a few moments as we grieved for the man who'd meant so much to us.

Then Aria blinked, her hair swishing over the pillow as she gazed over at me. "What do we do now? Will there still be Kruen to fight?"

"That, I don't know, Aria. Not until we sleep. But what I do know . . . ?" Shifting, I rolled on top of her. The thin towel was the only thing that separated us. I brushed back the pieces of hair clinging to her face, voice low with devotion when I said, "I'm going to keep every promise I've made you. I'm going to give you all the good things in life. The love and peace you deserve. A home." I glanced away for a beat before I returned my gaze to her. "A family."

Affection billowed through her features, and she reached up again, this time brushing her fingertips over my lips. "Together."

"Always, always together." I let a slight smile take to my mouth. "You just have to decide where that's going to be. I'm guessing some deserted island where you can bury your toes in the sand."

Joy swept through her expression, this lightness we found once we realized the chains that had bound us had been released.

The fear that she would be running forever.

That there would be nowhere to hide.

That one day her calling would catch up to her and bring her to her end.

But she had prevailed.

She had the power, just like she was promised.

"Well, a deserted island does sound pretty nice, but maybe only part-time."

My grin grew. "Ah, yeah, that's right. My princess needs two houses."

Her teeth clamped down on her bottom lip, her neck and cheeks flushed with the blood that rushed through her veins. "Princess. Nol. Wife. Whatever you want to call me."

She hiked a playful shoulder.

Sincerity took over when I murmured down at her, "What you are is my everything."

And there was no teasing after that. There were only impassioned kisses and searching hands and healed hearts.

Writhing bodies and sweat-slicked skin.

There was only us.

Together.

Forever, in every way, no matter what that looked like.

# Chapter Forty-Eight

## ARIA

Pax's arms were curled around me where we lay in the middle of the bed.

Legs and hearts tangled.

Our breaths long, steady, and in sync.

Night pressed in, hovering in the room, lulling and coaxing our exhausted bodies toward the bliss of sleep.

For my whole life, there had always been a bare space in between asleep and awake.

A sense of anticipation.

One of joy and fear and purpose.

I began to drift on it, hovering in that nothingness.

Where I was weightless.

Timeless.

And heard the voice whisper somewhere in my ear. In my spirit. In my heart.

"Aria, dear Valient. The last Laven born. The last of my power. Our last chance to defeat the ones who would destroy us all. Chosen for a specific time to stand in my weakness. For many times love comes with the greatest burden, and the love I bore for Kreed nearly became our destruction."

"Valeen," my spirit murmured as I floated through a wispy light.

"But your love conquered. Your strength prevailed. Because of you, this world is safe, and I am replenished. Because of your hope, we go on. And now, sweet child, rest."

I blinked my eyes open to the faintest rays of morning light. I was still wrapped in Pax's hold, his breaths steady and slow where he slept next to me.

For the first time ever, the sharpened, honed edges of his face were serene.

And there was no panic inside me, no fear or distress, since I had not emerged in Tearsith when I'd fallen asleep.

Because we were no longer needed.

That battle we'd thought would rage on forever in Faydor had been won.

We were free.

Truly, completely free.

# Epilogue

## ARIA

***Five years later***

Rays of late-afternoon light spread out over us, glistening against the bright blades of green grass that covered the entire yard. A massive tree stood proud in the middle, its dense branches stretching out to provide shade and protection from the summer heat.

We sat beneath it, softly swaying on the double swing that hung from one of its sturdy arms. In the peace, I sketched, my hand swishing a charcoal pencil over the thick paper.

Pax sat next to me, and he had an arm casually slung around my shoulders.

It was Sunday, and everyone had just left an hour ago after they'd been here for a barbecue.

What had become our large, extended family.

My mother and my father.

My brothers, who were still wild but in brand-new ways, both bragging to Pax that they were now taller than he was and were constantly wanting to wrestle him to the ground.

My baby sister, who wasn't such a baby any longer and was preparing to leave for West Virginia to attend a small university next month.

Dani and Timothy, who lived about twenty minutes away.

And Josephine, who'd moved into a small house directly across the street.

"It was a nice day," I whispered into the tepid breeze.

The swing faced the back of our little house, and I stared out over the yard.

This sweet, perfect place where we had made our home in Albany.

Pax had asked me where it was that I wanted us to be together forever.

The beach had been nice.

Once the dust had settled, after we'd mourned with the members of our Laven family, we spent four enchanted weeks at a secluded resort in the Caribbean.

But this place?

It'd called me back.

I'd once believed that I would be separated from my family forever. That I had to run. To start a new life because there was no way I could go on under the judgment and scrutiny, even though I knew doing it would break my heart.

But I was no longer misunderstood. Now they saw. And I'd long forgiven what they hadn't had the capacity to see.

"Yeah. Have to admit, these are my favorite kind of days," Pax rumbled quietly.

It was amazing to see my husband this way. At peace and surrounded by the people who loved him. By people who recognized him, too.

Maybe he still bore the scars of his childhood. Of his own judgment and rejection. But I knew sometimes when you went without love and support for so long—when you believed it impossible—once you had it, it was so much sweeter.

Truthfully, life was sweet for all of us.

Even my father had found his redemption. I wasn't sure if it was because of what he'd seen and experienced, or simply because many of the evils of the world had been wiped away.

Stricken down on that day we'd faced Kreed through Ambrose.

I thought the former, since he watched the world with caution. As if he were terrified he might succumb again, ensuring he had a pure heart and a firm mind to fight off any attacks that might come.

But those voices—those voices had been silenced.

Yes, there were still crimes and betrayals. I supposed it was intrinsic, human nature, though there was no longer the badgering of human minds and souls. That thing that tripped them over the edge and sent them toppling into wickedness and degeneracy.

Now there was a new peace that echoed over the land. In our hearts and in our homes. It extended out, traversing all borders and boundaries.

"We should definitely do it every week," I said with a soft smile pulling at the edges of my mouth.

Pax huffed out a teasing sound that echoed with tenderness. "You want to have everyone over every week, huh? I think it's just so you can watch me do all the work."

I shifted so I could slant him a grin. My chest squeezed in a fit of joy. Buzzed with the energy that would forever pull between us. "Really? Says the man who shooed me out of the kitchen and told me to go put up my feet."

"Well, I can't have my princess overexerting herself, can I?" Then he smoothed his palm over my protruding belly, and his voice went rough. "Neither of them."

That joy billowed, gliding through me on a fluttering of wings. Our little girl kicked against his hand. The laugh Pax emitted was nothing but awe and devotion.

"It seems she doesn't think we need the rest," I whispered, the words clogged with the adoration I felt.

Pax's mouth tipped up at the side. "Nah, she's just agreeing with her daddy."

"Is that so?"

"Oh, yeah."

I bit down on my bottom lip, and I turned back to the drawing pad and started sketching again. The charcoal pencil swished in rhythmic strokes over the thick, textured paper.

Coming to life with the imaginings in my head.

I shouldn't have been surprised that the face that emerged was Pax's. Those fierce eyes seeming to burn from the page.

White flames.

The way they had done for all the years I'd drawn him, back when he was my darkest secret.

But now, there was so much comfort in that warmth. So much comfort in the way the image formed with the infant held protectively in his arms.

"That's beautiful, Aria," he murmured as he peered down at what I'd drawn.

"That's what you've always been to me, Pax. Beautiful. So perfect in every way."

I rolled onto my back so I was staring up at him. His shock of white hair billowed in the breeze, a bit longer than it'd been when I'd first met him.

The scar that cut through the right side of his face was still prominent, our bodies still riddled with battle wounds.

Reminders of what we'd fought for.

Of the purpose we'd been given.

A prompt for us to cherish the gift we'd been bestowed.

"I'm so thankful I get to share this life with you. This dream that I never thought I could receive." Love flowed out with my words.

Pax brushed his thumb down my jaw. And he whispered a promise that he'd uttered long ago.

"You're every dream I've ever had. Every vision in the day. Every hope that I've dared to have. All of me, it's yours."

He paused, then murmured, "You, Aria Morrison, are the reason my heart still beats."

The rattled cry echoed through the night, dragging me from sleep. A tiny, sweet sound that squeezed my chest in a bout of love when I heard her need for me.

A dull glow filled our room when I flicked on the bedside lamp. I leaned over so I could scoop her out of her bassinet, and I sat up against the headboard and brought her to my breast.

Her cries were immediately stemmed when she latched on, and her little fist bounced around on my chest, trying to find something to hang on to.

I gave her my index finger, my insides fluttering with affection when she squeezed it tight.

Gently, I ran my thumb over the soft skin of the back of her hand as I gazed down at her.

Her precious, delicate face and the shock of black hair on her head.

This child who had become the fruition of our joy. An example of our love. The truest, purest gift that Pax and I had ever received.

That void of loneliness that he and I had once believed we'd forever be subject to filled with our devotion to each other. With our devotion to this family.

And she opened those eyes to me.

Big and wide and full of trust.

My daughter, with her beautiful pale-gray eyes.

# About the Author

*Photo © 2022 Wander Aguiar Photography*

A.L. Jackson is the *New York Times* and *USA Today* bestselling author of numerous series, including Darkness, Bleeding Stars, Fight for Me, Falling Stars, Redemption Hills, Moonlight Ridge, and Time River. She writes emotional, sexy, and heart-filled contemporary romances about boys who usually like to be a little bit bad. If she's not writing, you can find her hanging out by the pool with her family, sipping cocktails with her friends, or, of course, with her nose buried in a book. For more information, visit www.aljacksonauthor.com.